Also by Ana Huang

TWISTED SERIES
A series of interconnected standalones
Twisted Love
Twisted Games
Twisted Hate
Twisted Lies

IF LOVE SERIES
If We Ever Meet Again (Duet Book 1)
If the Sun Never Sets (Duet Book 2)
If Love Had a Price (Standalone)
If We Were Perfect (Standalone)

twisted LOVE

ANA HUANG

Bloom books

To my mom, for all her support and
encouragement over the years.

Mom, if you're reading this, turn back immediately.
There are scenes in here that will scar you for life.

Published by Bloom Books, an imprint of Sourcebooks
P.O. Box 4410, Naperville, Illinois 60567-4410
(630) 961-3900
sourcebooks.com

Originally self-published in 2021 by Ana Huang.

Cataloging-in-Publication Data is on file with the Library of Congress.

Printed and bound in the United States of America.
LSC 43

Content Warnings

This book contains explicit sexual content, profanity, a very possessive/morally gray antihero, and topics that may be sensitive to some readers.

For more detailed information,
click the QR code below.

Playlist

"Twisted"—MISSIO

"Ice Box"—Omarion

"Feel Again"—OneRepublic

"Dusk Till Dawn"—ZAYN & Sia

"Set Fire to the Rain"—Adele

"Burn"—Ellie Goulding

"My Kind of Love"—Emeli Sandé

"Writing's on the Wall"—Sam Smith

"Ghost"—Ella Henderson

"Stronger (What Doesn't Kill You)"—Kelly Clarkson

"Wide Awake"—Katy Perry

"You Sang to Me"—Marc Anthony

CHAPTER 1

Ava

THERE WERE WORSE THINGS THAN BEING STRANDED IN the middle of nowhere during a rainstorm.

For example, I could be running from a rabid bear intent on mauling me into the next century. Or I could be tied to a chair in a dark basement and forced to listen to Aqua's "Barbie Girl" on repeat until I'd rather gnaw off my arm than hear the song's eponymous phrase again.

But just because things could be worse didn't mean they didn't suck.

Stop. Think positive thoughts.

"A car will show up...*now*." I stared at my phone, biting back my frustration when the app reassured me it was "finding my ride," the way it had been for the past half hour.

Normally, I'd be less stressed about the situation because hey, at least I had a working phone and a bus shelter to keep me mostly dry from the pounding rain. But Josh's farewell party was starting in an hour, I had yet to pick up his surprise cake from the bakery, and it would be dark soon. I may be a glass half-full kinda gal, but I wasn't an idiot. No one—especially not a college girl with zero fighting skills to speak of—wants to find herself alone in the middle of nowhere after dark.

I should've taken those self-defense classes with Jules like she wanted.

I mentally scrolled through my limited options. The bus that stopped at this location didn't run on the weekends, and most of my friends didn't own a car. Bridget had car service, but she was at an embassy event until seven. My rideshare app wasn't working, and I hadn't seen a single car pass by since the rain started. Not that I would hitchhike anyway—I've watched horror movies, thank you very much.

I only had one option left—one I *really* didn't want to take—but beggars couldn't be choosers.

I pulled up the contact in my phone, said a silent prayer, and pressed the Call button.

One ring. Two rings. Three.

Come on, pick up. Or not. I wasn't sure which would be worse—getting murdered or dealing with my brother. Of course, there was always the chance said brother would murder me himself for putting myself in such a situation, but I'd deal with that later.

"What's wrong?"

I scrunched my nose at his greeting. "Hello to you too, Brother Dearest. What makes you think something is wrong?"

Josh snorted. "Uh, you called me. You never call unless you're in trouble."

True. We preferred texting, and we lived next door to each other—not my idea, by the way—so we rarely had to message at all.

"I wouldn't say I'm in *trouble*," I hedged. "More like... stranded. I'm not near public transport, and I can't find a rideshare."

"Christ, Ava. Where are you?"

I told him.

"What the hell are you doing there? That's an hour from campus!"

"Don't be dramatic. I had an engagement shoot, and it's a thirty-minute drive. Forty-five if there's traffic." Thunder boomed, shaking the branches of nearby trees. I winced and shrank farther back into the shelter, not that it did me much good. The rain slanted sideways, splattering me with water droplets so heavy and hard they stung when they hit my skin.

A rustling noise came from Josh's end, followed by a soft moan.

I paused, sure I'd heard wrong, but nope, there it was again. Another moan.

My eyes widened in horror. "Are you having *sex* right now?" I whisper-shouted, even though no one else was around.

The sandwich I'd scarfed down before I left for my shoot threatened to make a reappearance. There was nothing—I repeat nothing—grosser than listening to a relative while they're mid coitus. Just the thought made me gag.

"Technically, no." Josh sounded unrepentant.

The word *technically* did a lot of heavy lifting there.

It didn't take a genius to decipher Josh's vague reply. He may not be having intercourse, but something was going on, and I had zero desire to find out what that "something" was.

"Josh Chen."

"Hey, you're the one who called me." He must've covered his phone with his hand, because his next words came through muffled. I heard a soft, feminine laugh followed by a squeal, and I wanted to bleach my ears, my eyes, my *mind*. "One of the guys took my car to buy more ice," Josh said, his voice clear again. "But don't worry, I got you. Drop a pin on your exact location, and keep your phone close. Do you still have the pepper spray I bought for your birthday last year?"

"Yes. Thanks for that, by the way." I'd wanted a new camera bag, but Josh had bought me an eight-pack of pepper spray instead. I'd never used any of it, which meant all eight bottles—minus the one tucked in my purse—were sitting snug in the back of my closet.

My sarcasm went over my brother's head. For a straight-A med student, he could be quite dense. "You're welcome. Stay put, and he'll be there soon. We'll talk about your complete lack of self-preservation later."

"I'm self-preserved," I protested. *Was that the right word?* "It's not my fault there are no—wait, what do you mean 'he'? Josh!"

Too late. He'd already hung up.

Figured the one time I wanted him to elaborate, he'd ditch me for one of his bed buddies. I was surprised he hadn't freaked out more, considering Josh put the *over* in overprotective. Ever since The Incident, he'd taken it upon himself to look after me like he was my brother and bodyguard rolled into one. I didn't blame him—our childhood had been a hundred shades of messed up, or so I'd been told—and I loved him to pieces, but his constant worrying could be a bit much.

I sat sideways on the bench and hugged my bag to my side, letting the cracked leather warm my skin while I waited for the mysterious "he" to show up. It could be anyone. Josh had no shortage of friends. He'd always been Mr. Popular—basketball player, student body president, and homecoming king in high school; Sigma fraternity brother and big man on campus in college.

I was his opposite. Not *un*popular per se, but I shied away from the limelight and would rather have a small group of close friends than a large group of friendly acquaintances. Where Josh was the life of the party, I sat in the corner and daydreamed about all the places I would love to visit but would probably never get to. Not if my phobia had anything to do with it.

My damn phobia. I knew it was all mental, but it *felt* physical. The nausea, the racing heart, the paralyzing fear that turned my limbs into useless, frozen things...

On the bright side, at least I wasn't afraid of rain. Oceans and lakes and pools, I could avoid, but rain...yeah, that would've been bad.

I wasn't sure how long I huddled in the tiny bus shelter, cursing my lack of foresight when I turned down the Graysons' offer to drive me back to town after our shoot. I hadn't wanted to inconvenience them and thought I could call a car and be back at Thayer's campus in half an hour, but the skies opened up right after the couple left and, well, here I was.

It was getting dark. Muted grays mingled with the cool blues of twilight, and part of me worried the mysterious "he" wouldn't show up, but Josh had never let me down. If one of his friends failed to pick me up like he'd asked, they wouldn't have working legs tomorrow. Josh was a med student, but he had zero compunction about using violence when the situation called for it—especially when the situation involved me.

The bright beam of headlights slashed through the rain. I squinted, my heart tripping in both anticipation and wariness as I weighed the odds of whether the car belonged to my ride or a potential psycho. This part of Maryland was pretty safe, but you never knew.

When my eyes adjusted to the light, I slumped with relief, only to stiffen again two seconds later.

Good news? I recognized the sleek, black Aston Martin pulling up toward me. It belonged to one of Josh's friends, which meant I wouldn't end up a local news item tonight.

Bad news? The person driving said Aston Martin was the *last* person I wanted—or expected—to pick me up. He wasn't an *I'll do my buddy a favor and rescue his stranded little sister* kinda guy.

He was a *look at me wrong and I'll destroy you and everyone you care about* kinda guy, and he'd do it looking so calm and gorgeous you wouldn't notice your world burning down around you until you were already a heap of ashes at his Tom Ford–clad feet.

I swiped the tip of my tongue over my dry lips as the car stopped in front of me and the passenger window rolled down.

"Get in."

He didn't raise his voice—he never raised his voice—but I still heard him loud and clear over the rain.

Alex Volkov was a force of nature unto himself, and I imagined even the weather bowed to him.

"I hope you're not waiting for me to open the door for you," he said when I didn't move. He sounded as happy as I was about the situation.

What a gentleman.

I pressed my lips together and bit back a sarcastic reply as I roused myself from the bench and ducked into the car. It smelled cool and expensive, like spicy cologne and fine Italian leather. I didn't have a towel or anything to place on the seat beneath me, so all I could do was pray I didn't damage the expensive interior.

"Thanks for picking me up. I appreciate it," I said in an attempt to break the icy silence.

I failed. Miserably.

Alex didn't respond or even look at me as he navigated the twists and curves of the slick roads leading back to campus. He drove the same way he walked, talked, and breathed—steady and controlled, with an undercurrent of danger warning those foolish enough to contemplate crossing him that doing so would be their death sentence.

He was the exact opposite of Josh, and I still marveled at the fact that they were best friends. Personally, I thought Alex was an asshole. I was sure he had his reasons, some kind of psychological trauma that shaped him into the unfeeling robot he was today. Based on the snippets I'd gleaned from Josh, Alex's childhood had been even worse than ours, though I'd never managed to pull the details out of my brother. All I knew was Alex's parents had died when he was young and left him a pile of money he'd quadrupled the value of when he came into his inheritance at age eighteen. Not that he'd needed it, because he'd invented a new financial modeling software in high school that made him a multimillionaire before he could vote.

With an IQ of 160, Alex Volkov was a genius, or close to it. He was the only person in Thayer's history to complete its five-year joint undergrad/MBA program in three years, and at age twenty-six, he was the COO of one of the most successful real estate development companies in the country. He was a legend, and he knew it.

Meanwhile, I thought I was doing well if I remembered to eat while juggling my classes, extracurriculars, and two jobs—front desk duty at the McCann Gallery and my side hustle as a photographer for anyone who would hire me. Graduations, engagements, dogs' birthday parties, I did them all.

"Are you going to Josh's party?" I tried again to make small talk. The silence was killing me.

Alex and Josh had been best friends since they roomed together at Thayer eight years ago, and Alex had joined my family for Thanksgiving and assorted holidays every year since, but I still didn't *know* him. Alex and I didn't talk unless it had to do with Josh or passing the potatoes at dinner or something.

"Yes."

Okay then. Guess small talk was out.

My mind wandered toward the million things I had to do that weekend. Edit the photos from the Graysons' shoot, work on my application for the World Youth Photography fellowship, help Josh finish packing after—

Crap! I'd forgotten all about Josh's cake.

I'd ordered it two weeks ago because that was the max lead time for something from Crumble & Bake. It was Josh's favorite dessert, a three-layer dark chocolate frosted with fudge and filled with chocolate pudding. He only indulged on his birthday, but since he was leaving the country for a year, I figured he could break his once-a-year rule.

"So…" I pasted the biggest, brightest smile on my face. "Don't kill me, but we need to make a detour to Crumble & Bake."

"No. We're already late." Alex stopped at a red light. We'd made it back to civilization, and I spotted the blurred outlines of a Starbucks and a Panera through the rain-splattered glass.

My smile didn't budge. "It's a *small* detour. It'll take fifteen minutes, max. I just need to run in and pick up Josh's cake. You know, the Death by Chocolate he likes so much? He'll be in Central America for a year, they don't have C&B down there, and he leaves in two days so—"

"Stop." Alex's fingers curled around the steering wheel, and my wild, hormonal mind latched on to how beautiful they were. That might sound crazy, because who has beautiful *fingers*? But he did. Physically, *everything* about him was beautiful. The jade-green eyes that glared out from beneath dark brows like chips hewn from a glacier; the sharp jawline and elegant, sculpted cheekbones; the lean frame and thick, light brown hair that somehow looked both tousled and perfectly coiffed. He resembled a statue in an Italian museum come to life.

The urge to ruffle his hair like I would a kid's gripped me, just so he'd stop looking so perfect—which was quite irritating to the rest of us mere mortals—but I didn't have a death wish, so I kept my hands planted in my lap.

"If I take you to Crumble & Bake, will you stop talking?"

No doubt he regretted picking me up.

My smile grew. "If you want."

His lips thinned. "Fine."

Yes!

Ava Chen: One.

Alex Volkov: Zero.

When we arrived at the bakery, I unbuckled my seat belt and was halfway out the door when Alex grabbed my arm and pulled me back into my seat. Contrary to what I'd expected, his touch wasn't cold. It was scorching, and it burned through my skin and muscles until I felt its warmth in the pit of my stomach.

I swallowed hard. *Stupid hormones.* "What? We're already late, and they're closing soon."

"You can't go out like that." The tiniest hint of disapproval etched into the corners of his mouth.

"Like what?" I asked, confused. I wore jeans and a T-shirt, nothing scandalous.

Alex inclined his head toward my chest. I glanced down and let out a horrified yelp. Because my shirt? White. Wet. Transparent. Not even a little transparent, like you could *kind of* see my bra outline if you looked hard enough. This was full-on see-through. Red lace bra, hard nipples—thanks, air-conditioning—the whole shebang.

I crossed my arms over my chest, my face flaming the same color as my bra. "Was it like this the entire time?"

"Yes."

"You could've told me."

"I did tell you. Just now."

Sometimes, I wanted to strangle him. I really did. And I wasn't even a violent person. I was the same girl who didn't eat gingerbread man cookies for years after watching *Shrek* because I felt like I was eating Gingy's family members or, worse, Gingy himself, but something about Alex provoked my dark side.

I exhaled a sharp breath and dropped my arms by instinct, forgetting about my see-through shirt until Alex's gaze flicked down to my chest again.

The flaming cheeks returned, but I was sick of sitting here arguing with him. Crumble & Bake closed in ten minutes, and the clock was ticking.

Maybe it was the man, the weather, or the hour and a half I'd spent stuck under a bus shelter, but my frustration spilled out before I could stop it. "Instead of being an asshole and staring at my breasts, can you lend me your jacket? Because I really want to get this cake and send my brother, your best friend, off in style before he leaves the country."

My words hung in the air while I clapped a hand over my mouth, horrified. Did I just utter the word *breasts* to Alex Volkov and accuse him of ogling me? *And* call him an asshole?

Dear God, if you smite me with lightning right now, I won't be mad. Promise.

Alex's eyes narrowed a fraction of an inch. It ranked in the top five most emotional responses I'd pulled out of him in eight years, so that was something.

"Trust me, I was not staring at your breasts," he said, his voice frigid enough to transform the lingering drops of moisture on my skin into icicles. "You're not my type, even if you weren't Josh's sister."

Ouch. I wasn't interested in Alex either, but no girl enjoys being dismissed so easily by a member of the opposite sex.

"Whatever. There's no need to be a jerk about it," I muttered. "Look, C&B closes in two minutes. Just let me borrow your jacket, and we can get out of here."

I'd prepaid online, so all I needed was to grab the cake.

A muscle ticked in his jaw. "I'll get it. You're not leaving the car dressed like that, even wearing my jacket."

Alex yanked an umbrella out from beneath his seat and exited the car in one fluid motion. He moved like a panther, all coiled grace and laser intensity. If he wanted, he could make a killing as a runway model, though I doubted he'd ever do anything so "gauche."

He returned less than five minutes later with Crumble & Bake's signature pink-and-mint-green cake box tucked beneath one arm. He dumped it in my lap, snapped his umbrella closed, and reversed out of the parking spot without so much as blinking.

"Do you ever smile?" I asked, peeking inside the box to make sure they hadn't messed up the order. Nope. One Death by Chocolate, coming right up. "It might help with your condition."

"What condition?" Alex sounded bored.

"Stickuptheassitis." I'd already called the man an asshole, so what was one more insult?

I might've imagined it, but I thought I saw his mouth twitch before he responded with a bland, "No. The condition is chronic."

My hands froze while my jaw unhinged. "D-did you make a joke?"

"Explain why you were out there in the first place." Alex evaded my question and changed subjects so quick I had whiplash.

He made a joke. I wouldn't have believed it had I not heard it with my own ears. "I had a photo shoot with clients. There's a nice lake in—"

"Spare me the details. I don't care."

A low growl slipped from my throat. "Why are *you* here? Didn't figure you for the chauffeur type."

"I was in the area, and you're Josh's little sister. If you died, he'd be a bore to hang out with." Alex pulled up in front of my house. Next door, a.k.a. at Josh's house, the lights blazed, and I could see people dancing and laughing through the windows.

"Josh has the worst taste in friends," I bit out. "I don't know what he sees in you. I hope that stick in your ass punctures a vital organ." Then, because I'd been raised with manners, I added, "Thank you for the ride."

I huffed out of the car. The rain had slowed to a drizzle, and I smelled damp earth and the hydrangeas clustered in a pot by the front door. I'd shower, change, then catch the last half of Josh's party. Hopefully, he wouldn't give me shit for getting stranded or being late, because I wasn't in the mood.

I never stay angry for long, but right then, my blood simmered and I wanted to punch Alex Volkov in the face.

He was so cold and arrogant and...and...*him*. It was infuriating.

At least I didn't have to deal with him often. Josh usually hung out with him in the city, and Alex didn't visit Thayer even though he was an alumnus.

Thank God. If I had to see Alex more than a few times a year, I'd go crazy.

CHAPTER 2

Alex

"WE SHOULD TAKE THIS SOMEWHERE MORE...PRIVATE." The blond trailed her fingers down my arm, her hazel eyes bright with invitation as she swiped her tongue over her bottom lip. "Or not. Whatever you're into."

My lips curved—not enough to classify as a smile but enough to broadcast my thoughts. *You can't handle what I'm into.*

Despite her short, tight dress and suggestive words, she looked like the type who expected sweet nothings and lovemaking in bed.

I didn't do sweet nothings or lovemaking.

I fucked a certain way, and only a specific type of woman was into that shit. Not hard-core BDSM, but not soft. No kissing, no face-to-face contact. Women agreed, then tried to change it up halfway through, after which I'd stop and show them the door. I have no tolerance for people who can't keep to a simple agreement.

That was why I stuck to a roster of familiar rotating names when I needed a release; both sides knew what to expect.

The blond was not making it onto that roster.

"Not tonight." I swirled the ice in my glass. "It's my friend's farewell party."

She followed my gaze toward Josh, who was basking in female attention of his own. He sprawled on the couch, one of the few remaining pieces of furniture after he'd packed the house up in anticipation of his year abroad, and grinned while three women fawned over him. He'd always been the charming one. While I put people on edge, he put them at ease, and his approach toward the fairer sex was the opposite of mine. The more, the merrier, according to Josh. He'd probably fucked half the DC metro area's female population by now.

"He can join too." The blond edged closer until her tits grazed my arm. "I don't mind."

"Same." Her friend, a petite brunette who had been quiet up till now but who'd eyed me like I was a juicy steak since I walked in the door, piped up. "Lyss and I do *everything* together."

The insinuation couldn't have been clearer had she tattooed it across her exposed cleavage.

Most guys would've jumped at the opportunity, but I was already bored with the conversation. Nothing turned me off more than desperation, which reeked stronger than their perfume.

I didn't bother answering. Instead, I scanned the room for something more interesting to hold my attention. If it were a party for anyone else but Josh, I would've skipped it. Between my job as the COO of Archer Group and my side project, I had enough on my plate without attending pointless social gatherings. But Josh was my best friend—one of the few people whose company I could stand for more than an hour at a time—and he was leaving Monday for his gap year as a medical volunteer in Central America. So here I was, pretending like I actually wanted to be here.

A silvery laugh pealed through the air, drawing my eyes toward the source.

Ava. Of course.

Josh's little sister was so sweet and sunshiny all the time,

I half expected flowers to sprout on the ground wherever she walked and a coterie of singing woodland animals to trail behind her while she traipsed through meadows or whatever girls like her did.

She stood in the corner with her friends, her face bright with animation as she laughed at something one of them said. I wondered if it was a real laugh or a fake laugh. Most laughs—hell, most people—were fake. They woke up every morning and put on a mask according to what they wanted that day and who they wanted the world to see. They smiled at people they hated, laughed at jokes that weren't funny, and kissed the asses of those they secretly hoped to dethrone.

I wasn't judging. Like everyone else, I had my masks, and they ran layers deep. But unlike everyone else, I had as much interest in ass-kissing and small talk as I did in injecting bleach into my veins.

Knowing Ava, her laugh was real.

Poor girl. The world would eat her alive once she left the Thayer bubble.

Not my problem.

"Yo." Josh appeared beside me, his hair tousled and his mouth stretched into a wide grin. His hangers-on were nowhere—wait, nope. There they were, dancing to Beyoncé like they were auditioning for a gig at the Strip Angel while a circle of guys watched them with their tongues lolling out. *Men.* My gender could use a little more standards and a little less thinking with their small heads. "Thanks for showing up, man. Sorry I haven't said hi till now. I've been...busy."

"I saw." I arched an eyebrow at the lipstick print smeared on the corner of his mouth. "You have a little something on your face."

His grin widened. "Badge of honor. Speaking of which, I'm not interrupting, am I?"

I glanced at the blond and brunette, who'd moved on to making out with each other after failing to capture my interest.

"No." I shook my head. "A hundred bucks says you won't survive the full year in Bumfuck, Nowhere. No women, no parties. You'll be back before Halloween."

"O ye of little faith. There'll be women, and the party is wherever I am." Josh swiped an unopened beer from a nearby cooler and cracked it open. "I actually wanted to talk to you about that. Me being gone," he clarified.

"Don't tell me you're getting sentimental on me. If you bought us friendship bracelets, I'm out."

"Fuck you, dude." He laughed. "I wouldn't buy your ass jewelry if *you* paid *me*. No, this is about Ava."

My glass paused an inch from my lips before I brought it home and the sweet burn of whiskey flowed down my throat. I hate beer. It tastes like piss, but since it was the drink du jour at Josh's parties, I always brought a flask of Macallan whenever I visited.

"What about her?"

Josh and his sister were close, even if they bickered so much I wanted to duct-tape their mouths sometimes. That was the nature of siblings—something I'd never quite gotten to experience.

The whiskey turned sour in my mouth, and I set my glass down with a grimace.

"I'm worried about her." Josh rubbed a hand over his jaw, his expression growing serious. "I know she's a big girl and can take care of herself—unless she's getting stranded in the middle of fucking nowhere; thanks for picking her up, by the way—but she's never been on her own for so long, and she can be a little too... trusting."

I had an inkling of where Josh was going with this, and I didn't like it. At all. "She won't be alone. She has her friends." I inclined my head toward said friends. One of them, a curvy redhead in a gold skirt that made her look like a disco ball, chose that moment to hop onto the table and shake her ass to the rap song blasting through the speakers.

Josh snorted. "Jules? She's a liability, not help. Stella is as trusting as Ava, and Bridget...well, she has security, but she's not around as much."

"You don't need to worry. Thayer's safe, and the crime rate here is close to zero."

"Yeah, but I'd feel better if I had someone I trusted looking after her, ya know?"

Fuck. The train was heading straight off a cliff, and I couldn't do anything to stop it.

"I wouldn't ask—I know you've got a lot of shit going on—but she broke up with her ex a couple of weeks ago, and he's been harassing her. I always knew he was a little shit, but she wouldn't listen to me. Anyway, if you could keep an eye on her—just to make sure she doesn't get killed or kidnapped or anything? I'd owe you big."

"You already owe me for all those times I saved your ass," I said wryly.

"You had fun while doing it. You're too uptight sometimes." Josh grinned. "So is that a yes?"

I glanced at Ava again. Took her in. She was twenty-two, four years younger than Josh and me, and she managed to appear both younger and older than her years. It was the way she carried herself, like she'd seen it all—the good, the bad, the downright ugly—and still believed in goodness.

It was as stupid as it was admirable.

She must've felt me staring, because she paused her conversation and looked directly at me, her cheeks tinting pink at my unflinching gaze. She'd changed out of her jeans and T-shirt into a purple dress that swirled around her knees.

Too bad. The dress was nice, but my mind flashed back to our car ride, when her damp shirt had clung to her like a second skin and her nipples had strained against the decadent red lace of her bra. I'd meant what I'd said about her not being my type, but I'd enjoyed the view. I could imagine myself lifting that shirt, tugging her bra aside with my teeth, and closing my mouth around those sweet, hardened peaks—

I yanked myself out of that startling fantasy fast. What the fuck was wrong with me? That was Josh's *sister.* Innocent, doe-eyed, and so sweet I could throw up. The total opposite of the sophisticated, jaded women I preferred both in and out of bed. I didn't have to worry about feelings with the latter; they knew better than to develop any around me. Ava was nothing *but* feelings, with a hint of sass.

A ghost of a smile passed over my mouth when I remembered her parting shot earlier. *I hope that stick in your ass punctures a vital organ.*

Not the worst thing anyone's said to me, not by a long shot, but more aggressive than I'd expected coming from her. I'd never heard her say a bad word to or about anyone before. I took perverse pleasure in the fact that I could rile her up so much.

"Alex," Josh prompted.

"I don't know, man." I dragged my eyes away from Ava and her purple dress. "I'm not much of a babysitter."

"Good thing she's not a baby," he quipped. "Look, I know this is a big ask, but you're the only person I trust not to, you know—"

"Fuck her?"

"Jesus, dude." Josh looked like he'd swallowed a lemon. "Don't use that word in relation to my sister. It's gross. But... yeah. I mean, we both know she's not your type, and even if she was, you'd never go there."

A sliver of guilt flashed through me when I remembered my errant fantasy a few moments ago. It was time for me to call up someone from my roster if I was fantasizing about Ava Chen, of all people.

"But it's more than that," Josh continued. "You're the only person I trust, period, outside my family. And you know how worried I am about Ava, especially considering this whole thing with her ex." His face darkened. "I swear, if I ever see that fucker…"

I sighed. "I'll take care of her. Don't worry."

I was going to regret this. I knew it, yet here I was, signing my life away, at least for the next year. I didn't make a lot of promises, but when I did, I kept them. Committed myself to them. Which meant if I promised Josh I'd look after Ava, I'd fucking look after her, and I'm not talking about a text check-in every two weeks.

She was under my protection now.

A familiar, creeping sense of doom slithered around my neck and squeezed, tighter and tighter, until oxygen ran scarce and tiny lights danced before my eyes.

Blood. Everywhere.

On my hands. On my clothes. Splattered over the cream rug she'd loved so much—the one she'd brought back from Europe on her last trip abroad.

An inane urge to scrub the rug and tear those bloody particles out of the soft wool fibers, one by one, gripped me, but I couldn't move.

All I could do was stand and stare at the grotesque scene in my living room—a room that, not half an hour earlier, had burst with warmth and laughter and love. Now it was cold and lifeless, like the three bodies at my feet.

I blinked, and they disappeared—the lights, the memories, the noose around my neck.

But they'd come back. They always did.

"You're the best," Josh was saying, his grin back now that I'd agreed to take on a role I had no business taking. I wasn't a protector; I was a destroyer. I broke hearts, crushed business opponents, and didn't care about the aftermath. If someone was stupid enough to fall for me or cross me—two things I warned people never, ever to do—they had it coming. "I'll bring you back—fuck, I don't know. Coffee. Chocolate. Pounds of whatever is good down there. And I owe you a big, fat favor in the future."

I forced a smile. Before I could respond, my phone rang, and I held up a finger. "Be right back. I have to take this."

"Take your time, man." Josh was already distracted by the blond and brunette who'd been all over me earlier and who found a much more willing audience in my best friend. By the time I stepped into the backyard and answered my call, they had their hands beneath his shirt.

"*Djadko*," I said, using the Ukrainian term for *uncle*.

"Alex." My uncle's voice rasped over the line, scratchy from decades of cigarettes and the wear and tear of life. "I hope I'm not interrupting."

"No." I glanced through the sliding glass door at the revelry inside. Josh had lived in the same rambling, two-story house off Thayer's campus since undergrad. We'd roomed together until I graduated and moved to DC proper to be closer to my office—and to get away from the hordes of shrieking, drunken college students who paraded through campus and the surrounding neighborhoods every night.

Everyone had turned out for Josh's farewell party, and by everyone, I mean half the population of Hazelburg, Maryland, where Thayer was located. He was a town favorite, and I imagined people would miss his parties as much as they missed Josh himself.

For someone who always claimed to be drowning in school-work, he found a lot of time for drinking and sex. Not that it hurt his academic performance. The bastard had a 4.0 GPA.

"Did you take care of the problem?" my uncle asked.

I heard a drawer open and close, followed by the faint click of a lighter. I'd urged him to quit smoking countless times, but he always brushed me off. Old habits die hard; old, *bad* habits even more so, and Ivan Volkov had reached the age where he couldn't be bothered.

"Not yet." The moon hung low in the sky, casting ribbons of light that snaked through the otherwise inky darkness of the backyard. Light and shadow. Two halves of the same coin. "I will. We're close."

To justice. Vengeance. Salvation.

For sixteen years, the pursuit of those three things had consumed me. They were my every waking thought, my every dream and nightmare. My reason for living. Even in situations where I'd been distracted by something else—the chess play of corporate politics, the fleeting pleasure of burying myself in the tight, warm heat of a willing body—they'd lurked in my conscious-ness, driving me to greater heights of ambition and ruthlessness.

Sixteen years might seem like a long time, but I specialize in the long game. It doesn't matter how many years I have to wait as long as the end is worth it.

And the end of the man who had destroyed my family? It would be glorious.

"Good." My uncle coughed, and my lips pinched.

One of these days, I'd convince him to quit smoking. Life had driven any sentimentality out of me years ago, but Ivan was my only living relative. He took me in, raised me as his own, and stuck by me through every thorny twist of my path toward revenge, so I owed him that much at least.

"Your family will be at peace soon," he said.

Perhaps. Whether the same could be said of me...well, that was a question for another day.

"There's a board meeting next week," I said, switching topics. "I'll be in town for the day." My uncle was the official CEO of Archer Group, the real estate development company he'd founded a decade ago with my guidance. I'd had a knack for business even as a teenager.

Archer Group headquarters called Philadelphia home, but it had offices across the country. Since I was based in DC, that was the company's real power center, though board meetings still took place at HQ.

I could've taken over as CEO years ago, per my uncle's and my agreement when we started the company, but the COO position offered me more flexibility until I finished what I had to do. Besides, everyone knew I was the power behind the throne anyway. Ivan was a decent CEO, but it was my strategies that had catapulted it into the Fortune 500 after a mere decade.

My uncle and I talked business for a while longer before I hung up and rejoined the party. The gears in my head cranked into motion as I took stock of the evening's developments—my promise to Josh, my uncle's nudge about the minor hiccup in my revenge plan. Somehow, I had to reconcile the two over the next year.

I mentally rearranged the pieces of my life into different patterns, playing each scenario out to the end, weighing the pros and cons, and examining them for potential cracks until I reached a decision.

"Everything good?" Josh called out from the couch, where the blond kissed his neck while the brunette's hands became intimately acquainted with the region below his belt.

"Yes." To my irritation, my gaze strayed toward Ava again. She was in the kitchen, fussing over the half-eaten cake from Crumble & Bake. Her tanned skin glowed with a faint sheen of sweat from dancing, and her raven hair billowed around her face in a soft cloud. "About your earlier request...I have an idea."

CHAPTER 3

Ava

"I HOPE YOU APPRECIATE WHAT A GOOD FRIEND I AM."
Jules yawned as we tromped across our front yard toward Josh's
house. "For waking up at the butt crack of dawn to help your
brother clean and pack when I don't even like the dude."

I laughed and looped my arm through hers. "I'll buy you a
caramel mocha from Morning Roast after. Promise."

"Yeah, yeah." She paused. "Large, with extra crunch
toppings?"

"You know it."

"Fine." Jules yawned again. "That makes it somewhat worth
it."

Jules and Josh were not fans of each other. I'd always found
that strange, considering they were so similar. They were both
outgoing, charming, smart as hell, and total heartbreakers.

Jules was a human version of Jessica Rabbit, all shiny red hair,
creamy skin, and curves that made me look at my body with a
sigh. Overall, I was happy with how I looked, but as a member of
the Itty Bitty Titty Committee, I did wish for an extra cup size or
two without having to resort to plastic surgery. Ironically, Jules

sometimes complained about her double-Ds, saying they were hard on her back. There should be a Venmo for breasts that allows women to send and receive cup sizes with the press of a button.

Like I said, I was happy with how I looked most of the time, but no one—not even supermodels or movie stars—was immune from insecurities.

Besides her grievances with her breasts, Jules was the most confident person I'd ever met—aside from my brother, whose ego was so large it could house the entire East Coast of the United States with room left over for Texas. I suppose he had reason to be, considering he'd always been the golden boy, and though it pained me to admit it because he was my brother, he wasn't bad-looking either. Six feet tall with thick black hair and razor-sharp bone structure, which he *never* let anyone forget. I was convinced Josh would commission a sculpture of himself and display it on his front lawn if he could.

Jules and Josh never divulged why they disliked each other so much, but I suspected it might be because they saw too much of themselves in each other.

The front door was already open, so we didn't bother knocking.

To my surprise, the house was pretty clean. Josh had put most of his furniture into storage last week, and the only things left to pack were the couch (which someone would pick up later), a few stray kitchen items, and the weird abstract painting in the living room.

"Josh?" My voice echoed in the large, empty space while Jules sat on the ground and pulled her knees to her chest with a grumpy expression. She wasn't a morning person. "Where are you?"

"Bedroom!"

I heard a loud thump upstairs, followed by a muffled curse.

A minute later, Josh came down holding a large cardboard box. "Shit I'm donating," he explained, setting it on the kitchen counter.

I wrinkled my nose. "Put a shirt on. Please."

"And deprive JR of her morning eye candy?" Josh smirked. "I'm not that cruel."

I wasn't the only one who thought Jules looked like Jessica Rabbit; Josh always called her by the cartoon character's initials, which pissed her off to no end. Then again, everything Josh did pissed her off.

Jules lifted her head and scowled. "Please. I've seen better abs at the campus gym. Listen to Ava and put a shirt on before I lose last night's dinner."

"Methinks the lady doth protest too much," Josh drawled, slapping a hand against his six-pack. "The only thing you'll be losing is—"

"Okay." I slashed my arms through the air, cutting off the conversation before it went down a path that'd scar me for life. "Enough chitchat. Let's get you packed up before you miss your flight."

Fortunately, Josh and Jules behaved for the next hour and a half while we packed up the remaining items and loaded them into the SUV he'd rented for the move.

Soon, the only thing left to pack was the painting.

"Tell me you're donating this too." I eyed the massive canvas. "I don't even know how it'll fit in the car."

"Nah, leave it there. He likes it."

"Who?" As far as I knew, no one had taken over Josh's lease yet. But it was still July, and I expected the place to go fast closer to the start of the semester.

"You'll see."

I didn't like the smile on his face. At all.

The low purr of a powerful engine filled the air.

Josh's smile broadened. "As a matter of fact, you'll see right now."

Jules and I exchanged glances before we ran to the front door and pushed it open.

A familiar Aston Martin idled in the driveway. The door opened, and Alex stepped out, looking more gorgeous than any human had the right to look in jeans, aviators, and a black button-down shirt with the sleeves rolled up.

He took off his sunglasses and assessed us with cool eyes, unfazed by the mini welcoming party on the front steps.

Only I didn't feel particularly welcoming.

"But...but that's Alex," I stammered.

"Looking miiiighty fine, might I add." Jules nudged me in the ribs, and I scowled in response. Who cared if he was hot? He was a jerk.

"Hey, dude." Josh slapped hands with Alex. "Where's your stuff?"

"Moving company's bringing it later." Alex side-eyed Jules, who assessed him the way one would a shiny new toy. Besides Josh, Alex was the only guy who'd never fallen for her charms, which intrigued her more. She was a sucker for a good challenge, probably because most guys fell at her feet before she even opened her mouth.

"Wait." I put my hand up, my heart slamming a panicked rhythm against my rib cage. "Moving comp—you're not moving *here*."

"Actually, he is." Josh slung an arm over my shoulder, his eyes twinkling with mischief. "Meet your new neighbor, Little Sis."

My eyes ping-ponged between him and Alex, who couldn't look more bored by the conversation.

"No." There was only one reason Alex Volkov would leave his cushy DC penthouse and move back to Hazelburg, and I'd bet my new camera it had nothing to do with nostalgia for his college days. "No, no, no, no, no."

"Yes, yes, yes, yes, yes."

I glared at my brother. "I *don't* need a babysitter. I'm twenty-two years old."

"Who said anything about babysitting?" Josh shrugged. "He's looking after the house for me. I'm moving back in when I return next year, so it makes sense."

"Bullshit. You want him to keep an eye on me."

"That's a bonus." Josh's face softened. "It doesn't hurt to have someone you can rely on when I'm not here, especially given this whole thing with Liam."

I winced at the mention of my ex. Liam had been blowing up my phone since I caught him cheating on me a month and a half ago. He'd even shown up at the gallery where I worked a few times, begging for another chance. I wasn't devastated by our breakup. We'd dated for a few months, and I hadn't been in love with him or anything, but the situation had brought all my insecurities to the surface. Josh worried about Liam getting out of hand, but let's be honest, Liam was a Brooks Brothers–wearing, polo-playing trust fund baby. I doubted he'd do anything that would mess up his perfectly gelled hair.

I was more embarrassed I'd dated him than concerned about my physical safety.

"I can handle myself." I pulled Josh's arm off my shoulder. "Call the moving company and cancel," I told Alex, who'd been ignoring us and scrolling through his phone this whole time. "You do *not* need to move here. Don't you have...stuff to do in DC?"

"DC is a twenty-minute drive," he said without looking up.

"For the record, I am totally in favor of you moving in next door," Jules piped up. *Traitor.* "Do you mow the lawn shirtless? If not, I highly recommend it."

Alex and Josh frowned at the same time.

"You." Josh pointed at her. "Do *not* pull any of your shenanigans while I'm gone."

"It's cute how you think you have a say in my life."

"I don't give a shit what you do with your life. It's when you drag Ava into your harebrained schemes I'm concerned."

"News flash: you don't have a say in Ava's life either. She's her own person."

"She's my sister—"

"She's my best friend—"

"Remember when you almost got her arrested—"

"You *have* to let that go. That was three years ago—"

"People!" I pressed my fingers to my temple. Dealing with Josh and Jules was like dealing with children. "Stop arguing. Josh, stop trying to control my life. Jules, stop provoking him."

Josh crossed his arms over his chest. "As your big brother, it's my job to protect you and to appoint someone to fill in for me when I'm not here."

I grew up with him; I recognized that look on his face. He wasn't budging.

"I assume Alex is the fill-in?" I asked in a resigned tone.

"I'm not a 'fill-in' anything," Alex said icily. "Don't do anything stupid, and we'll be fine."

I groaned and covered my face with my hands.

This was going to be a long year.

CHAPTER 4

Ava

TWO DAYS LATER, JOSH WAS IN CENTRAL AMERICA AND Alex was all moved in. I'd watched the movers carry a giant flat-screen TV and boxes of varying sizes into the house next door, and Alex's Aston Martin was now a daily sight.

Since stewing over my situation wouldn't do me much good, I decided to make lemonade out of my lemons.

The gallery closed on Tuesdays during the summer, and I didn't have any shoots scheduled, so I spent the afternoon baking my signature red velvet cookies.

I'd just finished packaging them in a cute little basket when I heard the unmistakable roar of Alex's car pulling in the driveway, followed by a door slam.

Shit. Okay, I was ready. I was.

I wiped my sweaty palms against the sides of my thighs. I shouldn't be nervous about bringing the man cookies, for Pete's sake. Alex had sat at our Thanksgiving table every year for the past eight years, and for all his money and good looks, he was human. An intimidating one, but a human nonetheless.

Plus, he was supposed to look after me, and he couldn't do that if he bit my head off, could he?

With that reassurance in mind, I grabbed the basket, my keys, and my phone and made my way to his house. Thank God Jules was at her law internship. If I had to hear her talk about how hot Alex was one more time, I'd scream.

Part of me thought she did it to annoy me, but another part worried she was actually interested in him. My best friend hooking up with my brother's best friend would open up a can of worms I had no interest in dealing with.

I rang the doorbell, trying to still my rampaging heart while I waited for Alex to answer. I wanted to chuck the basket on the front step and run home, but that was the coward's way out, and I was no coward. Most of the time anyway.

A minute passed.

I rang the doorbell again.

Finally, I heard the faint sound of footsteps, which grew louder until the door swung open and I found myself face-to-face with Alex. He'd taken off his jacket, but otherwise, he still wore his work outfit—white Thomas Pink shirt, Armani pants and shoes, blue Brioni tie.

His eyes roved over my hair (tossed up into a bun), my face (hot as sun-scorched sand for no discernible reason), and my clothes (my favorite tank and shorts set) before settling on the basket. His expression remained unreadable the entire time.

"They're for you." I shoved the basket toward him. "They're cookies," I added unnecessarily, because duh, he had eyes and could see for himself that they were cookies. "It's a welcome-to-the-neighborhood gift."

"A welcome-to-the-neighborhood gift," he repeated.

"Yep. Since you're...new. To the neighborhood." I sounded like an idiot. "I know you don't want to be here any more than I want you here—" *Crap, that came out wrong.* "But since we *are* neighbors, we should call a truce."

Alex arched an eyebrow. "I wasn't aware a truce was necessary. We're not in a war."

"No, but—" I blew out a frustrated breath. He *had* to make this difficult. "I'm trying to be nice, okay? We're stuck with each other for the next year, so I want to make our lives easier. Just take the damn cookies. You can eat them, throw them out, feed them to your pet snake Nagini, whatever."

His mouth twitched. "Did you just compare me to Voldemort?"

"What? No!" *Maybe.* "I used the snake as an example. You don't seem like the type who'd have a furry pet."

"You're right on that account. But I don't have a snake either." He took the basket off my hands. "Thank you."

I blinked. Blinked again. Did Alex Volkov *thank* me? I'd expected him to take the cookies and shut the door in my face. He'd never thanked me for anything in my life.

Except maybe that one time I passed him the mashed potatoes at dinner, but I'd been drunk, so my recollection was hazy.

I was still frozen in shock when he added, "Do you want to come in?"

This was a dream. It had to be. Because the chances of Alex inviting me inside his house in real life were lower than me solving a quadratic equation in my head.

I pinched myself. *Ow.* Okay, not a dream. Just an incredibly surreal encounter.

I wondered if aliens had abducted the real Alex on his way home and replaced him with a nicer, more civil imposter.

"Sure," I managed, because hell, I was curious. I'd never been inside Alex's home before, and I was curious to see what he'd done with Josh's place.

He'd moved in two days ago, so I expected to see stray boxes lying about, but everything was so polished and put together, it looked like he'd been living here for years. A sleek gray couch and eighty-inch flat-screen TV dominated the living room, accented with a low, white lacquered coffee table, industrial-chic lamps, and Josh's abstract painting. I glimpsed an espresso machine in the kitchen and a glass-topped table with white-cushioned chairs in the dining room, but otherwise, there wasn't much furniture to speak of. It was a drastic difference from Josh's messy but cozy collection of random books, sports equipment, and items he'd collected from his travels.

"You're a minimalist, huh?" I examined a strange metal sculpture that looked like an exploding brain but probably cost more than my monthly rent.

"I don't see a point in collecting items I don't use and don't enjoy." Alex placed the cookies on the coffee table and walked to the bar cart in the corner. "Drink?"

"No, thanks." I sat on the couch, unsure of what to do or say.

He poured himself a glass of whiskey and sat opposite me, but it wasn't far enough. I caught a whiff of his cologne—something woodsy and expensive-smelling, with a hint of spice. It was so delicious I wanted to bury my face in his neck, but I didn't think he'd take too kindly to that.

"Relax," he said dryly. "I don't bite."

"I'm relaxed."

"Your knuckles are white."

I glanced down and realized I was clutching the edges of the couch so tightly my knuckles were, indeed, white.

"I like what you've done with the place." I winced. *Talk about a cliché line.* "No photos though." In fact, I didn't see any personal effects—nothing that showed I was in an actual home and not a model showroom.

"Why would I need photos?"

I couldn't tell if he was joking or not. *Probably not.* Alex didn't joke, except for that one blip in his car a few days ago.

"For the memories," I said, like I was explaining a simple concept to a toddler. "To remember people and events?"

"I don't need photos for that. The memories are here." Alex tapped the side of his forehead.

"Everyone's memories fade. Photos don't." At least not digital ones.

"Not mine." He set his empty glass on the coffee table, his eyes dark. "I have a superior memory."

My snort slipped out before I could stop it. "Someone has a high opinion of himself."

That earned me a shadow of a smirk. "I'm not bragging. I have hyperthymesia, or HSAM. Highly superior autobiographical memory. Look it up."

I paused. That, I hadn't expected. "You have a photographic memory?"

"No, they're different. People with photographic memory recall details from a scene they've observed for a short time. People with HSAM remember almost everything about their lives. Every conversation, every detail, every emotion." Alex's jade eyes morphed into emeralds, dark and haunted. "Whether or not they want to."

"Josh never mentioned this." Not once, not a hint, and they'd been friends for close to a decade.

"Josh doesn't tell you everything."

I'd never heard of hyperthymesia. It sounded fantastical, like something out of a science-fiction movie, but I heard the truth in Alex's voice. What would it be like to remember *everything*?

My heart rate picked up.

It would be wonderful. And terrible. Because while there were memories I wanted to keep close to my heart, as vivid as if they were happening right before my eyes, there were others I'd rather let fade into oblivion. I couldn't imagine not having the safety net of knowing horrible events would eventually recede until they were only faint whispers from the past. Then again, my memories were so twisted I remembered nothing before the age of nine, when the most horrible events of my life had occurred.

"What's it like?" I whispered.

How ironic the two of us were sitting here: me, the girl who remembered almost nothing, and Alex, the man who remembered everything.

Alex leaned toward me, and it was all I could do not to back away. He was too close, too overwhelming, too *much*.

"It's like watching a movie of your life play out before your eyes," he said quietly. "Sometimes it's a drama. Sometimes it's horror."

The air pulsed with tension. I was sweating so hard my top stuck to my skin. "No comedy or romance?" I tried to joke, but the question came out so breathless it sounded like a come-on.

Alex's eyes flared. Somewhere in the distance, a car horn honked. A bead of sweat trickled between my breasts, and I saw his gaze dip to it briefly before a humorless smile touched his lips. "Go home, Ava. Stay out of trouble."

It took me a minute to gather my wits and peel myself off the couch. Once I did, I all but fled, my heart pounding and knees shaking. Every encounter with Alex, no matter how small, left me on edge.

I was nervous, yes, and a bit terrified.

But I'd also never felt more alive.

CHAPTER 5

Alex

I SLAMMED MY FIST INTO THE MANNEQUIN'S FACE, reveling in the sharp burst of pain that jolted up my arm at the impact. My muscles burned and sweat dripped down my forehead into my eyes, blurring my vision, but I didn't stop. I'd done this so many times I didn't have to see to land my hits.

The smell of sweat and violence stained the air. This was the one place I allowed myself to unleash the anger I kept under careful wraps in all other areas of my life. I'd started Krav Maga training a decade ago for self-defense, but it had since become my catharsis, my sanctuary.

By the time I finished pummeling the mannequin, my body was a mess of aches and sweat. I toweled the perspiration off my face and took a swig of water. Work had been a bitch, and I'd needed this release to reset.

"Hope you worked off your frustration," Ralph, the owner of the training center and my personal instructor since I'd moved to DC, said dryly. Short and stocky, he had the powerful build of a fighter and a mean mug, but deep down, he was a teddy bear. He'd knock my lights out if I ever told him or anyone else that though. "You looked like you had a personal vendetta against Harper."

Ralph named all the training dummies after TV characters or real-life people he didn't like.

"Shitty week." We were alone in the private training studio, so I spoke more freely than I would have otherwise. Besides Josh, Ralph was the only person I considered a true friend. "I could go for the real thing right now."

Dummies were good for practice, but Krav Maga was a hand-to-hand combat method for a reason. It was all about the interaction between yourself and your opponent and responding quickly. Couldn't do that if your opponent was an inanimate object.

"Yeah, let's do it. Gotta end right at seven though—no overtime. There's a new class coming in."

I raised my eyebrows. "Class?"

The KM Academy catered toward intermediate to advanced practitioners and specialized in one-on-one or small group sessions. It didn't host large classes the way most other centers did.

Ralph shrugged. "Yeah. We're opening the center up to beginners. Just one class for now, see how it goes. Missy bugged me about it until I agreed—said people would be interested in learning it for self-defense and that we have the best instructors in the city." He barked out a laugh. "Thirty years of marriage. She knows how to stroke the ol' ego. So here we are."

"Not to mention it's a good business decision." KMA had little competition in the area, and there was likely pent-up demand for lessons, not to mention loads of yuppies who could afford the prices.

Ralph's eyes twinkled. "That too."

I took another swig of water, my mind spinning. *Beginner lessons...*

Might be a good idea for Ava. For anyone, really, man or

woman. Self-defense is a skill you never want to use but that could mean the difference between life and death when you *do* have to use it. Pepper spray only gets you so far.

I fired off a quick text to her before Ralph and I started our session.

I still wasn't happy playing babysitter, but Ava and I had settled into a wary "truce"—her word, not mine—since her olive branch the week before. Plus, when I commit to something, I commit to it one hundred percent. No half-assery or phoning it in.

I promised Josh I'd look after his sister, and that was what I'd do. Sign her up for self-defense lessons, upgrade her house's shitty alarm system—she'd thrown a fit when the security company woke her up at seven in the morning to install the new system, but she got over it—whatever it took. The more she stayed out of trouble, the less I had to worry about her and the more I could focus on my business and plan for revenge.

I wouldn't mind more of those red velvet cookies though. They were good.

I especially wouldn't mind if she delivered them wearing the tiny shorts and tank top she'd worn to my house. An unbidden image of a bead of sweat trailing down her bronzed skin into her cleavage flashed through my mind.

I grunted when Ralph landed a punch in my gut. *Fuck.* That was what I got for allowing my thoughts to stray.

I set my jaw and refocused on the training session, pushing all thoughts of Ava Chen and her cleavage out of my head.

An hour later, my limbs felt like jelly, and I had several blossoming bruises on my body.

I grimaced, stretching out my limbs while the low hum of voices filtered through the closed door to the private studio.

"That's my cue." Ralph clapped me on the shoulder. "Good session. You might even beat me one day—if you're lucky."

I smirked. "Fuck you. I can already beat you if I want."

I'd come close to doing it once, but part of me liked the fact that I wasn't the best—yet. It gave me a goal to strive toward. But I would win. I always did.

Ralph's laugh rolled through the sweat-dampened space like thunder. "Keep telling yourself that, kid. See you Tuesday."

After he exited the room, I checked my phone for new messages.

Nothing.

A tiny furrow creased my brow. I'd texted Ava almost an hour ago, and she was a compulsively fast replier unless she had a photo shoot. She didn't have one today. I knew because I made her promise to tell me every time she did, along with the location and clients' names and contact info. I always ran background checks on the clients beforehand. There were crazy people out there.

I sent a follow-up text. Waited.

Nothing.

I called. No answer.

Either she'd turned off her phone—something I told her never to do—or she could be in trouble.

Blood. Everywhere.

On my hands. On my clothes.

My heart rate ticked up. The familiar noose around my neck tightened.

I squeezed my eyes shut, focusing on a different day, a different memory—that of me attending my first Krav Maga lesson at sixteen—until the red stains of my past retreated.

When I opened them again, anger and worry coalesced into a block in my stomach, and I didn't bother changing out of my training clothes before I exited the center and took off for Ava's house.

"You better be there," I muttered. I blocked and flipped off a Mercedes that tried to cut in front of me at Dupont Circle. The driver, an overgroomed lawyer type, glared at me, but I didn't give a shit.

If you can't drive, get off the road.

By the time I arrived at Ava's place, I still hadn't received a reply, and a muscle pulsed dangerously in my temple.

If she was ignoring me, she was in deep shit.

And if she was hurt, I would bury the person responsible six feet beneath the ground. In pieces.

"Where is she?" I dispensed with the usual greetings when Jules swung open the door.

"Who?" she asked, all doe-eyed innocence. I wasn't fooled. Jules Ambrose was one of the most dangerous women I'd ever met, and anyone who thought otherwise because of the way she looked and flirted was an idiot.

"Ava," I growled. "She's not answering her phone."

"Maybe she's busy."

"Don't fuck with me, Jules. She could be in trouble, and I know your boss. Wouldn't take much more than a word from me to derail your internship."

I'd done my research on all Ava's closest friends. Jules was prelaw, and the internship between a student's junior and senior years was critical for admittance into a competitive law school.

All traces of flirty coquettishness melted. Jules narrowed her eyes. "Don't threaten me."

"Don't play games."

We glared at each other for a minute, precious seconds ticking by before she relented. "She's not in trouble, okay? She's with a friend. Like I said, she's probably busy. She's not glued to her phone."

"Address."

"You're hot, but you can be a real overbearing asshole."

"*Address.*"

Jules huffed out a sigh. "I'm only telling you if I can go with you. To make sure you don't do anything stupid."

I was already halfway to my car.

Five minutes later, we were speeding back to DC. I was going to bill Josh for all my gas expenses when he returned, just out of spite.

"Why are you so concerned? Ava has her own life, and she's not a dog. She doesn't have to jump every time you say fetch." Jules flipped down the visor mirror and retouched her lipstick when we stopped at a red light.

"For someone who claims to be her best friend, you're not concerned *enough*." Irritation coiled in my stomach. "When have you known her not to reply within minutes of receiving a text or a call?"

"Uh, when she's in the bathroom. Class. Work. Sleeping. Showering. A photo—"

"It's been almost an hour," I snapped.

Jules shrugged. "Maybe she's having sex."

A muscle jumped in my jaw. I wasn't sure which version of Jules was worse—the one who always tried to convince me to mow the lawn shirtless or the one who relished baiting me.

Why couldn't Ava have lived with one of her other friends? Stella seemed more accommodating, and given her background, Bridget wouldn't ever say the shit Jules said.

But no, I was stuck with the redheaded menace.

No wonder Josh always complained about her.

"You said she's with a friend." I pulled onto the street where said friend's house was located and parked.

"A *male* friend." She unbuckled her seat belt with a beatific smile. "Thanks for the ride and conversation. It was... enlightening."

I didn't bother asking her what she meant. She'd just feed me a heap of sugar-laced bullshit.

While Jules took her sweet time, I exited the car and banged an impatient fist against the front door.

It swung open a minute later, revealing a skinny, bespectacled man with confusion stamped on his face when he saw Jules and me standing there. "Can I help you?"

"Where's Ava?"

"She's upstairs, but who—"

I shouldered my way past him, which wasn't hard considering he weighed a hundred sixty, tops.

"Hey, you can't go up there!" he yelled. "They're in the middle of something."

Fuck. That. If Ava *was* having sex—a dangerous rhythm pulsed behind my temple at the thought—that was all the more reason for an interruption. Horny college guys were some of the most dangerous creatures in existence.

I wondered if she'd gotten back together with her ex. Josh mentioned the weasel had cheated on her, and she didn't seem like the type who'd crawl back to someone after they treated her terribly, but I wouldn't put anything past Miss Sunshine and Roses. That bleeding heart of hers would land her in a heap of trouble one day.

Once I reached the second floor, I didn't need to guess what room she was in—I heard sounds bleeding through the half-open door at the end of the hall. Behind me, Jules and Spectacles pounded up the steps, the latter still blabbering about how I couldn't be up here even though I was already fucking here.

I didn't know how humans survived this long. Most people were idiots.

I opened the door all the way and froze.

Not sex. *Worse.*

Ava stood in the middle of the room, clad in a skimpy black lace getup that left little to the imagination. She huddled next to a guy with spiked blond hair holding a camera. They were whispering and laughing while staring at the camera's display screen, so engrossed in their little tête-à-tête they didn't notice they had company.

My temple pulsed harder.

"What…" My voice sliced through the air like a whip. "Is going on here."

It wasn't a question. I knew what was going on. The setup, the rumpled bed, Ava's outfit…they were in the middle of a photo shoot. With Ava as the model. Dressed in something that wouldn't be out of place in *Playboy* magazine.

The strappy concoction Ava wore barely covered the necessary bits. It looped around her neck, baring her shoulders, and plunged to her navel in the front. The high-cut bottom left her legs and most of her ass bare, and other than the areas covering her breasts and between her legs, the sheer black lace revealed more than it covered.

I'd never seen her like this. It wasn't just the outfit; it was everything. The usually straight black hair that fell in luscious waves down her back, the made-up face with the smoky eyes and glossy red lips, the miles of golden skin and curves that etched themselves into my brain forever.

I was caught between disturbing lust—she was my best friend's sister, for fuck's sake—and inexplicable fury that other men were seeing her like this.

Ava's eyes widened with alarm when she spotted me. "Alex? What are you doing here?"

"I tried to stop him," Spectacles panted, out of breath. Living proof that skinniness does not equal fitness.

"He's here for you, babe." Jules leaned against the doorway, her amber eyes glowing with amusement. "You look super hot, by the way. Can't wait to see the pics."

"You are not seeing the *pics*," I ground out. "*No one* is seeing the *pics*." I yanked the blanket off the bed and tossed it over Ava's shoulders, covering her up. "We're leaving. Right now. And Blondie here is deleting every photo he took of you."

Her jaw dropped. "No, I'm not, and no, he's not. You can't tell me what to do." She threw the blanket on the ground and lifted her chin in defiance. "You're not my father or brother, and even if you *were*, you have no say in what I do in my free time."

"He's taking photos of you half-naked," I snapped. "Do you know how destructive those can be if they're leaked? If a future employer sees them?"

"I volunteered for this," she snapped back. "It's boudoir photography. Artistic. People do this *all the time*. It's not like I'm baring it all for a porn site. How did you even know I was here?"

"Oops," Jules said from behind us. She didn't sound sorry at all.

"You might as well be." The simmering in my blood had reached a full boil. "Get. Dressed."

"No-oh." Ava's glare intensified, and she dragged out the word *no* until it had two syllables.

"Hey, dude, I don't mean no harm." Blondie let out a nervous chuckle. "Like she said, this is art. I'll edit it so her face is in shadow and no one can tell it's her. I just need the photos for my port—what are you doing?" He squawked in protest when I snatched the camera out of his hands and started deleting photos but fell silent when I leveled him with a death glare.

"Stop! You're being ridiculous." Ava tried to retrieve the camera, to no avail. "Do you know how long those photos took? *Stop*. You are—" She yanked on my arm. It didn't budge. "Being—" Another yank, same result. "Unreasonable!"

"I'm protecting you, since you clearly can't do it yourself."

My mood darkened further when I saw the pictures of her lying on the bed, staring sultrily at the camera. How long had she and Blondie been doing this, alone? It didn't take a genius to figure out what had been going through his mind the entire time. It was the same thing that would've gone through any red-blooded man's mind. Sex.

I hoped Blondie enjoyed his working pair of eyes while he still had them.

Ava stepped back for a minute, then lunged for the camera in a poorly concealed attempt to catch me off guard. I'd expected the move, but I still grunted at the impact as she scrambled over me like a fucking spider monkey. Her breasts grazed my arm, and her hair tickled my skin.

My blood heated at the sensations.

She was so close I could hear her breath coming out in soft pants. I tried not to notice how her chest heaved or how smooth her skin felt pressed against mine. They were dangerous, twisting thoughts that had no place in my mind. Not now, not ever.

"Give it back," she ordered.

It was almost cute how she thought she could order me around. "No."

Ava narrowed her eyes. "If you don't give it back, I swear to God I'll walk out into the street wearing this outfit."

Another bolt of fury sizzled through me. "You wouldn't."

"Try me."

Our faces were inches apart, our words so soft no one could hear them except us.

Nevertheless, I lowered my head so I could whisper right in her ear. "If you step a foot outside this room in that outfit, I'll not only delete every picture on this camera, but I will destroy your 'friend's' career until he has to resort to advertising shitty five-dollar-an-hour headshots on Craigslist." A wintry smile touched my lips. "You wouldn't want that, would you?"

There are two ways to threaten people: attack them directly or attack those they care about. I wasn't above doing either.

Ava's mouth trembled. She believed me, as she should, because I meant every word. I wasn't a senator or a lobbyist, but an obscene net worth, thick files of blackmail material, and years of networking had granted me more than my fair share of influence in DC. "You're an asshole."

"Yes, I am, and don't you forget it." I straightened. "Get dressed."

Ava didn't argue, but she also refused to look at me as she disappeared into the bathroom across the hall to change.

Blondie and Spectacles gaped at me like the devil himself had poofed into their house. Meanwhile, Jules grinned like she was watching the most entertaining movie of the year.

I finished deleting the photos and shoved the camera back into Blondie's hands. "Never ask Ava to do something like this again." I towered over him, relishing the subtle shake of his shoulders as he tried not to cower. "If you do, I'll know. And you won't like what happens next."

"Okay," Blondie squeaked.

The bathroom door opened. Ava brushed past me and said something to Blondie in a low voice. He nodded. She placed a hand on his arm, and my jaw ticked.

"Let's go." The words came out sharper than I'd intended.

Ava finally looked at me, her eyes flashing. "We'll go when I'm ready."

I didn't know how Josh dealt with her all these years. Two weeks in, and I already wanted to strangle her.

She murmured something else to Blondie before she stalked past me without another word. Jules followed, still grinning.

I cast one last glare in Blondie's direction before I left.

Silence permeated the car as we drove back to Thayer. Jules sat in the back seat, tapping away on her phone, while a stone-faced Ava stared out the window from the passenger seat, her shoulders tight.

I didn't mind silence. I craved it. There were few things I found more irritating than incessant, pointless conversation. The weather, the latest blockbuster, who broke up with whom...who the fuck cared?

Still, something compelled me to turn on the radio halfway through the drive, though I left the volume so low I almost couldn't hear the music.

"It was for your own good," I said over the teeny-tiny beats of the latest rap hit.

Ava turned her body farther away and didn't respond.

Fine. She could be mad all she wanted. The only thing I regretted was not smashing Blondie's camera altogether.

It wasn't like I cared about her silent treatment. Not one bit.

CHAPTER 6

Ava

"THEN HE SAID, '*NEVER* ASK AVA TO DO SOMETHING like this again, or I will murder you and your entire family,'" Jules finished dramatically before taking a sip of her caramel mocha.

"Shut up." Stella leaned forward, her eyes wide. "He did not say that."

"No, he didn't." I shot Jules a disapproving look. "Stop exaggerating."

"How would you know? You were in the bathroom," she countered. When my frown deepened, she sighed. "Fine. He didn't say those *exact* words—at least not the last part—but the general idea was the same. He did warn Owen away from you though." Jules ripped off a piece of her cranberry scone and popped it in her mouth.

"Poor Owen." Guilt niggled at me as I traced absentminded patterns on the table. Jules, Stella, Bridget, and I were at Morning Roast for our weekly Tuesday coffee catch-up, and Jules had been regaling the other girls with a hyperbolized account of what happened at Owen's house on Saturday. "I wish he hadn't gotten dragged into this. All those hours of shooting, gone."

I worked with Owen at the McCann Gallery, where I'd served as a gallery assistant for the past year and a half. My father had never said outright he disapproved of me pursuing a photography career, but he'd made it clear that he wouldn't fund any of my equipment. He paid for my tuition and other school-related expenses, but if I wanted a new lens, camera, or even a tripod? That was all me.

I tried not to let his unspoken disapproval bother me. I was beyond lucky I'd graduate with no student loan debt, and I wasn't afraid of hard work. The fact that I'd shelled out my own money for every piece of equipment made me cherish them a little more, and I enjoyed my job at McCann. It was one of the most prestigious photography galleries in the Northeast, and I loved my coworkers, though I wasn't sure whether Owen would want anything more to do with me after what Alex had done.

Even now, my skin heated with anger at the memory of his overbearing attitude.

I couldn't believe he'd had the gall to show up and boss me around like that. To threaten my friend. To act like I was a...a servant or his employee. Even Josh had never gone that far.

I stabbed at my yogurt with my spoon, furious.

"Sounds like I missed an interesting time." Bridget sighed. "All the fun stuff happens while I'm away."

Bridget had been attending an event at Eldorra's New York consulate, as was required of the princess of Eldorra.

That's right. She was an honest-to-God, real-life princess, second in line to the throne of a small but wealthy European country. She looked the part too. With her golden hair, deep blue eyes, and elegant bone structure, she could've passed for a young Grace Kelly.

I hadn't known who Bridget was when she, Jules, Stella, and I found ourselves assigned to the same suite freshman year. Besides, I would've expected a freakin' princess to have a private room.

But that was the great thing about Bridget. Despite her insane upbringing, she was one of the most down-to-earth people I'd ever met. She never pulled rank, and she insisted on living life as a normal college student whenever she could. In that sense, Thayer was the best fit for her. Thanks to its proximity to DC and its world-class international politics program, the campus swarmed with political offspring and international royalty. Just the other day, I'd overheard the son of the Speaker of the House and the crown prince of a controversial oil kingdom arguing over video games.

You can't make that stuff up.

"Trust me, it was *not* fun," I grumbled. "It was humiliating. And I owe Owen a dinner at least."

My phone flashed with a new text. *Liam.* Again.

I swiped away the notification before any of my friends saw it. I wasn't in the mood to deal with him or his excuses right now.

"Au contraire, I thought it was hilarious." Jules finished the rest of her scone. "You should've seen Alex's face. He was *pissed.*"

"How is that hilarious?" Stella snapped a photo of her latte art before joining the conversation.

She was a big fashion and lifestyle blogger with over four hundred thousand Instagram followers, and we were used to her capturing everything for the 'gram. Ironically, for someone with such a big social presence, she was the shyest in the group, but she said the "anonymity" of the internet made it easier to be herself online.

"Did you hear me? He was *pissed.*" Jules placed extra emphasis on the last word like it was supposed to mean something.

Bridget, Stella, and I stared at her blankly.

She sighed, obviously exasperated by our lack of comprehension. "When was the last time any of us saw Alex Volkov pissed? Or happy? Or sad? The man doesn't show emotion. It's like God gave him extra helpings of gorgeousness and zero doses of human feeling."

"I think he's a psychopath," Stella said. She blushed. "No normal person is *that* controlled all the time."

I was still upset with Alex, but a strange part of me felt compelled to defend him. "You've only met him a few times. He's not so bad when he's not…"

"Being bad?" Bridget finished.

"All I'm saying is, he's Josh's best friend, and I trust my brother's judgment."

Jules snorted. "This the same brother who wore that hideous rat costume to last year's Halloween party?"

I wrinkled my nose while Bridget and Stella burst into laughter. "I said judgment, not *taste*."

"Sorry, I didn't mean to upset you." Stella tilted her head until her glossy dark curls cascaded over her shoulder. We always joked that she was the United Nations of humans because of her multicultural background—German and Japanese on her mother's side, Black and Puerto Rican on her father's side. The result was five feet eleven inches of leggy limbs, deep olive skin, and catlike green eyes. Supermodel material, if she had any interest in being a supermodel, which she didn't. "It was just an observation, but you're right. I don't know him well enough to judge. Statement retracted."

"I'm not upset. I'm…" I faltered. What the hell was I doing? Alex didn't need me defending him. It wasn't like he was here, listening to us. Even if he were, he wouldn't care.

If there was one person in the world who didn't give a shit what others thought of him, it was Alex Volkov.

"Guys, you're missing the point." Jules waved a hand in the air. "The point is, Alex *did* show emotion. Over Ava. We could have fun with this."

Oh no. Jules's idea of "fun" usually involved a heap of trouble and a potential dose of embarrassment on my part.

"What kind of fun?" Bridget looked intrigued.

"Bridge!" I kicked her under the table. "Don't encourage her."

"Sorry." The blond made a face. "But all I have going on lately are…" She glanced around to make sure no one was listening. They weren't, except for her bodyguard Booth, who sat at the table behind us and pretended to read the paper while actually keeping a sharp eye on the surroundings. "Diplomatic events and ceremonial duties. It's terribly boring. Meanwhile, my grandfather's sick, my brother's acting weird, and I need something to take my mind off it all."

Her grandfather and brother, a.k.a. King Edvard and Crown Prince Nikolai of Eldorra. I had to remind myself they were human beings like everyone else, but even after years of friendship with Bridget, I wasn't used to her speaking so casually about her family. Like they weren't literal royalty.

"I have a theory." Jules leaned forward, and the rest of us, even me, leaned in, eager to hear what she had to say. Call it morbid curiosity, because I was sure I wouldn't like what was about to come out of her mouth.

I was right.

"Ava somehow gets under Alex's skin," Jules said. "We should see how far it goes. *How much* can she make him feel?"

I rolled my eyes. "All those long hours you put in at your internship must've scrambled your brain, because you're not making any sense."

She ignored me. "I call it"—dramatic pause—"Operation Emotion." She looked up and drew an arc with her hand like the words would magically appear in the air.

"Creative," Stella teased.

"Hear me out. We all think Alex is a robot, right? Well, what if *she*"—Jules pointed at me—"can prove he isn't? Don't tell me you guys don't want to see him act like an actual human being for once."

"No." I tossed my empty coffee cup into the nearest trash can and almost beaned a passing student in a Thayer sweatshirt. I winced and mouthed "sorry" before returning to the ridiculous proposition at hand. "That's the dumbest idea I've ever heard."

"Don't knock it till you've tried it," my so-called best friend sang.

"What would be the point?" I threw my hands in the air. "How would it even work?"

"Simple." Jules pulled a pen and notepad out of her bag and started scribbling. "We come up with a list of emotions, and you try to make him feel each one. It'll be a test of sorts. Like giving him an annual physical to make sure he's functioning properly."

"Sometimes," Bridget said, "the way your mind works scares me."

"No," I repeated. "Not happening."

"It *does* seem kind of...mean." Stella tapped her gold-polished nails on the table. "What emotions did you have in mind?"

"Stel!"

"What?" She cast a guilty look in my direction. "I'm curious."

"Off the top of my head? We've already seen him angry, so happiness, sadness, fear, disgust..." A wicked smile slashed across Jules's face. "Jealousy."

I snorted. "Please. He'd never be jealous of me."

He was a multimillionaire executive with a genius-level IQ; I was a college student who worked two jobs and ate cereal for dinner.

No contest.

"Not jealous *of* you. Jealous *over* you."

Bridget perked up. "You think he likes Ava?"

"*No.*" I was tired of saying that word. "He's my brother's best friend, and I'm not his type. He told me so."

"Psh." Jules waved away my protest like she would a mosquito. "Men don't know *what* they want. Besides, don't you want to get back at him for what he did to Owen?"

"I don't," I said firmly. "And I'm not going along with this crazy idea."

Forty-five minutes later, we decided phase one of Operation Emotion would commence in three days.

I hated myself for caving.

Somehow, Jules *always* convinced me to do things against my better instincts, like that time we drove four hours to Brooklyn to watch some band perform because she thought the lead singer was hot, and we ended up stranded in the middle of the highway when our rental car broke down. Or that time she convinced me to write a love poem to the cute guy in my English lit class, only for his girlfriend—who I hadn't known existed—to find it and hunt me down in my dorm.

Jules was the most persuasive person I'd ever met. A good quality for an aspiring lawyer, but not so much for an innocent friend, i.e. me, who wanted to stay out of trouble.

That night, I climbed into bed and closed my eyes, trying to sort through my racing thoughts. Operation Emotion was supposed to be a fun, lighthearted experiment, but it made me nervous, and not just because it erred on the side of mean-spirited. Everything about Alex made me nervous.

I shuddered, thinking of how he'd retaliate if he found out what we were up to, and thoughts of being flayed alive consumed me until I fell into a light, fitful sleep.

"Help! Mommy, help me!"

I *tried to scream those words, but I couldn't. I shouldn't. Because I was underwater, and if I opened my mouth, all the water would rush in, and I would never see Mommy and Daddy and Josh again. That was what they told me.*

They also told me not to go near the lake by myself, but I wanted to make pretty ripples in the water. I liked those ripples, liked how throwing one little stone could cause such a big effect.

Only those ripples were suffocating me now. Thousands and thousands of them, dragging me farther and farther from the light above my head.

Tears trickled from my eyes, but the lake swallowed them and buried my panic until it was just me and my silent pleas.

I'm never getting out never getting out never getting out.

"Mommy, help!" I couldn't hold it in any longer. I screamed, screamed as loud as my little lungs allowed. Screamed until my throat was raw and I felt like I would pass out, or maybe that was the water rushing in, filling my chest.

So much water. Everywhere. And no air. Not enough air.

I thrashed my arms and legs in hopes it would help, but it didn't. It made me sink faster.

I cried harder—not physically, because I couldn't tell the difference between crying and existing anymore, but in my heart.

Where was Mommy? She was supposed to be here. Mommies were always supposed to be with their daughters.

And she had been there with me on the deck, watching me... until she hadn't. Had she returned? What if she was sinking beneath the water too?

The blackness was coming. I saw it, felt it. My brain went fuzzy, and my eyes drooped.

I didn't have the energy to scream anymore, so I mouthed the words. "Mommy, please..."

I jerked upright, my heart beating a million drums of warning while my faded screams soaked into the walls. My covers twisted around my legs, and I threw them off, my skin crawling at the sensation of being entangled—of being trapped with no way to free myself.

The glowing red numbers on my alarm clock told me it was 4:44 a.m.

A pinprick of dread blossomed at the base of my neck and slithered down my spine. In Chinese culture, the number four is considered unlucky because the word for it sounds like the word for death. *Sì*, four; *sì*, death. The only difference between their pronunciation is a tone inflection.

I've never been a superstitious person, but chills swamped me every time I awoke from one of my nightmares during the 4:00 a.m. hour, which was almost always. I couldn't remember the last time I'd awoken during a different hour. Sometimes I woke up not remembering I had a nightmare, but those blessed occasions were few and far between.

I heard the soft patter of footsteps in the hall and schooled my features into something other than stark terror before the door opened and Jules slipped inside. She flicked on the lamp, and guilt swirled through me when I saw her rumpled hair and exhausted face. She worked long hours and needed sleep, but she always checked on me even after I insisted she stay in bed.

"How bad was it?" she asked softly. My bed sank beneath her weight as she sat next to me and handed me a mug of thyme tea. She'd read online that it helped with nightmares and started making it for me a few months ago. It helped—I hadn't had a nightmare in over two weeks, which was a record, but I guess my good luck ran out.

"Nothing out of the ordinary." My hands trembled so much, liquid spilled over the side of the mug and dripped onto my favorite

Bugs Bunny shirt from high school. "Go back to sleep, J. You have a presentation today."

"Fuck that." Jules raked a hand through her tangled red hair. "I'm already up. Besides, it's almost five. I bet there are dozens of overambitious, Lululemon-wearing fitness junkies jogging outside right now."

I mustered a weak smile. "I'm sorry. I swear, we can sound-proof my room." I wasn't sure how much that would cost, but I'd deal with it. I didn't want to keep waking her up.

"How about no? That's totally unnecessary. You're my best friend." Jules wrapped me in a tight hug, and I allowed myself to sink into her comforting embrace. Sure, she led me into dubious situations sometimes, but she'd been my ride or die since freshman year, and I wouldn't have anyone else by my side. "Everyone has nightmares."

"Not like me."

I'd had these nightmares—these awful, vivid nightmares that I feared weren't nightmares at all but actual memories—for as long as I could remember. For me, that was the age of nine. Everything before that was a haze, a canvas peppered with faint shadows of my life before the Blackout, as I called the divide between my forgotten childhood and my later years.

"Stop. It's not your fault, and I don't mind. Seriously." Jules pulled back and smiled. "You know me. I'd never say something was okay if I wasn't actually okay with it."

I let out a soft laugh and set the now-empty mug on my night-stand. "True." I squeezed her hand. "I'm fine. Go back to sleep, jog, or make yourself a caramel mocha or something."

She scrunched up her nose. "Me, jog? I don't think so. Cardio and I parted ways a long time ago. Plus, you know I can't work a coffee machine. That's why I blow all my paychecks at Morning Roast." She examined me, a tiny crease marring her smooth brow.

"Give me a holler if you need anything, okay? I'm right down the hall, and I don't leave for work until seven."

"'Kay. Love you."

"Love you, babe." Jules gave me one last hug before she left and closed the door behind her with a soft *click*.

I sank back into bed and pulled the covers up to my chin, trying to fall asleep again even though I knew it was a futile exercise. But even though I was tucked beneath my comforter in a well-insulated room in the middle of summer, the chill remained—a ghostly specter warning me that the past is never past, and the future never unfolds the way we want it to.

CHAPTER 7

Alex

"DON'T DO THIS."

I poured myself a cup of coffee, leaned against the counter, and took a leisurely sip before responding. "I'm not sure why you're calling me, Andrew. I'm the COO. You should talk to Ivan."

"That's bullshit," Andrew spat. "You pull the strings behind the scenes, and everyone knows it."

"Then everyone is wrong, which wouldn't be the first time." I checked my Patek Philippe watch. Limited edition, hermetically sealed and waterproof, the stainless-steel timepiece had set me back a cool twenty grand. I'd bought it after I sold my financial modeling software for eight figures, one month after my fourteenth birthday. "Ah, it's almost time for my nightly meditation session." I didn't meditate, and we both knew it. "I wish you the best. I'm sure you'll have a flourishing second career as a busker. You took band in high school, didn't you?"

"Alex, please." Andrew's voice turned pleading. "I have a family. Kids. My oldest daughter is starting college soon. Whatever you have against me, don't drag them or my employees into it."

"But I don't have anything against you, Andrew," I said

conversationally, taking another sip of coffee. Most people didn't drink espresso this late for fear of not being able to sleep, but I didn't have that problem. I could never sleep. "This is business. Nothing personal."

It baffled me that people still didn't get it. Personal appeals had no place in the corporate world. It was eat or be eaten, and I for one had no grand aspirations of becoming prey.

Only the strongest survived, and I had every intention of remaining at the top of the food chain.

"Alex—"

I tired of hearing my name. It was always Alex this, Alex that. People begging for time, money, attention or, worst of all, affection. It was a fucking chore. It really was.

"Good night." I hung up before he could make another plea for mercy. There was nothing sadder than seeing—or, in this case, hearing—a CEO reduced to a beggar.

The hostile takeover of Gruppmann Enterprises would go ahead as planned. I wouldn't have cared about the company, except it was a useful pawn in the grand scheme of things.

Archer Group was a real estate development company, but in five, ten, twenty years, it'd be so much more. Telecommunications, e-commerce, finance, energy...the world was ripe for my taking. Gruppmann was a small fish in the finance industry, but it was a stepping-stone toward my bigger ambitions. I wanted to iron out all the kinks before I took on the sharks.

Besides, Andrew was an asshole. I knew for a fact that he'd quietly settled with several of his past secretaries out of court over sexual harassment charges.

I blocked Andrew's number for good measure and made a mental note to fire my assistant for allowing my personal cell information to slip into the hands of someone outside my tightly controlled contacts list. She'd already fucked up several times—paperwork with errors, appointments scheduled for the wrong times, missed calls from VIPs—and this was the last straw. I'd only kept her on so long as a favor to her father, a congressman who wanted his daughter to get "real work experience," but her experience was over as of 8:00 a.m. tomorrow.

I'd deal with her father later.

Silence hummed in the air as I placed my coffee cup in the sink and walked toward the living room. I sank onto the couch and closed my eyes, letting my chosen images play through my mind. I didn't meditate, but this was my own fucked-up form of therapy.

October 29, 2006.

My first birthday as an orphan.

It sounded depressing when I put it like that, but it wasn't sad. It just...was.

I didn't care about birthdays. They were meaningless, dates on a calendar that people celebrated because it made them feel special when, in reality, they weren't special at all. How could birthdays be special when everyone had one?

I used to think they were special because my parents always made a big deal out of them. One year, they took the entire family and six of my closest friends to Six Flags in New Jersey, where we ate hot dogs and rode roller coasters until we puked. Another year, they bought me the latest PlayStation, and I was the envy of my class. But some things were the same every year. I'd stay in bed, pretending to be asleep while my parents "snuck" into my bedroom wearing goofy paper cone hats and carrying my favorite breakfast— blueberry pancakes drenched in syrup with hash browns and crispy bacon on the side. My dad would hold my breakfast while my mom tackled me and yelled, "Happy birthday!" and I'd laugh and scream while she tickled me fully awake. It was the one day of the year they let me eat breakfast in bed. After my sister was old enough to walk, she'd join them, climbing over me and messing up my hair while I complained about girl cooties getting all over my room.

Now they were gone. No more family trips, no more blueberry pancakes and bacon. No more birthdays that mattered.

My uncle tried. He bought me a big chocolate cake and brought me to a popular arcade in town.

I sat at a table in the dining area, staring out the window. Thinking. Remembering. Analyzing. I hadn't touched any of the arcade games.

"Alex, go play," my uncle said. "It's your birthday."

He sat across from me, a powerfully built man with salt-and-pepper hair and light brown eyes almost identical to my father's. He wasn't a handsome man, but he was vain, so his hair was always perfectly coiffed and his clothes perfectly pressed. Today, he wore a sharp blue suit that looked woefully out of place among all the sticky children and haggard-faced, T-shirt-clad parents roaming through the arcade.

I hadn't seen Uncle Ivan often before "that day." He and my father had a falling-out when I was seven, and my father never spoke of him again. Even so, Uncle Ivan had taken me in instead of letting me drift through the foster system, which was nice of him, I guess.

"I don't want to play." I rapped my knuckles against the table. Knock. Knock. Knock. One. Two. Three. Three gunshots. Three bodies falling to the floor. I squeezed my eyes shut and used all my strength to shove those images out of my head. They'd return, as they had every day since that day. But I wasn't dealing with them now, in the middle of a stinky suburban arcade with cheap blue carpet and water ring stains on the table.

I hated my "gift." But short of carving out my brain, I couldn't do anything about it, so I learned to live it with it. And one day, I would weaponize it.

"What do you want?" Uncle Ivan asked.

I shifted my gaze to meet his. He held it for a few seconds before dropping his eyes.

People never used to do that. But ever since my family's murder, they acted differently. When I looked at them, they would look away—not because they pitied me but because they feared me, some base survival instinct deep inside them screaming at them to run and never look back.

It was silly, adults fearing an eleven—now twelve—year-old boy. But I didn't blame them. They had reason to be afraid.

Because one day, I would tear the world apart with my bare hands and force it to pay for what it had taken from me.

"What I want, Uncle," I said, my voice still registering the clear, high pitch of a boy who had not yet hit puberty, "is revenge."

I opened my eyes and exhaled slowly, letting the memory wash over me. That was the moment I'd found my purpose, and I'd replayed it every day for fourteen years.

I'd had to see a therapist for a few years after my family's death. More than one, actually, because none made any inroads and my uncle kept replacing them in the hopes one would stick. They never did.

But they all told me the same thing—that my obsessive focus on the past would impede my healing process and that I needed to focus my energy on other, more constructive pursuits. A few suggested art, while others suggested sports.

I suggested they shove their suggestions up their ass.

Those therapists didn't get it. I didn't *want* to heal. I wanted to burn. I wanted to bleed. I wanted to feel every scorching lick of pain.

And soon, the person responsible for that pain would feel it too. One thousandfold.

CHAPTER 8

Ava

Operation Emotion: Phase Sadness.

I came armed for battle.

I applied makeup, brushed my hair, and wore my favorite white cotton sundress with yellow daisies at the bottom. It was both pretty and comfortable, and it showed off just enough cleavage to intrigue. Liam had loved it. Whenever I wore it, we ended up at his place and my dress ended up on the floor.

I'd considered throwing the outfit away after we broke up *because* he'd loved it, but I thought better of it. I refused to let him ruin the good things for me, whether it was a dress or mint chocolate chip ice cream, which he used to buy me whenever I had my period cravings.

I figured looking good couldn't hurt if I was angling for an unannounced evening moviethon with Alex.

I couldn't think of any good ideas to make him sad without being a total bitch, so I'd chosen the neutral option of sad movies. They worked on everyone. Yes, even men.

I saw Josh cry once at the end of *Titanic*, though he claimed it was allergies and threatened to toss my camera from the top of the Washington Monument if I told anyone.

Yeah, right. A decade later, and he still couldn't shut up about how there'd been room for Jack on the door. I agreed with him, but that didn't mean I couldn't make fun of him.

Since Alex was a *teensy* bit more reserved than Josh, I skipped *Titanic* and brought out the big guns: *A Walk to Remember* (sadder than *The Notebook*) and *Marley & Me*.

I knocked on the door to Alex's house. To my surprise, it opened less than two seconds later.

"Hey, I—" I stopped. Stared.

I'd expected to see Alex in a suit from the office or casual loungewear, though nothing he owned was really *casual*. Even his T-shirts cost hundreds of dollars. Instead, he wore a deep gray shirt tucked into dark denim jeans and a tailored black Hugo Boss blazer.

Awfully dressy for a Thursday night.

"Did I catch you on your way out?" I tried to peer behind him and see if he had company, but Alex's frame blocked most of the doorway.

"Should I move so you have a clearer view of my living room?" he asked sardonically.

Heat scorched my cheeks. *Busted.* "I don't know what you're talking about. Your living room isn't that interesting," I fibbed. "Lack of color. No personal effects." *What am I saying? Someone stop me.* "The painting's ugly too." *Stop me* now. "Could use a woman's touch." *Fuck. Me. Sideways.*

I did *not* just say that.

Alex's lips pressed together. Had he been anyone else, I could've sworn he was trying not to laugh. "I see. The painting technically belongs to Josh, you know."

"Which should've been the first red flag."

This time, a tiny smirk did touch Alex's mouth. "To answer your question, I *was* on the way out. I have a date."

I blinked. Alex on a date. *Did not compute.*

Because of course the guy dated. *Look* at him. But I'd never heard or seen evidence of activity in his love life, unless you counted the women throwing themselves at him wherever he went, so I'd assumed he was one of those workaholics who had an exclusive relationship with his job.

I mean, we'd been neighbors for over a month, and I hadn't seen him bring a single woman home, though admittedly, I wasn't watching his house 24/7 like a total creep.

The thought of Alex dating was…strange.

That was the only word I could use to describe the niggling feeling in my stomach, the one that made my skin itch and my pulse beat double time.

"Ah, don't want to hold you up then." I stepped back and tripped over nothing, because of course I did. He reached out to steady me, and my heart jumped. It wasn't a big, cheerleading competition–worthy jump. It was just a tiny skip, really. But it was enough to fluster me further. "I'll see you later."

"Since you're already here, might as well tell me why." Alex was still holding my arm, and the heat from his touch seared me to the bone. "I assume this means the cold shoulder treatment is over."

I'd been ignoring him for days since he stormed into Owen's house like an overbearing, green-eyed tornado. It was the longest I'd ever held on to my anger. Being upset was exhausting, and I had better things to do with my time, but I'd wanted to make a point, which was that he couldn't barge in and try to take over my life without consequences.

"For the most part." I narrowed my eyes. "Don't do that again."

"Don't parade in front of other men half-naked, and I won't have to."

"I was not parading—" His words clicked into place. "*Other* men?"

Alex dropped my arm, his eyes growing even more glacial. "Tell me why you're here, Ava. Is someone bothering you?" His gaze sharpened. "Liam?"

An obvious attempt to change the subject, but my head spun too much for me to call him out on it. "No. It was nothing. Jules is on a date, and I'm bored, so I thought I'd see if you wanted to hang out."

I realized I should've come up with a less pathetic, more convincing excuse for why I'd shown up to his house unannounced on a Thursday night, especially since we weren't friends per se, but it was too late.

See, this was why I'd never make it as a spy *or* lawyer. Jules would be so disappointed in me.

"You're a terrible liar." Alex looked unimpressed. "Tell me the real reason you're here."

Crap. I had to come up with *another* excuse? It wasn't like I could let him know about Operation Emotion.

"I figured you could use the company now that Josh isn't here," I said. "I haven't seen you hang out with anyone else since he left, so I thought you might be lonely?" The sentence morphed into a question when I realized how dumb that logic was, because duh, Alex's life didn't revolve around his house. He may not throw house parties every week like Josh, but he probably ate out with friends and attended sports games like everyone else. "Which obviously isn't the case, since you're going on a date," I added quickly. "So I'll hop on back to my place, and you can forget this ever happened. Enjoy your date!"

"Stop."

I froze, my heart thundering against my chest as I wondered how this encounter had gone so off the rails. The funny thing was, it wasn't *actually* off the rails; it just felt like it.

Alex widened the door and stepped aside. "Come in."

What? "But your date."

"Let me worry about her. I don't know what's going on with you, but since you broke your silent treatment to come over and 'hang out,' something must be wrong."

The seed of guilt blossomed into a full-blown tree, trunk and all, in my stomach. This was supposed to be a harmless experiment. I didn't want him to cancel his scheduled plans for me.

But as I followed Alex into the living room, the thought that he was no longer going to dinner or whatever he'd had planned with some beautiful, mysterious woman pleased me more than it should have.

I stifled a laugh at Alex's expression when he caught sight of the movies I'd brought over.

"Not a Mandy Moore fan?" I teased, popping the DVD into the player and curling up on the couch while the previews played. I still owned DVDs the way I still owned paperback books. There was just something so magical about holding your favorite items rather than seeing them on-screen.

"I don't have anything against Mandy Moore, but I'm not a fan of maudlin or melodrama." Alex shrugged off his blazer and draped it over the back of the couch. His shirt stretched across his broad shoulders, and the top two buttons were undone, revealing a sliver of his chest and sexy collarbones.

I hadn't thought collarbones could be sexy, but here we were.

I swallowed hard. "It is *not* maudlin or melodrama. It's romantic."

"Doesn't she die in the end?"

"Way to spoil it," I grumbled.

He shot me a disbelieving look. "You've already watched it."

"But have you?"

"I know what happens."

"Shh." I nudged his leg with my foot. "Movie's starting."

He sighed.

I loved *A Walk to Remember*, but I snuck peeks at Alex throughout the film, hoping to catch *some* sort of reaction.

None. Nada. Zilch, even during Jamie and Landon's wedding.

"How are you not crying?" I demanded, brushing away my tears with the back of my hand after the end credits rolled. "This movie is *so sad*."

"It's fiction." Alex grimaced. "Stop crying."

"I can't stop when I feel like it. It's a biological reaction."

"Biological reactions can be mastered."

I couldn't resist—I scooted closer to him on the couch and pushed his shoulders forward so I could run my palm down his back.

His muscles bunched beneath my touch. "What," he said in a tight, controlled voice, "are you doing?"

"I'm searching for your control panel." I patted his back, trying—and failing—not to notice the sculpted contours of his muscles. I'd never seen Alex shirtless, but I imagined it was glorious. "You must be a robot."

I received a stony glare in response. See? Robot.

"Do you have to swap out your batteries, or are you rechargeable?" I teased. "Should I call you R2-D—"

I yelped when he grabbed my arm and spun me around until I straddled one of his legs. My blood roared in my ears as he tightened his grip on my wrist—not enough to hurt but enough to warn me he could easily break me if he wanted.

Our eyes locked, and the roaring intensified. Beneath those jade pools of ice, I glimpsed a spark of something that sent heat curling through my stomach.

"I'm not a toy, Ava," Alex said, his voice lethally soft. "Don't play with me unless you want to get hurt."

I swallowed my fear. "You wouldn't hurt me."

That mysterious spark crystallized into anger. "This is why Josh was so worried about you. You are trusting to a fault." He leaned forward a fraction of an inch, and it was all I could do not to lean back. Alex's presence crackled with coiled energy, and I had the unnerving sense that beneath all that ice lay a volcano waiting to erupt—and God help whoever was around when that happened. "Don't try to humanize me. I'm not a tortured hero from one of your romantic fantasies. You have *no idea* what I'm capable of, and just because I promised Josh I'd look after you doesn't mean I can protect you from yourself and your bleeding heart."

Pink blossomed on my face and chest. I was torn between fear and fury—fear of that hard, unyielding look in his eyes; fury over how he spoke to me like I was a naïve child who couldn't tie her shoelaces without hurting herself. "This seems like an overreaction to a simple joke," I said, my jaw tight. "I'm sorry I touched you without permission, but you could've told me to stop instead of giving me an entire speech about how you think I'm a helpless idiot."

His nostrils flared. "I don't think you're a helpless idiot."

My anger edged out my fear. "Yes, you do. You and Josh both. You always say you want to 'protect' me like I'm not a grown woman who's perfectly capable of handling herself. Just because I see the good in people doesn't mean I'm an idiot. I think optimism is a *good* trait, and I feel sorry for people who go through life believing the worst of others."

"That's because they've seen the worst."

"People see what they want to see," I countered. "Are there awful people in the world? Yes. Do awful things happen? Yes. But wonderful people exist and wonderful things happen too, and if you focus too much on the negative, you miss all the positive."

Utter silence, made all the more awkward by the fact that I was still straddling Alex's leg.

I was sure he would yell at me, but to my shock, Alex's face relaxed into a hint of a smile. His fingers grazed the small of my back, and I almost jumped out of my skin.

"Those rose-tinted glasses look good on you, Sunshine."

Sunshine? I was sure he meant that mockingly, but the butterflies in my stomach stirred to life anyway, fanning away my anger. *Traitors.*

"Thanks. You can borrow them. You need them more than I do," I said pointedly.

A low chuckle slipped from his throat, and I almost fell to the floor in shock. Tonight was turning out to be a night of firsts.

Alex's hand trailed up my spine until it rested on the back of my neck, leaving a cascade of tingles in their wake. "I feel it dripping all over me."

He did not—what? An inferno consumed my body.

"You're—you—no, I'm not!" I sputtered, pushing him away and scrambling off him. My core pulsed. *Oh my God, what if I was?* I couldn't look, afraid I'd see a telltale wet spot on his jeans.

I'd have to move to Antarctica. Build myself an ice cave and learn to speak penguin because I could never show my face in Hazelburg, DC, or any city where I could run into Alex Volkov again.

His chuckle blossomed into a full-blown laugh. The effect of his real smile was so devastating, even amid my mortification, that all I could do was stare at the way his face lit up and the sparkle that transformed his eyes from beautiful to downright breathtaking.

Holy crap. Perhaps I should be grateful he never smiled, because if *that* was what he looked like while doing it...womankind didn't stand a chance.

"I'm talking about your bleeding heart," he drawled. "What did you think I was talking about?"

"I—you—" Forget Antarctica. I had to move to Mars.

Alex's laughter subsided, but the twinkle in his eyes remained. "What's the next movie?"

"Excuse me?"

He angled his chin toward the DVD on the table. "You brought two movies. What's the second one?"

The sudden subject change gave me whiplash, but I wasn't complaining. I didn't want to speak about my dripping anything with Alex. Ever.

My thighs clenched, and I gritted out, *"Marley & Me."*

"Put it in."

Put it—oh, the DVD.

I needed to get my mind out of the gutter.

While the opening credits played, I sat as far away from Alex as possible and "casually" placed two throw pillows between us for good measure. He didn't say anything, but I saw his smirk out of the corner of my eye.

I was so focused on *not* looking at him I barely paid attention to the movie, but an hour later, when my eyes drooped and sleep beckoned, I was still thinking about his smile.

CHAPTER 9

Alex

I SILENTLY CURSED JOSH AS I CARRIED AVA UPSTAIRS. That asshole always put me in situations I didn't want to be in.

Case in point: sleeping in the same room as his sister.

I'm sure he would be even less happy about it than I was, but I hadn't set up the guest room—I never had guests, not if I could help it—and it was pouring outside, so I couldn't bring her home without both of us getting drenched. I could've left her on the couch, but she would've been damn uncomfortable.

I kicked open the door to my room and set her on the bed. She didn't stir.

My eyes lingered on her form, noticing details I had no business noticing. Her dark hair fanned out beneath her like a blanket of black silk long enough for me to wrap my fist around, and her skirt rode up, baring an inch more thigh than modest. Her skin looked smoother than silk, and I had to clench my hands to refrain from touching her.

My mind flashed back to earlier in the night. Her skin had turned the prettiest shade of red when I made my "dripping" comment, and while I'd joked about her bleeding heart, a part of me—a very large part—had wanted to bend her over my knee, yank up her skirt, and find out just how wet she was. Because I'd seen the lust in those big, brown eyes—she'd been turned on. And if she hadn't moved away when she did...

I tore my gaze away, my jaw clenching at the unwelcome thoughts crowding my brain.

I shouldn't have been thinking about my best friend's sister this way, but something had shifted. I wasn't sure when or how, but I'd started seeing Ava less as Josh's baby sister and more as a woman. A beautiful, pure-hearted but feisty woman who might be the death of me one of these days.

I never should've invited her in earlier. I should've gone on my date with Madeline like I'd planned, but truth be told, I couldn't stand Madeline's company outside the bedroom. She was gorgeous, rich, and sophisticated, and she understood she'd get nothing more than a physical relationship out of me, but she insisted on being wined and dined before each of our sex sessions. I only obliged because the woman fucked like a porn star.

A night in with Ava, as bad of an idea as it had turned out to be, had sounded far more appealing than another tiresome meal at a generic fancy restaurant where Madeline preened and pretended we were a couple in front of DC's movers and shakers.

She didn't expect any strings from our arrangement, but she liked status symbols, and I—as one of the richest, most eligible bachelors in the DMV area, according to *Mode de Vie*'s latest power issue—was a status symbol.

I didn't care. I used her; she used me. We got orgasms out of it. It was a mutually beneficial relationship, but my arrangement with Madeline had run its course. Her less-than-pleased reaction when I called to tell her I couldn't make it tonight had cemented my decision.

Madeline had no claim over me, and if she thought a few

dinners and blowjobs would change my mind, she was sorely mistaken.

I lifted Ava so I could tuck her beneath the covers. I'd expected her to sleep with a dreamy smile like the one she always wore when she was awake. Instead, her brows were drawn, her mouth tight, her breathing shallow.

I almost smoothed a hand over her brow before I caught myself.

Instead, I changed into a pair of black sweats, flicked off the light, and climbed into the other side of bed. A gentleman would sleep on the couch or the floor, but of all the insults people had thrown my way over the years, "gentleman" wasn't one of them.

I laced my hands behind my head, trying to ignore the soft female presence beside me. Sleep wasn't forthcoming, as usual, but instead of flipping to a specific day in my mental scrapbook, I let my mind wander as it pleased.

November 27, 2013.

"Trust me, dude, my dad will be thrilled he has someone to talk football with." Josh hopped out of the car. "Me being an NBA instead of NFL guy is his biggest disappointment."

I smirked, following him up the driveway toward his family's imposing brick house in the Maryland suburbs. It wasn't as large as my mansion on the outskirts of Philadelphia where I lived with my uncle, but it must've cost at least a million or two. Thick hedges lined the stone path leading up to the massive mahogany front door, and a fall-themed wreath of flowers accented with a silky bow hung over the brass door knocker.

"My sister's doing, most likely," Josh said, noticing my gaze. "My dad hates all that shit, but Ava loves it."

I knew little about his sister other than that she was a few years younger than us, and she liked photography. Josh had bought her

*a secondhand DSLR camera from eBay for Christmas because she
kept dropping hints about it whenever they spoke on the phone.*

I met Josh's father first. He sat in the living room, watching
the Cowboys versus Lions game like Josh had predicted. Michael
was shorter than his son, but his chiseled face and sharp eyes made
him appear taller than his five feet eight inches.

"Nice to meet you, sir." I held his gaze, unflinching, when I
shook his hand.

Michael grunted a response.

Josh was a second-generation Chinese American, which meant
his father had been born in the U.S. Michael had been the model
son, a straight-A student who'd attended top-tier schools and
founded a successful company despite the fact that his own parents
never finished high school. Similar to my father, except mine had
been born in Ukraine and immigrated to the U.S. in his teens.

My chest tightened. When Josh found out I had no family to
celebrate Thanksgiving with other than my uncle, who couldn't
care less about the holiday, he'd invited me to celebrate with the
Chens. I was both grateful and somewhat irritated. I hated being
the object of anyone's pity.

"Josh, have you—oh." The female voice behind me halted.

I turned, my cool gaze assessing the petite brunette in front
of me. She wasn't actually that short—probably five foot five—
but compared to my six three, she was miniature-sized. With her
rosebud lips and delicate face, she resembled a doll.

She beamed, and I fought a grimace. It wasn't normal for
smiles to be that bright.

"Hi! I'm Ava, Josh's sister. You must be Alex." She held out
her hand.

I stared at it long enough that her smile faded, replaced with
an uncomfortable expression, and Josh nudged me in the ribs.

"Dude," he coughed out the side of his mouth.

I finally shook her hand. It was tiny and delicate, and I couldn't help thinking how easy it would be to crush it.

This girl and her sunshiny smile wouldn't last a day in the real world, where monsters lurked around every corner and people hid their dark intentions behind masks. I was sure of it.

A scream yanked me out of my memories and into real life again, where the shadows grew long and the body next to mine writhed with distress.

"Stop!" Stark terror drenched Ava's voice. "No! *Help!*"

Five seconds later, I'd turned on the bedside lamp and was out of bed, gun in hand. I always kept a firearm by my side, and I'd installed a new, top-of-the-line security system right after I moved in. I didn't know how an intruder got past all the defenses without triggering an alarm, but they picked the wrong house to break into.

When I looked around, though, I didn't see anyone else in the room.

"Please, stop!" Ava twisted on the bed, her face pale. Her eyes were wide open but unseeing. "He—" She choked like she couldn't get enough air in her lungs.

Nightmare.

My shoulders relaxed before tensing again.

She wasn't having a nightmare; she was having night terrors. Powerful ones, if her reaction was anything to go by.

Ava screamed again, and my heart tripped. I almost wished there *were* an intruder so I had something physical to fight.

I couldn't wake or restrain her; that was the worst thing you could do when someone had night terrors. All I could do was wait for the episode to pass.

I left the bedside lamp on and kept an eye on her in case she hurt herself with all the thrashing. I hated feeling helpless, but I knew better than anyone that no one can fight our mental battles for us.

Half an hour later, Ava's screams had quieted, but I continued my vigil. It wasn't like I could sleep. My insomnia meant I only slept two or three hours a night, though I often crashed for naps in the middle of the day when I could.

I opened my laptop and was reviewing new business documents when my phone pinged.

Josh: Yo, I'm bored.

Guess I wasn't the only person who couldn't sleep tonight.

Me: What do you want me to do about it?
Josh: Entertain me.
Me: Fuck you. I'm not your circus monkey.
Josh: I woke up my roommate, I snorted so loud. You should def dress up as a circus monkey for Halloween.
Me: Only if you dress up as an ass. Sorry, I mean donkey.
Me: You're already an ass.
Josh: What a comedian. Don't quit your day job.
Josh: P.S. You think I won't do it? I'll do it just so I can blackmail you with the monkey pics.
Me: You don't tell someone you want to blackmail them before getting the blackmail material, dumbass.

As Josh and I joked and gave each other shit, I glanced to my side, where Ava slept with her face buried in one of my pillows. A trickle of something that might've been guilt wormed its way into my stomach, which was ridiculous. It wasn't like we'd messed around.

Besides, sleeping in the same bed as my best friend's sister wasn't the worst thing I'd ever done...or would do.

Not by a long shot.

CHAPTER 10

Ava

SOMETHING SMELLED DELICIOUS, LIKE SPICE AND HEAT. I wanted to wrap it around myself like a blanket.

I snuggled closer to the source, enjoying the strong, solid warmth beneath my cheek. I didn't want to wake up, but I'd promised Bridget I would volunteer at a local pet shelter with her this morning before my afternoon shift at the gallery.

I allowed myself one more minute of coziness—had my bed always been this big and soft?—before I opened my eyes and yawned.

Weird. My room looked different. No photograph prints papering the walls, no vase of sunflowers by the bed. And did my bed just move by itself?

My eyes latched onto the broad expanse of bare skin beneath me, and my stomach dropped. I looked up, up—straight into a pair of familiar green eyes. Eyes that stared back at me with no hint of the humor from last night.

He flicked his gaze down. I followed it...and realized, to my abject horror, that I was touching Alex Volkov's dick. Unintentionally, and he had on sweats, but still.

I. Was. Touching. Alex. Volkov's. Dick.

And it was hard.

Mortification washed over me in a tidal wave. *Move your hand. Move it now!* My brain screamed, and I wanted to. I really did. But I stayed frozen, paralyzed by shock and humiliation and something else I would rather not name.

A brief image flashed through my mind of what Alex must be packing beneath his pants. I had a feeling—pun intended—it would rival that of any male porn star.

"Please remove your hand from my cock unless you plan on doing something with it," Alex said coolly.

I finally yanked my hand away and scrambled back, my heart beating a wild rhythm in my chest as I tried to get my bearings.

"What happened? Why am I here? Did we— Did you and I—" I gestured between us, sick with anticipation.

Oh God. Josh would kill me, and I couldn't even blame him.

I'd slept with my brother's best friend.

Shit!

"Relax." Alex rolled out of bed, lithe and graceful as a panther. Sunlight streamed through the windows and illuminated his sculpted frame, casting his perfectly carved chest and abs in a pale glow. "You fell asleep during that dog movie and it was raining, so I brought you up here. The end."

"So we didn't..."

"Fuck? No."

"Oh, thank God." I pressed a hand to my forehead, relief a cool balm to the heat on my cheeks. "That would've been awful."

"I'll try not to take offense to that," Alex said dryly.

"You know what I mean. Josh would've murdered us, brought us back to clean up the mess, then murdered us again. Not that I want to sleep with you either way." *Liar*, an annoying voice in my head whispered. I shoved it aside. "You're not my type."

Alex's eyes narrowed. "No? Then who, pray tell, *is* your type?"

It was too early for this. "Um…" I scrambled to think of a safe answer. "Ian Somerhalder?"

He let out a derisive snort. "Better than the sparkly vampire," he muttered. "News flash, Sunshine. You and Ian aren't happening."

I rolled my eyes and got out of bed, flinching when I saw my reflection in the mirror. Wrinkled dress, tangled hair, pillow creases on my cheek, and was that a line of crusted drool on the side of my lips? Yeah, I wouldn't win a beauty contest anytime soon.

"Thanks, Captain Obvious," I said, discreetly wiping the drool from my face while Alex pulled a T-shirt over his head. His bedroom was as sparse as the living room, with nothing except his massive bed, a nightstand with a lamp and alarm clock, and a dresser decorating the space. "Don't get your panties in a twist. I'm not your type either, remember? Or maybe I am…" I raised my eyebrows at the obvious tent in his pants.

He wanted to be a jerk again? Two could play this game.

"Don't read too much into it. It's morning wood. Every guy gets it." Alex ran a hand through his hair, which of course was still perfect after a night's sleep. "And my panties are *not* in a twist."

"If you say so," I sang. "Also, stop calling me Sunshine."

"Why?"

"Because it's not my name."

"I'm aware. It's a nickname."

I released an exasperated breath. "We don't know each other well enough for nicknames."

"We've known each other for eight years."

"Yes, but we don't have that type of relationship! Plus, I'm sure you're mocking me, bleeding heart and all."

Alex raised an eyebrow. "Enlighten me. What type of relationship *do* we have?"

We were treading dangerous ground. "We're neighbors. Friendly acquaintances." I racked my brain for more, because those terms didn't seem right. "Movie buddies?" ⌐

He closed the distance between us, and I gulped, holding my ground even though I wanted to run. "You always sleep in the same bed as your acquaintances?" he asked softly.

"I didn't *ask* to sleep in the same bed as you." I tried not to stare at the region below his waist, but it was difficult to ignore. My nipples hardened and scraped against my bra, and my skin flushed with arousal.

What the hell was happening? This was *Alex*, for Pete's sake. The Antichrist. The asshole. The robot.

Except my body must've not gotten the memo, because I was suddenly fantasizing about pushing him on the bed and finishing what my hand had inadvertently started earlier.

No. Get it together. You are not sleeping with Alex Volkov, now or ever.

"Anyway, I—I have to go. Volunteer. Pets," I stammered, barely making sense to myself. "Thanksforlettingmestayoverseeyou laterbye!"

I beat a hasty retreat down the stairs and ran home.

I needed a cold shower, ASAP.

Phase Sadness status: Failed.

"You *touched* Alex's dick?" Bridget's eyes widened. "What did it feel like?"

"*Shh!*" I glanced around to see if anyone was listening, but everyone was too busy with their duties to pay attention to us. Bridget had volunteered at the shelter long enough that the staff didn't blink an eye at the princess in their midst, and we were always the only volunteers on the days Bridget came in, per the royal family's request. "It's unbecoming for a princess to say the word 'dick.'"

Especially in Bridget's posh, lightly accented voice, which sounded like it was made to discuss fancy galas and Harry Winston diamonds, *not* male genitalia.

"I've said worse things than dick."

As someone who'd been friends with her for almost four years, I could confirm. It still sounded wrong though.

"So?" she prompted. "What did it feel like?"

"I don't know what you want me to say. It felt like a penis." A big, hard—*nope*. *Not* going there.

Not now. Not ever.

Bridget and I were cleaning and sanitizing the cages at Wags and Whiskers, a pet rescue shelter located near campus. She was a huge animal person and had been volunteering here since sophomore year. I accompanied her when I had time, as did Stella. Jules was allergic to cats, so she stayed away. But this shelter was Bridget's baby. She came twice a week without fail, much to Booth's consternation.

I stifled a smile at the sight of the burly, redheaded bodyguard eyeing a parrot with suspicion. Despite its name, Wags and Whiskers took in all sorts of animals, not just dogs and cats, and it had a small but robust bird section.

Booth wasn't scared of birds per se, but he disliked them; he said they reminded him of giant flying rats.

"Hmm." Bridget seemed disappointed by my uninteresting response. "And the movies really didn't make him sad? At all?"

"Nope." I rolled up the newspaper from my cage and dumped it in the garbage can. "Well, I fell asleep before the end of *Marley & Me*, but I doubt he cried or anything like that. He looked bored the entire time."

"Yet he continued watching *both* movies." Bridget raised a perfect blond brow. "Interesting."

"He didn't have a choice. I was already at his house."

"Please. This is Alex Volkov we're talking about. He'd throw someone out in a heartbeat if he wanted."

True.

I frowned and considered her words. "He's nicer to me because I'm Josh's sister."

"Right." Bridget let out a soft laugh. "Which phase is up next again?"

Ugh, the stupid Operation Emotion, or OE as I'd started calling it. It was the bane of my existence.

"Disgust." I had no clue what I'd do, but that phase seemed easier. I had a feeling lots of things disgusted Alex.

"I'd pay good money to see that." Bridget tossed a laughing glance in Booth's direction. "Are you all right, Booth?"

"Yes, Your Highness." He grimaced when the parrot squawked, "Ooh, yes! Spank me, master!"

"I am not your master," he told the bird. "Go away."

The parrot drew itself up and ruffled its feathers in indignation.

Bridget and I burst into laughter. Apparently, the parrot's old owner had been quite active sexually...and kinky. Its outburst today was tame compared to its previous tirades.

"I'll miss you." Bridget sighed. "I hope my next bodyguard has a sense of humor."

I stopped scrubbing the cage. "Wait, what? Booth, you're leaving us?"

Booth scratched the back of his neck, looking sheepish. "My wife is giving birth soon, so I'll be on paternity leave."

"Congrats." I smiled, even though I was pretty sad. He was Bridget's employee, but we'd accepted him as an honorary member of our group. He'd bailed us out of many dodgy situations in the past, and he gave pretty good boy advice too. "We'll miss you, but that is so exciting!"

His face flushed with pleasure. "Thank you, Miss Ava."

He was unfailingly polite and insisted on calling me "Miss" no matter how many times I told him he could use just my first name.

"We're throwing you a going-away party when the time comes," Bridget said. "You deserve it for putting up with me all these years."

Booth's blush deepened. "That's not necessary, Your Highness. It was—is—a pleasure serving at your side."

Bridget's eyes twinkled. "See, this is why you deserve a going-away party. You're the best."

Before Booth could explode from how red he was turning, I added, "We'll make it parrot themed."

Bridget and I collapsed into laughter again while the bodyguard shook his head with a half-resigned, half-embarrassed smile.

It was almost enough to take my mind off Alex.

CHAPTER 11

Ava

Operation Emotion: Phase Disgust.

"You already brought me welcome-to-the-neighborhood cookies." Alex stared at the basket on the dining table.

"These aren't welcome cookies." I pushed the basket toward him. "These are an experiment. I tried a new recipe and wanted to see what you think."

He made an impatient noise. "I don't have time for this. I have a conference call in half an hour."

"It won't take you half an hour to eat one cookie."

Yes, I had finagled an invitation inside Alex's house *again*, this time for the second phase of OE. Neither Alex nor I mentioned his, er, morning wood situation a few days earlier. I didn't know about him, but I'd prefer if we forgot about that morning altogether.

"Fine." He peered at the confections with suspicion. "What flavor?"

Asparagus, raisins, and garlic brittle. I'd picked the most disgusting ingredient mixture I could think of because this was, after all, Phase Disgust. Part of me felt bad because he'd been pretty nice the night we watched those movies and he'd canceled his date for me; the other part was still a little annoyed by how he'd treated Owen, who was afraid to talk to me now because he feared Alex would pop up out of nowhere and kill him.

I cleared my throat. "It's a, um, surprise."

I tucked my hands beneath my thighs and jittered my foot as Alex brought a cookie to his mouth. I almost dove for him and knocked it out of his hand, but I was curious how he would react.

Would he spit it out? Gag? Throw the cookie at me and kick me out of the house?

He chewed slowly, his face not betraying any emotion whatsoever.

"Well? What do you think?" I injected fake pep in my voice. "Good?"

"You baked these." Not a question.

"Yep."

"You baked the red velvet cookies, and you baked...these."

My bottom lip disappeared behind my teeth. "Uh-huh." I couldn't look him in the eye. Not only was I terrible at lying, I was terrible at keeping a straight face.

"They're fine."

My head snapped up. "What?" The cookies weren't fine; they were *gross*. I'd tried one myself and almost threw up. Asparagus and garlic brittle did *not* mix.

Alex finished chewing, swallowed, and dusted the crumbs from his hands. "They're fine," he repeated. "Now, if you'll excuse me, I have a call to take."

He left me in the dining room, mouth agape.

I picked up a cookie from the basket and nibbled on it, just in case—

Blech! I gagged and ran into the kitchen to spit out the abomination, then rinsed my mouth with water from the sink to erase the lingering aftertaste.

Alex must have messed-up taste buds, because no normal person would've been able to swallow those cookies without at least grimacing.

I came to the only conclusion that made sense.

"He's definitely a robot."

Phase Disgust status: Failed.

Operation Emotion: Phase Happiness.

What makes men happy?

The question had plagued me in the lead-up to the third phase of OE. Most of the things that would make men happy didn't apply to Alex or my situation.

Money? He had plenty of it.

Job satisfaction? Nothing I could do about it.

Spending time with friends? Josh was Alex's only friend that I knew of, and I was pretty sure Alex did not enjoy most people's company.

Sex? Um, I wasn't having sex with him for an experiment. Or any other reason, even if I was the *teeniest* bit curious about what it would be like.

Love? Lol, okay. Alex Volkov in love. Sure.

Jules suggested a blowjob, which fell under sex and which I vetoed.

It took days of brainstorming, but I came up with something that *might* work. Perhaps it wouldn't make Alex soul happy, but it would help him relax and laugh a little.

Maybe.

"I dislike sitting on the ground." He stared at the grass like it was a mud pit. "It's uncomfortable and unsanitary."

"It's not. How is it unsanitary?" I laid a blanket out and anchored it with the picnic basket so it wouldn't blow away. I'd convinced him to go for a picnic at Meridian Hill Park. When I brought it up, he'd acted like I'd suddenly sprouted two heads, but he'd agreed.

Now, if only he would stop acting like such a grouch, we could enjoy the last days of summer.

"The grass is probably soaked with dog urine," he said.

I winced at the mental image. "That's what the blanket is for. *Sit.*"

Alex heaved an aggrieved sigh and sat, looking unhappy about it the entire time.

Undeterred, I unpacked the picnic basket, which contained summer pasta (my favorite), lobster rolls (Alex's favorite, according to Josh), assorted fruit, cheese and crackers, strawberry lemonade, and, of course, my red velvet cookies, which Alex seemed to like.

"This is so much better than being cooped up inside." I stretched my arms over my head, luxuriating in the sunshine. "Fresh air, good food. Don't you feel happier already?"

"No. There are children screaming everywhere, and a fly just landed in your salad."

Damn flies. I quickly shooed it away.

"Why are we here, Ava?" Alex's brow pinched.

"I'm trying to help you relax, but you're making it damn hard." I threw my hands in the air, pretty exasperated myself. "You know that magical thing you did during movie night called a laugh? You did it once, you can do it again. Come on," I encouraged while he stared at me like I was crazy. "You must have *some* warm, fuzzy feelings left inside you somewhere."

And that was the moment a dog from a nearby party wandered over and peed on Alex's shoes.

Phase Happiness status: Failed.

Operation Emotion: Phase Fear.

We were stuck.

Between my friends and I, none of us could think of a single thing that would inspire fear in Alex—at least none that weren't illegal or fucked up.

Jules, who was more comfortable with "fucked up" than the rest of us, joked about pretending to rob him at knifepoint—at least I hoped she was joking—until Stella pointed out Alex would likely turn the situation around and kill *me* before he figured out it was a prank.

I agreed.

I was too young to die, so we scrapped any ideas that would involve a physical confrontation.

In the absence of any light-bulb moments, I turned to my last resort, Josh.

We video chatted every week, catching each other up on our lives, and right now, he was telling me about his new "friend with benefits."

Seriously.

Trust Josh to find women even while doing medical volunteer work in the middle of a tiny Central American village.

"How is that possible?" I demanded. "There's less than a hundred people in that village!" I knew because I'd Googled it after Josh announced his placement.

"What can I say? I'm charmed," he drawled. "Wherever I go, women follow."

"I think she was there before you, dickhead, and I hope you're not neglecting your work to make out with your new 'friend.'"

"Da fuck? Tell me you're kidding."

I waved my hand in the air. "I am, I am. Don't get your knickers in a twist."

As much of a horndog as my brother was, he took his work

seriously. Whereas I had to bust my ass for my A's, he was one of those annoying people who didn't have to study much to excel in school. But he loved medical work and helping people. Even when we were young, he was the one who'd bandaged me up after I scraped my knee and looked up ways to help me with my nightmares while our father threw himself into work.

It was why I let Josh get away with his overprotectiveness. He could be annoying as hell, but he was still the best brother.

I'd never tell him that though. If his head inflated any more, he'd have trouble walking.

"By the way." I tried to sound casual as I fiddled with the sleeve of my shirt. "Halloween is coming up, and I was thinking of pulling some pranks. Is there anything Alex is scared of? Clowns, spiders, heights…"

Suspicion crawled into Josh's face. "Halloween is more than two months away."

"Yeah, but it sneaks up on you, and I want to prepare."

"Hmm." Josh tapped his fingers on his thigh. "*Hmm…*"

"Any time before I'm eighty would be great."

"Shut up. You know how hard it is to think of something Alex is scared of? I've known him for eight years, and I've never once seen him afraid."

My face fell. *Well, shit.*

"You could try the usual stuff people hate, but I doubt you'd get anywhere." Josh shrugged. "One time, we ran into a bear while hiking and the fucker didn't even blink. Just stood there looking bored and annoyed until the bear wandered off. Jump scares don't work either. Trust me—I've tried many times to prank him in the past and failed every time."

"Good to know."

Perhaps this phase was a lost cause. If Josh, who knew Alex better than anyone, couldn't scare him, none of us could.

The suspicion returned to Josh's eyes. "Is this your idea or a certain redhead's?"

"Umm...mine?"

"Bullshit." Josh scowled. "Don't tell me she's still infatuated with Alex. He's a lost cause when it comes to relationships—won't ever get into one, and he only fucks certain women."

I was dying to ask who these "certain women" were, but I couldn't without sounding like I was interested in Alex. Which I wasn't.

"I don't think Jules was ever *infatuated* with him," I said. "She just thinks he's hot."

"Whatever." Josh raked a hand through his hair. "Hey, I have an early morning tomorrow, so I'm gonna crash. Let me know if you succeed in pranking him, and take a video of it for me. I could use the laugh."

"Sure." Concern replaced my earlier discomfort at hearing about Alex's "certain women." I could tell Josh was worn out despite his jokes and wiseass comments. There were dark circles beneath his eyes, and lines of tension bracketed his mouth. He'd begged off early our last few calls, and usually, he could stay up all night talking about the dumbest stuff.

Once, he'd waxed poetic about his new sneakers until three in the morning.

"Get some rest. If I have to fly down to Central America to kick your ass, I'll be pissed."

"Ha." Josh snorted. "You *wish* you could kick my ass."

"Night, Joshy."

"*Don't* call me that," he grumbled. "Night."

After I hung up, I took out my notebook and scratched out phase three.

Phase Fear status: On hold (indefinitely).

CHAPTER 12

Ava

"THE EXPERIMENT IS A FAILURE, BUT AT LEAST IT'S over." I sucked down the rest of my cranberry vodka. I'd nursed it for so long all the ice had melted and it tasted like fruity water. "Thank God."

"Too bad." Bridget looked disappointed. "I was looking forward to seeing Alex lose his cool."

"He still can. The experiment isn't over yet." Jules wagged her finger in the air.

Unease crawled down my neck. "Yes, it is. We decided on four phases: sadness, disgust, happiness, and fear."

"There are *five* phases." Jules's hazel eyes sparkled with mischief. "The last is jealousy, or did you forget?"

"I never agreed to that!"

We were at the Crypt, Thayer's most popular off-campus bar, for one last hurrah before classes started Monday. Students had started trickling back, and the bar was way more packed than earlier this summer.

"But it's the best one," Jules argued. "Don't—"

"Ava."

I stiffened at the sound of my name said in *that* voice. The voice that used to whisper to me at night and tell me it—he—loved me. The voice I hadn't heard in two months, not since he showed up outside the gallery one day in July and demanded I speak with him.

I tilted my head until hazel eyes clashed with my dark brown ones.

Liam towered over me, handsome and preppy as ever in a navy-blue polo and khakis. He'd cut his hair, the blond strands no longer the mess of soft curls I'd loved running my fingers through but shorter, closer cropped to his skull.

My peripheral vision revealed my friends' reactions to his unexpected appearance in one sweep: nervousness on Stella's face, trepidation on Bridget's, anger on Jules's.

"What are you doing here?" I told myself I didn't need to be scared. We were in public, sitting smack-dab in the middle of a crowded bar. I was surrounded by my friends and Booth, who eyed Liam like he'd like to drop-kick the guy.

I was safe.

Still, my skin tingled with unease. I thought Liam had given up his quest to win me back, but here he was, looking at me like nothing had changed. Like I hadn't caught him with his pants down and buried inside a strange blond the night he'd claimed to have a "fever." I'd dropped by his apartment hoping to surprise him with chicken soup and ended up being the one surprised instead.

"Can we talk?"

"I'm busy." I could smell the alcohol on his breath, and I wasn't interested in talking to a sober Liam, much less a drunk one.

"Ava, please."

"She said she's busy, asshole," Jules snapped.

Liam glared at her. They'd never gotten along. "I don't remember speaking to you," he sneered.

"See if you remember when I stick my—"

"Five minutes." I stood, my shoulders stiff.

"What—"

"Ava—"

"Are you sure—"

My friends all spoke at once.

I nodded. "Yeah. I'll be back in five, okay? If I'm not"—I glared at Liam—"you can come looking for me with torches and pitchforks." He'd hover all night unless I spoke with him, and I'd rather get it over with.

"I have more than torches and pitchforks," Booth growled.

Liam flinched.

I followed him outside the bar and crossed my arms over my chest. "Make it quick."

"I want you to give me another chance."

"I've already told you a thousand times—no."

Frustration bled into his face. "Babe, it's been *months*. What do you want me to do, fall to my knees and beg? Haven't you punished me enough?"

"It's not about punishment." For someone who'd graduated cum laude, Liam couldn't seem to grasp such a simple concept. "It's about the fact that *you cheated on me*. I don't care how long it's been or how sorry you are. Cheating is unacceptable, and we are not getting back together. Ever."

The frustration morphed into anger. "Why? You got a new man?" he growled. "You have new dick and you don't need me anymore, is that it? I never knew you were such a slut."

"Fuck you." My heart pumped fast. Liam had never said such nasty things to me. Ever. "Your five minutes are up. This conversation is over."

I tried to leave, but he grabbed my wrist and yanked me back. It was the first time he'd laid a hand on me out of anger.

My heart was racing triple speed now, but I forced myself to remain calm. "Get your hands off me," I hissed. "Or you'll regret it."

"Who is he?" Liam's eyes were wild, and I realized with a sinking stomach that he was not only drunk but high. A dangerous combination. "Tell me!"

"There *is* no other guy, and even if there were, it's none of your business!" I wished I'd brought my pepper spray. Since I hadn't, I settled for the next best thing: kneeing him in the balls. Hard.

Liam released his hold on me and doubled over in pain. "You bitch," he wheezed. "You—"

I didn't wait to hear what he said next. I fled back to the safety of the bar, my pulse roaring in my ears.

I can't believe that happened. Liam had never acted so out of control. He'd been persistent and kind of douchey, but he'd never physically hurt me.

By the time I told my friends what happened and they ran outside to confront Liam over my protests, he was gone, but my queasiness remained.

You think you know someone until something happens that proves you never really knew them at all.

CHAPTER 13

Alex

THAYER UNIVERSITY'S ANNUAL ALUMNI CHARITY GALA was the event of the season, but while it did raise money for the latest cause du jour, it wasn't really about charity. It was about ego.

I attended every year.

Not because I wanted to be a philanthropist or reminisce about my college days but because the gala was a fountain of information. Thayer counted the most powerful people in the world among its alumni, and they all congregated in the ballroom of the Z Hotel DC every August. It was the perfect opportunity to network and gather intel.

"...pass the bill, but it'll get killed in Congress..."

I pretended to listen while Colton, an old classmate who now worked in government affairs for a major software company, droned on about the latest piece of tech legislation.

He rarely had anything interesting to say, but his father was high up in the FBI, so I kept him in my orbit in case I needed him in the future.

It was always about the long game—measured not in weeks or months but in years. Decades.

Even the tiniest of seeds can sprout into the mightiest of oaks.

It was a simple concept most people didn't understand because they were too busy chasing short-term gratification, and it was the reason most people fail. They spent their lives sitting on their asses and telling themselves "someday" when preparation should've started yesterday. By the time "someday" came, it was too late.

"...this IP issue with China—" Colton stopped abruptly. *Thank God.* If I had to listen to his nasal voice one more second, I would've walked over to the bar and stabbed myself in the eye with a fork.

"Who is *that*?" he asked, a hungry look overtaking his face as he stared over my shoulder. "She's *hot*." His voice was as hungry as his expression. "I've never seen her before. Have you?"

I turned out of mild curiosity. It took me a second to latch on to whatever unsuspecting girl had captured his attention. Colton was almost as big a womanizer as Josh.

When I finally located the source of Colton's ravenous gaze, my muscles snapped into a rigid line and my fist closed around the stem of my champagne glass, tight enough the delicate glass could shatter at any moment.

She glided into the ballroom, her lithe body poured into a sleek gown that flowed over her curves like liquid, shimmering gold. She'd gathered her hair up in a fancy hairdo, exposing her swanlike neck and smooth shoulders. Dark eyes. Bronze skin. Red lips. All smiles and sunshine, unaware she'd walked into a pit of vipers.

A goddess entering the gates of hell, and she didn't even know it.

A pulse ticked in my jaw.

What the *hell* was Ava doing here, wearing that dress? She wasn't an alumna yet. She shouldn't be here. Not around these people.

I wanted to gouge out the eyes of every man staring at her like they were starved and she was a juicy steak, which was pretty much every man here—including Colton. If he didn't put his tongue back in his mouth soon, I'd cut it out for him.

I left him salivating behind me without a word and stalked toward Ava, my strides eating up the distance between us with angry, purposeful steps. I made it halfway before someone blocked my path.

I recognized her scent before I saw her face, and my muscles tightened further.

"Alex," Madeline purred. "I haven't heard from you in a while."

Her scarlet gown matched the glossy lipstick coating her pouty lips. Blond hair spilled over her shoulders in sculpted waves, and I was close enough to see the faint outline of her nipples through the silky material of her dress.

Once upon a time, that might've turned me on. Now, she might as well be wearing a potato sack for all the reaction her outfit and seductive smile elicited.

"I've been busy." I sidestepped her; she mimicked my action and blocked my path again.

"You never made it up to me for canceling our date." She trailed her fingers over my arm. It was a light, practiced touch, meant to leave the receiver wanting more.

All I wanted was for her to get out of my way.

My eyes strayed toward Ava again, and my already tense muscles bunched up further at the sight of Colton by her side. How the fuck did he get over there so fast? I'd played basketball with him once in college; the man was slower than a turtle on morphine.

"And I never will." I removed Madeline's hand from my arm. "It's been fun, but it's time for us to part ways."

Shock scattered over her face before coalescing into a mask of stunned anger. "You're *breaking up* with me?"

"To break up, we'd have to be dating." I nodded at one of the men staring at her ass. "The congressman looks interested. Why don't you go say hi?"

Red tinted her creamy skin. "I'm not a prostitute," Madeline hissed. "You can't pimp me out to another man when you're done with me. And we are *not* done. Not until I say so. I'm Madeline fucking Hauss."

"That's where you're wrong. We're all prostitutes in our own ways." My smile lacked any semblance of warmth. "I'll give you a pass for your tone tonight, given our history. But don't contact me again, or you'll find out the hard way how I earned my reputation for being ruthless. I'm not above ruining women."

This conversation was over.

I left a sputtering Madeline behind me and walked away, irritated by the interruption and furious at the sight of what awaited me in the middle of the dance floor.

Ava and Colton swayed to music from the live band the university had hired for the gala. His hands rested on her hips, and I saw them inching lower with each passing second.

I arrived next to them right as she laughed at something he said. It rang through the air like silver bells, and the tic in my jaw pulsed harder.

He didn't deserve her laugh.

"Something funny?" I asked, masking my ire with an expression of cool indifference.

Surprise and wariness flared in Ava's eyes at the sight of me. *Good.*

She should be wary. She should be fucking home, safe and sound, instead of dancing with a manwhore like Colton and letting him put his hands all over her.

"I was just telling her a joke." Colton chuckled but shot me a warning look that said, *Why are you cockblocking, man?* He was lucky if all I did was cockblock. I was tempted to break every bone in his hand for touching her like that. "You mind? We're in the middle of a dance."

"Actually, it's my turn." I maneuvered myself between them and pulled him off her with a little more force than necessary. Colton flinched. "You have to leave the gala early. Business calls."

His brow pinched. "I..." His eyes roved between me and Ava, whose own eyes did the same between me and Colton. Realization dawned on his face. Guess he wasn't so slow after all. "Ah, you're right. Sorry, man. I forgot."

"We'll get lunch one day," I said. I didn't burn bridges unless it was a business rival or I had to. *Seeds. Oaks.* "At Valhalla."

The Valhalla Club was the most exclusive private club in DC. It capped its membership at one hundred members, each of whom was allowed to bring one guest for a meal each quarter. I'd just handed Colton the ticket of a lifetime.

His eyes widened. "Oh, y-yeah," he stuttered, trying and failing to hide the awe in his voice. "I'd like that."

"Good night." It was a dismissal and a warning rolled into one.

Colton scurried off, and I turned my displeasure on Ava. We were close enough that I could see the way the lights from the chandeliers reflected in her eyes, like tiny star beams streaking across an endless night. Her lips parted, lush and wet, and an insane desire to find out whether they tasted as sweet as they looked gripped me.

"You ran off my dance partner." Her voice came out breathier than usual, and my cock jerked at the sound.

I gritted my teeth and tightened my hold on her until she gasped. "Colton is not a dance partner. He is a womanizer and a slimeball, and it's in your best interest to stay far, far away from him."

It would be in her best interest to stay far away from me too, and the irony wasn't lost on me. *If she only knew why I'm in DC...*

But fuck it, I was okay with hypocrisy. It didn't even crack the top ten of my worst traits. "You don't know what's in my best interest." The star beams morphed into fire, sparking with challenge. "You don't know me at all."

"Is that so?" I guided her across the floor, my skin prickling from the strange, electric charge in the air. It was a thousand needles piercing my flesh, searching for a weakness. A crack. A doorway, however tiny, through which it could slip and jump-start my long-dead, long-cold heart.

"Yes. I don't know what Josh tells you about me—if he tells you anything at all—but I assure you, you have no idea what I want or what's in my best interest."

I paused, causing her to stumble into my chest. My thumb and forefinger grasped her chin, forcing her to look up at me. "Try me."

Ava blinked, her breaths coming out in short, shallow puffs. "My favorite color."

"Yellow."

"My favorite ice cream flavor."

"Mint chocolate chip."

Her chest rose and fell harder. "My favorite season."

"Summer, because of the warmth and sunshine and greenery. But secretly, winter fascinates you." I lowered my head until my own breath skated over her skin and her scent crawled into my nostrils, drugging me, turning my voice into a hoarse, sinful version of itself. "It speaks to the darkest parts of your soul. The manifestations of your nightmares. It's everything you fear, and for that, you love it. Because the fear makes you feel alive."

The band played, and the people around us whirled and danced, but in this world we'd carved for ourselves, it was silent save for our ragged intakes of breath.

Ava shivered beneath my touch. "How do you know all that?"

"It's my job to know things. I observe. I watch. I remember." I gave into my desire—a tiny one—and traced her lips with my thumb. A shudder rolled through us, our bodies so in sync we reacted the exact fucking way at the exact fucking time. I brought my thumb down and tightened my grip on her chin. "But those are shallow questions, Sunshine. Ask me something real."

She stared up at me, those eyes liquid chocolate beneath the lights. "What do I want?"

A dangerous, loaded question.

Humans want a lot of things, but in every heart, there beats one true desire. One thing that shapes our every thought and action.

Mine was vengeance. Sharp, cruel, bloodthirsty. It had bloomed from the bloody corpses of my family's bodies, inking itself into my skin and soul until my sins were no longer mine but ours. Mine and vengeance's, two shadows walking the same twisted path.

Ava was different. And I'd known what her true desire was the moment I set eyes on her for the first time eight years ago, her face shining and her mouth stretched into a warm, welcome smile.

"Love." The word floated between us on a soft gust of air. "Deep, abiding, unconditional love. You want it so much you're willing to live for it." Most people thought the biggest sacrifice they could make was to die for something. They were wrong. The biggest sacrifice you could make was to *live* for something—to allow it to consume you and turn you into a version of yourself you didn't recognize. Death was oblivion; life was reality, the harshest truth that had ever existed. "You want it so much you'd say yes to anything. Believe in anyone. One more favor, one more kind gesture...and maybe, just maybe, they'll give you the love you want so desperately you'd whore yourself out for it."

My tone turned biting; the conversation made a U-turn and headed straight for harsh and brutal.

Because what I admired most about Ava was also what I hated about her. Darkness craves light as much as it wants to destroy it, and here, in this ballroom, with her in my arms and my cock straining against my zipper, that had never been more clear.

I hated how much I wanted her, and I hated that she wasn't smart enough to run away from me while she still had a chance.

Though let's be honest, it was already too late.

She was mine. She just didn't know it yet.

I hadn't known it myself until I saw her in Colton's arms and every instinct raged at me to tear her away. To claim what belonged to me.

I'd expected her to grow angry at my words, to cry or run away. Instead, she stared at me, unflinching, and said the most unbelievable thing I'd heard in a long, long time.

"Are you talking about me, or are you talking about yourself?"

I almost laughed at the sheer ludicrousness of the statement. "You must have me confused with someone else, Sunshine."

"I don't think I do." Ava stood on tiptoes so she could whisper in my ear. "You don't fool me anymore, Alex Volkov. I've been thinking about it, the way you noticed all those things about me. How you agreed to look after me, even though you could've said no. How you stayed in to watch those movies with me when you thought I was upset and let me stay the night in your bed after I fell asleep. And I've come to a conclusion. You want the world to think you have no heart when in reality, you have a multilayered one: a heart of gold encased in a heart of ice. And the one thing all hearts of gold have in common? They crave love."

I tightened my grip on her, equal parts furious and turned on by her foolish, stubborn *goodness*. "What did I tell you about romanticizing me?"

I wanted her, but it wasn't a sweet, tender kind of want.

It was a dirty, ugly want, tainted by the blood on my hands and a desire to drag her out of the sunshine and into my night.

"It's not romanticizing if it's true."

A growl slipped out of my throat. I allowed myself to hold on to her for one more moment before I pushed her away. "Go home, Ava. This isn't the place for you."

"I'll go home when I want to go home."

"Stop being difficult."

"Stop being a jerk."

"I thought I had a heart of gold," I mocked. "Choose a side and stick to it, Sunshine."

"Even gold can tarnish if you don't take care of it." Ava stepped back, and I tamped down the ridiculous urge to follow her. "I paid for my ticket, and I'm staying here until I decide I want to leave. Thank you for the dance."

She walked away, leaving me in fuming silence.

———

I made a concerted effort to ignore Ava for the rest of the night, though she hovered in my peripheral vision like a golden spark that wouldn't go away. Luckily for every man in the room, she didn't dance with anyone else; she spent most of her time chatting and laughing with alumni.

I spent mine gathering intel—information about congressmen I'd need if I wanted to expand Archer into a conglomerate, tidbits about competitors, interesting nuggets about friends and foes.

I'd just wrapped up an enlightening conversation with the head of a major consulting company when I lost sight of Ava. One minute, she was there; the next, she was gone. She was still gone twenty minutes later—far too long for a bathroom break.

It was getting late; perhaps she'd left. We hadn't parted on the best note, but I'd check on her to make sure she got home safely. Just in case.

I was already on my way out when I heard a thump from the small room by the ballroom, which served as an overflow space for guests' bags and jackets.

"Get *off* me!"

I froze, my blood icing over. I opened the door, and the ice erupted into scalding flames.

Ava's soon-to-be-dead ex Liam had her pinned against the wall with her wrists above her head. They were so focused on each other they didn't notice me enter.

"You told me you didn't have a new man," Liam slurred. "But I saw you dancing and watching *him*. You lied, Ava. Why did you lie?"

"You're crazy." Even from here, I saw her eyes flashing fire. "Let go of me. I mean it. Or do you want a repeat of last week?"

Last week? What the *hell* happened last week?

"But I love you." His voice turned plaintive. "Why won't you love me back? It was one mistake, babe." He pressed his body against hers, preventing her legs from moving. Fire scorched my veins as I stalked over, my approach muffled by the plush carpet beneath my feet. "You *do* still love me. I know it."

"I'm giving you three seconds to move, or I can't be held accountable for my actions." A burst of pride shot through me at Ava's flinty tone. *Attagirl.* "One...two...three."

I'd just reached them when she headbutted him. A howl ripped out of his throat; he stumbled back, clutching his nose, which now gushed blood.

"You broke my nose!" he spat. "You asked for it, you slut."

He lunged for her, but he only made it halfway before I closed my fist around the back of his shirt and yanked him back.

It was only then that Ava noticed me. "Alex. What—"

"Mind if I join the fun?" I hauled Liam up by his collar, my lip curling at the sight of his watering eyes and bleeding nose, and socked him in the gut. "That's for calling her a slut." Another blow to the jaw. "That's for holding her against her will." A third hit to his already suffering nose. "That's for cheating on her."

I continued my blows, letting the fire wash over me until Liam was unconscious and Ava had to drag me off him.

"Alex, stop. You'll kill him!"

I adjusted my shirtsleeves, breathing hard. "Is that supposed to deter me?"

I could go all night and not stop until the bastard was nothing more than a pile of bloodied flesh and broken bones. A film of red tinted my vision, and my knuckles were bruised from the force of my blows.

The image of him pinning Ava against the wall flashed through my mind, and my anger erupted anew.

"Let's just go. He learned his lesson, and if someone sees you, you'll get in trouble." Ava's face was the color of porcelain. "Please."

"He wouldn't dare say anything." Nevertheless, I relented because of how bad she was trembling. Despite her toughness earlier, Ava was shaken up over the incident. Plus, she was right; we were lucky no one had stumbled in on us yet. I didn't give a shit if they did, but there was no need to drag out an already unpleasant evening.

"We should call an ambulance." She eyed Liam's prone form with unease. "What if he's seriously hurt?"

Of course she still cared about his well-being after he tried to fucking assault her. I didn't know whether to laugh in disbelief or shake her.

"He won't die." I'd controlled my hits so they were punishing but not fatal. "He'll wake up with a helluva banged-up face and a couple of broken ribs, but he'll survive." *Unfortunately.*

The worry remained on Ava's face. "We should call 911 anyway."

For fuck's sake. "I'll place an anonymous call from the car." I had a burner phone in the glove compartment.

I placed a steadying hand on the small of her back as we exited the hotel. Thankfully, we didn't pass anyone except the doorman along the way. "Now." I pinned Ava with a glare. "Tell me what the *hell* happened between you two last week."

CHAPTER 14

Ava

HE WAS FURIOUS.

He was alive with it, pulsing with it. One hand clutched the steering wheel, knuckles white, while the other rested on the gearshift, flexing and unflexing like he wanted to strangle someone. The glow from passing streetlights illuminated the beautifully carved planes of his face as we sped down the dark streets, throwing into sharp relief the tense set of his mouth and the way his brows bunched over his eyes.

When I told him about the incident with Liam outside the Crypt, I almost disintegrated from the force of his fury.

"I'm okay," I said, wrapping my arms around my torso. My voice sounded scratchy and unsure. "Really."

That only made him more furious.

"If you'd attended Krav Maga lessons like I'd asked, he wouldn't have been able to corner you like that." Alex's voice was soft. Deadly. I remembered his face when he'd pounded Liam's face into a pulp, and a shiver skated down my spine. I wasn't scared of Alex hurting me, but the sight of all that coiled strength unleashed was unnerving. "You have to learn to protect yourself. If anything had happened to you..."

"I defended myself fine." I pressed my lips together. I hadn't seen Liam at the gala, but there had been so many people it would've been impossible for me to pick him out in the crowd. Bridget had finagled me an invite to the ball so I could connect with an alumnus who'd been a World Youth Photography fellow a few years ago. We'd had a great conversation about the WYP program, but I tired of the small talk with the rest of the gala's guests and had been on my way out when Liam cornered me in the coatroom.

He'd been high tonight too. I'd seen it in his dilated pupils and manic energy. He never used drugs when we were together, at least not that I knew of, but whatever he was on, it made him swing between bouts of rage and sadness.

Despite what he did and the things he'd said, I couldn't help feeling sorry for him.

"This time." Alex's jaw flexed. "Who knows what might happen the next time you're alone?"

I opened my mouth to respond, but before I could get the words out, images and sounds slammed into my brain, rendering me mute.

I threw a stone into the lake and giggled at the ripples that spread over the smooth surface.

The lake was my favorite part of our backyard. We had a dock that ran out to the middle of the water, and during the summers, Josh would cannonball off it while Daddy fished and Mommy read magazines and I skipped stones. Josh always teased me about not being able to swim, much less cannonball.

I would though. Mommy signed me up for swimming lessons, and I would be the best swimmer in the world. Better than Josh, who thought he was the best at everything.

I'd show him.

My mouth turned down at the corners. There would be no more summers by the lakeside with all of us though. Not since Daddy moved out and took Josh with him.

I missed them. It got lonely sometimes, especially since Mommy didn't play with me like she used to. All she did now was yell into the phone and cry. Sometimes, she sat in the kitchen and just stared into space.

It made me sad. I tried to cheer her up—I drew her pictures and even gave her Bethany, my nicest, bestest doll to play with, but it didn't work. She still cried.

Today was a better day though. It was our first time playing by the lake since Daddy moved out, so maybe it meant she felt better. She'd gone into the house for more sunscreen—she always worried about freckles and stuff like that—but when she got back, I planned to ask her to play with me like we used to.

I picked up another stone from the ground. It was smooth and flat, the type that would make really pretty ripples. I drew my arm back to throw it, but I smelled something flowery—Mommy's perfume—that distracted me.

My aim veered and the stone thudded onto the ground, but I didn't mind. Mommy was back! We could play now.

I turned, smiling a big gap-toothed smile—my front tooth fell out last week, and I found five dollars from the tooth fairy under my pillow after, which was super cool—but I only made it halfway before she pushed me. I pitched forward—down, down, off the edge of the deck, my scream swallowed up by the water rushing toward my face.

Reality yanked me back into the present with jarring force. I bent over double, chest heaving, tears streaming down my face. *When had I started crying?*

It didn't matter. All that mattered was I *was* crying. Huge, heaving sobs, the kind that made my nose all snotty and my stomach hurt. Thick, salty rivulets ran down my cheeks and dripped off my chin onto the floor.

Maybe I'd finally broken, split apart for the world to see. I'd always known I wasn't normal, me with my forgotten childhood and fragmented nightmares, but I'd been able to hide it behind smiles and laughter. Until now.

My nightmares were usually confined to when I was sleeping. They had never consumed me when I was awake.

Maybe the adrenaline rush from what happened with Liam triggered something in my brain. If I had to worry about my waking hours *and* my sleeping ones...

I pressed the heels of my palms to my eyes. I was losing it.

A cool, strong hand touched my shoulder.

I jerked, remembering in a rush that I wasn't alone. That someone bore witness to my sudden, humiliating breakdown. I also hadn't noticed that Alex had pulled over to the side of the road until now.

If he'd been furious before, he was crazed now. Not in a psycho, angry way—well, maybe a little—but more in a panicked way. His eyes were wild, that muscle in his jaw jumping so fast it had a life of its own. I'd never seen him like that. Pissed, yes. Annoyed, definitely. But not like *that*.

Like he wanted to burn the world down at seeing me hurt.

My naïve heart sang, cutting a swath of hope through my lingering panic. Because no one looks at someone like that unless they care, and I realized that I wanted Alex Volkov to care. Very much.

I wanted him to care because of *me*, not because of a promise he'd made to my brother.

Talk about a terrible time to come to such a realization. I was a freaking mess, and he'd just beat the living daylights out of my ex-boyfriend.

I sucked in a shaky breath and wiped the tears from my face with the backs of my hands.

"I will destroy him." Alex's words sliced through the air like lethal blades of ice. Goose bumps blossomed on my skin and I shivered, my teeth chattering from the cold. "Everything he has ever touched, everyone he has ever loved. I will ruin them until they're nothing more than a pile of ashes at your feet."

I should've been terrified by the leashed violence flickering in the car, but I felt oddly safe. I always felt safe around him.

"I'm not crying because of Liam." I took a deep breath. "Let's not talk or think about him anymore, okay? Let's salvage the rest of the night. Please."

I needed to take my mind off everything that happened tonight, or I'd scream.

A few beats passed before Alex relaxed his shoulders, though his face remained tight. "What do you have in mind?"

"Food would be good." I'd been too nervous to eat at the gala, and I was starving. "Something greasy and bad for you. You're not one of those health nuts, are you?"

His body was so cut he looked like he subsisted on lean protein and green shakes.

Disbelief shadowed his eyes before he let out a short laugh. "No, Sunshine, I'm not one of those health nuts."

Ten minutes later, we pulled up in front of a diner that looked like it served nothing *but* food that was bad for you.

Perfect.

Heads swiveled in our direction when we walked into the diner. I couldn't blame them. It isn't every day you see a duo in black tie enter a roadside diner. I'd tried my best to fix myself so I was presentable before I left the car, but there's only so much a girl can do without her makeup bag.

Something warm and silky enveloped me, and I realized Alex had taken off his jacket and draped it over my shoulders.

"It's cold," he said when I shot him a questioning look. He glared at a group of guys who were ogling me—or rather, my breasts—from a nearby table.

I didn't protest. It *was* cold, and my gown didn't cover much.

I also didn't protest when Alex insisted we sit in the back and positioned me in the booth facing the wall, so I was out of the other diners' sight.

We placed our orders, and I shifted beneath the weight of his stare.

"Tell me what happened in the car." For once, his tone was gentle, not commanding. "If not Liam, what made you…"

"Freak out?" I fiddled with a loose strand of hair. No one knew about my lost memories or nightmares except my family and closest friends, but I had a strange urge to spill the truth to Alex. "I had a… flashback. Of something that happened when I was young." I'd been in denial all these years, telling myself they were fictional nightmares instead of fragmented flashbacks, but I couldn't lie any longer.

I swallowed hard before I told Alex, in halting sentences, about my past—or what I remembered of it. It wasn't the lighthearted conversation I'd envisioned when I'd suggested we "salvage the rest of the night," but I felt ten times lighter by the time I finished.

"They told me it was my mom," I said. "My parents were going through a nasty divorce, and apparently, my mom had some sort of breakdown and pushed me into the lake, knowing I couldn't swim. I *would've* drowned had my dad not come by to drop off some papers and seen what happened. He saved me, and my mom's condition deteriorated further until she killed herself. They told me I was lucky to be alive but…" I drew in a shuddering breath. "Sometimes, I don't feel lucky."

Alex had listened patiently the entire time, but his eyes flickered dangerously at my last statement. "Don't say that."

"I know. It's super self-pitying, which is not what I want. But what you said at the gala earlier? About me craving love? You're right." My chin wobbled. Call me crazy, but something about being tucked away in this corner of a random diner, sitting across from a man who I thought didn't even like me until a few hours ago, made me voice my most insidious thoughts. "My mom tried to kill me. My dad barely pays attention to me. Parents are supposed to be the most loving forces in their children's lives, but..." A tear slipped down my cheek, and my voice broke. "I don't know what I did wrong. Maybe if I tried harder to be a good daughter—"

"Stop." Alex's hand curled around mine on the table. "Don't blame yourself for fucked-up things other people do."

"I try not to, but..." Another shaky breath. "That's why Liam cheating on me hurt so much. I wasn't really in love with him, so I wasn't heartbroken per se, but he's yet another person who was supposed to love me but didn't." My chest ached. If I wasn't the problem, why did this keep happening to me? I tried to be a good person. A good daughter, good girlfriend...but no matter how hard I tried, I always ended up hurt.

I had Josh and my friends, but there was a difference between platonic love and the deep bonds that bound a person to their parents and significant other. At least there was supposed to be.

"Liam is an idiot and an asshole," Alex said flatly. "If you let lesser people determine your self-worth, you'll never reach higher than their limited imagination." He leaned forward, his expression intense. "You don't have to work overtime to get people to love you, Ava. Love isn't earned. It's given."

My heart rattled in my chest. "I thought you didn't believe in love."

"Personally? No. But love is like money. Its worth is determined by those who believe in it. And you obviously do."

Such a cynical, Alex way to look at it, but I appreciated his straightforwardness.

"Thank you," I said. "For listening to me and...everything."

He released my hand, and I curled it into a loose fist, mourning his warmth.

"If you really want to thank me, you'll take Krav Maga lessons." Alex arched an eyebrow, and I laughed softly, grateful for the small break. It'd been a heavy night.

"Okay, but you have to sit for a portrait with me."

The idea came to me on a whim, but the more I thought about it, the more I realized I'd never wanted to photograph someone as much as I wanted to photograph Alex. I wanted to peel back those layers and reveal the fire I knew beat within that cold, beautiful chest.

Alex's nostrils flared. "You're negotiating with me."

"Yes." I held my breath, hoping, praying...

"Fine. One session."

I couldn't hold back my smile.

I was right. Alex Volkov did have a multilayered heart.

CHAPTER 15

Ava

I AGONIZED FOR DAYS OVER WHETHER TO SHOOT ALEX in a studio or outdoors.

I took all my photo shoots seriously, but this one felt different. More intimate. More...life-changing, like it had the power to make or break me, and not just because I might submit it as part of my portfolio for the WYP fellowship.

I would have Alex Volkov all to myself for two hours, and I wouldn't squander a single second.

I eventually chose to shoot him in a studio. I booked the space in the university's photography building and waited, pulse thumping, for him to arrive.

I was more nervous than I should have been, but maybe that had something to do with the wildly inappropriate dream I'd had last night. One that featured me, Alex, and positions that would make an acrobat's jaw drop.

Even now, I flushed at the memory.

To stave off the onslaught of unbidden, erotic images, I fiddled with my camera and stared out the window, where the green leaves of summer bloomed on the trees and swirled lazily on soft gusts of wind.

Despite the lush foliage, it was an unusually chilly day for early September, but it didn't take long before a different kind of winter whooshed in on a cloud of delicious spice and cool reserve.

Alex entered the room, cutting a sleek, powerful figure in his all-black outfit—black coat, black pants, black shoes, black leather gloves. A sharp contrast to the pale beauty of his face.

My fingers tightened around my camera. My creative soul salivated, desperate to capture that mystery and lay it bare on the page.

I've found that the quietest, most reserved people often make the best portrait subjects because the exercise doesn't require them to speak; it requires them to *feel*. Those who bottle up their emotions every day feel the strongest and love the hardest; the best photographers are the ones who can capture each drop of emotion as it spills out and mold it into something visceral, relatable. Universal.

Alex and I didn't greet each other. No words, not so much as a nod.

Instead, the air hummed with silence as he divested himself of his coat and gloves. It wasn't overtly sexual, but *everything* about the man was sexual. The way his strong, deft fingers slid each button from its hole without so much as a pause or stumble; the way his shoulders and arms flexed beneath his shirt as he hung his coat on the hook by the door; the way he moved toward me like a panther stalking its prey, his eyes bright with scorching intensity.

The velvety tips of butterfly wings brushed my heart, and I clutched my camera tighter, willing myself not to step back or tremble. Liquid warmth pooled in my stomach, and every inch of my body became a nerve ending, hypersensitized and throbbing with arousal.

He hadn't touched me, and I was already so turned on I trembled. I hadn't thought that was possible outside romance novels and movies.

Those green eyes flared, like he knew exactly what he did to me. How tight my nipples were beneath my thick sweater, how wet I was between my thighs. How much I wanted to devour him, to pour myself into the cracks of his soul so he would never be alone.

"Where do you want me?" Gravel rasped his voice for the first time since I'd met him, turning the clear, authoritative tone into something darker. More sinful.

Where did I want him? *Everywhere. Over me. Beneath me. Inside me.*

I licked my suddenly dry lips. Alex's gaze dropped to my mouth, and my entire body pulsed.

No. I wasn't a schoolgirl on a date. I was a professional. *This* was professional.

A portrait session with a subject, just like countless other sessions I'd had in the past.

Of course, I hadn't wanted to throw any of my previous subjects on the floor and ride them until kingdom come, but that was a minor detail.

"Uh, here is fine," I croaked, gesturing to the stool I'd set up on a plain white background.

I'd kept today's setup simple. I didn't want anything to detract from Alex, not that they could. His presence obliterated everything around him until he was the only thing left standing.

He folded himself gracefully on the stool while I checked my settings and snapped a few test shots. Even unposed, his photos jumped off the screen, his gorgeous features and piercing eyes tailor-made for the camera.

I reined in my shameless lust and spent the next hour coaxing him out of his shell, moving him into various poses, and encouraging him to relax.

I wasn't sure Alex understood the meaning of the word.

The pictures so far were beautiful, but they lacked emotion. Without emotion, a beautiful photo is just a photo.

I attempted to open him up with chitchat, talking to him about everything from the weather to Josh's latest update to that day's news, but he remained aloof and guarded.

I tried a different tactic. "Tell me about your happiest memory."

Alex's lips thinned. "I thought this was a photo shoot, not a therapy session."

"If it were a therapy session, I'd be charging you five hundred dollars an hour," I quipped.

"You have an inflated sense of your worth as a therapist."

"If you can't afford me, just say so." I snapped more pictures. *Finally*. A sign of life.

The click and whir of the shutter filled the air.

"Sweetheart, I could get you with a snap of my fingers, and I wouldn't have to shell out a single penny."

I lowered my camera and glared at him. "What the hell is that supposed to mean?"

A tiny smirk tugged at the corner of Alex's mouth. "It means you want me. You wear your emotions all over your face."

My thighs clenched, and my skin burned until I thought I'd collapse into a pile of ashes on the ground.

"Now who's the one with an inflated sense of self-worth?" I managed, my heart racing. Alex had never said anything so direct to me before. He usually shut down any hint of attraction between us, but here he was, talking about me wanting him.

He was right, but still.

Alex leaned forward and clasped his hands loosely together. Graceful, casual but alert. Waiting to lure me into his trap.

"Tell me it's not true."

I licked my lips again, my throat parched, and his gaze zeroed in on my mouth. The small but unmistakable movement bolstered my confidence and compelled me to say something I would've never had the guts to say otherwise. "It's true." I almost smiled at the flare of surprise in his eyes. He hadn't expected honesty. "But you want me too. Question is, are you too scared to admit it?"

Alex's thick, dark brows lowered. "I'm not scared of anything."

Lies. I would've believed him a month ago, but now I knew better. Everyone fears something; it's what makes us human. And Alex Volkov—for all his control, all his power—was still wonderfully, frighteningly, heartbreakingly human.

"That doesn't answer my question." I walked over to him, my camera swaying from the strap looped around my neck. He didn't move an inch, not even when I brushed my fingers along his jaw. "Admit you want me too."

I wasn't sure where my boldness came from. I wasn't Jules. I always waited for the guy to ask me out—partly out of fear of rejection, partly because I was too shy to make the first move.

But I had a feeling if I waited for Alex, I might have to wait forever.

It was time to take matters into my own hands.

"If I wanted you, I would've taken you already," Alex said with lethal softness.

"Unless you're too scared."

I was playing with fire, but that was better than standing out in the cold alone.

I stiffened when Alex trailed his fingers down my neck and over my shoulder. His lips curved into a smirk. "Nervous? I thought this was what you wanted," he taunted. His hand dipped lower, closer to the curve of my breast. The ice pools in his eyes melted, revealing a blazing inferno that heated me from head to toe.

My head spun. My nipples tightened into firm beads, and my pulse throbbed through every inch of my body. Somehow, it was *worse* that he wasn't touching me where I ached most; the anticipation heightened my senses, and my skin tingled with phantom caresses.

"That's not what I said," I wheezed. Oh God, this was embarrassing. What had I been thinking? I wasn't a femme fatale or a...a...whatever else was like a femme fatale.

I couldn't think straight.

Alex grazed his thumb over my breast, and I moaned. *Moaned.* From a touch that lasted less than two seconds.

I wanted to die.

His pupils dilated until the green irises were eclipses ringed with jade fire. He dropped his hand, and cool air rushed in to replace the warmth of his touch.

"Finish the photo shoot, Ava." The roughness of his voice scraped against my skin.

"What?" I was too shocked by the sudden change in the atmosphere to process his words.

"The photo shoot. Finish it," he gritted out. "Unless you want to start something you're not ready to finish."

"I—" The photo shoot. Right.

I backed away on unsteady legs and tried to refocus on the task at hand. Alex sat straight-backed, his face hard, while I circled him and captured every angle I could think of.

The low hum of the heater was the only sound breaking the silence.

"Okay. We're done," I said after twenty minutes of excruciating quiet. "Thanks—"

Alex stood, grabbed his coat, and walked out without another word.

"—for doing this," I finished, my words echoing in the empty room.

I exhaled a long-held breath. Alex was the most mercurial

person I knew. One minute, he was gentle and protective; the next, he was closed off and distant.

I scrolled through the photos, curious as to how they'd turned out.

Oh. Wow. Alex's emotions leaped off the screen after our... interaction, and yes, most of it was irritation, but irritation on him looked better than contentment on anyone else. The way the shadows hit the sharp lines of his brows, the glare of his eyes, the set of his jaw...these were possibly the best photos I'd ever taken.

I paused at one of the last shots, and my heart stuttered to a stop.

I'd been so busy snapping away I hadn't paid attention in the moment, but now I saw it clear as day. Stark desire scrawled across Alex's face as he stared at me, his eyes burning through the camera and straight into my soul. It was the only photo where he wore that expression, so it must've been a momentary slip on his part.

A stripping of his mask, if only for a few seconds.

But here's the thing: even a few seconds can change someone's life. And as I turned off the camera and packed up my equipment with shaky hands, I couldn't shake the feeling that mine had been altered forever.

CHAPTER 16

Alex

"IT'LL BE OVER IN A FEW MONTHS." I LEANED BACK IN my chair and rolled my whiskey glass in my hands, watching dust mites dance in the air before me.

"Hmm." My uncle rubbed his jaw, his eyes sharp as he examined me through the screen. I'd turned the guest room into my home office, as I preferred to work from home on the days I didn't *have* to be in the office. Fewer tiresome interactions that way. "You don't seem excited for someone who's been working toward this since you were ten."

"Excitement is overrated. All I care about is that it'll be done."

Despite my words, my chest pinched, because my uncle was right. I *should* feel excited. Vengeance was so close I could taste it, but instead of sweet relief, it coated my tongue with bitterness and turned my stomach sour.

What came after vengeance?

Every other purpose I could have paled in comparison to the force that had driven me all these years. It'd held me together while I shattered on the inside. It'd revived me as I lay bleeding, comatose in a pool of guilt and horror. It'd created the chessboard on which I'd painstakingly lined up all the pieces one by one, year over year until the moment came for me to topple the king.

I didn't fear much, but I feared what would happen after I lost my purpose.

"Speaking of done..." I set my glass on the table. "I assume you signed the papers for the Gruppmann deal today."

Ivan smiled. "Congratulations. You're one step closer to world domination."

Me. Because Archer Group had always been mine.

I'd funded its inception with my money, and the company had flourished under my guidance over the years. My father had started his own successful construction company after immigrating to the U.S., and it'd been his dream to see me take it over one day. The company had collapsed in the wake of his death—I'd been too young to prevent its demise—but I'd built upon his legacy and created something new. Something bigger.

All my parents had wanted was for me to grow up happy and successful. While the "happy" part may be a reach, I could damn well work on the "successful" part.

After my uncle and I wrapped up our weekly check-in, I opened my burner laptop and pulled up the encrypted folder where I kept all the documents detailing my enemy's finances, business dealings—both legal and illegal—and upcoming contracts. I'd chipped away at his empire over the years, slow enough that he thought he was just going through a long string of shitty luck. Now I needed just one more piece of evidence before I felled him for good.

I stared at the screen, the numbers blurring before my eyes as I envisioned my endgame. The prospect didn't excite me as much as it used to.

At least I'd taken satisfaction in the fall of Liam Brooks. A few well-placed calls, and he'd been fired and blacklisted from every company that mattered in the northeastern United States. A few whispers in the right ears, and he'd landed on DC society's blacklist. Honestly, I'd just sped up his inevitable fall from grace— according to the information my people dug up, Liam had picked up a nasty drug habit and several DUIs since graduating. It was only a matter of time before he fucked up at his job or pissed off the wrong people on his own.

He was a man who'd had everything handed to him on a silver platter, and he threw it away for a temporary high. *Excuse me while I cry a nonexistent river.*

Then again, he'd cheated on Ava, so he clearly lacked the good-judgment gene.

My phone pinged with a social media notification. I despised social media, but it was the world's biggest gold mine of information. It was amazing how much personal information people shared online with little to no regard for who might be watching.

I tapped on the notification so it would go away and accidentally clicked into the app, where a shaky video of two people arguing autoplayed. I was about to exit when I paused. Looked closer.

Fuck!

The video was still playing when I left and sped toward Madeline's house.

CHAPTER 17

Ava

OF ALL THE WAYS I'D PICTURED MY FRIDAY NIGHT going, getting trapped in a pool room by a blond who eyed me like I'd stolen her favorite Prada purse wasn't one of them.

"I'm sorry, do I know you?" I strove for politeness even as I took a step back. The woman looked familiar, but I couldn't place where I'd seen her before.

"I don't believe we've met." Her smile could've cut glass. Objectively, she was one of the most beautiful women I'd ever met. With her spun-gold hair, cerulean eyes, and statuesque body, she was what I imagined Aphrodite would look like had she been a real person. But there was something hard about her expression that made her not attractive at all. "Madeline Hauss of the petrochemical Hausses. This is my house."

"Oh. I'm Ava. Chen," I added when she continued staring at me. "Of the, uh, Maryland Chens. Can I...help you?" I hoped that didn't come off rude, considering this was her house, but I hadn't wanted to attend this party in the first place. Stella, who was friends with what must be Madeline's sister, had persuaded me to go out after I spent the past few days buried in school, work, and my fellowship application. Jules and Bridget were both busy tonight, so it was only the two of us.

"I wanted a good look at you," Madeline purred. "Since you captured so much of Alex's attention during the gala."

The gala. Of course. This was the woman I'd seen Alex talking to while I danced with Colton. I'd tried not to look, but I couldn't help staring and comparing myself to her the whole time.

To Jules's dismay, I'd nixed the jealousy part of Operation Emotion, but I'd admittedly used Colton to make Alex jealous at the gala. It was stupid and petty, but Colton had shown up around the same time I saw Alex with Madeline, and I'd been so consumed with jealousy myself I went for it. Judging by Alex's reaction when he saw us dancing, it had worked—a little too well, judging by Madeline's glare.

"I didn't realize you knew Alex," I fibbed. My stomach churned, and not because of Madeline's poisonous tone.

The Hausses' pool room looked like a luxurious, modern Roman bath, all white marble and gilded columns. The pool itself gleamed turquoise beneath a glass dome that revealed the night sky in all its glory, and I spotted the colorful swirl of mosaics beneath the water forming the shape of a mermaid. But the smell of chlorine and sight of all that water...

My dinner rose in my throat.

The Hausses lived in a giant house in Bethesda, and Stella and I had spent the night room hopping, enjoying the different music and entertainment options in each space. While Stella left to find us fresh drinks, I'd wandered into the room next to the one we'd been in and found myself facing my worst, watery nightmare. Madeline had cornered me before I could leave, and here we were.

"Oh, I know Alex *very* well," Madeline said, and I knew, with a sickening drop in my stomach, that she was one of the "certain women" he'd been involved with. Were they still involved? Was she the one he'd almost gone on a date with before I ambushed him for movie night?

Jealousy gnawed at me, almost overpowering my nausea from the chlorine.

"What I don't get is why he would be interested in *you*." She flicked her gaze over me. "I doubt you can keep up with his tastes in the bedroom."

Despite myself, curiosity reared its ugly head. *What tastes?* "You'd be surprised," I bluffed, hoping she'd reveal more information.

My mind flashed back to my sex dream starring Alex, and my heart raced.

Madeline smirked. "Please. You look like the type who expects tender kisses and sweet nothings in bed. But as you probably know"—her smirk turned vicious—"Alex doesn't do either of those things. It's well known among a certain segment of DC's female population. No kissing, no face-to-face contact during sex." She lowered her head so she could whisper in my ear. "But he will take you from behind. Choke and fuck you till you see stars. Call you the filthiest names and treat you like a slut." She straightened, her eyes gleaming with triumph at my scarlet face. "Some women like that. You…" She looked me over again with a laugh. "Go back to your bake sales, honey. You're way out of your league."

My body throbbed at her words, both out of anger at her condescension and stunning arousal at the picture she'd painted.

We were attracting attention. Other partygoers gathered around us, hungry for drama. A few even had their phones out, recording. I guessed Madeline was the draw, because I wasn't well-known enough to be that interesting.

"Maybe," I said, matching the blond's honey-laced poison, "he just doesn't like looking at *you* during sex. Because he's never had that problem with me."

Lies. But she didn't need to know that.

I kept my head above the fray best I could, but I could play dirty when the situation called for it.

Madeline's smile disappeared. "He'll be sick of you in a week. There's only so much sugar a man like Alex can take before he gets a stomachache."

"And there's only so much bitterness he can take before he kicks it to the curb." I raised my eyebrows. "But you already know that, don't you?" I wasn't sure where my sass came from, since I wasn't a sassy person, but Madeline brought out all my claws.

I hated being the type of girl who fought with other girls over a guy, but she'd attacked me first. I wouldn't stand here and let her walk all over me.

Madeline's creamy skin flushed with anger. "Are you calling me bitter?"

Walk away, my better angels encouraged me. I almost did, until I pictured Madeline and Alex together, and the words fell out of my mouth. "Yes, and? What are you going to do about it?"

Childish. So freakin' childish. But the taunt was out there, and I couldn't—

My mind blanked when my body pitched backward and hit the pool with a splash.

She'd pushed me. Into the pool.

The pool.

Ohgodohgodohgod.

Grotesque, echoing laughter broke out, but it sounded dim compared to the roaring in my ears. Shock and panic suffused me, freezing my limbs, and all I could do was stare at Madeline's twisted smirk until my face sank beneath the water.

I'm going to die.

CHAPTER 18

Alex

"WHERE IS SHE?" I GRASPED MADELINE BY THE THROAT, resisting the urge to squeeze until I wiped the smug look off her face.

I'd never raised a hand to a woman outside the bedroom—and then only if they consented—but I was this close to losing my shit.

After I saw the video of Madeline pushing Ava into the pool, which I recognized from my previous visits to the Hauss mansion, I broke every speed limit to get here. By the time I arrived, the party had ended and only a few stragglers remained. I found Madeline laughing with her cronies in the kitchen, but it had only taken a glare from me for her to excuse herself and follow me into the hall.

"Why don't you tighten your hold a little?" she purred. "You know you want to."

"I'm not here to play games." I was holding on to my patience by a thread. "Answer my question, or Hauss Industries is over."

"You don't have that kind of power."

"Don't underestimate me, sweetheart." It wasn't an endearment. "Just because we've fucked a few times doesn't mean you know what—or who—I have in my back pocket. So unless you want to explain to dear old Dad why regulators are breathing down his neck and his precious company stock is tanking, I suggest you answer me. Now."

Madeline's lips compressed into a thin line. "Her friend pulled her out of the pool, and they left," she said, sullen. "How was I supposed to know she can't swim?"

My grip tightened, and my lips curled into a sneer when I saw the resulting flare of desire in her eyes. "Pray she's all right, or the downfall of Hauss Industries will be the least of your worries," I said softly. "Do not contact or come near her or me again. Understand?"

Madeline lifted her chin in defiance.

"Do. You. Understand." I pressed my thumb into the soft flesh of her neck—not enough to injure but enough to make her flinch.

"Yes," she choked out, resentment coating her voice.

"Good." I released her and walked away, keeping my steps calm when all I wanted was to race to Ava's house and check if she was okay. She hadn't answered any of my calls and texts, and while I understood why, it still made me nervous.

"Is she really worth it?" Madeline called after me.

I didn't bother answering her.

Yes.

When I reached my car, I floored the gas and nearly mowed over a group of drunk frat boys. My grip strangled the steering wheel as I imagined how Ava must have felt when she fell into the pool—or how she must feel right now.

A mixture of worry and anger coiled in my stomach. Fuck what I told Madeline earlier. She'd put a huge target on her family's back, and I wouldn't rest until Hauss Industries was no more than a footnote in corporate history.

I pulled up to Ava's house in time to see Stella exiting. I cut the engine and made it to the front door in half a dozen long strides.

"How is she?" I demanded.

Worry etched itself on Stella's face. "She could be worse, given the circumstances. I was getting us drinks when she went into the pool room…" She gnawed on her bottom lip. "Anyway, I found her when that woman pushed her into the pool. I got her out before she passed out or anything like that, but she's pretty shaken. Jules isn't home yet, and I wanted to stay with her, but she said she's going to sleep and insisted I leave." Stella's brows knit together. "You should check on her. Just in case."

That was a big ask coming from Stella, who liked me the least out of Ava's friends, and it said a lot about Ava's current state.

"I'll take it from here." I brushed past her into the living room.

"How did you find out what happened so fast?" Stella called after me.

"Online," was all I said. I made a mental note to call my tech guy and have him scrub every trace of the video off the internet. He was the same person I relied on to hack into my competitors' computers and dig up offshore accounts. Five years of working together, and there hadn't been a single leak or job he couldn't complete. In return, I'd paid him enough money over the years that he could buy a private island off the coast of Fiji if he wanted.

I took the stairs two at a time until I reached Ava's room. The light spilling through the crack in the door told me she was still awake, despite what she'd told Stella.

I rapped my knuckle twice against the wood. "It's Alex."

There was a short pause. "Come in."

Ava sat in bed, her hair damp and her gaze wary as she took me in. Worry edged out my anger when I saw how pale her cheeks were and the way she shivered, even though the heat was on and she'd tucked herself beneath a thick comforter.

"I saw what happened. Some fucker filmed it live on social." I sat on the edge of the bed and resisted the insane urge to tuck her into my chest. "I'm sorry."

"It's not your fault. Don't blame yourself for fucked-up things other people do."

A smile ghosted my mouth as she threw my words back at me.

"You have terrible taste in women though." Ava sniffled. "Do better."

"Madeline and I are over. We never even started."

"That's not what she told me."

I cocked my head at her stiff tone. "Are you...jealous?" The thought pleased me more than it should've.

"No." With her scowl and fluffy gray top, she looked like an angry kitten. "As if. So what if she's tall and blond and looks like a Victoria's Secret model? She's a horrible person. Next time I see her, I'm going Krav Maga on her ass."

I bit back a full smile. Ava had attended all of one lesson. It'd be a while before she went anything on anyone's ass, but her indignation was adorable.

"She won't be bothering you again." I grew serious. "The pool—"

"I thought I was going to die."

I flinched, horror skating through me at the thought.

"I thought I was going to die because I can't swim and I have this stupid phobia and I am *so sick of it*." Ava fisted her covers, her mouth tight. "I hate feeling helpless and out of control in my own life. Do you know one of my biggest dreams is to travel the world and I can't even do that because the idea of flying over an ocean makes me sick?" She took a deep, shaky breath. "I want to see what's out there. The Eiffel Tower, the pyramids of Egypt, the Great Wall of China. I want to meet new people and try new things and live life, but I can't. I'm trapped. When I was in that pool, thinking those were my last moments...I realized I've done none of the things I want to do. If I died tomorrow, I'd die with a lifetime of regrets, and that terrified me even more than the water." She looked up at me, her big brown eyes wide and vulnerable. "That's why I need you to do something for me."

This time, I was the one who swallowed hard. "What is it, Sunshine?"

"I need you to teach me to swim."

CHAPTER 19

Ava

IF I HAD TO DESCRIBE ALEX VOLKOV, A LITANY OF words came to mind. Cold. Beautiful. Ruthless. Genius.

"Patient" wasn't one of them. It wasn't even in the top thousand.

But over the past few weeks, I had to admit I might have to bump it up on the list, because he'd been nothing *but* patient as he guided me through a series of visualization and meditation exercises to prepare me for my first real swimming session.

If you'd told me two months ago that I would be "visualizing" and "meditating" with Alex freakin' Volkov, I would've laughed my ass off, but sometimes reality is stranger than fiction. And you know what? The exercises helped. I'd visualize myself standing near a body of water, then use deep breathing and relaxation techniques to calm myself. I started small, with pools and ponds, and worked my way up to lakes. Alex also started taking me to bodies of water so I could get more comfortable near them. I even dipped my toe into a pool.

I wasn't cured of my fear of water, but I could think about it now without having a panic attack—most of the time. The thought of flying over an ocean still made me sick to my stomach, but we'd get there.

The most important thing was I had hope. If I worked long and hard enough, then maybe one day, I would finally conquer the fear that had haunted me for as long as I could remember.

But that wasn't the only seismic change in my life. Something had shifted in my relationship with Alex. He was no longer just my brother's best friend but my friend too, though some of the thoughts I had toward him were less than platonic. What I'd felt during our photo shoot was nothing compared to the fantasies running through my mind now.

He will take you from behind. Choke and fuck you till you see stars. Call you the filthiest names and treat you like a slut.

That was the one snippet from my horrible conversation with Madeline I couldn't forget. Every time I thought about it, my thighs clenched and warmth flooded my lower belly. I was also ashamed to admit that yes, I'd masturbated to fantasies of Alex doing those things to me more than once.

Not that he would. He'd been frustratingly composed since my pool incident—no heated gazes, no lingering touches, no trace of the desire I'd seen on his face in that photo from our shoot.

I hoped that would change tonight.

"I'm nervous." Stella crouched behind the couch; she was so tall she had to bend all the way so her dark curls didn't peek out from the top. "Are you nervous?"

"No," I lied. I was definitely nervous.

It was Alex's birthday, and I was throwing him a surprise party. There was every chance he hated both surprises and parties, but I felt compelled to do *something* for him. Besides, no one should be alone on their birthday. I'd asked Alex what his plans for tonight were—not letting on that I remembered it was his birthday—and he said he had business documents to look over.

Business documents. On his birthday.

I don't think so.

Since I didn't know any of his friends except Ralph, our Krav Maga instructor, I'd kept the guest list small. Jules, Stella, Bridget, Booth, and a few other students from the KM Academy hid in Ralph's living room. Ralph had agreed to host the shindig and trick Alex into thinking it was a casual Halloween get-together for academy regulars; he and Alex should arrive any minute now.

I'd nixed the costume party idea—Alex didn't strike me as a costume sort of guy—but I hoped the party itself was a good idea. Most people liked parties, but he wasn't most people.

A car door slammed, and my stomach tightened with anticipation. "Shh! They're here," I said in a loud whisper.

The lingering murmurs in the dark room quieted.

"...help me set up," Ralph said, opening the door and flipping on the light.

We all jumped out. "Surprise!"

I wished I'd had my camera ready, because the expression on Alex's face? Priceless. He looked like a frozen mannequin except for his eyes, which moved from the balloons I'd tied to various pieces of furniture to the handmade poster spelling out *Happy birthday, Alex!* in glittery blue cursive before resting on my face.

"Happy birthday!" I chirped, trying to tamp down my nerves. I couldn't tell if he liked or hated the surprise or if he was indifferent. The man was harder to read than a Latin textbook in the dark.

No response. Alex remained frozen.

Jules came to the rescue, turning on the music and encouraging people to eat and mingle. While the rest of the party scattered, I edged my way toward him and pasted on a bright smile.

"Fooled you, huh?"

"How did you know it's my birthday?" Alex peeled off his

jacket and tossed it over the back of the couch. At least that meant he was staying.

I shrugged, feeling self-conscious. "You're Josh's best friend. Of course I know."

He frowned. "You've never celebrated my birthday before."

"There's a first time for everything. C'mon." I pulled at his wrist. "You're twenty-seven! That means you have to take twenty-seven shots."

His frown deepened. "Absolutely not."

"It was worth a try." I grinned. "Just wanted to see if you were dumb enough to do it."

"Ava, I'm a genius."

"A humble one too."

Alex cracked a smile. Not a big one, but we were getting there.

It took some effort, but he eventually relaxed more and more throughout the night until he was eating and chatting with people like a normal human. I'd baked him a red velvet cake since he liked red velvet, and we sang "Happy Birthday" while he blew out the candles. All normal stuff.

He did, however, refuse to participate when a half-drunk Ralph broke out his karaoke machine.

"Come on!" I insisted. "You don't have to be a *good* singer. I'm terrible, but I do it anyway. It's all in good fun."

Alex shook his head. "I don't do anything unless I'm good at it, but don't let me stop you."

"That's silly. How can you be good at something unless you practice?"

He still wouldn't budge, so I sighed and serenaded the party with an off-key solo rendition of Britney Spears's "Oops!... I Did It Again" while they cheered me on. Alex lounged on the couch, one arm draped over the back, the top few buttons of his shirt unbuttoned. A lazy smile graced his face as he watched me sing my heart out.

He looked so gorgeous and at ease I stumbled over the lyrics, but everyone gave me a standing ovation anyway.

The party wrapped up a few hours later, and I insisted on staying and cleaning up even after Ralph told me he'd take care of it. Everyone offered to pitch in as well, so we split into different groups—garbage duty, sweeping duty, et cetera.

Alex and I somehow ended up on dish duty together. Ralph didn't have a dishwasher, so I hand-washed while he dried.

"I hope you had a good time," I said, scrubbing caked-on sugar from a plate. "Sorry if we gave you a heart attack."

His chuckle sent the butterflies in my stomach into a tizzy. "It would take more than a surprise party to give me a heart attack." He took the plate from me and wiped it dry before setting it on the dish rack. Seeing Alex do something as domestic as dishes sent another flutter through my system. *I have serious issues.* "I had a good time though." He cleared his throat, his cheeks coloring. "This was my first birthday party since my parents died."

I froze. Alex had never brought up his parents before, but I knew from Josh they'd died when he was young, which meant he hadn't had a birthday party in at least a decade.

My heart ached for him. Not because of the party but because he could no longer celebrate with his family. For the first time, I realized how lonely Alex must be with no relatives left in the world except for his uncle.

"So what do you usually do on your birthday?" I asked in a soft voice.

He shrugged. "Work. Grab a drink with Josh. It's not a big deal. My parents made it a big deal, but after their deaths, it seemed pointless."

"How did—" I stopped myself before I finished the question. A guy's birthday was *not* the right time to bring up the method of his family's death.

Alex answered anyway. "They were murdered." After a beat of hesitation, he added, "My father's business rival ordered the hit and made it look like a home invasion gone wrong. My parents hid me right before the intruders found us, but I saw..." His throat bobbed with a hard swallow. "I saw it happen. My mom, dad, and little sister, who didn't hide in time."

Horror suffused me at the thought of someone having to witness their own family's murder. "I'm so sorry. That's—I have no words."

"It's all right. At least they caught the bastards who pulled the trigger."

"And the business rival?" I asked softly.

His eye twitched. "Karma will get him."

My heart weighed heavy in my chest even before something more horrifying occurred to me. "Your HSAM—"

Alex flashed a humorless smile. "Is a real bitch. I relive that day every day. Sometimes I think about whether I could've saved them, even though I was just a kid. I used to rage at the unfairness of it all until I realized no one gives a shit. There's no entity out there listening to me yell at them. There's only life and luck, and sometimes both those things deal you a crap hand."

Tears stung my eyes. I'd forgotten all about the dishes; my heart hurt too much.

I stepped closer to Alex, who watched me approach with a tense expression.

"Sometimes, but not all the time." I heard the faint chatter of other guests in the living room, but they might as well be light-years away. Here, in the kitchen, Alex and I had entered our own little world. "There's something beautiful waiting for you, Alex. Whether you find it tomorrow or years from now, I hope it'll restore your faith in life. You deserve all the beauty and light in the world."

I meant every word. Beneath the icy shell, he was human like everyone else, and his broken heart broke mine a hundredfold.

"There you go, romanticizing me again." Alex didn't move as I took another step toward him, but his eyes burned with intensity. "It's too late for me, Sunshine. I destroy everything beautiful that comes into my life."

"I don't believe that," I said. "And that wasn't romanticizing you. This is."

Before I could lose my nerve, I stood on tiptoes and kissed him.

It was a soft, chaste kiss, but the effect was the same as a full-on make-out session. Sparks consumed my skin, and the heat in my stomach flared to life. I shuddered at the sensation, my pulse beating so wildly I couldn't hear anything else. Alex's lips were cool and firm, his taste like that of spice and red velvet, and I wanted to wrap myself around him and devour him until every bit of him was inside me.

Alex remained still, his chest rising and falling with harsh breaths beneath my tentative touch. I pressed a firmer hand against his chest and ran my tongue along the seam of his lips, seeking entry—

I gasped when Alex yanked me toward him and deepened the kiss. His hand fisted my hair and tugged, forcing my back to arch while his tongue plundered my mouth.

"Not the romance you were thinking of, is it?" he growled, his grip so tight my eyes watered. He'd spun me around so the edge of the counter dug into my flesh, and he used his other hand to hitch my leg up around his waist. His thick erection pressed against my core, and I ground against it shamelessly, desperate for the friction. "Tell me to stop, Sunshine."

"No." Tell him to stop? A herd of wild horses couldn't drag me away.

I inched my hand beneath his shirt, eager to explore the

expanse of smooth skin and hard muscles beneath my fingers. My entire body pulsated with need, and the possibility of someone walking in on us any moment further heightened my arousal. It was only a kiss, but it seemed so much more illicit. Dangerous.

Alex groaned. His mouth claimed mine again, and the kiss turned fierce. Wanting. Hungry. He was ruthless in his invasion of my senses, his touch so hot and possessive it branded itself into my skin, and I surrendered to him without a shred of resistance.

I was on the verge of unbuckling his belt when he pulled away so forcefully I stumbled forward, disoriented by the sudden loss of contact. My core throbbed, my nipples could cut diamonds, and my skin was so sensitive even the brush of air caused me to tremble. But when the fog of sensation dissipated, I realized Alex was glaring at me.

"Fuck." He scrubbed a hand over his face, his scowl fierce enough to make grown men quake. "Fuck, fuck, *fuck*."

"Alex—"

"No. What the hell were you thinking?" he bit out. "Did you think we would fuck in the kitchen while your friends are in the other room?"

Heat scorched my cheeks. "If this is about Josh—"

"It's not about Josh." Alex pinched the bridge of his nose and exhaled a slow, controlled breath. "Not entirely."

"Then what is it?" He wanted me. I knew he did; I felt it, and I'm not just talking about the massive bulge straining his pants. Yes, Josh would attempt to murder us both if he found out what happened, but he couldn't stay mad at us *forever*. Besides, he didn't return to DC until Christmas. We had time.

"It's me. And you. Together. It won't work." Alex's glare intensified. "Whatever fantasies you have of us swirling in that pretty head of yours, kill them. That kiss was a one-time mistake. It'll never happen again."

I wanted to die of mortification. I wasn't sure what would've been worse—Alex not kissing me back at all or him kissing me back and saying those things. I wanted to argue, but I'd used up my boldness quota for tonight. It had taken a helluva lot for me to kiss him first, and a girl can throw herself at a guy only so many times before it becomes humiliating.

"Fine." I picked up a random dish in the sink and scrubbed, unable to look him in the eyes. My face felt so hot I thought I'd explode. "I get it. Let's pretend that never happened."

"Good." Alex didn't sound as pleased as I'd expected.

We worked in silence save for the clank of the porcelain.

"I'm trying to save you, Ava," he said out of nowhere, right as we finished all the dishes and I prepared to flee.

"From what?" I refused to look at him, but I could see him watching me out of the corner of my eye.

"From me."

I didn't respond, because how was I supposed to tell the man determined to save me that I didn't want to be saved?

CHAPTER 20

Alex

I WAS ON A WARPATH, AND EVERYONE GAVE ME A WIDE berth as I stalked down the hall toward the elevators. My new assistant, who I'd hired after firing the congressman's insipid daughter for leaking my cell number to the Gruppmann CEO, pretended to be on the phone when I passed, and the rest of the staff kept their eyes glued to their computer screens like their lives depended on it.

I didn't blame them. I'd been biting people's heads off left and right for the past week.

Incompetent, every single one of them.

I refused to entertain any other reason I'd been so cranky since my birthday, especially if that "other reason" happened to be five five with black hair and lips that tasted sweeter than sin.

I ignored the two people who scrambled off the elevator when they saw me enter, and I jabbed the button for the lobby.

That fucking kiss. It'd tattooed itself onto my mind, and I found myself thinking about it—about the way Ava tasted and felt in my arms—far more than I should. Thanks to the "gift" of my memory, I relived those few minutes in Ralph's kitchen like they were real every night in the shower, my fist wrapped tight around my cock and my chest burning with self-loathing.

I hadn't seen or heard from Ava since that night. She'd skipped our swimming prep sessions this week, and I didn't even hear from her directly. Jules was the one who texted saying Ava was busy.

Her absence chafed more than I cared to admit.

I got into my car and deliberated. *One. Two. Three. Four.* I tapped my fingers against the steering wheel, torn, before I finally gritted my teeth and set the GPS for the McCann Gallery in Hazelburg.

Nineteen minutes later, I strode into the gallery, my eyes flitting over the pale wood floors, the framed prints hanging on the stark white walls, and the half dozen well-dressed patrons wandering the space before I zeroed in on the brunette behind the counter.

Ava rang up a customer, her face animated and her smile bright as she said something that caused the woman to smile in return. She had a knack for doing that, bringing out the joy in others.

She hadn't noticed me yet, and for a while, I simply watched her, letting her light creep into the shadowed corners of my soul.

Once the customer left, I walked over, my custom-made loafers silent against the polished floors. It wasn't until my shadow enveloped her that Ava looked up with a polite, professional smile that wilted the second she saw me.

She swallowed hard, and the sight of that small throat bob sent an unwelcome jolt of desire straight to my dick.

I hadn't fucked anyone except my right hand in months, and the celibacy was addling my brain.

"Hi." She sounded wary.

"Here." I placed a brand-new phone—the latest model, which wasn't available on the market yet and cost me several grand—on the counter.

Her brow knit in confusion.

"Your current phone is clearly broken, since I haven't received so much as a text from you in the past five days," I said icily.

The confusion lingered for a beat before it melted into a teasing expression, and my heart kicked like a damn Rockette at Radio City Music Hall. I made a mental note to discuss this with my doctor during my annual checkup.

"You miss me," she said.

My hands curled around the edge of the counter. "I do not."

"You showed up at my work and bought me a new phone because I didn't text you for a few days." Ava's eyes gleamed with mischief. "I think that amounts to missing me."

"You think wrong. I bought you the phone in case you needed a new one for *emergencies*."

"In that case"—she pushed the box toward me—"I don't need it. My phone works fine. I've just been busy."

"Doing what? Attending a silent ashram in the middle of the desert?"

"That's for me to know and for you never to find out."

A vein throbbed at my temple. "Dammit, Ava, this isn't funny."

"I never said it was." She threw her hands in the air. "I don't know what you want me to say. I kissed you, you kissed me back, then you said it was a mistake, and we agreed never to do it again. I thought you wanted space, and I gave it to you. I'm not one of those girls who chases after guys who don't want them." Ava pressed her lips together. "I know everything's been messed up between us since Saturday. Maybe we need to...not spend as much time together. I can do the visualizations on my own, and when the time comes, I can find another swim instructor—"

My blood pressure hit a record high. "The hell you will," I snapped. "You asked *me* to teach you how to swim. *I'm* the one who worked with you all these weeks. If you think I'm going to let some

fucker swoop in and take what's mine, you don't know me at all."
Ava stared at me, her eyes wide with shock. "We're resuming lessons
this weekend. Don't even *think* of trying to find someone else."

"Fine, no need to yell."

"I'm *not* yelling." I never raised my voice. Period.

"Then why is everyone staring at us?" Ava winced. "Shit,
including my manager. He's looking right at us." She busied herself
with papers behind the counter. "I promise to learn swimming
only with you, okay? Now leave before I get in trouble."

I turned and saw an older man with an unfortunate toupee
glowering at us.

"Do you get sales commission?" I asked Ava without taking
my eyes off her manager, who marched toward us, his paunch
jiggling over his belt with each step.

"Yes. Why?"

"I'd like to buy a piece from the gallery." I turned back to Ava
when her manager reached us. His name tag read "Fred." Figured.
He was a Fred if I ever saw one. "The most expensive one you
have."

Her jaw dropped. "Alex, the most expensive piece in the
gallery is—"

"Perfect for your needs, I'm sure," Fred cut in. He'd lost his
scowl and now beamed at me like I was the second coming of
Jesus. "Ava, why don't you ring this gentleman up for the Richard
Argus moonlight piece?"

She looked uneasy. "But—"

"Now."

My smile cut across my face with the precision of a honed
knife. "Careful with the tone, Fred. Ava is your best employee.
You wouldn't want to alienate her or any customers who value her
opinion *very* highly, would you?"

He blinked, his eyes darting around as his tiny brain struggled to process the not so subtle threat behind my words. "N-no, of course not," Fred stuttered. "In fact, Ava, you stay right here with this gentleman. I'll pack the piece myself."

"But she'll get the commission." I arched an eyebrow.

"Yes." The manager nodded so fast he resembled a bobble-head doll. "Of course."

While he scurried off to another part of the gallery, Ava leaned in and hissed, "Alex, the piece costs $40,000."

"Really? Shit."

"I'm sure we can—"

"I thought it was expensive." I allowed myself a soft laugh at her stunned expression. "It's not a big deal. I'll own a new piece of art, you'll receive a hefty commission, and your manager will kiss your ass until the end of days. Win-win."

Fred returned with a large black-and-white print.

Fifteen minutes later, the print had been packaged with the same care one would use to handle a newborn baby, and my bank account was $40,000 lighter.

"This weekend, our usual time, Z Hotel," I told Ava after dismissing Fred.

Her eyebrows shot up. We usually practiced at one of our houses or near a lake or Thayer's pool so she could get more comfortable near water.

"It has the best indoor pool in DC," I explained. "You're ready for actual swimming lessons."

She'd been ready for a while, but I'd wanted to make sure before throwing her into the deep end, so to speak.

Ava sucked in a breath. "Really?"

"Yeah." I flashed a crooked smile. "See you Saturday, Sunshine."

I left the gallery in a remarkably better mood than when I'd entered.

CHAPTER 21

Ava

THE DAY HAD FINALLY COME.

I stood five feet away from the pool, my skin etched with goose bumps even though the temperature hovered at a toasty eighty-four degrees thanks to the hotel's state-of-the-art heating system.

I wore a one-piece Eres swimsuit, courtesy of Alex, who'd handed me the shopping bag without a word when he picked me up for our lesson today.

After weeks of learning relaxation techniques and acclimating myself to the thought of being in water, it was time for me to get *in* the water.

I wanted to throw up. Panic gripped me, its icy claws digging into my sweat-slicked skin and drawing invisible blood. My stomach pumped in rhythm with my wild heart, causing my breakfast to slosh around like rubber ducks in a bath.

"Breathe." Alex's calm voice steadied me somewhat. "Remember our lessons."

"Okay." I dragged in a lungful of air and almost gagged at the smell of chlorine. "I can do this, I can do this," I chanted.

"I'll go in first." He stepped into the pool until he was waist-deep in the water and held out his hand.

I stared at him, willing my feet to move.

"I'll be right here. I won't let anything happen to you." He radiated calm confidence. "Do you trust me?"

I gulped. "Y-yes."

I realized with a start that I did. One hundred percent. Alex may not be the nicest or easiest person to get along with, but I trusted him with my life. Literally.

I edged toward the pool and held my breath as I stepped in and grabbed his hand, letting his strength calm my thundering nerves. The water sloshed around my thighs, and I stumbled.

The hotel's pool room spun, the pale-blue walls and terra-cotta tiles flashing before me in a blur. *Oh God, I can't do this. I can't—*

"Close your eyes. Deep breaths," Alex said. "That's it..."

I did as he instructed, allowing his voice to wash over me until most of the panic subsided.

"How do you feel?" he asked.

"Better." I cleared my throat and tried to focus on the small radius around us instead of the entire pool. It was a standard Olympic-size pool, but it might as well be the Atlantic Ocean. "I—I'm ready."

As ready as I'll ever be.

We started in the shallow end, and Alex had me walk around so I could get used to the feeling of the water and my body's buoyancy. After that, we went deeper until I was submerged up to my shoulders. I clung to the relaxation techniques I'd learned over the past few months, and they worked—until we reached the part of the lesson where I had to put my head underwater.

I closed my eyes before I dipped my face in, unable to bear the sight of the water rushing toward me.

"Help! Mommy, help me!"

The words echoed in my head.

So cold. So dark.

I couldn't breathe.

Something glinted at the edges of my consciousness. A faint memory, perhaps, but it floated away every time I tried to grasp it.

"Please!"

I sank deeper.

Deeper.

Deeper still.

Pleasepleaseplease.

Icantbreathecantbreathecantbreathe.

"Ava!"

I gasped, the sound of my name jerking me back to the present. My screams echoed against the stone walls before fading into oblivion. I wasn't sure how long I'd been under. It felt like mere seconds, but judging by how cold I was and how much my throat hurt, it must've been longer.

Alex clutched my arms, his face white. "Jesus," he breathed, pulling me roughly into his chest while I choked out a sob. We were no longer in the pool—he must've carried me out during my mini blackout. "It's okay. You're okay. We're out."

"I'm sorry." I buried my face in his chest, embarrassed and furious with myself. "I thought I could do it. I thought—"

"You did great," he said firmly. "This is your first lesson. There'll be more, and you'll get better each time."

"Promise?"

"I promise."

I shuddered, curling into his warmth. He felt strong and solid beneath my touch, and I was once again struck by the contradiction that was Alex Volkov. So cold and uncaring to the world, yet so warm and protective when he wanted to be. I'd known him for eight years, yet I hadn't known him at all.

He wasn't the man I thought he was. He was so much better, even when he tried to convince me he was worse, and I wanted him like nothing before. Not only physically but mentally and emotionally. I wanted every shadow of his soul and every piece of his beautiful, multilayered heart. I wanted to pour into him every drop of light I had to give until he consumed me whole. Until I was his and he was mine.

We stayed there—me cuddled up against his chest, him with his arms wrapped around me—until my lingering panic faded and I worked up the courage to say what I said next.

"Alex…"

"Yes, Sunshine?" He ran a gentle hand through my hair.

"Kiss me."

His touch stilled, and he stiffened.

"Please." I licked my lips. "Forget about Josh or…whatever else may be on your mind. If you want me, kiss me. I know what we said on your birthday, and I'm sorry for going back on my word, but I need…" *You.* "I need this."

Alex closed his eyes, his expression pained. "You have no idea what you're asking me."

"Yes, I do." I pressed a hand against his abdomen, feeling it tremble beneath my touch. "Unless you don't want to."

He left out a half laugh, half groan. "Does this feel like I don't want to?" He grasped my hand and pulled it down until it rested on the most masculine part of him. My breath stuttered at his sheer heat and size—obvious even under his swim trunks—and I curled my fingers around the thick rod, fascinated by the power I held in my palm.

A low growl rumbled out of Alex's chest. "What did I say about staying out of trouble, Sunshine? Keep doing that, and you'll be in a *world* of trouble."

"Maybe I like trouble." I tightened my grip, and he hissed out a curse. "Maybe I want to stay there."

"I'm beginning to think *you're* the trouble I need to stay away from," he muttered. He pinned my wrist to my side, and a jolt of excitement flashed through me. "But we can't. You just—" He gestured toward the pool with his free hand.

"I just what? Had a panic attack? I get those all the time when I'm near water. If that bothers you, we're in a hotel. We can find a room." It seemed like I'd recovered all the boldness I'd lost after kissing Alex on his birthday.

His mouth tilted up. "When did you get so feisty?"

"When I got sick of everyone treating me like I'm a fragile flower who'll break if someone breathes on me the wrong way. Just because I have a phobia over one specific thing doesn't mean I'll freak out in other areas of my life." I paused, then added, "Madeline told me. About what you—what you like in bed."

His expression darkened. The air turned ominous, and my heart gave an anxious thud.

"What, exactly, did she tell you?" His voice lowered to a dangerous decibel.

"She told me—" I gulped. "She told me you only do it from behind. That you don't like kissing or face-to-face contact during sex. That you..."

"That I what?" Alex asked silkily.

"That you like choking and calling women names. In bed." The danger in the air thickened until I could almost taste it, and my bravado faltered. *Maybe baiting the tiger wasn't the best idea...*

"Yet you're still here, asking me to kiss you." His grip on my wrist turned to iron. "Why is that, Sunshine?"

He hadn't denied it, which meant it must be true.

My heart raced.

"Maybe—" I wet my lips with my tongue, conscious of his

eyes tracking the movement the way a lion would a gazelle. "I like those things too."

Flames burned away the ice pools in his eyes until the heat seared me to my core. I couldn't believe I'd ever thought him cold. In that moment, he was a supernova waiting to erupt and swallow me whole.

And I'd love every second.

Alex released me and stood, no trace of the patient, soothing man from earlier tonight in sight. In his place was something hungry and depraved that caused me to tremble with lust.

"Get up," he said, his voice soft but so commanding I obeyed without thinking. "You're about to find out what happens when you invite yourself into the lion's den."

CHAPTER 22

Alex

IT DIDN'T TAKE LONG FOR ME TO SECURE THE penthouse and all but drag Ava into the luxurious suite. I was so fucking hard my cock almost punched a hole through my pants, and the images I had running through my mind...

Fuck. I was going to destroy her, but any remaining shred of conscience I possessed had disappeared the moment she'd uttered those words.

Maybe I like those things too.

My blood roared at the memory.

Baby, you have no idea what you got yourself into, I thought, shutting the door behind me.

Ava stood in the middle of the bedroom, wearing a dress over her swimsuit and a half-nervous expression. With her doe eyes and innocent features, she resembled a sacrificial virgin awaiting defilement.

My cock throbbed harder.

"Take off your clothes," I said, my soft voice a whip crack in the silence.

Part of me wanted to bury myself deep inside her as soon as possible; the other part wanted to savor every moment.

Despite a slight shake in her hands, Ava didn't hesitate. She kept her eyes trained on mine as she unzipped her dress and the gauzy material pooled around her ankles. The swimsuit went next, sliding down inch by torturous inch until a masterpiece of bare golden flesh unveiled itself.

I devoured her with my eyes, taking in every detail and imprinting it in my mind. Her skin glowed bronze beneath the suite's dim lights, and her body... Christ. Round ass, long legs, the sweetest little pussy, and firm, perky tits—not big, but enough for a handful and tipped with hard, rosy nipples that were perfect for sucking and nibbling.

Her chest rose and fell with every breath, and she stared at me with nothing but trust in those big, brown eyes.

Oh, Sunshine. If you only knew.

I circled her, a predator toying with its prey, so close I could smell the tang of her arousal.

I stopped behind her and pressed my body against hers until she could feel my angry, steel-hard erection against the soft curve of her ass. She was naked as the day she was born while I was fully clothed, and somehow that made the scene even filthier.

I pressed my lips to her neck, enjoying the rapid flutter of her pulse beneath my mouth.

"You want me to take you, Sunshine?" I murmured. "Ruin you, pound you into a pathetic mess, turn you into my little fuck doll?"

A whimper escaped her mouth and shot straight to my groin, hardening my already aching cock. "Y-yes."

"You say yes so easily." I licked the hollow between her neck and lower jaw. True to my nickname for her, she tasted like sunshine and honey, and I wanted to devour her. Feed off her light, consume every inch of her until she was mine and mine alone. "But do you know what it means to be taken by me?"

Ava shook her head, a quick, small movement that under-scored her innocence and naïveté.

Not for much longer. Once I got my hands on her, she'd be filthy. Broken. Just like everything I touched. But she'd be mine. And I was selfish and cruel enough that I'd take her with me while I burned down the world.

"It means you're mine. Your mouth is mine." I rubbed my thumb over her bottom lip before trailing it down her chest and pinching her nipples. She moaned. "Your breasts are mine." I drifted lower, adjusting my position so I could squeeze her ass. Hard. "Your ass is mine." I reached around and parted her thighs, sliding my fingers past her slippery folds. She was so wet they were drenched within seconds. "And your pussy is mine. Every inch of you belongs to me, and if you ever let another man touch you—" My other hand closed around her throat. "He'll end up in pieces, and you'll end up tied to my bed and fucked in every hole until my name is the only one you remember. Do you understand?"

Her cunt clenched around my fingers. "Yes."

"Say it. Who do you belong to?"

"You," Ava whispered. "I belong to you."

"That's right." I slipped my fingers out of her pussy and thrust them into her mouth. I hummed in approval when she sucked and licked her own juices off without my asking. "Do you taste that, Sunshine? That's the taste of you signing your life away. Because from now on, I own you. Body, mind, and soul."

Another moan, this one even more eager than the last.

I released my hold on her and made short work of my belt and pants. "Get on your knees." She sank to the floor, so beautiful it made my chest hurt and my cock throb. I fisted her hair and tugged it back until she stared straight up at me. "If it gets to be too much, tap my thigh." When she nodded, I tugged her hair harder and ordered, "Open your mouth."

I slipped the head of my cock into her waiting mouth, slowly pushing deeper until I was buried all the way down her throat.

"*Fuck.*" The sensation of her mouth engulfing me was so hot a shudder rippled through my entire body, and I almost shot my load right there. I hadn't done that since I was a teenager having sex for the first time.

Ava blinked up at me, her eyes watering from my size and how deep I was, but she didn't tap out, so I stayed still while she adjusted. After what felt like an eternity but was in actuality a few seconds, she started licking and sucking—slowly at first, but quickly building up to a rhythm that had her bobbing her head up and down with enthusiasm.

My other hand shot to the back of her head, and my abs shook from the effort not to come down her throat before I was ready. "That's it," I growled. "Suck that cock like a good little whore."

The vibrations from her ensuing moan traveled all the way up my spine. I started thrusting into her, faster and faster until the only sounds were that of my ragged breaths, flesh slapping against flesh, and the gurgles coming from her throat. I was so rough I half expected her to finally tap out, but she never did.

I pulled out at the last second and came all over her face and chest, the thick white streaks coating her skin in a glistening sheen. My orgasm burned through me, wild and hot, razing any lingering doubts that stood in its way, and I watched my cum drip off Ava's chin with possessive, lust-filled eyes.

A pale pink flush of arousal stained her face, and her gaze remained locked to mine as her tongue darted out to lick a drop of cum from the corner of her mouth.

Holy fuck.

I'd witnessed or partaken in just about every filthy sex act imaginable, but that small movement might've been the hottest thing I'd ever seen.

"Get on the bed," I ordered, my voice thick with gravel. "All fours. Now."

Her hands and knees barely had time to hit the mattress before I stripped off the rest of my clothes and came up behind her, spreading her thighs with my hands.

"You are so very wet, my beautiful whore." I licked her glistening juices off her skin, savoring the taste and delicate female scent that drove every man crazy. I pushed a finger inside her tight, slick folds and was rewarded with a loud whimper. "Do you want me to eat out this gorgeous cunt of yours?"

"Please," Ava gasped, pushing back at me. "I need—*oh God.*" She dropped her head, her squeal muffled by the pillows when I flattened my tongue against her clit, alternating between long, slow licks and fast flicks. I was so fucking hungry—for her, for her taste, for the innocence shattering beneath me at this very moment. I feasted on her like a man possessed, my hand digging into her flesh, my fingers curling inside her until I found the spot that had her bucking against my face. I gently tugged on her clit with my teeth, flicking over the sensitive nub with my tongue, and she exploded, her screams reverberating off the walls.

"You taste so fucking good," I growled, lapping up every drop while she shook and trembled beneath my touch. "The perfect appetizer for tonight."

Ava twisted her head to look at me, her face flushed from her orgasm and her eyes round with shock. "*That* was an appetizer? I thought—you—"

"Sunshine, this is a twelve-course meal." I rolled on a condom and slid my already hard again cock along her drenched folds. "And we're just getting started."

I gripped her throat and slammed into her, and all conversation ground to a halt, unless you counted her moans and my grunts as conversation. She felt like heaven to my hell, the closest

I'd ever get to salvation, and yet I still wanted to drag her into the depths of Hades with me. I fucked her so hard I was afraid I'd break her, but every time I eased up, Ava uttered tiny warning growls that had my lips curving in a mixture of satisfaction and amusement.

It turned out my sweet, innocent lamb was actually a dirty little slut in disguise, and I'd never been happier to be wrong.

I flipped her over in time to see her shatter once more, her pleasure-glazed eyes and sighs urging me to go faster and deeper until I too came apart in a powerful orgasm that ripped through me with the force of a Category 5 hurricane.

When my breathing slowed and I came down from my high, I found Ava staring up at me with a strange expression.

"What is it, Sunshine?" I brushed my lips over hers, already preparing myself for the next round. If I was going to hell for this, I might as well enjoy every second.

"No kissing or face-to-face contact during sex," she murmured. "I thought those were your rules."

I paused. She was right. Those *were* my rules—ones I created after I was old enough to realize emotions had nothing to do with sex and feelings had no place in the bedroom. I'd never once broken them—until tonight. And I hadn't even thought about it or realized it until Ava reminded me. I enjoyed fucking from the back more than the average man—there was a sense of removal that came with it, which was why it was my position of choice—but I'd wanted to *see* her. To watch the way she reacted to each shift in movement, to see her face when she fell apart and screamed my name.

And that was when I realized I was well and truly fucked.

"You're right, sweetheart," I said, dropping my forehead to hers with a resigned sigh. *So. Fucked.* "But the rules don't apply to you."

CHAPTER 23

Ava

BY THE TIME ALEX AND I FINISHED, I WAS EXHAUSTED and wrung out, and I would wake up sore as hell tomorrow, but I didn't care. Alex hadn't held back, and that was what I'd wanted. Needed.

Somehow, in choosing to let go, I'd never felt more powerful. Strength in weakness, control in submission.

"Aren't you tired?" I yawned, watching Alex through half-droopy eyes. We'd gone at it for what must've been hours, but whereas I was ready to pass out, he looked alert and awake as ever.

"If by 'tired' you mean you wore me out, perhaps," he said in an uncharacteristically teasing tone. "But if you're asking whether I'm sleepy, no."

"How is that possible?" I mumbled into my pillow.

"Insomnia, Sunshine. I sleep a few hours a night—if I'm lucky."

I frowned. "But that's..." Another huge yawn. "Not good." Humans need sleep. How had Alex survived all this time on only a few hours a night? "We should fix that. Chamomile tea.

Meditation. Melatonin..." My voice drifted off. If only my head didn't feel so heavy and the bed weren't so comfortable, I could make him tea or find a guided YouTube meditation or something.

"Let's talk about it later. You're exhausted." He smoothed a hand over my head, and I purred as I nestled into his touch. "Good night."

My breaths slowed as sleep took over. I thought I felt an arm wrap around my waist and pull me close, but I was out before I could confirm.

That night, for the first time in a long time, I slept soundly with no nightmares.

CHAPTER 24

Ava

ALEX AND I SPENT THE REST OF THE WEEKEND LOCKED in our suite, subsisting on room service and orgasms and christening every surface—though I'm not sure "christening" was the right word to use, considering how filthy our activities were.

Sex with Alex was sex like I'd never known it. Raw. Animalistic. Soul destroying in the best possible way. It shattered every preconceived notion of who I was and molded me into something darker, more depraved. He called me Sunshine one moment and his whore the next.

And I loved it.

Even at his coldest, Alex had always treated me with respect outside the bedroom, but inside the bedroom, I was his toy. His to fuck and use—in the shower, pressed against the window, bent over the desk—and I craved it as much as he did.

I screamed, my core clenching around his cock for what must've been the thousandth time as another orgasm ripped through and broke me into a million pieces of ecstatic agony.

When the fog of pleasure finally faded, I found Alex staring down at me with a smirk.

"What?" I murmured, too drowsy with content to utter more words.

"I love watching you come apart." His hands gripped my hips possessively. "Only for me, Sunshine. Never forget that."

"What would you do if I did?" I'd meant it as a tease, but Alex's eyes glittered with danger as his fingers dug into my flesh.

"You'd have a man's murder on your hands. Is that what you want?" He grazed my skin with his nose before he sank his teeth into the side of my neck—punishing and marking me at the same time.

Pain and pleasure burst through me. "Careful," I breathed. "Or you'll ruin your reputation for unfeeling sex."

"No one else will see me this way. Only you."

Before I could rein in the out-of-control butterflies in my stomach, someone knocked on the door. "Who is that?" I asked, still trying to wrap my head around his words. *No one else will see me this way. Only you.*

A grin tugged at my mouth.

"Room service. We ordered it before you cornered me and had your way with me." Alex rolled out of bed and laughed softly when I mock glared at him from my pile of wonderful, fluffy pillows.

"For someone with a supposedly 'superior' memory, you seem to have forgotten that *you're* the one who woke me up with an urgent...issue." I arched an eyebrow, remembering the sensation of his hands cupping my breasts and his cock rubbing against my ass this morning.

"Did I?" He flashed a lazy smile, and I all but melted into a pile of goo. I would never tire of Alex's smiles. *I'm sorry, honey, but it's over*, I told my poor heart. *You don't belong to me anymore.* "How inconsiderate of me."

It wasn't until he brought back our breakfast that I realized I was starving.

Sex, I decided as I nibbled on a croissant, *is my favorite form of exercise.*

But as incredible as the weekend had been, we had to return to reality tomorrow, and there were things we still needed to discuss.

"Alex…"

He sighed and set his coffee down. "I know."

"What will we tell Josh?" I winced, imagining my brother's reaction. I should buy full-body armor, just in case.

"We're both adults. It's our decision what we do with our lives." Nevertheless, Alex grimaced. "We'll tell him in person when he comes home for Christmas."

I nodded. Okay, that gave us over a month to prepare—though I wasn't sure anything would prepare us for the shitstorm Josh would unleash once he found out his baby sister and best friend were sleeping together. Which brought me to my next question…

"So what exactly will we say? I mean—" I stabbed at a strawberry, hating myself for bringing this up during such a blissful weekend but also knowing we needed to figure out where we stood before we spiraled into a mess of misunderstandings and uncertainty. "Are we friends with benefits? Dating? Exclusive or nonexclusive?"

Alex gripped my chin and brought my gaze to his. "What did I tell you? You're mine, Sunshine. You're never touching another man unless you want him six feet in the ground. So yes, we're fucking exclusive."

Was it bad that his words turned me on so much? Probably, but I didn't care. "Same for you and other women." I scowled, remembering Madeline. "No matter how much they throw themselves at you or…or look like a supermodel. How many women have you slept with anyway?"

His grip loosened, and his dark chuckle set off flutters in my stomach. "Jealous, Sunshine?" he purred. "I like this side of you."

"You didn't answer my question."

"It doesn't matter." Alex rolled me over until I was beneath him again. "All that matters is I'm only sleeping with one woman from now on."

"So is that what we are?" I gasped when he slid his rapidly hardening cock along my already wet slit. "Fuck buddies?"

"Among other things." He fished a condom from our dwindling supply—he'd had to run out yesterday for a box—and pinned my wrists above my head before thrusting into me. "You want to fuck, we fuck. You want to date, we date. You want to call me your boyfriend, I'll call you my girlfriend. But for now, let me take care of that needy little pussy of yours, hmm?"

And he did.

My shameless moans soaked the air as Alex pounded me into the mattress, his thrusts so rough the bedsprings squeaked and the headboard slammed against the wall.

A tingling sensation blossomed at the base of my spine. I reached up to play with my nipples, my breaths coming out in short pants. I was close. *So close.* I was going to—

The unwelcome ring of an incoming call interrupted our obscene symphony of moans and grunts, followed by a cool voice.

"This is Alex."

My eyes flew open. I gaped at Alex, who stared down at me with a calm expression as he listened to whoever was on the other end of the call. Gone was passionate, playful Alex; in his place was the composed businessman Alex.

"No, I'm free to talk. What happened with the Wilbur development?"

Free to talk? He was *still inside me!*

He wasn't moving, but I could feel every hard inch of him buried in between my thighs.

I opened my mouth to protest, but he shot me a warning

look and pressed the fingers of his free hand into my hip, silencing me.

"Bastard," I mouthed. I knew Alex was ambitious, but I'd never expected him to take a business call in the middle of freakin' sex.

What was worse, I'd been about to come, and I was left squirming with need while he discussed square footage and building plans.

I rolled my hips up, desperate for friction. His eyes flared and his grip tightened before he slid out of me. He muted his end of the call, placed it on speaker, and hauled me off the bed with one arm while he carried his phone in the other.

"What are you doing?" I wrapped my legs around his waist while the man on the other end of the line droned on about zoning laws.

Alex deposited me next to the couch. "Bend over and spread your legs."

Lust speared through me at his authoritative tone. I trembled but obeyed, placing my hands on the armrest, arching my back, and spreading my legs until every inch of me was bared to him.

Satisfaction curled in my stomach when I heard his sharp intake of breath.

The man stopped talking, and Alex unmuted the line to answer his question.

I could see my reflection in the large glass window opposite the couch. Wanton and flushed, my hair tousled from our sex marathon and my breasts hanging heavy and full. Behind me, Alex stood proud as a sculpted god, his face carved with brutal lust as he squeezed my ass.

My soft moan turned into a squeal when he slammed into me hard enough that the couch scraped forward an inch.

"Don't make a sound," he warned. "This is an important call."

The flames of desire burned hotter. I should be upset that he was on a business call of all things while fucking me, but I was so turned on I couldn't see straight. There was something so dirty and delicious about fucking while his partners prattled on, clueless.

Alex's thrusts picked up a steady, punishing rhythm until I was no longer gripping the armrest—I was on the couch itself, my hips draped over the arm, my face buried in the cushions, my rock-hard nipples and swollen clit scraping against the fabric as he fucked me so viciously my feet lifted off the ground.

All the while, he continued his call, taking it off mute only when he had to speak. When he did, his voice remained calm and even, though I could hear his harsh breathing in the moments when he was silent. I had no clue what they were talking about anymore, too lost in a fog of lust to decipher specific words and phrases.

An unbidden yelp erupted from my throat when he hit a spot that caused my back to bow.

Alex fisted my hair and tugged my head back until I was half-upright again while his other hand closed around my throat. A warning and a reminder rolled into one. *Don't make a sound.*

I tried my best. I really did. But I was a mess—I could see it in the window, my tear-streaked face and glazed eyes, my mouth hanging slack as orgasm after orgasm crashed over me in an endless, white-hot wave of sensation. Was it possible to die from too much pleasure? If so, that was what was happening. I was dying a million tiny deaths, each one ripping me apart and piecing me back together only for the next to destroy me again.

Another sob of pleasure, one that had Alex releasing my hair so he could cover my mouth and muffle my whines.

One hand over my mouth, one hand around my throat.

I came again, my entire body shuddering with the force of my explosion.

Alex fucked me harder, deeper, the couch screaming with protest—it had slid halfway across the floor by now, its progress impeded only by the wall—and I realized it was otherwise quiet.

The call was over.

"I thought you were better at following directions, Sunshine," he said silkily. "Didn't I tell you not to make a sound?"

I responded with an incoherent mumble—my failed attempt at apologizing.

"No words?" Alex slid his hand down from my throat to my nipples. He pinched them hard, one after the other, eliciting another jumbled moan. "Did I fuck your brains out, my gorgeous slut?"

Considering I couldn't even remember my name, probably.

And as the minutes—hours—rolled into each other, I lost myself in him. In us.

In sweet, filthy, depraved oblivion.

CHAPTER 25

Ava

MY FRIENDS HAD MIXED REACTIONS TO ALEX'S AND MY new relationship status. Jules was ecstatic, claiming she *knew* Alex had a thing for me and demanding to know what he was like in bed. I refused to answer but flushed a deep crimson, and that had told her all she needed to know. I think Jules would have died of disappointment had Alex's bedroom skills not lived up to the promise of his devastating looks and intimidating presence. Luckily for me, they did.

Stella, meanwhile, was worried. Happy for me, but worried. She warned me to take things slow and not fall too hard, too fast. I didn't have the heart to tell her that train had left the station ages ago. Maybe not the "too fast" part, as Alex Volkov had stolen my heart, bit by bit, over the years, even before I thought I liked him, but the "too hard"? *Heart, meet free fall.*

Bridget was neutral. I supposed princesses were inherently more diplomatic, which was why she said nothing other than if I was happy, she was happy.

The specter of Josh lingered in the background, and I'd acted so jumpy during our last call he'd demanded to know what was wrong. I told him I had period cramps, which shut him up. Periods sucked, but they were a useful weapon for shutting down questions from men.

Today, though, I had another family member on my mind.

I waved goodbye to Bridget and Booth, who'd driven me to my father's house—an hour and a half from Hazelburg—so I didn't have to take the train or bus, and unlocked the front door. The house smelled like pine-scented air freshener, and my sneakers squeaked against the polished floors as I searched for my father.

It was his birthday on Tuesday. Since I had class, work, *and* a photo shoot that day, I'd decided to surprise him today with his favorite cake from Crumble & Bake.

I heard sounds coming from the den, and when I entered the room, I found my dad poring over papers at the table in the corner.

"Hey, Dad." I slid my bag strap off my shoulder and let the leather tote thump on the ground.

He glanced up, surprise scrawled over his face when he saw me standing there. "Ava. I didn't know you were coming home this weekend."

Michael Chen was not a conventionally good-looking man, but I'd always considered him handsome the way all little girls thought their fathers were handsome. Black hair peppered with gray at the temples, broad shoulders, and a dusting of stubble on his chin. He wore a striped polo shirt and jeans, his casual outfit of choice, and a pair of wire-rimmed glasses rested on the bridge of his nose.

"I'm not. Well, not the whole weekend." I flashed an awkward smile. "I wanted to drop by and wish you a happy early birthday." I placed the cake box on the table. "I'm sorry Josh and I can't be here on your actual birthday, but I brought your favorite cheese-cake from C&B."

"Ah. Thank you." He stared at the box but didn't touch it.

I shifted my weight from foot to foot, restless in the silence.

We had never been good at talking to each other. Luckily, we'd had Josh to fill our conversations with chatter about med school, sports, and his latest adrenaline-inducing adventure. Skydiving, bungee jumping, zip-lining—he did it all.

But now Josh was in Central America, and I realized how little my dad and I had to say to each other. When was the last time we'd had a real, one-on-one conversation?

Probably not since he sat my fourteen-year-old self down and explained what happened with my mother.

"I don't understand." My face twisted with confusion. "You told me Mom died of a heart condition."

I didn't remember Mom. I didn't remember anything before the Blackout other than brief moments that flashed through my mind at unpredictable times—a snippet of a lullaby sung in a haunting voice, the splash of water followed by screams and laughs, the burn of a scraped knee after I fell off my bike. Glimpses into the past that were too small and fragmented to mean anything.

Of course, there were my nightmares, but I tried not to think about them except in therapy, and only because I had to. Phoebe, my therapist, believed detangling my nightmares was the key to unlocking my repressed memories. I wasn't a trained psychiatrist like her, but sometimes I wanted to snap back at her maybe I'd be better off not remembering. My brain had repressed the memories for a reason, and no good could come of unleashing those horror-scapes into the present.

Other times, I wanted to dig that key out of my twisted mind with my own hands and unlock the truth, once and for all.

My father braced his hands on his knees and leaned forward with an intensity that unnerved me. "That's not entirely true," he rumbled in that deep voice of his. "We told you that because we didn't want to distress you, but Phoebe and I agreed you're old enough to know the truth now."

My pulse thumped in warning. It knew. A storm was rolling in, ready to rain all over my life as I knew it. "Wh-what's the truth?"

"Your mother died of an overdose. She...took too many pills one day, and her heart stopped."

Funny. That was what my heart did too. Just for a beat or two, not enough to kill me. Not like it'd killed my mom.

Because "heart stopped" was just a euphemism for "died," and "took too many pills" was just a euphemism for "committed suicide."

My lower lip trembled. I dug my nails into my thigh until crescent grooves etched into my flesh. "Why would she do that?"

Why would she leave me and Josh? Didn't she love us? Weren't we enough?

Parents were supposed to be there for their children, but she took the easy way out and left.

I knew that was unfair, because I had no idea what she'd been going through, but that only angered me more. Not only did I not have my mother, but I also didn't even have memories of her. That wasn't her fault, but I blamed her anyway.

If she were here, we could've made new memories, and the absence of the old ones wouldn't matter as much.

My father rubbed a hand over his face. "She didn't leave a letter." Of course she didn't, I thought bitterly. "But I imagine she felt...guilty."

"About what?"

He flinched.

"About what, Dad?" My voice rose. My pulse was roaring now, so loud I almost didn't hear his answer.

Almost.

But I did, and when I registered his words, tasted the poison of their truth, my chest collapsed on itself.

"About what happened at the lake when you were five. How you almost drowned. How she pushed you in."

I gulped in a deep breath, my lungs greedy for the oxygen.

My dad shattered my world that day in my bedroom. That was why I'd been so happy when I left for college. I hated the memory of that conversation and the way his words had soaked into the walls. They whispered to me every time I walked down the halls, taunting me, twisting my past into new truths.

Your own mother didn't love you. Your own mother tried to kill you.

I blinked back sudden tears and pasted a smile on my face. The smiles had gotten me through tough times. I'd read online that the physical act of smiling—even if you were unhappy— could improve your mood by tricking your brain into releasing happiness-inducing hormones. So I'd smiled all the time as a teenager, and people probably thought I was crazy, but it was better than sinking into a darkness so deep I might've never clawed my way out.

And when smiling on my own became too hard, I looked for other reasons to be "happy," like the beauty of a rainbow after a storm, the sweet taste of a perfectly baked cookie, or gorgeous photographs of glittering cities and epic landscapes around the world. It had worked...for the most part.

"...of the cake?"

My father's voice shook me out of my trip down memory lane. I blinked. "I'm sorry, what?"

He hitched an eyebrow. "Do you want a piece of the cake?" he repeated.

"Oh, uh, sure."

He picked up the cake box, and we walked silently to the kitchen, where he silently cut us slices and we silently chewed.

Awkward with a capital A.

I wondered where it had gone wrong with us. My father never had issues talking and laughing with Josh. Why did he act so weird around me? And why did I act so weird around him? He was my *dad*, yet I'd never been able to open up to him fully.

He paid my bills and fed and sheltered me until I went to college, but Josh had been my real sounding board over the years, the one I went to whenever I wanted to talk about my day or had problems—with school, friends, or, much to his disgust, boys.

It was more than the fact that my dad was an authority figure and Josh was closer to my age. I had no trouble connecting with professors and my friends' parents.

It was something else. Something I couldn't name.

But perhaps that's just the nature of Asian parents of a certain age. It's not in our culture to show affection openly. We didn't say *I love you* or hug all the time like Stella's family. Chinese parents show their love through actions, not words—working hard to provide for their children, cooking food, taking care of their kids when they're sick.

I grew up not wanting for any material goods, and my father paid my full tuition at Thayer, which wasn't cheap. Sure, he disapproved of my photography career, and I had to fund all my equipment myself. And yeah, he played favorites with Josh, probably because he retained a deep-seated cultural preference for sons over daughters. But in the grand scheme of things, I'd lucked out. I should be grateful.

Still, it would be great if I could hold a normal conversation with my own father without it devolving into awkward silence.

I stabbed at my cake, wondering whether any early birthday surprise had ever been as pathetic as this one, when my skin tingled.

I looked up, and the tingles morphed into chills.

There.

Maybe that was why I'd never opened up to my dad, because sometimes I caught him staring at me like that.

Like he didn't know me.

Like he hated me.

Like he feared me.

CHAPTER 26

Ava

"IT'S NOT SAFE."

Bridget drew herself up to her full five feet, nine inches and leveled an icy glare at the dark-haired man glowering right back at her. Ballsy, considering she was the princess and he was the bodyguard, but Rhys Larsen wasn't Booth. That much was clear in the week since he'd arrived in Hazelburg to take over Booth's protection duties.

We'd thrown a big going-away celebration for Booth at the Crypt and sent quick prayers that Bridget's new bodyguard would be as cool as Booth.

Prayers not answered.

Rhys was gruff, surly, and arrogant. He drove Bridget mad, which was quite something, since she never lost her temper. In the past seven days, however, I'd seen her on the verge of *yelling*. I'd been so shocked I almost dropped my camera.

"Fall Fest is an annual tradition," she said in a regal voice. "I've attended every year for the past three years, and I don't intend to stop now."

Rhys's gray eyes flickered. He was a little younger than

Booth—maybe early thirties, with thick black hair, eyes the color of gunmetal, and a broad, muscled frame that towered over Bridget's leggy grace, even when she wore heels. Dark stubble shadowed his chin, and a small, jagged scar slashed across his left eyebrow. Without the scar, he would've been disconcertingly gorgeous; with it, he was still disconcertingly gorgeous, but also dangerous. More menacing.

Good quality to have in a bodyguard, I supposed.

"It's a crowd management issue." His voice rumbled through the car, deep and authoritative, even though he was technically Bridget's employee. "Too many people, too close quarters."

Stella, Jules, and I wisely stayed quiet while Bridget matched him glare for glare. "It's a college event. There's bound to be a crowd, and I've never had issues before. Half the people there don't even know who I am."

"It only takes one person one time," Rhys countered, his tone even. "One look and I know the festival is over max capacity."

"This is ridiculous. I'm not entering a war zone, and there are fewer people than at a sports game. No one ever said I couldn't attend one of *those*."

"The security measures and layout at sports games are—"

"Enough." Bridget held up a hand. "I refuse to stay in my house like a princess locked in a tower my senior year of college. I'm going, and you can either stay in the car or come with me." She opened the car door and exited without a backward glance.

Rhys's nostrils flared, but he followed her a heartbeat later, those sharp eyes of his constantly roving, searching for danger.

Jules, Stella, and I scrambled after them.

Fall Fest was one of the most anticipated events of the school year. Local businesses set up booths hawking seasonal food and products discounted for students—decadent hot chocolate and apple cider doughnuts, pumpkin pies and pulled-pork sandwiches. There were classic games and activities like bobbing for apples, tarot readings, and—because this was college—a tailgate where local alumni and students gathered to drink to their heart's content.

Rhys was right—there were more people than expected at the festival, but it was nothing compared to the spring break parties we'd attended in the past. I understood why he was concerned, but I also agreed with Bridget he was overreacting a *tiny* bit.

Bridget ignored him as we took advantage of all the food and activities on offer. Fall Fest was a necessary stress reliever between midterms and finals, and we had a blast—for the most part.

"He's driving me crazy," Bridget said a while later in a low voice. She sipped her hot chocolate with a morose expression. "I miss Booth."

I glanced over my shoulder at Rhys, who followed us with an impassive expression. Either he didn't hear what she said, or he had the world's best poker face.

I'd bet the latter. I had a feeling there wasn't much, if anything, that Rhys Larsen didn't see, hear, or notice.

"It's his first week." Stella snapped a picture of her drink before tasting it. "Booth has been with you for years. It's only natural that Rhys would be more overprotective. Give him time."

"I suppose." Bridget sighed. "I don't know how Nik does it. He has double the security I do because he's the crown prince, and there's so much riding on his shoulders." She shook her head. "I'm glad I'm second in line to the throne."

"You mean you don't want to rule, Your Majesty?" I teased. "You could be a queen and see your face on a postage stamp."

Bridget laughed. "No, thank you. As tempting as a postage stamp with my face is, I'd rather have a modicum of freedom." She shot a dark look in Rhys's direction. "Unless my bodyguard has other ideas."

"He's strict, but at least he's delicious," Jules said in a stage whisper. "No offense to Booth, but *whew*." She fanned herself.

"Is that all you think about?" Bridget asked, clearly torn between laughter and frustration.

A shadow slid across Jules's face before it disappeared. "Most of the time. I like to think about pleasant things. Speaking of which…" She turned to me. "Where's Lover Boy?"

I rolled my eyes, a blush spreading over my cheeks. "Don't call him that, and he's busy running a company. He doesn't have time for college events."

"You sure about that?" Stella tilted her chin at something behind me.

I whipped around, my heart jumping in my throat when I saw Alex standing behind me. In his navy cashmere sweater and jeans, he cut a sophisticated figure among the crowds of drunk college students and rumpled professors.

I couldn't help it—I ran and threw my arms around him. "I thought you had work!"

"I took off early." He pressed a kiss to my lips, and I sighed with pleasure. "I miss Fall Fest."

"Uh-huh. I'm sure *that's* what you miss," Jules teased.

My friends stared at us with fascination, and I realized this was the first time they'd seen us together as a…couple? I wasn't sure what to call our relationship. "Couple" sounded too mundane, but I guessed that was what we were.

We went on dates, talked through the night, and had wild, explosive sex. Alex Volkov and I were a couple.

The butterflies in my stomach quivered with excitement.

Alex stayed with us through the end of Fall Fest. He declined to play most of the festival games, but we convinced him to take pictures at the pumpkin-themed photo booth.

"Do you realize these are the first photos we have of the two of us?" I waved the Polaroids in triumph. "If you don't hang them in your living room, I'll be offended."

"I don't know. You don't match my decor," he said in a bland tone.

I swatted him on the arm, earning myself a rare laugh. Stella nearly choked on her hot chocolate, she was so shocked.

It was the perfect afternoon: great food, great weather, great company. The only hiccup occurred when Alex nicked himself on something sharp at one of the booths. The cut was deep enough that blood welled and streaked down his finger.

"It's fine," he said. "It's just a scratch."

"You're bleeding." I planted my hands on my hips. "We have to clean and bandage it. Let's go." My tone brooked no opposition.

No way in hell was he walking around with blood dripping down his hand. What if it got infected?

Alex's mouth quirked up. "Yes, ma'am."

I huffed at his amusement—he was *bleeding*—and dragged him to the campus health center, where the bored-looking student assistant supplied us with a gauze pad and Band-Aid.

I rinsed the cut under running tap water in the bathroom and dabbed at it with the gauze. "Hold still." I tossed the gauze in the trash and peeled open the Band-Aid. "You should've been more careful," I grumbled. "You're lucky you weren't seriously hurt. What the hell were you thinking?"

I looked up and found Alex staring at me with a small smile.

"What?"

"You're cute when you're worried."

I pressed my lips together, struggling to contain my smile. "Don't try to act all sweet so you can get out of trouble."

"Am I in trouble?" he drawled. He kicked the door shut with his foot and locked it with his free hand.

My pulse ratcheted up a notch. "Yes."

"You think I'm acting sweet?"

I gave a tiny nod.

Alex hefted me up onto the sink. "We better remedy both those things, shouldn't we?"

My teeth dug into my bottom lip as he shoved my dress up over my chest and grazed his teeth over my nipples through the thin lace of my bra.

"Alex, we're in the student health center," I squeaked, wanting him to both stop and keep going. Everyone was at Fall Fest so the center wasn't busy, but the receptionist sat a few feet away outside the door, and the flimsy walls were anything *but* soundproof.

"I'm aware." He pulled my bra aside with his teeth and lavished attention on my breasts while his nonbandaged hand found the sweet spot between my legs. I was already soaked for him, my thighs slick with my juices as he drove me crazy with his mouth and fingers. His erection pressed against my leg, thick and hard as a steel pipe, but when I reached for it, he batted my hand away.

"I hope you're not attached to your underwear," he said.

My brows drew together. "Wha—" The sound of fabric tearing answered my incomplete question.

Alex's mouth curled into a sly grin at my shocked expression. "Since we've established that you're a screamer," he said. "Open your mouth."

My resistance collapsed.

I opened my mouth, and he shoved my underwear in, muffling my moan. I shivered when I tasted the slickness of my arousal.

I was throbbing now, so turned on I couldn't see straight. There was something so freakin' erotic about knowing someone could catch us any minute.

Alex returned his attention to my breasts while he slid one finger, then two, into my slippery folds. I gripped his hair, tugging so hard it must've hurt as he worked me into a frenzy, but if it did, he didn't show it.

He lifted his head from my chest and watched me with smoldering eyes. "That's it, Sunshine," he murmured, his muscles taut as he finger fucked me harder. He was knuckles deep inside me now, the obscene sounds of him sliding in and out of my drenched core creating a dirty symphony that intensified my arousal. I rode his hand shamelessly, drool leaking from the corners of my mouth as I screamed around my makeshift gag. "Come for me like a little slut."

I did. Hard, fast, and endlessly, flying high in an explosion of starry bliss.

When I finally came down, I saw that he had unbuttoned his pants and was fisting his cock. It didn't take long before he erupted, spurting thick, hot jets all over my thighs.

"No," he said when I reached to clean myself. He pulled my shredded panties out of my mouth and pocketed them, his movements crisp and precise. "I want you to walk around with my cum on you so you know exactly who you belong to."

Heat blistered my cheeks. "Alex," I hissed. "I can't walk out there with no underwear and...and—"

"You can, and you will." His fingers brushed my thighs, where the cum was already drying. "The faster you obey, the faster we can leave and go home, where you can shower. With help," he added with a wicked smile.

"You're crazy." But I did as he asked, pulling my sweater dress down and fixing my hair. I couldn't look the receptionist in the eye as we walked out. She probably knew what we'd done, because it didn't take *that* long to bandage a wound.

The wind brushed against my bareness as we rejoined our friends and I jumped, earning myself a smirk from Alex and strange looks from everyone else.

"Are you okay?" Stella asked. "You look flushed."

"Yes," I squeaked. "Just, ah, a bit chilly." While the others got distracted by the start of the pie-eating contest, I slapped Alex's arm. "You'll pay for this."

"Looking forward to it."

I rolled my eyes, but I couldn't stay mad at him, especially since part of me loved how dirty I felt walking around like this.

"I have a serious question," I said as we watched two seniors destroy their pumpkin pies. "What are you doing for Thanksgiving?"

"I imagine I'll be eating turkey somewhere," he said casually.

"Do you...want to come to my place for the weekend? Since your uncle doesn't celebrate and all. Not that you have to," I added quickly.

"Sunshine, I've spent every Thanksgiving with your family for the past eight years."

"I know, but Josh isn't here this year, and I didn't want to assume. I mean, meeting the dad..."

Alex's eyes gleamed with laughter. "I've already met your dad."

"Right. But..." I faltered. "I guess it doesn't matter. We can't tell him we're dating until we tell Josh, but would it be suspicious if we show up together? Parents have a weird lie-detecting radar. What if he—"

"Ava." He placed his hands on my shoulders. "Do you want me to spend Thanksgiving with you?"

I nodded.

"Then that's what I'm doing. Don't overthink it."

"Says the king of overthinking," I muttered, but I was smiling.

CHAPTER 27

Ava

EVERY YEAR, MY FAMILY CELEBRATED THANKSGIVING with a Chinese twist. Instead of turkey and mashed potatoes, we ate roast duck, rice, dumplings, and fish cake soup. Food-wise, this year was the same, but without Josh, the dinner had been two hours of silence and awkwardness. Alex and my dad held a few brief conversations about football and work, and that was it. I think my dad was stressed about something at his office. He seemed more irritated than usual.

I also suspected my dad didn't like Alex much. It was a surprise, considering he had a soft spot for smart, accomplished people, and Alex was as smart and accomplished as they came. I'd always chalked it up to the fact that Alex didn't kiss ass as much as Chinese parents liked—he wasn't one for flattering words. Plus, I was 90 percent sure my dad knew something was up with me and Alex, though he didn't say anything.

"He knows," I whispered when my dad excused himself to use the restroom. "I swear, he *knows*."

"No, he doesn't. Even if he does, he has no proof, and he won't say anything to Josh," Alex said. "Relax. It's supposed to be your weekend off."

"There's no such thing as a weekend off for students."

It may have been a holiday, but I had to study for finals and finish my fellowship application. It was all done except for a few paragraphs of my personal statement. I'd included the photos I took of Alex in my portfolio, though I hadn't told him yet. They were some of my best work, but I didn't want to say anything until I heard from the WYP committee. I didn't want to jinx it.

"It's too bad we're not sleeping in the same room." Alex's eyes glinted. "I could help relieve your stress."

I laughed. "Is that all you think about?"

Except I wasn't much better. I wanted to sleep in the same room as Alex too—especially here, in this house, where the nightmares were always darker. But since my dad didn't know about our relationship, Alex was staying in the guest room.

"Only when I'm around you." While my dad seemed more stressed, Alex was more relaxed these days. Smiling, laughing... he even made the occasional joke. I liked to think I had a part in loosening him up. I was still taking Krav Maga lessons with Ralph, and Alex was still giving me swim lessons—I panicked way less now than I did at the beginning—and after everything he'd helped me with, I wanted to help him too. He came off invincible and unflappable, but everybody, no matter how strong, needs a little care and attention of their own.

"Alex Volkov, when did you become so cheesy?" I teased.

He left out a playful growl and reached for me right as my father reentered the dining room. We sobered and maintained a safe distance between us the rest of the night, but my dad's raised eyebrows confirmed my suspicions. He knew.

I couldn't breathe. The hand tightened around my neck, and I thrashed my arms and legs, desperate to throw it off.

"Stop," I tried to say. "Please stop."

But I couldn't. The hand was too tight.

Tears blurred my vision. Snot ran down my nose.

I was dying. Dying...dying...

I awoke with a gasp. My sweat-drenched sheets slid off my body, and I looked around wildly, certain I'd find an intruder in my room. Deep shadows skulked in the corners, and an eerie splash of silvery white moonlight filtered through the white lace curtains fluttering in the window.

But there was no intruder.

"It was a dream," I whispered, my voice a gunshot in the silence. "It was just a dream."

A different one from the ones I usually had. I wasn't underwater. I didn't scream. But I was terrified—more terrified than I had been in a long, long time.

Because my dreams were never just dreams—they were memories.

I always had worse "dreams" at home. Maybe it was because of the lake out back. It was a different lake than the one at my mother's house before she died, but it was a lake nonetheless.

I wished my family didn't like lakes so much.

I glanced at my digital clock, and the icy fingers of dread scratched down my spine when I saw the time. 4:44 a.m. Again.

I wanted to run down the hall and throw myself into Alex's arms. With him, I was safe. Even my nightmares had decreased in frequency and intensity since we'd started sleeping together every night—me tucked into his side, his arms wrapped around me in a protective embrace. While I wanted his insomnia cured, wanted him to get the peace and rest he deserved every night, a tiny, shameful part of me liked that he was awake to watch over me in the long hours between dusk and dawn.

He was probably awake, but I forced myself to stay put in case he wasn't. I didn't want to risk interrupting the two or three precious hours of sleep he got every night.

I crawled back beneath my covers and tried to catch more shut-eye, but my skin itched, and something called to me beyond the walls. I resisted for as long as I could, until twilight melted into dawn.

7:02 a.m. A more respectable time to wake up than 4:44 a.m.

I changed into a sweatshirt and yoga pants, shoved my feet into fuzzy boots, and tiptoed through the silent house toward the backyard. The air smelled fresh and crisp, and a light fog hung over the lake, cloaking the scene in mystery.

The itching on my skin intensified. The call grew louder.

I walked toward the lake, my boots crunching over the tiny gravel stones of the barbecue area my dad had set up for summer get-togethers. Drops of dew dusted the empty wood furniture, and the charcoal grill looked sad and lonely, rendered useless until Memorial Day weekend.

My breaths formed tiny puffs in the air. It was colder than I'd expected, but I didn't stop walking until I reached the edge of the lake—close enough to smell the damp earth beneath my feet.

It was the first time I remembered visiting the lake.

I'd shied away from it growing up, going only as far as the barbecue seating area. Even then, I'd get so nervous I would excuse myself halfway through parties and run to the bathroom to bring myself under control.

I wasn't sure what compelled me to come out here this morning, but the lake's siren song enveloped me, coaxing me closer—like it was trying to tell me a secret it didn't want others to hear.

I was better with water now after all my lessons with Alex, but a tremor of unease still spiraled through me when I thought about the watery depths before me.

Deep breaths. You're fine. You're on solid ground. The lake will not rise up and drag you—

A car alarm blared in the distance, and I flinched, all relaxation techniques forgotten as my nightmare played out in broad daylight.

I picked up another stone from the ground. It was smooth and flat, the type that would make really pretty ripples. I drew my arm back to throw it, but I smelled something sweet and flowery— Mommy's perfume—and got distracted.

My aim veered, and the stone thudded onto the ground, but I didn't mind. Mommy was back! We could play now.

I turned, smiling a big gap-toothed smile, but I only made it halfway before something pushed me. I pitched forward—down, down, off the edge of the deck, my scream swallowed up by the water rushing toward my face.

"Ava?" My father's worried voice penetrated my daze. "What are you doing out here?"

I forgot. He came out here every morning to exercise, rain or shine. He was religious about his morning routine.

I spun, trying to escape the images flashing through my brain, but they wouldn't stop. Old nightmares. New revelations.

No. No, no, nononononono.

My father's gold signet ring flashed in the light, and I saw his face.

And I screamed.

CHAPTER 28

Alex

SOMETHING WAS WRONG.

I felt it deep in my bones as I pulled into my driveway, my sixth sense blaring.

Ava stared straight ahead, her face pale, her eyes unseeing. She'd been like this since the morning after Thanksgiving, when her father found her by the lake and she'd screamed so loud she woke me up from one of my rare bouts of sleep. I'd raced outside, my mind conjuring all sorts of horrible scenarios while I cursed myself for leaving her alone. For failing her.

But I found her outside, safe and unharmed—at least physically—while her father tried to soothe her. Lines of distress had marred Michael's face as she shook like a leaf in the wind, tears streaming down her face. She refused to tell us what was wrong, and it wasn't until hours later that she confessed she'd freaked out about being that close to the lake. She wasn't sure why she'd gone out there in the first place, but her aquaphobia had kicked in late.

Bullshit.

Ava could enter the pool now without panicking, and she'd

stayed calm when we visited lakes before. No, something else had terrified her to the point where she'd screamed the house down, and once I found out what it was, I would hunt it to the ends of the earth and tear it apart with my bare hands.

I guided her into my house, where I tucked her beneath a blanket on the couch and made her a hot drink. I'd turned off the heat since I'd gone away for the weekend, and until it caught up, the house was freezing.

"Hot chocolate with oat milk and three marshmallows." I kept my tone light as I handed Ava the drink. "Just like you like it."

"Thanks." She wrapped her hands around the mug and stared at the marshmallows bobbing in the liquid but made no move to drink it.

Normally, she'd have downed half the mug by now. She loved hot chocolate. It was her favorite part of winter.

I grasped her chin and angled her face toward mine. "Tell me who or what I need to kill," I growled. "What happened at your father's house?"

"I told you, nothing. It was just the lake." Ava eked out a wobbly smile. "You can't kill a lake."

"I'll drain every fucking lake and ocean in the world if I have to."

A tiny crystal tear slipped from her eye. "Alex..."

"I mean it." I rubbed the tear away with my thumb. My heart raged in my chest, a snarling beast furious at the sight of her distress and the thought that there was something in the world that would dare hurt her. *Hypocrite*, my conscience whispered. *Cruel, selfish hypocrite. Look in the mirror. Think about the things you've done.* I gritted my teeth and ignored the taunting voice in my head. "I'd do it for you." I kissed the spot where her tear had been. "I'd do anything for you. No matter how twisted or impossible."

A shudder rolled through her body. "I know. I trust you. More than anyone else in this world."

If only she knew, my conscience sang. *If only she knew what kind of man you are. She wouldn't touch you with a ten-foot pole, much less trust you.*

Shut. Up.

Great. I was now having silent conversations with an imaginary voice.

How the mighty have fallen.

"I don't know if it's even...if it's true," Ava whispered. "I could have imagined it."

My knuckles turned white around my knee. "Imagined what?"

"I—" She gulped, her eyes haunted. "My childhood memories. They came back."

The confession hit me like a freight train, blindsiding me.

Of all the things I'd expected her to say, that had not been one of them.

Repressed memories were usually the result of a traumatic event and could resurface if the person encountered a trigger—a sound, a smell, an event. But Ava had been at home, where she'd grown up her entire life. What had happened over Thanksgiving that could've triggered her? The lake?

"Okay." I kept my voice calm and even. Soothing. "What do you remember?"

Ava's shoulders trembled. "I don't remember everything. But I remember the day I...the day I almost died."

My entire body flushed hot, then cold. *Almost died.* If she had died, if she was no longer somewhere in this world...

The invisible noose around my neck tightened; a tiny bead of sweat trickled down the back of my neck.

Her near-death experience wasn't my fault. It'd happened long before I met her, but still...

My breath grew shallow.

"I was playing by the lake." She licked her lips. "There used to be a dock that ran out to the middle of the water. My dad took it down after The Incident—that's what I call what happened—but we used to go out there all the time until my parents' divorce. My dad moved out, and my mom fell into a depression. It was a really nasty divorce, from what I gleaned over the years, and now I remember all the shouting and threats. I was too young to understand what they were mad about; all I knew was that they were angry. So angry sometimes I thought they would kill each other. Anyway, my mom stopped taking me out to the lake until one day...she did. We were playing on the dock, and we ran out of sunscreen. My mom was really big on sunscreen—said it was the most important thing we could do for our skin. I didn't want to stop playing to go with her, so she made me promise to stay put while she ran inside. She was supposed to be gone for only a few minutes."

Ava traced the rim of the mug with her finger, her eyes gaining that far-off quality that told me she was lost in her unearthed memories. "I did. I stayed put. Watched the fish, threw stones in the water—I loved the ripples they made. I waited for her to come back so we could play again. I've had nightmares about this day for as long as I could remember, so not all this is new. I remembered her leaving, and I remembered her returning and me falling into the water. Only..." She drew in a deep breath. "I don't think she returned. I thought I smelled her perfume, but in my nightmares—my memories—I never got a good look at the face of the person who pushed me. It all happened so quickly. But when I was by the lake a few days ago...more memories returned, and I realized I'd seen more than I'd thought. Before I fell in the water, I saw a flash of gold. A signet ring. *MC*."

Dread and shock coiled at the base of my spine and flared their wings, enveloping me in their dark embrace.

"Michael Chen." Ava shook harder. "Alex, my mom didn't try to kill me. My dad did."

CHAPTER 29

Ava

I COULDN'T STOP THROWING UP.

I heaved into the toilet, my stomach roiling, my skin drenched with sweat as Alex held my hair back and rubbed circles on my back.

He was livid. Not at me but at my father, my past, the entire situation. I could feel it in the tenseness of his hands and the aura of barely leashed violence that'd swirled around him since I confessed my memories.

The day at the lake had only been the tip of the iceberg.

I'd remembered something else—something that cemented my father's guilt.

"Daddy, look!" I ran into his office, brandishing the paper in my hands with pride. It was an essay I wrote for class on who we admired most. I wrote about Daddy. Mrs. James gave me an A-plus on it, and I couldn't wait to show him.

"What is it, Ava?" He raised his eyebrows.

"I got an A-plus! Look!"

He took the paper from me and skimmed it, but he didn't look happy like I'd expected.

My smile dimmed. Why was he frowning? Weren't A's good? He always praised Josh when he brought home A's.

"What's this?"

"It's a paper about who I admire most?" I twisted my hands, growing more nervous. I wished Josh was here, but he was at his friend's house. "I said you, because you saved me."

I didn't remember him saving me, but that was what everyone told me. They said I fell into a lake a few years ago and would've died if Daddy hadn't jumped in after me.

"I did, didn't I?" He finally smiled, but it wasn't a nice smile.

I suddenly didn't want to be here anymore.

"You look so much like your mother," Daddy said. "A carbon copy of when she was your age."

I didn't know what a carbon copy was, but based on his tone, it probably wasn't a good thing.

He stood, and I instinctively stepped back until my legs hit the couch.

"Do you remember what happened at the lake when you were five, darling Ava?" He brushed his fingers over my cheek, and I flinched.

I shook my head, too scared to speak.

"That's for the best. Makes things easier." Daddy smiled another ugly smile. "I wonder if you'll forget this too?" He picked up a throw pillow and pushed me onto the couch.

I didn't have time to respond before I lost the ability to breathe. The pillow pressed into my face, cutting off my oxygen supply. I tried to push it off, but I wasn't strong enough. A strong hand locked my wrists together until I couldn't struggle anymore.

My chest tightened, and my vision flickered.

No air. Noairnoairnoair—

Not only had my father tried to drown me, he'd also tried to suffocate me.

I retched again and again and again. I'd managed to stay calm for most of Thanksgiving weekend, but saying the words out loud—*my father tried to kill me*—must've triggered a delayed physical response.

After I'd thrown up what must've been all the contents in my stomach, I sank onto the floor. Alex handed me a glass of water, and I downed it with long, grateful gulps.

"I'm sorry," I rasped. "This is so embarrassing. I'll clean up—"

"Don't worry about it." He ran a gentle hand over my hair, but an inferno raged in his eyes. "We'll figure everything out. Leave it to me."

A week later, Alex and I waited for my father to arrive in one of Archer Group's conference rooms. It was my first time seeing Alex's workplace, and the building was exactly how I'd pictured it: sleek, modern, and beautiful, all glass and white marble.

I couldn't appreciate it though. I was too nervous.

The clock ticked on the wall, deafening in the silence.

I drummed my fingers on the polished wood table and stared through the tinted glass windows, both willing and dreading my father's appearance.

"Security here is top-notch," Alex reassured me. "And I'll be by your side the entire time."

"That's not what I'm worried about." I had to press my other hand against my knee to keep it from bouncing. "I don't think he would..."

Physically hurt me? But he had. Or at least he'd tried.

The day he pushed me into the lake and the day he suffocated me. And those were only the instances I remembered.

I flashed back over the years, trying to remember anything else amiss. I thought he'd been a decent father during my teenage years. Not the most present or affectionate, but he hadn't tried to kill me, which begged the question: why hadn't he? There'd been plenty of opportunities, plenty of times when he could've made my death look like an accident.

But that question paled in comparison to the biggest one of all, which was why he wanted to kill me in the first place. I was his *daughter*.

A single broken sob erupted from my throat. Alex squeezed my hand, his brows drawn tight over his eyes, but I shook my head.

"I'm okay," I said, gathering the strength to pull myself together. I could do this. I wouldn't break down. *I wouldn't*. Even if my heart hurt so much I might combust. "I—"

The door opened, and my words died in my throat.

My father—Michael; I couldn't think of him as my father anymore—walked in, looking confused and a little annoyed. He wore his favorite striped polo and jeans again, as well as that damn signet ring.

I choked back bile. Beside me, Alex tensed, wrath radiating from him in dark, dangerous waves.

"What's going on?" Michael frowned. "Ava? Why did you ask me to come here?"

"Mr. Chen." Alex's voice seemed pleasant enough; only those who knew him could detect the lethal blade beneath his words, waiting to strike. "Please, take a seat." He gestured at the leather chair on the other side of the table.

Michael did, his expression growing more irritated. "I have work to do, and you made me come all the way to DC for a supposed emergency."

"I sent a car," Alex said, still in that deceptively pleasant tone.

"Your car or mine, it takes the same amount of time."

Michael's eyes flicked between Alex and me before settling on me. "Don't tell me you're pregnant."

Confirmation he knew Alex and I had been an item at Thanksgiving. Not that I cared what he thought anymore.

"No." I raised my voice so I could hear it over my pounding pulse. "I'm not."

"Then what's the emergency?"

"I—" I faltered. Alex squeezed my hand again. "I—"

I couldn't say it. Not with an audience.

Alex already knew everything, but what Michael and I had to discuss seemed too personal to air out in front of other people. It was between us. Father and daughter.

Pinpricks of light danced before my vision. I dug the nails of my free hand into my thigh so hard I would've drawn blood had I not been wearing jeans.

"Alex, can you let us have a moment alone, please?"

His head whipped toward me, his expression thunderous.

Please, I begged with my eyes. *I need to do this on my own.*

Knowing how protective he was, I expected more resistance, but he must've seen something in my face—my unshakeable belief that I had to fight my own battles—because he released my hand and stood.

Reluctantly, but he did it.

"I'll be right outside," he said. A promise and a warning.

Alex shot a dark look at Michael before he exited.

And then there were two.

"Ava?" Michael raised his eyebrows. "Are you in trouble?"

Yes.

I'd run through this conversation in my mind hundreds, if not thousands, of times before I stepped foot in this room. I'd labored over how to bring up the topic and how I'd react to his response, whatever it may be. *Oh hey, Dad, nice to see you. By the way, did*

you try to murder me? Yes? Oh damn, okay. But I couldn't drag
it out any longer.

I needed answers before the questions killed me.

"I'm not in trouble," I said, proud of how steady I sounded.
"But I have something to tell you about what happened over
Thanksgiving weekend."

Wariness crept into his eyes. "Okay…"

"I remembered."

"Remembered what?"

"Everything." I watched him closely for a reaction. "My childhood. The day I almost drowned."

Wariness morphed into shock and a faint tinge of panic. Deep
grooves appeared in his forehead.

My stomach dropped. I'd hoped I'd been wrong, but the wild
look in Michael's eyes told me all I needed to know—I wasn't
wrong. He really had tried to kill me.

"Really?" His chuckle sounded forced. "Are you sure? You've
been having nightmares for years—"

"I'm sure." I straightened my shoulders and looked him
straight in the eye, trying to keep my trembles under control.
"Were you the one who pushed me into the lake that day?"

Michael's face collapsed, the shock in his eyes tripling.
"What?" he whispered.

"You heard me."

"No, of course not!" He raked a hand through his graying
hair, agitated. "How could you think that? I'm your *father*. I
would never do anything to hurt you."

Hope whispered through my heart even as my brain shook its
head in skepticism. "That's what I remember."

"Memories can deceive. We remember things that didn't
actually happen." Michael leaned forward, his face softening.
"What exactly do you think happened?"

I gnawed on my bottom lip. "I was playing by the lake. Someone came up behind me and pushed me. I remembered turning around and seeing a flash of gold. A signet ring. *Your* signet ring." My gaze dropped to said ring on his finger.

He glanced down and rubbed it. "Ava." He sounded pained. "I was the one who saved you from drowning."

That was the part that didn't make sense. I'd passed out, so I hadn't seen who'd saved me, but the paramedics and police said Michael had been the one who called them. Why would he do that if he was the one who pushed me in?

"I came over to speak with your mother about the divorce, and no one answered the door even though her car was in the driveway. I went around back to see if she was out there, and I saw—" Michael swallowed hard. "It was the worst few minutes of my life, thinking you were dead. I jumped in and saved you, and all the while, your mother...she just stood there in shock. Like she couldn't believe what had happened." His voice dropped. "Your mother wasn't well, Ava. She didn't mean to harm you, but sometimes she did things out of her control. She felt so guilty afterward, and between the divorce and criminal charges...that's why she overdosed."

Pain ripped through my head. I pressed my fingers to my temples, trying to sort through my father's words and my own memories. What was real? What wasn't?

Memories were unreliable. I knew that. And Michael sounded sincere. But had I really been that off base? Where did those visions come from, if not my memories?

"There's another instance," I said shakily. "Third grade. I brought home an essay from Mrs. James's class and showed you. We were in your office. You looked at me and said I was a carbon copy of Mom and you...you pushed a pillow into my face and tried to suffocate me. I couldn't breathe. I would've died, but Josh came home and called for you, and you stopped."

The story sounded ridiculous beneath the bright lights of the conference room. My head pounded harder.

Alarm spread across Michael's features. "Ava," he said softly, calmly, like he didn't want to spook me. "You never had a teacher named Mrs. James."

My heart crashed against my chest. "I did! She had blond hair and glasses, and she gave us sugar cookies on our birthdays..." Tears prickled my eyes. "I swear, Mrs. James was real."

She had to be real. But what if she wasn't? What if I'd made everything up and *thought* they were memories? What was wrong with me? Why was my brain so messed up?

I couldn't breathe. I felt crazy, like nothing in my life was real and I'd dreamed it all up. I pressed my palms into the table, half expecting it to dissolve in a shower of dust.

"Honey..." He reached for me, but before he could touch me, the door banged open.

"That's enough. Stop lying." Alex strode in, his face like thunder. Of course he had this place wired. "I had my people investigate after Ava told me what she remembered," he said coldly. *He did?* He never told me that. "You'd be surprised how much—and how quickly—one can find out with the right amount of money. She *did* have a third-grade teacher named Mrs. James—one who reported suspicious bruising on Ava's wrists when she came into class the next day. You claimed it was a playground injury, and they believed you." Alex's eyes burned with disgust. "You're a good actor, but drop the mask. We're onto you."

I stared at Michael. I didn't know what to believe anymore. "Is that true? You were gaslighting me this whole time?"

"Ava, I'm your father." Michael rubbed a hand over his face, his eyes bright. "I would never lie to you."

I looked between him and Alex. My head pounded harder.

There was too much going on, too many secrets to reveal. But in the end, I had to trust myself.

"I think you would," I said. "I think you've been lying to me my entire life."

Michael's face remained anguished for several more seconds before it twisted and morphed into a hideous mask. His eyes gleamed with delighted malice, and his mouth spread into a mocking smile.

He didn't look like my father anymore. He didn't look human at all. He looked like a monster straight from my nightmares.

"Bravo." He slow-clapped. "I almost had you," he told me. "You should've seen yourself. *I swear, Mrs. James was real,*" he mimicked, laughing. The ugly sound raised every hair on my body. "Classic. You really thought you were crazy."

I gave a subtle shake of my head when Alex moved toward Michael. I wanted to run and hide, but adrenaline pushed the words out of my mouth. "Why? I was a *kid.*" My chin wobbled. "I'm your daughter. Why would you do those things to me? Tell me the truth." I tightened my jaw. "No. More. Lies."

"The truth is subjective." Michael leaned back in his chair. "But you want to know so bad? Here's my truth—you're not really my daughter." He flashed a humorless smile at my sharp intake of breath. "That's right. Your bitch of a mom cheated on me. Must've been one of those times I was away for business. She always complained I wasn't around enough, like it wasn't my fucking business that put the roof over her head and kept her nice and warm in designer clothes. I'd always suspected you weren't mine—you look nothing like me, but I figured, hey, maybe you just have a strong resemblance to Wendy. I took a secret paternity test, and lo and behold, you really aren't mine. Your mother tried to deny it, but there wasn't much she could do with the evidence staring her in the face." His expression darkened. "Of course, we couldn't mention that in the divorce proceedings. Those things always leak, and we would've both lost face."

There were few things worse than losing face in Chinese culture. Except, of course, trying to murder your daughter.

"If I'm not your daughter, why did you fight so hard for custody?" I demanded, my tongue thick in my mouth.

Michael's lips curled into a sneer. "I didn't fight for custody for *you*. I did it for Josh. He's *actually* my son. Test confirmed it. My legacy, my heir. But since no one other than your mother and I knew you weren't mine, you and Josh were a package deal. Unfortunately, courts almost always side with the mother except in extraordinary circumstances, so..." He shrugged. "I had to engineer an extraordinary circumstance."

I felt sick, but I stayed frozen while Michael unraveled the tangled web of our past.

"I was lucky your mom was stupid enough to leave you alone. Honestly, that was negligence on its own. But I snuck into the house, intending to plant evidence of her 'drug addiction,' and I found you playing by the lake instead. It was like God dropped the opportunity into my lap. Sometimes, courts side with the mother even if she's a drug addict, but trying to *drown* her child? Guaranteed win for me. Not to mention, it'd be punishment for her. So I pushed you in. I was tempted to let you drown for real." Another flash of teeth. "But I wasn't *that* coldhearted. You were just a kid. So I fished you out, told the authorities I saw Wendy push you in. She kept screaming she didn't do it, but you wanna know the real genius of my plan?" He leaned forward, his eyes sparkling. "*You* were the one who implicated your mother."

"No." I shook my head. "I didn't. I didn't even see—I didn't remember—"

"Not after. But in the moment?" He smirked. "It's quite easy to implant false memories, especially in the mind of a confused, traumatized child. A few suggestions and leading questions from me, and you were convinced it was your mom. Said you smelled her perfume, plus she was the only person there. Either way, the authorities had to investigate, and they gave me custody of you and Josh while they gathered evidence. Your mom became depressed and, well, you know what happened with the pills. It's pretty poetic, actually. She died of the very thing I'd wanted to frame her for—at 4:44 a.m., no less. The unluckiest time."

My stomach lurched. *4:44 a.m.* The time I awoke from my nightmares.

I've never been a superstitious person, but I couldn't help wondering if that had been my mom screaming at me from the other side, urging me to remember. To leave the sociopath whose house I'd been living in all these years.

"What about that day in your office?" I asked, determined to see this through even though I wanted to throw up.

Michael snorted. "Right. That stupid essay about how I 'saved' you. You know, I did a pretty good job of hiding how much I resented having to raise you, the 'daughter' who's not even my own, all those years. I played the role of the quiet, awkward, grief-stricken father to a tee." His ugly smile reappeared. "But sometimes, you push my limits, especially since you look so much like *her*. A living reminder of her infidelity. It would've been so easy if you were out of the picture, but Josh chose that moment to come home. Alas." He lifted his shoulder in a shrug. "Can't have it all. To be fair, the office incident was a moment of weakness on my part—you were very much aware of what was going on, and I would've had a helluva time explaining what happened, though I'm sure I would've come up with *something*. But imagine my pleasant surprise when you woke up with not only no recollection of the office but no recollection of your entire childhood up to that point. Doctors couldn't explain it, but it didn't matter. All that mattered was you forgot." He smiled. "God really does smile on me, doesn't he?"

I felt Alex's hands on my back. I hadn't even noticed him approach. I leaned into the comfort of his touch while my mind spun. I remembered running to my room and locking the door after Michael released me and greeted Josh like nothing had happened. I stayed there all night, refusing to eat dinner no matter how much Josh tried to persuade me to come out. He'd only been thirteen at the time—too young to help me—and I had no one else to turn to.

I wondered if I'd been so panicked and traumatized that I'd blacked out *all* my experiences with Michael, which was basically my entire childhood.

"I couldn't be sure I'd be as lucky again though," Michael continued. "So I left you alone after that. Even sent you to therapy because I had to play the part of the concerned father, but it was a good thing those incompetent idiots didn't know what they were doing."

No wonder he'd been so adamant about stopping my therapy sessions. He must've been terrified I would remember and implicate him. Which begged the question...why the hell was he so willing to tell me all this *now*?

It was like Alex read my mind. "There's no statute of limitations for attempted murder, and this entire conversation is recorded," he said. "DC has a one-party consent law for recordings, and Ava"—he gestured at me—"consented beforehand. You're going to jail for a long, long time."

Michael's mask of malice melted, leaving behind the "father" who took me on college visits and planned my birthday parties again. It was terrifying how easily he switched between the two. "If I have to go to jail to save her, I will," he whispered. He turned to me, his eyes shining with actual tears. "Ava, honey, Alex is not who you think he is. His driver picked me up, and on the way here, he threatened me—"

"Enough," Alex hissed. "No more gaslighting her. You're done, and my friends would agree."

I watched in shock as two FBI agents burst into the room and hauled Michael out of his chair. Alex hadn't mentioned the FBI when we'd planned this.

"This won't hold up in court," Michael said, sounding quite calm for someone entering federal custody. "I'll fight it. You won't win."

"With what money?" Alex raised his eyebrows. "You see, my people found some interesting things about your business during their digging as well. Interesting, *illegal* things. Tax evasion. Corporate fraud. Ring any bells?"

For the first time since he arrived, Michael's composure slipped. "You're lying," he hissed. "You had no authority—"

"Au contraire. I worked with the FBI on that part. My friends at the agency were quite interested in what I had to say and what they found." Alex smiled. "You can use your untainted assets to hire an attorney, but most of your assets *are* tainted and will be frozen before your trial. You'll receive the official notice before the end of today."

"Josh will never forgive you for this." Michael's eyes burned. "He worships me. Who do you think he'll believe? Me, his father, or you, a punk he met a few years ago?"

"In this case, Father—" Josh walked in, his face darker than I'd ever seen it. "I think I'll believe 'the punk.'"

He slammed his fist into Michael's face, and all hell broke loose.

CHAPTER 30

Ava

SEVERAL HOURS LATER, JOSH AND I SAT IN THE BACK booth of a restaurant near Archer Group. Alex had booked the entire place and dismissed most of the staff. Other than a waiter who hovered by the entrance, out of earshot, we were the only ones here. Alex, too, had retreated to his office to give us more privacy.

"I'm so sorry, Ave." Josh looked terrible. Lackluster complexion, huge bags beneath his eyes. Stress and worry carved deep grooves in his face, and his usual cocky, charming grin was nowhere to be seen. "I should've known. I should've—"

"It's not your fault. Dad—Michael—fooled *all* of us." I shuddered, thinking about how well Michael had played his role. "Besides, he loved you. He treated you perfectly. You wouldn't have noticed anything."

Josh's lips thinned. "He didn't love me. People like him can't love. He saw me as a...vessel to continue his legacy. Nothing else."

Alex and I had contacted Josh and told him what I remembered a few days ago. He'd been shocked, but he'd believed me. He'd also insisted on flying back for the confrontation and received emergency leave from his program to do so. He'd watched and listened to the conversation via the conference room's secret cameras the entire time, and Alex's security team had had to restrain him so he didn't burst in too early.

I could only imagine. Josh was nothing if not hot-tempered.

After he punched Michael, the situation had devolved into chaos, with the FBI agents, Josh, Michael, and various security guards grappling with each other. Josh would have beaten the hell out of our—his—father had Alex not finally pulled him back. The FBI agents hauled a bruised and bleeding Michael into custody, and now we awaited his trial.

Thanks to Alex, whose friend's father was apparently high up in the FBI, Josh didn't get charged with assault for attacking Michael.

The entire situation felt surreal.

"Either way, it wasn't your fault," I repeated. "You were just a kid too."

"If I'd been there that day in his office…"

"Stop it. Do you hear me, Josh Chen?" I said sternly. "I will *not* let you blame yourself. Mom and Michael were adults. They made their own choices." I swallowed, feeling guilty about my suppressed rage toward my mother over the years when, in fact, she'd been a victim too. "You've *always* been there when I needed you, and you are an amazing brother. I'll only say that once, so don't ask me to repeat it. Your ego doesn't need more inflation."

He cracked a small smile. "Are you going to be okay?"

I took a deep breath. The past week and a half had been…a lot. The revelations, the mind fucks, the sinking realization that I was practically an orphan. My mother was dead, my father wasn't my real father—and would probably be locked up for a long time—and I had no clue who my actual father was. But at least I knew the truth, and I had Josh, Alex, and my friends.

Maybe the import of what happened would hit me later, but for now, all I felt was relief mingled with sadness and lingering shock.

"Yeah," I said. "I will."

Josh must've heard my conviction, because his shoulders relaxed the tiniest bit. "If you need to talk or anything, I'm here. Can't guarantee I'll give good advice, but I'll be a sounding board or whatever."

I smiled. "Thanks, Joshy."

He made a face at his hated nickname. "How many times do I have to tell you? *Don't* call me that."

We spent the next half hour talking about lighter topics—his time in Central America, what DC luxuries he'd indulge in before he returned to his volunteer program, and his now-dead relationship with the girl he'd told me about. Apparently, he'd ended things immediately after she brought up marriage. Typical Josh.

As annoying as he was, I had missed him, and I would be sad to see him leave. He was coming home for Christmas, but he couldn't take the entire period between now and then off, so he was leaving tomorrow and flying back in two weeks.

However, we still had one elephant in the room we needed to discuss.

"Now that we got all the small stuff out of the way..." A scowl overtook Josh's face. "You and Alex. What. The. Fuck?"

I cringed. "We didn't plan it, I promise. It just sort of... happened."

"You just 'happened' to fall into bed with my best friend?"

"Don't be mad."

"I'm not mad at you," Josh snapped. "I'm mad at *him*. He should've known better!"

"And I *don't* know better?"

"You know what I mean. You're a romantic. I can see you

falling for that broody asshole thing he has going on. But Alex...
Jesus Christ, Ave." Josh rubbed a hand over his face. "He's my best
friend, but even I shudder at the things he does. In all the years I've
known him, he's never once been in a relationship. Never shown
an interest in it. He cares about work, and that's it."

"Yes, he can be an asshole sometimes, but he's still human.
He needs love and care like anyone else," I said, feeling protective
of Alex even though he was the last person on earth who needed
protection. "As for the relationship part, there's a first time for
everything. He's been..." I swallowed hard. "You have no idea
how much he's helped me these past few months. He was there for
everything. The nightmares, the panic attacks...he taught me how
to swim. *Swim*, Josh. He helped me get over my fear of water, at
least a little bit, and he was so patient the entire time. But beyond
how much he's helped me, he's smart and funny and wonderful.
He makes me laugh and believe in myself, more than anyone else
ever has. And he may not show it to the world, but he *does* have a
heart. A beautiful one."

I cut myself off before I rambled further, my cheeks a deep,
bright red.

Josh stared at me, shock stamped on every inch of his face.
"Ava," he said. "Do you...love him?"

A lot of things in my life had been hazy up to this point, but my
feelings about this were clear. I didn't hesitate before answering.

"Yes." I may not have known what was in my mind, but I
knew what was in my heart. "I do."

———————

Josh left the next morning after threatening to kill Alex if he ever
broke my heart. He was still uncomfortable with our relationship,
but he'd grudgingly accepted it after he saw how much I cared
about Alex.

Alex had urgent business to take care of after he dropped Josh off at the airport, so I spent the rest of the day with my girls. Since it was drizzling and I wasn't up for going out, we had an at-home spa day, complete with DIY facials, mani-pedis, and a marathon of feel-good movies.

I'd told them what had happened with Michael. They'd been stunned, but none of them pressed me on it, for which I was grateful. It had been a heavy twenty-four hours, and I needed light-hearted downtime.

Stella checked her phone before pushing it away with an uncharacteristic frown.

"Is it that creep again?" Jules asked, blowing on her freshly polished gold nails.

Some random guy had been messaging Stella nonstop for the past two weeks, and it was making her nervous. As an influencer, she received her fair share of unsolicited DMs from creepy guys, but this one put her on edge more than normal.

"Yeah. I blocked him, but he keeps making new accounts." Stella sighed. "That's the sucky part about being a semipublic figure."

"Be careful." A shadow of worry crossed Bridget's face. "There are crazy people out there."

Rhys, who kept watch from the armchair, snorted, no doubt because that was what he always told her—and she always ignored him, like she did now.

Bridget refused to look at him as she lowered the volume on *Mean Girls*. That must've been the thousandth time we'd watched it, but it never got old. Regina George was iconic.

"I will. He's likely another internet weirdo." Stella made a face. "That's why I never post my stories until after I've left a place."

I couldn't imagine documenting my life online the way Stella did. I worried for both her physical safety and mental health sometimes, but she'd handled it well so far. Maybe I was just being a worrywart.

Someone knocked on the door.

"I'll get it." Rhys unfolded himself to his full six feet, five inches. Seriously, the man was enormous. He probably wore custom-made clothes because no way would an off-the-rack shirt fit those big shoulders and broad chest.

"Look at that ass." Jules sighed. "Talk about a tight end."

"Stop objectifying him. That's Bridget's *bodyguard*," I said, nudging her in the ribs.

"Exactly. Bodyguards are hot. Don't you think so, Bridge?"

"No," Bridget said flatly.

"You guys are no fun." Jules twisted her red hair into a messy topknot. "Ooh, look who comes bearing gifts."

My stomach fluttered when Alex walked in with Rhys on his heels. He carried a distinctive pink-and-green-striped box.

"Cake?" Stella perked up. She'd warmed up to Alex over the past month after seeing he was "capable of human emotion after all."

"Cupcakes," Alex confirmed, setting the goodies on the table.

My friends dove for the box like treasure hunters diving for gold.

I smiled and tilted my head up so I could kiss him. "Thank you. You didn't have to do that."

"It's just cupcakes." He returned my kiss before sitting next to me and curling a protective arm around my waist. "Figured you could use the sugar rush."

I peeled the wrapper away from my red velvet cupcake with a small frown. It would take a long time to get over what Michael did. I wasn't sure I would *ever* get over what Michael did. My entire life was a lie. Sometimes, I'd lie awake at night, so anxious

I couldn't sleep or think straight. Other times, like now, I'd look around me and comfort myself with the knowledge that I would be all right. That old saying was true: what doesn't kill you makes you stronger. I'd almost died twice in my life—that I knew of—and I was still standing. I'd continue to stand tall, long after Michael rotted in jail.

Thanks to a nudge from Alex, who knew half the judges in this town, Michael was locked up with no bail until his court date. He'd sent a message asking me to see him, but I refused. I had nothing left to say to him. He'd shown me his real face, and I would be happy if I never saw it again for the rest of my life.

But yeah, sometimes a girl needed a cupcake or two to get her through the rainy days.

Part of me was grateful Michael and I had never been close. If we had, I wasn't sure I'd be able to take the heartbreak. That was why I worried about Josh, who was his real son and who'd had a much closer relationship with him. But Josh insisted he was fine, and there was no arguing with him. He was even more stubborn than me.

We ate in silence for a while before Stella cleared her throat. "Um, thanks for the treat, but I should head out. I have a brand collab I need to shoot."

"Me too," Bridget added, picking up on Stella's cue. "I have a political theory paper to write."

After Stella, Bridget, and Rhys beat a hasty retreat, Jules announced she had a date tonight and needed to get ready. She swept up the stairs, taking half the remaining cupcakes with her.

"You know how to clear a room," I teased, running an absent-minded hand down Alex's arm. What would I do without him? Not only had he helped me confront my father—I mean, Michael—but he was helping me deal with the aftermath, including all the finan- cial and legal webs I was now tangled up in. Most of Michael's assets had been frozen, but luckily, he'd already paid my tuition for the year, and I had a steady income from my job and side gig. The commission I received for selling the Richard Argus piece to Alex helped too. Josh, who'd received a full-ride scholarship plus living stipend for the duration of med school, was also set money-wise. At least that was one less thing we had to worry about.

"It's one of my many talents." Alex captured my mouth in a searing kiss, and I melted into him, letting his tongue and taste and touch carry me away to a land where my troubles didn't exist.

God, I loved this man, and he didn't even know it. Not yet.

My pulse thundered in my ears when we pulled apart. "Alex…"

"Hmm?" He brushed his fingers over my skin, his gaze still locked on my mouth.

"I have something to tell you. I—" *Tell him. It's now or never.* "I love you," I whispered, my heart beating fast, my confession a breathless rush.

A beat passed, followed by a second. Third.

Alex's hand stilled, his expression fierce and strangely haunted. A wisp of unease niggled at my stomach.

"You don't mean that."

"Yes, I do," I said, hurt and a little angry at his reaction. "I know what I feel."

"I'm not an easy person to love."

"Good thing I never cared much about taking the easy road." I sat up straight and looked him straight in the eyes. "You are cold and infuriating and, I admit, a little scary. But you are also patient and supportive and brilliant. You inspire me to chase my dreams and drive away my nightmares. You are everything I didn't know I needed, and you make me feel safer than anyone else on the planet." I took a deep breath. "What I'm trying to say—again—is, I love you, Alex Volkov. Every part of you, even the parts I want to slap."

A smile ghosted his mouth. "That was quite the speech." The smile faded as quickly as it had come, and he dropped his forehead to mine, his breath ragged. "You are the light to my dark, Sunshine," he said in a raw voice. His lips brushed against mine as he spoke. "Without you, I'm lost."

Our kiss was even deeper this time, more urgent, but his response played on a loop in the back of my mind.

You are the light to my dark. Without you, I'm lost.

Beautiful words that made my heart pound...but I couldn't help noticing none of them were "I love you too."

CHAPTER 31

Alex

THE IRON GATES SLID OPEN, REVEALING A LONG DRIVE-way lined with northern red oak trees, their branches bare and brown in the harsh cold of winter, and the large brick mansion looming in the distance.

My uncle's house—my house as well, before I'd moved to DC—stood behind a virtual fortress on the outskirts of Philadelphia, and that was the way he liked it.

I hadn't wanted to leave Ava so soon after the shitshow with Michael, but I'd put off this meeting with my uncle long enough.

I found him in his office, smoking and watching a Russian drama on the flat-screen TV hanging in the corner. I never understood why he insisted on watching TV in here when he had a perfectly good den.

"Alex." He blew a smoke ring in the air. A half-empty cup of green tea sat before him. He'd been obsessed with the drink ever since he read an article that said it helped with weight loss. "To what do I owe this surprise?"

"You know why I'm here." I sank into the overstuffed chair opposite Ivan and picked up the ugly gold paperweight on his desk. It looked like a deformed monkey.

"Ah, yes. I heard. Checkmate." My uncle smiled. "Congratulations. Though I have to admit, it was a bit anticlimactic. I'd expected your final move to go off with more of a...bang."

My jaw tightened. "The situation changed, and I had to adapt."

Ivan's gaze turned knowing. "And what about the situation changed?"

I stayed silent.

I'd labored over my revenge plan for more than a decade, moving and manipulating every piece until I had them where I wanted them. *Always play the long game.*

But even I had to admit I'd gotten...distracted these past few months. Ava had swept into my life like a sunrise after dark, awakening creatures within my soul that I thought had died a long time ago—guilt, conscience, remorse—making me question whether the ends justified the means.

Around her, my thirst for vengeance was slaked, and I almost— almost—gave it up, if only so I could pretend to be the man she thought I was. *You have a multilayered heart, Alex. A heart of gold encased in a heart of ice.*

The sharp edges of the paperweight dug into my palm.

Ava knew I'd committed my fair share of unsavory deeds for Archer Group, but that was business. She didn't condone it or endorse it, but she wasn't naïve either. For all her romantic notions and soft heart, she'd grown up near the DC viper pit and understood that in certain situations—whether it be business or politics—it was eat or be eaten.

But if she found out the lengths to which I'd gone in order to wreak havoc on those responsible for my family's death—no matter how much they deserved it—she would never forgive me.

There are some lines you never cross.

A tiny well of blood blossomed on my hand. I released the

paperweight, wiped the blood off on my conveniently dark pants, and set it back on the table.

"Don't worry about it, Uncle." I kept my face and posture relaxed. I didn't want him finding out how much Ava had burrowed inside my heart.

My uncle had never been in love, had never married or fathered children of his own, and he wouldn't understand my dilemma. For him, wealth, power, and status were all that mattered.

"Ah, but I do worry." Ivan puffed on his cigarette with a small frown. He'd slicked his hair back and wore a suit and tie even though he was alone in his office, watching a stupid drama about Cold War spies. He was always conscious of his appearance, even when there was no one else around. He switched from English to Ukrainian for the next part of our conversation. "You have not been acting like yourself. You've been distracted. Unfocused. Carolina mentioned you only go into the office a few days a week, and you leave before seven each time."

I tamped down my flare of irritation. "My assistant shouldn't be blabbing about my schedule to others."

"I'm the CEO, so she didn't have much choice." Ivan stubbed out his cigarette and leaned forward, his eyes intense. "Tell me about Ava."

Tension rocketed down my spine at the sound of her name on his lips. I didn't have to ask how he knew about her—I wasn't the only one with spies everywhere. "There's nothing to tell. She's a good lay," I said, the words poison on my tongue. "That's it."

"Hmm." My uncle looked skeptical. "So, your revenge. That's it?" He switched topics so abruptly it took me half a second longer than usual to respond.

"No." I wasn't done with the man I'd destroyed. Not yet. "There's more."

I had one final ace up my sleeve.

I wanted to take everything from the man who'd taken every-thing from me. His business, his family, his *life*.

And I did. I would.

But was it worth it?

"Good. I thought you'd gone soft." Ivan sighed and stared at the framed picture on his desk of him and my father when they were young. They'd just moved to the U.S., and they both wore cheap, happy suits and matching hats. While my uncle looked stern and serious, my father's eyes twinkled like he was in on a grand secret no one else knew. My throat squeezed at the sight. "Never forget what happened to your parents and poor little Nina. They deserve all the justice in the world."

As if I would ever forget. Even if I didn't have HSAM, the scene would forever be engraved in my mind.

"Don't cheat!" I yelled over my shoulder as I ran to the bathroom. I'd had two apple juices this morning, and I was about to burst. "I'll know."

"You're losing, anyway!" my little sister, Nina, yelled back, causing my parents to chuckle.

I stuck my tongue out at her before slamming the bathroom door behind me. I was annoyed I'd never beaten Nina at Scrabble for Kids, even though she was two years younger than me and I had a "genius" IQ, according to my teachers and parents. She'd always been good at words. Mama said she'd probably grow up to be a writer.

I used the toilet and washed my hands.

I was supposed to be at a special camp for gifted children this summer, but camp was so boring. All the activities were too easy; the only one I'd liked was chess, but I could play that anywhere. I complained to my parents, who pulled me out yesterday and brought me home.

I was drying my hands when I heard a loud bang in the distance, followed by shouts.

I ran back to the living room, where I found my parents ushering Nina toward the secret passageway behind the fireplace. That was one thing I loved about our house—it was full of secret passageways and hidden corners. Nina and I had spent countless hours exploring every nook and cranny; it made hide-and-seek more exciting, that was for sure.

"Alex, get in there. Quick!" Mama's face was tight with panic. She grabbed my arm, more roughly than she ever had before, and pushed me into the darkness.

"What's going on? Who's here?" My heart beat a fast rhythm. I heard strange voices, and they were getting closer.

Nina cowered in the passageway, clutching her beloved cat, Smudges, to her chest. We'd stumbled on the stray one day during a family picnic in the park, and she cried and begged until my parents agreed to let her keep it as a pet.

"It'll be okay." Papa had a gun in his hand. He always kept one in the house, but I'd never seen him use it. The sight of that shiny black metal glinting beneath the lights made my blood run cold. "Get in there with your sister and mother, and don't make a sound. Everything will be fine—Lucia, what are you doing?"

Mama swung the passageway shut while Nina and I stared with wide eyes.

"I'm not leaving you out here alone," she said fiercely.

"Dammit, Lucy. You have to—"

The sound of a vase crashing to the floor interrupted Papa and startled Smudges, who yowled and broke free of Nina's arms. He darted through the narrowing gap between the wall and passageway door.

"Smudges!" Nina yelled, scrambling after him.

I tried to grab her, but she wriggled out of my grasp and chased after him.

"Nina, no," I whisper-yelled, but it was too late. She was gone, and the door shut, enveloping me in darkness. I sat there, my blood roaring in my ears while my eyes tried to adjust to the dark.

Mama and Papa put me in here for a reason, and I didn't want to worry them by leaving. But I also needed to know what was going on, even though something screamed at me to turn away, to cover my eyes and hide.

I was hiding, but I wouldn't cover my eyes.

The fireplace passageway had a peephole disguised as the eyes in a painting that hung above the mantel. I was a little too short, but if I stood on tiptoes and really stretched, I could look out into the living room.

What I saw made my blood run cold.

There were two strange men in the living room. They wore ski masks and carried guns—bigger than the one Papa had, which now lay at his feet. One of those guns pointed at Papa, the other at Mama and Nina. Mama covered Nina protectively while my sister cried and hugged Smudges tight. The cat was freaking out and yowling at the top of its lungs.

"Shut that damn thing up," one of the men growled. "Or I'll do it for you."

Nina cried harder.

"Take whatever you want," Papa said, his face pale. "Just don't hurt my family."

"Oh, we'll take whatever we want," the second man said. "Unfortunately, I can't guarantee the second part. In fact, let's make this quick, shall we? No use dragging out the inevitable. We don't get paid by the hour, y'know."

A gunshot rang out. Somewhere, Mama and Nina screamed.

I should've screamed too, but I didn't. I could only watch, eyes wide and frozen, legs burning from how long and hard I stood on tiptoes, as a bright red stain blossomed on Papa's chest. He staggered, his mouth moving but forming no words. Perhaps he would've survived one shot, but then another gunshot rang out, and another, until Papa's big, strong body thudded to the ground. It lay there, still and unmoving.

"It," not "he." Because the corpse wasn't my Papa. It had his face and hair and skin, but Papa was gone. I'd seen him leave, the light fading from his eyes.

"No!" Mama wailed. She crawled toward Papa, but she only made it halfway before her body jerked and her mouth fell open. She, too, collapsed, her blood staining the floors.

"Damn, what d'you do that for?" the first man complained. "I wanted to have some fun with her first."

"Bitch was getting on my nerves. Can't stand all the wailing, and we're here for a job, not your dick," the second man growled.

The first man scowled but didn't argue.

The pair stared at Nina, who cried so hard her face turned bright red and her body shook from the force of her sobs. Smudges hissed at the men, its eyes glowing ferociously in its tiny face. It was a kitten, but in that moment, it had all the trappings of a lion.

"Too young," the first man said in disgust.

The second man ignored him. "Sorry, kiddo," he told Nina. "Nothing personal. Your bad luck for being born into this family."

My blood roared and roared. Liquid dripped down my wrist, and I realized I'd dug my nails into my palms so hard I was bleeding.

Drip. Drip. Drip.

Each drip sounded like a sonic boom in the dark, cramped space. Could they hear it? Could they hear me, crouched behind the fireplace like a coward while they murdered my family?

I wanted to run out. I wanted to jump on the men and kick and claw. I wanted to bash their heads in with the heavy sculpture on the fireplace mantel and strip the flesh from their bones piece by piece until they begged for death.

It was the first time I'd had such violent thoughts. Mama was sweet and loving, and Papa was tough but fair. Honorable. They had raised Nina and me to be the same.

But after seeing what those men did, I wanted to torture them slowly. Endlessly.

Except I couldn't. If I went out there, they would kill me too, and there would be no vengeance. No justice.

Drip. Drip. Dripdripdrip.

I bled faster. I couldn't look away as the second man raised his gun again and fired.

One shot. That was all it took.

Smudges went berserk. He flew at the men, hissing and clawing. One of them cursed and tried to kick him, but he dodged just in time.

"Forget about the damn cat," the second man snapped. "Let's finish the job and get outta here."

"I fucking hate animals," the first man muttered in disgust. "Hey, didn't he say there was another kid? Where's the little snot?"

"Not here." His partner glanced around, his eyes flickering past the fireplace and settling on the small, fancy jade statue on a side table. "At camp or something."

"Shit, I've never been to camp. You ever been to camp? I've always wanted—"

"Shut. Up."

They swept through the living room, pilfering the most valuable items and putting their filthy hands all over my family belongings before they finally left and silence fell.

My breath rasped in the quiet. I waited and waited. When

I was sure they wouldn't come back, I pushed open the heavy passageway door, my face reddening from the effort, and stumbled toward the bodies in the living room.

Mama. Papa. Nina.

I should call the police. I also knew I shouldn't disturb the crime scene, but this was my family. This was the last chance I'd ever have to hold them.

So I did.

My breathing slowed, my head cleared.

I should feel angry.

I should feel sad.

I should feel something.

But I didn't. I didn't feel anything at all.

The clawing pressure around my neck tightened. I couldn't protect them. The people I'd loved most in the world, and I'd been useless. Helpless. A coward.

I could take revenge all I wanted, but it wouldn't change the fact that they were gone and I was here. Me, the most fucked-up one. If there was ever proof that the universe had a sick sense of humor, this was it.

"I have to go," my uncle said, smoothing his hand over his tie. "I'm meeting an old friend. Are you staying for the weekend?"

I blinked away my memories and nodded.

"Excellent. We'll play chess when I get back, hmm?"

My uncle was the only person who could hold his own against me in chess.

"Of course." I rubbed my thumb over the wound on my hand. "Looking forward to it."

After my uncle left, I spent an hour in the home gym working off my frustrations, but something niggled at me.

Something Ivan said and the way he'd said it...

I'm the CEO, so she didn't have much choice.

Why the hell was my uncle checking in on me, and why did he want to know my schedule so bad he'd threaten Carolina for the information? She was a good assistant, and she wouldn't divulge the information unless she had to.

I turned off the shower and dried myself, my mind running through the possibilities. I hadn't gotten this far in life without listening to my instincts, so I got dressed, pulled on a pair of leather gloves, and returned to my uncle's office. He had hidden security cameras in there, but the top-of-the-line jammer I'd bought off the black market took care of them in no time.

I wasn't sure what I was looking for, but after an hour of searching—including for false drawers and secret compart-ments—I didn't find it. Same went for his bedroom.

Perhaps I *was* being paranoid.

My stomach growled, reminding me I hadn't eaten since my coffee and bagel at breakfast. It was now near sunset.

I gave up on my uncle's private quarters and walked toward the kitchen. Ivan had hired a housekeeper who came by twice a week to clean up, but otherwise, he had no staff; he was too paranoid about corporate spies, whom he claimed could pop up anywhere.

Don't trust anyone, Alex. It's always the people you least expect who'll stab you in the back.

At the last minute, I veered toward the library, my uncle's favorite room in the house. The soaring, two-story room looked like something out of an English manor, with its Tiffany stained glass lamps and wall of mahogany shelves groaning beneath the weight of leather-bound tomes. Soft Oriental rugs muffled the sound of my footsteps as I walked around the room, examining the shelves. I hoped whatever I was looking for wasn't hidden in a fake book—there were thousands of books in here.

Knowing my uncle, though, he wouldn't choose any book. He'd choose something with significance.

I checked the sections for his favorite authors. Leo Tolstoy, Fyodor Dostoyevsky, Taras Shevchenko, Alexander Dovzhenko… he had a soft spot for Russian and Ukrainian classics. Said they grounded him in his roots.

But no, all the books were real.

My eyes flitted over the rest of the library and landed on the limited-edition chess set in the corner. The pieces were still arranged in the same pattern from our last game.

While I examined the set and the surrounding area for anything that could give credence to my suspicions, I knocked against the table, and a pawn tumbled to the floor.

I cursed under my breath and bent to pick it up. As I did, my eyes snagged on the outlet beneath the table. It was a simple, ordinary outlet, except…

My gaze traveled to the left.

There was another outlet, less than a foot away. The U.S. National Electrical Code stipulated outlets must be positioned no more than six feet apart measured along the floor line, but it was rare to see two so close together.

I paused, listening for any noises—the purr of my uncle's Mercedes pulling into the driveway, the thud of his footsteps against the parquet floors.

Nothing.

I fished a heavy-duty paper clip from the library's writing desk and crawled under the chess table, bending the clip until it was straight. I jiggled the screw in the middle of the outlet, feeling ridiculous, but my instincts screamed at me to continue.

Just when I was about to give up, the outlet popped open, revealing a stash of papers in the wall.

Fake outlet. *Of course.*

My heart thudded as I reached for the papers—right as an engine roared in the distance.

My uncle was home.

I unfolded the documents—letters, written in two familiar sets of handwriting.

I speed-read them, unable to believe my eyes.

I'd expected corporate politics. Boardroom foul play. I wouldn't have been surprised if my uncle tried to hold on to his CEO position, even though I was supposed to take over soon. But *this?* This, I never saw coming.

The puzzle pieces in my brain clicked into place, and a strange cocktail of betrayal, fury, and relief knotted in my gut. Betrayal and fury over the revelation; relief that—

The front door banged open. Footsteps, coming closer.

I shoved the letters into the wall, folding them the way I'd found them, and screwed the outlet cover back on. I crawled out from beneath the table, placed the pawn in the same position it'd been in before I knocked it over, and pocketed both the paper clip and my gloves, which were sleek enough that they didn't create a visible bulge in my pants.

I plucked *The Count of Monte Cristo* by Alexandre Dumas— one of my favorite books—off the shelf on my way to the door.

"Alex," my uncle said when he saw me in the hall. He chuck-led. "Dumas again? You can't get enough of that book."

I smiled. "No, I can't."

All the while, my blood raged.

CHAPTER 32

Ava

HE WAS LATE.

I tapped my fingers on the table, trying not to check the time on my phone. *Again.*

Alex and I had agreed to meet at the Italian restaurant near campus at seven. It was now 7:30, and all my texts and calls had gone unanswered.

Half an hour wasn't *that* long, especially when you took rush hour traffic into account, but Alex was never late. And he always, always answered my messages.

I'd called his office, but his assistant told me he'd left an hour ago, so he *should* be here by now.

Worry unspooled in my stomach and gnawed at my insides.

Had something happened to him? What if he'd gotten into an accident?

It was easy to think of Alex as invincible, but he bled and hurt like anyone else.

Ten more minutes. I'll give him ten more minutes, and then I'll...hell, I don't know. Send out the freakin' National Guard. If he was hurt, I wouldn't sit here and do nothing.

"Can I get you anything, dear?" The waitress swooped by again. "Other than water," she added pointedly.

The tips of my ears turned red. "No, thanks. I'm, um, still waiting for my friend." That seemed slightly less pathetic than admitting I was waiting for my boyfriend.

Slightly.

She let out an aggrieved sigh and moved on to the older couple next to me.

I felt bad about hogging the table on a Friday night, but I'd barely seen Alex over the past week, and I missed him. We slept in the same bed every night, and our sex was as explosive as ever, but he seemed more distant during the day. Distracted.

"Ava?"

My head jerked up, and my chest deflated when I realized it wasn't Alex.

"Remember me?" The guy smiled. He was cute in a geek-chic way, with black-rimmed glasses and longish brown hair. "I'm Elliott. We met at Liam's birthday party last spring."

"Ah, right." I suppressed a flinch at the sound of Liam's name. I hadn't seen or heard from him since the charity ball, but Jules—ever tuned in to the gossip—informed me he'd gotten fired and had moved back to his parents' house in Virginia. I couldn't say I felt sorry for him. "Nice to see you again."

"You too." Elliott ran an awkward hand through his hair. "Hey, sorry about what happened with Liam. We haven't kept in touch since we graduated, but I heard about your breakup and… uh…what happened. He was a real jerk."

"Thanks." I couldn't blame him for being Liam's friend. *Ex-friend?* I was the one who'd dated the asshole, and guys usually treated their friends better than they did their girlfriends. It was a sad truth.

"Sorry to bother you during dinner—" His gaze flicked to

my water glass. "But I'm looking for a photographer who can do an engagement shoot for me, and none of the ones I checked out fit what Sally, my fiancée, is looking for. But I saw you and remembered you're a photographer, so I figured it's a sign." Elliott flashed a sheepish smile. "Hope this doesn't sound creepy, but I pulled up your website and showed it to Sally, and she *loves* your pictures. If you're free in the next few weeks, we'd love to hire you."

I spotted a pretty blond at a neighboring table watching us. She grinned and waved at me. I waved back.

"Congrats," I said, my smile genuine this time. "I'd love to help. Give me your number, and we can sort out details later."

While we exchanged contact information, an icy voice sliced through the din of the restaurant.

"You're in my way."

Alex stood behind Elliott, pinning him with a glare so dark I was surprised the poor man didn't disintegrate into ashes.

"Oh, sorry—"

"Why are you getting my girlfriend's number?"

Elliott shot me a nervous glance, and I clenched my jaw. *Seriously?* Alex was almost an hour late, and he had the nerve to act like a jealous ass the minute he showed up?

"He's a client," I said, struggling to remain calm. "Elliott, I'll call you later, okay? Congratulations again on your *engagement*." I emphasized the last word.

Alex's frown eased a smidge, but he didn't fully relax until Elliott ran back to his table.

"What the hell was that?" I demanded.

"What was what?" Alex slid into his seat.

"You're late, and you were rude to Elliott for no reason."

He snapped his napkin open and placed it in his lap. "I had urgent business to take care of, and my phone died, so I couldn't call you. As for *Elliott*, I showed up and saw some random guy flirting with my girlfriend. How did you expect me to react?"

"He. Wasn't. Flirting. With. Me." I exhaled a long breath. This wasn't how I'd pictured the evening going. "Look, I don't want to fight. This is the first time we've had a meal together in over a week, and I want to enjoy it."

"Me too." Alex's face softened. "I'm sorry I'm late. I'll make it up to you."

"You better."

His lips quirked.

We placed our orders, the waitress looking much happier after Alex ordered the most expensive white wine on the menu. I couldn't drink red or my face would explode. I blame my Asian genes—one sip of alcohol, especially red wine, and I turn the color of a tomato.

I waited until the server brought out our entrees before I revealed my big news. "I heard back from the photography fellowship today."

Alex's fork paused halfway to his mouth.

"I got in." I bit my lower lip, my chest wild with the drumbeat of excitement and nerves. "New York. I got in."

"I knew you would." Simple and matter-of-fact, like he'd never doubted me, but Alex's eyes shone with pride. "Congratulations, Sunshine."

He leaned across the table and pressed a kiss to my lips. I was so giddy I couldn't stop grinning, and my earlier irritation melted away. So what if he'd been a little late? *I got in!*

I'd nearly dropped my phone when I received the email this morning. I'd had to reread it several times before the words sunk in.

I, Ava Chen, was going to be a World Youth Photography fellow. I would spend a year in New York, studying with the world's best photographers. My only regret was not being able to study under Diane Lange, who taught the London cohort, because while I'd made progress with my aquaphobia, I wasn't ready to fly over an ocean yet.

But that was okay. I'd meet her one day. In the meantime, I'd work on honing my craft and *holy crap, I was going to be a WYP fellow!* One of the most prestigious honors in the industry.

My heart soared before reality dragged me down.

"I'll be in New York," I said after Alex and I broke apart. "You'll be in DC."

"No, I won't." His eyes gleamed at my questioning look. "Archer Group has an office in Manhattan."

My hopeful heart flapped its wings again. "But you've built your base here. Your house, your friends…"

"It's not my house; it's Josh's. I'm keeping it safe for him. And most of the people I know here are acquaintances, not friends." Alex lifted his shoulder in an elegant shrug. "It's a simple equation, Sunshine. If you're in New York, I'm in New York."

The last vestiges of my hesitation floated away. I grinned, so happy I could dance right here in the middle of a crowded restaurant. "You know how—"

Something buzzed. Alex stiffened, and my eyes dropped to his coat pocket, which buzzed again.

My grin faded. "You said your phone died."

Just like that, the tension returned, simmering in the air until it became a full-on boil.

The night was an emotional roller coaster, and I couldn't keep up.

"I charged it in the car." Alex sipped his wine, his shoulders tense.

"But you didn't reply to any of my messages or calls." I tucked my hands beneath my thighs, suddenly cold even though the heat was on. "Why were you really late, Alex?"

"I told you, I had urgent business to take care of."

"That's not good enough."

"I don't know what you want me to tell you."

"The *truth*!" I lowered my voice when the diners at the next table shot me an alarmed look. "That's all I want. Please. My fath—Michael lied to me my entire life, and I don't want you to start."

A shadow passed over Alex's face before it disappeared. "I won't lie unless the truth hurts you."

My teeth clenched. "Alex—"

"Plausible deniability exists for a reason, Sunshine." He cut into his pasta with more force than necessary.

"What did you do?" I whispered.

Alex tightened his grip on his fork. "I'm not always a good person. I don't always do the right thing. You know that, even if you seem determined to see the good in me. I won't—" He released a pent-up breath, looking frustrated. "Just drop it, Ava. For your own sake."

"Sure. I'll drop it." I tossed my napkin on the table, my own frustration boiling over. "I'm also leaving. I've lost my appetite."

"Sunshine—" He reached for me, but I shrugged him off and ran out before he could stop me.

My chest felt tight as I speed walked home. What should've been one of the best nights of my life had turned into one of the worst.

CHAPTER 33

Alex

I PAID AND LEFT THE RESTAURANT IMMEDIATELY AFTER Ava. She hadn't gotten far, and I followed discreetly to make sure she got home safe before I drove back to DC.

I hated seeing her upset, especially on a night when we should've been celebrating instead of fighting. I wanted to run after her and apologize for being an ass, but the clock was ticking, and I needed to finish what I'd started.

Only then could I put the past behind me, once and for all.

I stared at my computer screen, watching the minutes tick by. *11:55 p.m.* I'd given the man a midnight deadline.

11:56 p.m.

I *hadn't* told Ava the truth...about many things. I didn't have urgent business to take care of before dinner, at least none relevant to Archer Group. Instead, I'd been talking to my family's killers' killer.

The police had ruled my parents' and sister's murders a home invasion gone wrong, but I knew better. The men had said it was a job and mentioned a "he," someone who knew I was supposed to be at camp that summer, though that was something anyone with internet access and a bare modicum of computer skills could figure out—the camp posted a list of its attendees online every year.

I'd kept the knowledge of their true motives to myself though. I'd been young but old enough to know the criminal justice system wouldn't deliver the type of justice I craved: total annihilation.

So I'd waited.

11:57 p.m.

My uncle was the only person I'd told. He, too, hadn't believed it was a simple invasion.

But the police caught the culprits a few days later thanks to street security footage that IDed their license plate, and they'd confirmed it was a home invasion. The "burglars" said they hadn't wanted to leave witnesses, so they'd killed everyone. They also hadn't made it to trial before they "mysteriously" died in jail.

My uncle did some digging and found the man who'd hired the killers' killer. Apparently, he was one of my father's business rivals and had a history of shady dealings and ruthless practices. By logic, he had to have been the one who'd ordered the hit on my family too.

I'd spent every second of my life since plotting his downfall.

11:58 p.m.

I'd been a kid, and I'd trusted my uncle, but what I'd read in the library threw everything I knew about him out the window.

Ava was right—I'd been distracted this past week, busy with my chess game. Not the unfinished one with my uncle in the library but the one playing out in real life.

I'd had my tech guy hack into Ivan's financial records dating back to my family's deaths and paid him a hefty sum to work day and night until he found what I'd expected to find all along. A large sum of money had been wired from one of my uncle's secret offshore accounts to an anonymous account two days before my family's death, and another equal sum had been sent the day after.

An even larger amount had been sent to a second anonymous account the day after the "burglars" died.

I'd paid the hacker another eye-watering sum to track down the second killer. He'd contacted me when I was on my way to meet Ava, saying he'd located the person, a notorious killer for hire who went by the name of Falcon. They'd apparently retired, but I didn't need their "skills." I only needed a name.

As a gesture of goodwill, I'd wired Falcon twenty-five percent of the fifty grand I'd promised them if they would confirm who hired them to kill the burglars.

Now, I waited.

11:59 p.m.

I stared at the blank black screen of Vortex, a fully encrypted messaging site popular among those in the criminal underworld. Unhackable and untraceable, it was where most of the world's seediest transactions took place.

A chill whipped around me.

I hadn't bothered to turn the heater on. I'd bought this house in DC under a shell company name because I wanted a place where I could carry out my more illicit activities without anyone knowing, not even my uncle. It boasted a security system the Pentagon would be jealous of, including a hidden jammer that disabled all electronic devices inside the house unless you had the code, which only I knew.

12:00 a.m.

A new message flashed on-screen.

Midnight on the dot. Gotta appreciate a punctual killer.

I read the message calmly, my blood colder than the chill creeping along the floorboards and bare walls.

No greeting, no questions. Just a name, like I'd requested.

I wired the rest of the money to Falcon and sat there in the dark, mulling over the news.

I knew. Of course I knew. All the evidence had pointed to it, but now I had my confirmation.

The man responsible for my family's death wasn't Michael Chen, Ava's father.

It was Ivan Volkov, my uncle.

CHAPTER 34

Alex

I MADE PANCAKES.

I rarely cooked—why waste my time doing something I didn't enjoy and that I could pay other people to do? But I made an exception today. I was waiting for a visitor, and I didn't want to miss them by eating out.

The doorbell rang.

It was 9:07 a.m., according to the clock on my microwave. Earlier than I'd expected, which meant he was eager.

I shut off the stove and sipped my tea as I answered the door. When I did, I had to mask my surprise.

Not who I was expecting.

"What are you doing here, Sunshine?"

Not the warmest greeting, but she needed to leave before he arrived.

Mild panic shot through me at the thought of them meeting.

Ava frowned. She looked exhausted, and I wondered if she was having nightmares again. They'd eased since she recovered her memories, but they still popped up from time to time.

Worry and guilt washed over me. We hadn't spoken in

days. She was still angry with me, and I'd been caught up in my plans. It was hard to convene a corporate board the week before Christmas—in secret, no less—but I held enough blackmail info over every member that they'd acquiesced to my request.

"We need to talk. About us," Ava said.

Not words any man wants to hear come out of his girlfriend's mouth, especially when he and said girlfriend were on rocky ground. I couldn't wait until this mess with my uncle was over so I could give her the attention she deserved.

As for my twisted and apparently ill-placed revenge plan against her "father"…that was a confession for another day.

If I ever confessed.

Michael Chen was a sociopathic bastard even if he hadn't plotted my family's murder, and I was tempted to follow through with my original plan to hire someone to off him in prison. But I wouldn't…yet.

"Can we talk later?" A familiar gray Mercedes came into view, and my muscles tensed. "Now isn't a good time."

Ava shook her head. "It's been a week, Christmas is in two days, and I'm tired of us tiptoeing around each other. You've been acting weird for a while now, and I deserve to know what's going on. If you don't want to be with me any longer—" She exhaled a sharp breath, her face tinting red. "Just tell me. Don't string me along."

Goddamn it. If only Josh had come home for Christmas like he'd planned, he would've kept Ava away. But there'd been an earthquake in his volunteer region—he was okay, thank God—and the people needed all the medical help they could get in the aftermath, so he'd stayed. I'd donated a hefty sum to help with his organization's expenses as well. Partly out of charity, mostly out of guilt.

Ava wasn't the only Chen I'd fucked over these past few years.

My uncle parked and got out of his car, his face thunderous.

My grip tightened around my mug.

"Of course I want to be with you," I said in a low voice while keeping an eye on Ivan. "I'll always want to be with you. But I—"

"Alex." My uncle's pleasant tone belied the fury simmering in his eyes. When Ava turned, startled, he smoothed his face into a gracious smile. "Who's this lovely creature?"

If the mug were glass, it would've cracked by now.

"Ava, Uncle Ivan," I responded, voice clipped.

"Ah, the infamous Ava. How lovely to meet you, dear."

She smiled, looking uncomfortable. "I didn't realize you were expecting company," she told me. "Um, you're right. We can talk later—"

"Nonsense. I'm just here for a friendly chat with my nephew." Ivan placed a hand on Ava's back and guided her into the house. *Get your fucking hands off her.* Anger streaked through me, but I tamped it down.

I couldn't lose my cool. Not now.

We settled in the dining room—Ava and I on one side, Ivan on the other. Tension laced the air.

"Anyone want a drink?" I set my near-empty mug on the table. "Tea? Hot chocolate?"

Ava shook her head. "No, thanks."

"Green tea for me." Ivan patted his stomach.

I returned a few minutes later with his drink and found him in deep conversation with Ava.

My uncle took the tea from me with an oily smile. "Alex, Ava was telling me about how you spent your Thanksgiving. He loves his holidays with the Chens," he told her. "He finds them so... enlightening."

My muscles burned from how tense I was while Ava returned his smile with her own uncertain one.

"What can I do for you, Uncle?" I asked, taking my seat with careful nonchalance. "It must be important if you're here this early. Long drive from Philly."

"I wanted to congratulate my favorite nephew." Ivan's smile tightened. I didn't bother pointing out I was his *only* nephew. "Ava, dear, did you know you're sitting next to the new CEO of Archer Group?"

I betrayed no emotion while Ava's head whipped toward me, her eyes wide.

"My uncle graciously stepped aside," I said. I addressed Ivan. "I'm grateful for your tutelage and all the years you've dedicated to the company, but now you can retire and indulge in fishing, crossword puzzles, TV dramas...a life of leisure, just like you deserve."

"Yes," he said coldly. "I'm looking forward to it."

It was all bullshit, this show we were putting on. My uncle didn't resign, though that would be the official story we fed to the press. He'd toppled from power thanks to the secret boardroom coup I'd spent the past week executing. I'd had to use more dirty tricks than usual to get it done in such a short time, but anger is the world's greatest motivator.

I was now CEO of Archer Group, and Ivan was nothing. After I finished with him, he wouldn't *have* anything either.

"Congratulations. That's amazing." Ava looked genuinely happy for me, but she also sounded confused and a little hurt, probably because I hadn't mentioned something so huge to her. Then again, the changeover hadn't been official until yesterday afternoon. No doubt the board notified Ivan, and he'd driven here first thing in the morning, intent on reaming me out.

He didn't take his eyes off me as he said, "You and Ava should visit one day. I'm an old man who doesn't have many friends, and I don't like to leave the house much." He chuckled. "I'm a bit paranoid about security, you see. I have cameras all over my home—my office, the kitchen...the library. I rarely go through all the tapes, but—" He sipped his tea. "What's a man with too much free time to do?"

I read between the lines in an instant.

Fuck. How had I missed the cameras in the library? I'd jammed the ones in his bedroom and office and adjusted them afterward so they didn't show any suspicious missing time periods, but my uncle had never had cameras in the other rooms before. He must've checked the feeds to see what I'd been up to after he received word of the coup.

He'd grown more paranoid—and I'd grown more lax.

I wouldn't make that mistake again.

Ivan and I stared at each other. The jig was up. He knew I'd seen the letters between him and my mother—the ones where he'd professed his love and begged her to leave my father, the ones where she'd rebuffed him until he grew more and more aggressive and she had to threaten him with a restraining order...the ones where he promised she would regret spurning him.

Once I had that piece of information, the rest of the puzzle fell into place—why my father and Ivan fell out, how the burglars knew so much about our family, why my uncle sometimes got a weird look on his face when we talked about my parents. I'd known all along how narcissistic my uncle could be, and my mother's rejection must've hit hard—hard enough that he'd plot his own brother's death.

That didn't explain why he chose Michael Chen as the scapegoat, but I'd figure it out. I wouldn't stop until I'd peeled back every layer of Ivan's deception and strangled him with them.

I now understood how Ava felt. I'd been lied to most of my life too, only my reaction was far less benign than hers.

"Um, sure." Ava glanced at me. "We'll visit someday."

Yes. Over my dead body. Or, to be more accurate, my uncle's dead body.

"Excellent." Ivan set his empty mug on the table. "Well, I think I've overstayed my welcome. I'll leave you kids alone. Alex, I'm sure we'll talk soon."

"I'm sure we will," I drawled.

After he left, Ava and I sat in silence, eyeing each other warily. I wanted to pull her to me, kiss her and reassure her, but everything had gotten so fucking complicated. Not to mention she still didn't know the truth about me and what I did.

She won't find out. The only other person who knew was my uncle, and he would be out of the picture soon.

A better person would tell her the truth, but I'd rather be the villain with her by my side than the hero who risked losing her because of a misguided sense of morality.

What she doesn't know won't hurt her.

"Your uncle is not what I expected," she finally said. "He's very...slick."

That pulled a small smile out of me. She didn't like him either. *Attagirl.*

"Why didn't you tell me about your promotion?" she asked. "That's huge news! We should've celebrated or something."

"It wasn't official until yesterday. Thought I'd announce it as a Christmas surprise." That was partly true.

Ava sighed, her expression growing sad. "I miss you, Alex."

God, this girl. She had no clue what she did to me. "I miss you too, Sunshine." I opened my arms, and she climbed into my lap, wrapping her arms around my neck. I breathed in her scent, my heart aching. I wanted to keep her here, safe and cherished, forever. Fuck the rest of the world. It could burn for all I cared.

"I don't want to fight, but..." Her bottom lip disappeared between her teeth. "You *have* been acting strange lately. If

246 | ANA HUANG

something is wrong, you know you can tell me and we'll figure it out together, right?"

"I know." How was she so amazing? Anyone who'd gone through what she had would've locked themselves away from the rest of the world by now, but not Ava. She was always thinking of others.

I didn't deserve her.

"Is it because I told you I—" She paused, pink blossoming on her cheeks. "I loved you?"

"Of course not." I tightened my hold and kissed her. "You know I'd do anything for you."

"Okay, because you started acting weird right after..."

"It's work," I lied. "I've been stressed about the CEO transition." Also partly true.

It was a testament to Ava's trust that she took my words at face value. "You'll be a great CEO." She brushed her lips over a sensitive spot on my neck, and my cock jumped with interest. I hadn't touched her in a week, and I was dying to tie her down and have my way with her. "Now, how about we alleviate that stress..."

I responded with a wicked grin. "I like the way you think."

But as I carried her upstairs and fucked her in every position until she couldn't scream anymore, the sense of impending doom hovering over me remained.

CHAPTER 35

Alex

MY WORLD CRASHED DOWN TWO WEEKS AFTER MY uncle's visit.

I was driving to work when I received a call from Ivan "requesting" I visit him ASAP. He'd been suspiciously quiet since he was dethroned as CEO, but I knew why. I also knew why he'd asked for a visit—I'd been expecting it.

I called my assistant and told her to cancel the rest of my meetings for the day and made it to Philadelphia in two hours flat.

I slowed my steps as I walked up the stairs to my uncle's office, sure he had cameras monitoring my every move since I pulled up to the estate's gates.

I found him sitting behind his desk, watching his beloved Russian drama on the TV.

"Hello, uncle." I leaned against the wall and stuffed my hands in my pockets, the picture of casual indifference.

Ivan's eye twitched. "So you finally made it, you little shit."

I suppressed a smile. My uncle rarely cursed; he must have been out of his mind with anger. I could see why; he looked horrible. I spotted a bald spot in his hair, as well as scaly red patches and a few nasty-looking pustular eruptions on his skin. His face looked haggard, his complexion wan.

For someone as vain as my uncle, the deterioration of his looks must be a living nightmare.

"I'll always make time to visit my favorite uncle." My *only* uncle, though not for much longer. "You don't look so well. Stressed over losing your job?"

A muscle ticked in his jaw. "You're handing the CEO position back to me."

I almost laughed out loud. "Why would I do that?"

"Because." Ivan leaned back and laced his hands over his stomach. "I have something you want, and I have a feeling you'll do anything to get it back—including resigning from Archer Group, reinstating me as CEO, and wiring me fifty million dollars. For the emotional distress," he explained.

His mental facilities must be deteriorating faster than his physical appearance if he thought I would do *any* of those things.

"Sure you do," I said indulgently. "Let's see what this magical 'something' is first."

"Did I say 'something'?" Ivan's eyes glowed with malice. "I meant 'someone.' Bring them in." He barked the last statement in Russian.

There was a scuffle outside the door, and my blood ran cold when a massive man in camo pants and dog tags entered, dragging two bound and gagged girls behind him.

Ava and Bridget.

They stared at me, fear stamped on every inch of their faces.

It took every ounce of willpower not to display a visible reaction.

"I see," I said in a bored voice. "Sorry, Uncle, but I don't see anything—or anyone—that would make me consider giving you dog shit, much less fifty million dollars."

A small cut marred Ava's face. Tears stained her cheeks, and she stared at me with wide eyes, her distress evident. Bruises marked her arms from where Camo grabbed her, and I glimpsed red, chafed skin from where the rope dug into her wrists.

Ava. Hurt.

Wild, all-consuming anger erupted in my stomach until it filled every inch of my being.

I stared at Camo, and he stared back, smugness oozing from his ugly mug.

Not for much longer.

He was going to die today. Slowly. Painfully.

I was pleased to note he had several cuts and bruises of his own. Ava and Bridget had clearly put up a fight, but that didn't matter.

He'd dared touch what was mine, and for that, I'd make him beg for something as sweet as death.

The guard I'd hired to look after Ava in case my uncle pulled shit like this? He would die too for failing at his job.

Beside Ava, Bridget shifted, her face pale. The small movement prompted Camo to yank her arm in warning, but to her credit, she didn't flinch. Instead, she glared at him, her gaze flinty.

The regal princess, even when kidnapped.

Speaking of which, where the fuck was *her* bodyguard? Rhys was an ex-Navy SEAL. He should be more competent than the apparent moron I'd hired.

I didn't have time to dwell on that question. I shifted my attention back to my uncle, who wore a knowing smirk.

"You can't fool me, Alex," he said, his voice thin and reedy. "I saw the way you looked at her. She's the reason you pulled your punches with the revenge plan. You love her. But will she love you after she finds out what you did?"

A thick pressure circled my neck, squeezing. My breath quickened.

I knew what my uncle was doing. He was forcing me to confess—the biggest lie I'd ever told, the worst thing I'd ever done. He wanted Ava to hate me.

And the worst part was, I had to do it. I would give her up if it meant saving her.

"That's where you're wrong," I drawled, keeping my gaze locked on Ivan's. "You underestimate me, Uncle. She was never more than a pawn in my game. Why do you think I pulled back after her father went to jail? She was useless to me after that. I admit, the sex was good." I shrugged. "That was the only reason I didn't cut her off entirely."

I saw Ava's head jerk up out of the corner of my eye.

"Sorry, Sunshine." I forced myself to inject a mocking lilt into her nickname. "The cat's out of the bag, so I might as well tell you the whole story. The man I told you about, the one who murdered my parents? That was your father—well, fake father. Michael Chen."

Ava's eyes popped, and Bridget finally stirred, her sharp intake of breath audible even through her gag.

"I always knew." I pushed off the wall and walked toward her. Camo tensed and stepped in my direction, but Ivan waved him off with a delighted smile. He was enjoying this, that bastard. "You think it was a coincidence that Josh and I were assigned to the same room our freshman year? A hefty bribe with the right person goes far, and there's no better way to destroy your enemy than from the inside. I played the 'dead parents' card to gain his sympathy until he invited me over for the holidays, and while everyone was asleep, I snooped. I bugged your house, went through your father's files...found lots of interesting information. Why do you think his business took so many hits over the years?"

A tear rolled down Ava's cheek, but I kept going. *I'm sorry, Sunshine.*

"I dismantled his empire, piece by piece, and you and Josh

had no clue." I uttered a soft laugh even as my chest burned. "This year was going to be the grand finale. The year in which my plan to take down his company publicly and humiliatingly came together. But I needed one more piece of information, one more excuse to search through his office. Then Josh—my ticket into your house every Thanksgiving—announced he was volunteering in Central America. Most inconvenient. I needed another in." I cupped her face with one hand, knowing this might be the last time I touched her. "That's where you entered the picture. Josh did most of the heavy lifting himself when he asked me to look after you, but I planted the idea of moving into his house." I smiled, my heart slowly shredding itself apart. "After all, it was much easier to make you fall in love with me when you had to see me every day. And you did. It was so easy it was almost embarrassing. Sweet, trusting Ava, so eager to fix broken things. So desperate for love she'd take it anywhere she could find it."

She shook her head, her chest heaving. She'd stopped crying, but her eyes burned with anger and betrayal. *That's my girl. Hate me. Don't cry over me. Never cry over me. I'm not worth it.*

"That night after Thanksgiving dinner? I found the information I was looking for," I said. "Your father got desperate over the years as his business crumbled, and he made a few bad deals with bad people. I had it all lined up...the FBI bust, the media circus." I left out the part where I'd planned to have Michael killed in prison. The jury was still out on whether I'd pull that plug. "But imagine my surprise when you regained your memories. It was like an early Christmas surprise. If I couldn't nail him on the corporate stuff, I could nail him on attempted murder. And it worked. Except..." I turned back to my uncle, whose eyes gleamed with malice. "I was wrong. It was never Michael. Was it, Uncle?"

Ivan's lips stretched into a thin grin. He bore no resemblance to the man who'd brought me into his house and treated me like his son—or so I thought. It took years to build a relationship and a second to destroy one, and ours had been ruined beyond repair.

Don't trust anyone, Alex. It's always the people you least expect who'll stab you in the back.

"That's the beauty of it," he said even as he winced. I reveled in the pleasure of that small movement—it'd been two weeks; he must be in serious pain by now—even as my heart tore itself apart at the way Ava looked at me. Like she didn't know me at all.

In some ways, she didn't.

"Michael *was* one of your father's business rivals when Anton started expanding into Maryland. They'd never gotten along—Anton hated the way Michael conducted business, and Michael hated that anyone dared encroach on 'his' territory. They eventually reached a truce, but Michael made an easy scapegoat. It didn't take much to plant 'evidence' that an impressionable teen like yourself would believe." Ivan coughed. "You're a smart kid, but your desire for vengeance blinded you. I always hated the man anyway. He humiliated me once at a party your father invited him to as a 'gesture of goodwill'—even though I told Anton not to—and I wasn't surprised to learn Michael's a psychopath as well."

"You're one to talk," I said coldly. My uncle *would* be deranged enough to hold on to a grudge over some slight at a party that happened decades ago.

I'd gone to painstaking lengths to ensure Michael wouldn't know of Ivan's nor my connection with my father, because he wouldn't exactly welcome the son of the man he'd murdered (or so I thought) into his home. I'd changed our last names and erased any evidence that would tie us to Anton Dudik. My uncle and I had been born Ivan and Alex Dudik; we were now Ivan and Alex Volkov. I was lucky my uncle was so paranoid—there were few public photos or traces of him before we started Archer Group, which made my job easier.

Apparently, that had all been for naught, since Michael had already met Ivan and knew of his connection to my father. He hadn't liked me, but he also hadn't cared about having me in his house, because he wasn't the murderer.

I couldn't believe my uncle pulled the wool over my eyes for so long. I was supposed to be a genius. A master strategist. But I'd fallen prey to the same failing as all other humans—believing the best of someone simply because they were there for you at your worst. He was my only living relative left, and I'd let that color my perception of him.

Now, because of my fuckup, Ava was hurt.

My stomach clenched. I kept my gaze averted from her—if I looked at her, I would lose it, and I couldn't afford to lose it. Not with Camo pointing a gun at her and my uncle's sharp eyes watching everything. He may be dying, but I wouldn't underestimate him until he was six feet in the ground.

"I can say the same for you." Ivan winced again, though he tried to hide it. I hoped the bastard suffered until his last breath on earth. "You, me, Michael. We're all cut from the same dark cloth. We're willing to do whatever it takes to achieve what we want. I knew it was smart taking you in," he said. "You were so grateful, and I couldn't let that intellect of yours go to waste. We've done well for ourselves, haven't we?" He swept an arm around his grand office.

"*I* did well. You leeched off me like the parasite you are."

Ivan clucked in disappointment. "Is that any way to speak to the man who kept you from being put into the *horrid* foster system? Really, you should be more grateful."

He really was deranged. "No wonder my mom wanted nothing to do with you," I said. "She must've smelled the crazy from a mile away."

Ivan's fake smile melted, and his face twitched with anger.

"Your mother was a stupid whore," he spat. "I loved her, but she turned me down—*me*, the one who'd been there for her long before she met your father—for naïve, softhearted Anton. I waited and waited for her to come to her senses, but she never did." He snorted. "When she told Anton about my letters, he stopped speaking to me. Wasn't man enough to confront me face-to-face, but he ran his mouth to our mutual friends, all of whom cut me off too." His eyes shone with hatred. "*No one* crosses me like that. He took what I loved from me, so I took what he loved from him."

"Not what. Who," I said through gritted teeth. "My mother was not an object."

Ivan cackled. "Oh, Alex, love *did* make you soft after all."

I clenched my jaw. "I'm not in love."

"That's not what a little birdie told me." A cough rattled in his lungs. "I had some interesting conversations with a pretty little blond by the name of Madeline. She had a lot to say about how you reacted when she pushed poor Ava into a pool."

Fury sliced through me. *Madeline.* I didn't know how she and my uncle met, but Ivan must've been tracking me longer than I thought.

Once again, I cursed myself for letting my guard slip.

By this time next month, Hauss Industries would be toast. I'd make sure of it. I'd already gathered the kindling after the pool incident; I just needed to set it on fire.

"All you have to do is give me the money and position, sign a contract saying you'll never come after me or hold corporate office again, and I'll let Ava and her little friend go," Ivan said. "It's a simple trade."

I wondered if he knew Bridget was the princess of Eldorra. If he did, he was an idiot for dragging her into this. If he didn't, he was an idiot for not doing his research.

And if he thought I'd believe he would let any of us go after he all but admitted to murder in front of us, he must think *I* was an idiot.

I weighed my options. Ivan wouldn't do anything to me, Ava, or Bridget until I'd wired the money and given him back his position, but that wouldn't take long. He knew I had the board under my thumb. I could make him CEO again with one call.

"To be clear, that wasn't a request," Ivan said.

I smiled, the gears in my brain clicking into place. "Sure. I can agree to your request—"

My uncle smirked.

"—or I can save your life. You choose."

The smirk disappeared. "What the hell are you talking about?"

I stepped toward him. Camo raised his gun in warning, but Ivan waved him off, his rheumy eyes narrowing as I stared pointedly at his skin, his hair, and the way his hand shook with barely concealed pain.

Realization dawned. "How?" he growled.

My smile slashed across my face. "You were quite thirsty after your drive to my house a few weeks ago."

"The tea." Ivan's face pinched. "I checked after the symptoms started showing. The doctors said—"

"That you had Guillain-Barré syndrome?" I sighed. "It is unfortunate that the symptoms are so similar. But no, I'm afraid it's not Guillain-Barré."

"What did you do, you little shit?"

A flash of movement behind Camo—visible only from where I stood—caught my eye. I showed no reaction even as my mental calculations adjusted to account for the new development.

"You can buy anything on the black market these days," I said, playing idly with the ugly monkey paperweight on the desk. "Including deadly poisons. The one currently destroying your system? Quite similar to thallium. It's odorless, tasteless, colorless.

Hard to identify because it's so rare, and its symptoms often point to a range of other illnesses. But unlike thallium, it has no widely known antidote. Luckily for you, Uncle, there *is* a secret antidote—and I have a vial stashed away."

My uncle trembled with rage. "How do I know you're not lying?"

I shrugged. "Guess you'll have to trust me."

Three things happened at once. Ava threw herself at a distracted Camo and knocked the gun out of his hand, Bridget's bodyguard tackled Camo from behind and caught him in a choke-hold, and I whipped out the gun hidden in the shoulder holster beneath my coat and pointed it at my uncle. I used my other hand to send a quick, one-number message on my phone without taking my eyes off Ivan.

"Stop!" he shouted.

Everyone froze until we resembled a grotesque comedic tableau—Rhys with one arm around Camo's neck and the other pressing a gun to his temple, Ava and Bridget wriggling out of their restraints, me ready to shoot my uncle point-blank in the chest.

"Alex." Ivan let out a nervous chuckle. "My dear nephew, is this necessary? We are, after all, family."

"No, we're not. You murdered my family." I cocked my gun, and he paled. "Ava, Bridget, leave the room."

They didn't move.

"*Now.*"

Camo hadn't tied their legs, so they could scramble out of the room even though their hands were still bound.

"Think of all the good times we had together," my uncle coaxed, his affable mask falling back into place. "When I took you to your first Krav Maga lesson, when we visited Kiev for your sixteenth birth—"

The shot rang out loud and clear over his pleas.

Ivan froze, his mouth hanging open in shock. A crimson stain bloomed across his chest.

"Unfortunately for you, I'm not someone who waxes poetic before I pull the trigger," I said. I felt no hint of remorse for the man who'd raised me. He was a murderer and a liar. I was too, but I'd resigned myself to hell a long time ago. "You'll die today, looking as ugly on the outside as you are on the inside."

"You ungrateful—"

A second shot rang out. His body jerked. "That was for my mother. The first was for my father. This"—a third shot—"is for Nina. For Ava. For Bridget. And this"—I cocked my gun for the last time—"is for me." I fired the bullet straight between his eyes.

My uncle was long dead by this point, his body riddled with holes and his feet steeped in a glistening pool of blood, but my words, like my bullets, weren't for him. They were for me, my own fucked-up version of closure.

I turned to Camo, whose complexion now resembled the color of chalk. Rhys still had him pinned to the ground.

I picked Camo's gun up from the floor and examined it. "You can let him go," I told Rhys. "He's mine."

To his credit, the bodyguard didn't even blink. He'd maintained the same stoic expression from the moment he entered the room. I had a feeling the man wouldn't blink an eye even if aliens in silver tutus poofed into existence before him and started dancing the Macarena.

"You sure?" He dug his gun harder into Camo's temple.

"I'm sure. Your princess is waiting for you"—my mouth formed a half smirk—"so let me take care of the trash." I pointed my gun at Camo while holding the second weapon in my other hand.

Rhys pulled back, keeping his gun aimed at Camo but his gaze on me.

Smart man.

I could tell he wanted to fuck up Camo himself, but Bridget was his priority, and a bodyguard's mandate was cover and evacuation, not combat.

The second he disappeared, I fired two shots into Camo's kneecaps—not to kill, merely to hobble him while I went to work. I ignored his pained screams as I locked the door.

"You made a mistake today," I said conversationally, kneeling next to him. Images of Ava's bruises and terrified face flashed through my mind, and my expression hardened. "You touched what was mine." I pulled a wicked-looking knife from my boot. Camo's eyes popped in terror. "You hurt what was mine." The smell of urine filled the air as he pissed himself. For such a tough-looking dude, he scared easily. My lips curled in distaste. "And now, it's time to pay. Don't worry." I pulled his shirt up and dug the tip of the blade into his abdomen. "I'll make it slow and sweet."

If Ava and Bridget had already called the police—which I was sure they had—I only had precious minutes before they arrived. But with a few handy tools and creativity? One could make a minute feel like an eternity.

We didn't pass the ten-second mark before Camo's screams started again.

CHAPTER 36

Ava

THE NEXT HOUR PASSED IN A BLUR. THE POLICE AND paramedics arrived, peppering me with questions and medical checkups and lots of somber-looking faces. I endured them all, my answers flat and robotic.

By the time they finished, I wanted to crawl into my bed and never get out—*if* I could bring myself to move.

"Ava?" Bridget placed a tentative hand on my arm. "The police said we can go. Rhys will drive us back."

The massive bodyguard hovered so close he was practically on top of us, his usual stoic mask replaced with pure fury.

I didn't blame him. We'd gotten ourselves into this mess.

Bridget and I had wanted to see one of our favorite bands perform in DC last night. Cool indie bands didn't visit the city often, and when they did, we took advantage. Except...Rhys had flat-out *forbidden* Bridget from going because it wasn't safe, and instead of arguing with him—which we all knew by now was useless—Bridget snuck out in the middle of the night. Everything had gone according to plan until the camouflage-wearing psycho yanked us off the street after the concert and into the back of his van. It'd happened so fast we didn't have time to scream. We'd fought back as hard as we could, and my amateur self-defense training allowed me to land a few hits, but he'd eventually knocked us out. When we woke up, we found ourselves in freakin' Philadelphia.

A shudder rippled down my spine. Our kidnapper must've been watching us for God knew how long before he made his move, which creeped me out more than the actual kidnapping part.

"Are you ready?" Despite her calm tone, I detected a small shake in Bridget's shoulders, and I suspected that was the reason Rhys hadn't torn us a new one yet. In fact, he hadn't said a word to us except to explain he'd found us via the chip he'd placed in Bridget's phone, which he'd activated when he discovered she wasn't in her room that morning. It was a testament to how much we'd fucked up that Bridget didn't utter a peep about him secretly tracking her.

My eyes strayed toward Alex, who looked remarkably composed for someone who'd shot his uncle, killed our kidnapper, and almost died himself.

He spoke with a police officer, his face not betraying a hint of agitation.

You were nothing more than a means to an end.

"Almost," I said. My voice sounded strange to my ears. Low and hollow, almost lifeless. "I need to talk to him."

Bridget and Rhys exchanged glances, their mutual concern for me overshadowing their animosity.

"Ave, I'm not sure that's a good idea—"

I ignored her. I stood, stepped around Bridget, and walked toward Alex, keeping the blanket the EMT gave me wrapped tight around my shoulders.

One foot in front of the other.

This entire day felt surreal. I kept thinking it was a new type of nightmare and that I would wake up at any moment, but I never did. Even when I told the police what happened, I felt like I was talking about a movie, not my life.

The story came out in pieces and half-truths. I told the officers Alex's uncle hired someone to kidnap us as leverage because Alex had ousted him as CEO, but I didn't mention their twisted family history. That wasn't my story to tell. I could honestly say I didn't know what happened after Bridget and I left—how Alex's uncle had ended up with four bullets in him or how the kidnapper had, according to the queasy-looking officer, ended up more carved up than a jack-o'-lantern on steroids. I technically *didn't* know, but it didn't take a genius to figure out what had happened.

I wasn't sure what Alex told the police, but considering they hadn't arrested him for killing two people yet, I assumed he'd spun a convincing tale of self-defense.

He was, after all, the consummate liar. Right? Or had he been lying about lying?

There was only one way to find out.

Alex noticed me first. He said something to the officer, who nodded and left.

I stopped two feet from him, my hands strangling the blanket.

He looked like the old Alex again—unruffled and uncaring, with eyes like chips of jade-colored ice. I didn't see a hint of the Alex I'd gotten to know over the past few months. The one who'd stayed and canceled a date to watch movies with me, the one who'd choked down one of the most disgusting cookies ever made and lied about it being "fine" because he didn't want to hurt my feelings, the one who'd taught me to swim and showed me a world I'd thought only existed in fantasies. A world in which I loved and had been loved in return. He hadn't said it, but I thought... I'd really thought he loved me and had just been too scared to say it.

Now, I questioned whether the Alex I "knew" had ever

existed. Perhaps it really had all been a ruse, a role played by a psychopath bent on vengeance and taking advantage of my unsuspecting heart.

Or he'd been lying, and he'd said all those things in front of his uncle to save me because he didn't want his uncle to know he cared. His tale seemed too elaborate to be fake, but Alex was a genius. He could do anything.

I clung to the tattered remains of my hope with bloody fingers.

"I thought you would've left by now." He slid his hands into his pockets, the picture of cool nonchalance.

"I wanted to speak to you first."

"Why?"

Heat rose on my face. *Leave before you embarrass yourself any further!* my pride screamed, but that horrible flicker of hope insisted I stay until the end.

"I wanted to know."

He lifted a bored brow.

"You and me." I was almost afraid to ask, but I had to know. "Was any of it real?"

Alex stilled, and I held my breath, hoping, praying...

"I tried to warn you, sweetheart," he said, his face impassive. "I told you not to romanticize me, to harden that soft heart. It was my one courtesy for the kindness you've shown me over the years. But you fell for me anyway." His jaw tightened. "Consider it a lesson for the future. Pretty words and pretty faces don't equal pretty souls."

My hope turned to ashes.

My soft heart? No. I didn't have a heart at all, not anymore. He'd torn it out of my chest, sliced it to ribbons with the blades of his words, and tossed the shreds aside without a second thought.

I should say something. Anything. But I couldn't think of a single thing.

I wished for an iota of my earlier anger and hurt, but none came. I was numb.

I might've stood there forever had gentle hands not guided me into Rhys's waiting car. I thought I heard Bridget hiss something at Alex, but I couldn't be sure. It didn't matter.

Nothing mattered.

Bridget didn't try to talk to me or feed me platitudes. That would've only made things worse. Instead, she let me sit in silence and stare out the window, watching dead tree after dead tree fly by. I couldn't remember why I liked winter. Everything looked dull and gray. Lifeless.

I made it all the way to the border of Maryland. There, it started raining, the tiny drops sprinkling over the window like scattershot crystals. I remembered the day Alex picked me up when I was stranded in the rain, and I broke down.

All my pent-up emotion from the past few hours—the past few *months*—burst forth at the same time. I was an ant swept up in a tidal wave, and I didn't bother fighting. I let it wash over me—the hurt, the anger, the heartbreak and betrayal and sadness—until my eyes burned and my muscles ached from the force of sobs.

Somehow, I found myself curled up in Bridget's lap while she stroked my hair and murmured soothing sounds. It would've been terribly embarrassing, crying into a royal princess's lap, except I was beyond caring.

Why was it always me?

What about me made me so damn unlovable? So *gullible*?

My favorite color.

Yellow.

My favorite ice cream flavor.

Mint chocolate chip.

You are the light to my dark, Sunshine. Without you, I'm lost.

Lies. All of it.

Every kiss, every word, every second that I had treasured…
tainted.

My eyes burned with liquid fire. I couldn't breathe. Everything
hurt, from the outside to the inside, as I sobbed terrible, wretched,
soul-racking tears.

Michael had lied to me. Alex had lied to me. Not for days,
weeks, or months but for *years*.

Something inside me broke, and I was no longer only crying
for my shattered heart but for the girl I used to be—the one who'd
believed in light and love and the goodness of the world.

That girl was gone.

CHAPTER 37

Alex

I WATCHED AVA LEAVE, MY CHEST HOLLOW, MY EYES burning with a foreign, pent-up emotion.

I wanted to run after her and snatch her out of Bridget's arms. To fall to my knees and beg her forgiveness for the unforgivable. To keep her by my side for the rest of our days so nothing and no one could hurt her again.

Except I couldn't, because *I* was the one who'd hurt her. I was the one who'd lied and manipulated. I was the one who'd endangered her with my thirst for vengeance and twisted plans against my uncle.

The only way to protect Ava was to let her go, even if that meant destroying myself.

The car taking Ava back to Maryland and away from me disappeared from sight, and I released a shuddering breath, trying to make sense of the pain clawing at my insides. It felt like someone was ripping out pieces of my heart and soul and grinding them beneath their feet. I had never felt so acutely, so *much*.

I hated it. I longed for the icy indifference of numbness, but I feared this was my penance—to burn in the flames of my self-inflicted agony for the rest of eternity.

My personal living hell. My own walking damnation.

"Alex." The head of my Philly team approached me, his movements sharp and precise. He wore a Philadelphia police uniform, the badge gleaming in the afternoon sun, but he was no officer of the law. "The house is ready."

"Good." I noticed Rocco staring at me with a strange expression. "What?" I snapped.

"Nothing." He cleared his throat. "You just look like you're about to—never mind."

"Finish the sentence. About to what?" My voice dropped to a dangerous decibel. I had cleanup teams on standby in various cities, ready to swoop in in case any of my many plans went awry. No one knew about them, not even my uncle when he'd been alive. They were discreet, efficient, and looked like normal people who held normal jobs—not fixers who could bury any body, erase any evidence, and jam any communications...including outgoing calls to local police stations.

Every "police officer" and "paramedic" who'd showed up today was on my team, and they'd played their roles convincingly.

Rocco looked like he wished he'd never opened his mouth. "Like you're about to, ah, cry." He flinched, no doubt aware that even though he'd intercepted Ava's 911 call and pulled the team together in record time, that wouldn't shield him from my wrath.

The fire in my veins matched the burning behind my eyes. I didn't dignify Rocco's statement with a response; I merely glared at him until he wilted. "Are there any other foolish observations you'd like to share with me?" My voice could've frozen the Sahara.

He gulped. "No, sir."

"Good. I'll take care of the house."

There was a short pause. "Personally? Are you—" He stopped when he saw the look on my face. "Of course. I'll tell the others."

While he rounded up the rest of the team, I walked into the

mansion where I'd spent the better part of my life. It was home, but it'd never felt like home, not even when my uncle and I had been on good terms.

It made what I had to do that much easier.

Rocco gave me the go signal from outside the entrance.

I retrieved the lighter from my pocket and flicked it open. The smell of kerosene soaked the air, but I didn't hesitate as I walked to the nearest set of curtains and tossed the flame at the thick gold material.

It was amazing how fast fire could spread across a ten-thousand-square-foot building. The flames licked the walls and ceiling, ravenous in their pursuit of destruction, and I was tempted to stay there and let them consume me. But my sense of self-preservation kicked in at the last minute, and I escaped through the open front door, the scent of charred ashes lingering in my nose.

My team and I stood a safe distance away, watching the proud brick manor burn until it came time to contain it before it spread out of control. The manor sat on acres of private property, and no one would know about the fire until hours, if not days, later. Not unless I told them.

Eventually, I would. It'd be a tragic story of how an errant cigarette caught fire and how the ailing lord of the manor, who'd refused to hire a full staff and lived alone, failed to put it out in time. It would be a small news item, buried in the back pages of the local paper. I'd make sure of it.

But for now, I simply stood and watched the flames inciner-ate the corpses of my uncle, Camo, and my past until there was nothing left.

CHAPTER 38

Alex

JOSH'S FIST SLAMMED INTO MY FACE, AND I HEARD AN ominous *crack* before I stumbled back. Blood dripped from my nose and lip, and judging by the pain radiating from the right side of my face, I was going to wake up with one hell of a shiner tomorrow.

Still, I made no move to defend myself while Josh pummeled me. "You fucking bastard," he hissed, his eyes wild as he kneed my stomach. I doubled over, the breath stolen from my lungs in a wet, crimson-stained gasp. "You. Motherfucking. *Bastard*. I trusted you!" Another punch, this time to the side of my rib. "You were my. Best. Friend!"

The hits continued until I dropped to my knees, my body a mess of cuts and bruises.

But I welcomed the pain. Reveled in it.

It was what I deserved.

"I always knew you had bad taste," I rasped. *Note to self: work from home until the injuries heal.* I didn't need the office running wild with rumors. Everyone was still whispering about my uncle's death, which was officially attributed to the fire that'd reduced the manor and everything in it to ashes.

Josh grabbed me by the collar and hauled me up, his face tight with pain and fury. "You think this is funny? Ava was right. You *are* a psychopath."

Ava. The name sliced through me like a razor-sharp knife. No physical beating could hurt more than thinking of her. Her face before she walked away would haunt me for the rest of my days, and thanks to my fucking cursed memory, I remembered every detail of every second. The scent of blood and sweat staining my skin, the way her shoulders trembled as she clutched the blanket with white-knuckled hands…the moment the faint light of hope died in her eyes.

My gut wrenched.

I may not have killed her physically, but I had killed her spirit, her innocence. The part of her that believed the best in people and saw beauty in the ugliest of hearts.

Was any of it real?

Yes, Sunshine. All of it. Realer than I ever thought possible.

Words I wished I'd been able to say, except I hadn't. She'd gotten hurt and almost killed because of me. I'd failed to protect her, just like I'd failed to protect my sister, my parents. Perhaps it was my curse to watch everyone I loved suffer.

I was a genius, but I'd been so arrogant I'd overlooked a crucial weakness in my plan. I'd anticipated my uncle might go after Ava, but I should've had a team monitoring her 24/7 instead of just during the day. That one error of judgment had almost cost me the one thing I couldn't live without.

Except I lost her anyway. Because while I may be a selfish son of a bitch, the only thing that would gut me more than not having her by my side was seeing her hurt again. I'd made plenty of enemies over the years, and once they discovered my weakness— because she *was* my weakness, the only one I ever had—they wouldn't hesitate to do what my uncle did. Ava would never be safe as long as she was with me, so I let her go.

She was mine...but I let her go.

I didn't think I had a heart before I met her, but she proved I did—it lay in pieces at her feet.

"Fight back," Josh growled. "Fight back so I can kill you, you bastard."

"No. And not because I'm afraid to die." Hell, I'd welcome it. I flashed a grim smile. The movement sent another burst of pain through my skull. "This is your freebie. One session of unlimited beating for eight years of lies."

His mouth twisted, and he shoved me away with disgust. "If you think one beatdown will make up for what you've done, you're delusional. You wanted to use me? Fine. But you brought my sister into this, and for that, I will never forgive you."

That makes two of us.

"I'm not wasting any more energy on you. You don't deserve it." Josh's jaw flexed. "You were my best friend," he repeated, his voice cracking on the last word.

Another, altogether different type of pain lanced through me. I'd originally befriended Josh because he was Michael's son, but over the years, he really had become my best friend. My uncle had been my last living relative, but Josh had been my brother. It had nothing to do with blood and everything to do with choice.

Truth was, I could've taken Michael down a long time ago, but I'd stalled out of loyalty to Josh. I'd made excuses as to why I dragged out my plan, even to myself, but deep down, I hadn't wanted to hurt him.

You were my best friend too.

Josh's face hardened once more. "If I ever see you near me or Ava again, I *will* kill you." He shot one last disgusted glance in my direction before he left.

The door banged shut, and I lay there, staring at the ceiling for what felt like hours. Movers had already packed up my belongings and transported them to my new penthouse in DC. I couldn't stay in this house any longer—it was too full of memories, of faded laughs and conversations that stretched deep into the night. Not just with Ava but with Josh. We'd lived here together in college, and it had been some of the best years of my life.

I closed my eyes, and for once, I allowed myself to sink into a good memory instead of a painful one.

"Sing one song. Just one," Ava pleaded. "It'll be my birthday present."

I shot her an unimpressed look, even as I held back a laugh at her exaggerated pout and puppy-dog eyes. How could someone so sexy also be so fucking adorable? "Your birthday isn't until March."

"It'll be my early *birthday present."*

"Nice try, Sunshine." I wrapped my arms around her waist from behind and brushed my lips over her neck, smiling when I heard her sharp inhale. My quickly hardening cock fit perfectly against her ass, like we were tailor-made for each other. "I'm not singing."

"What do you have against music?" she huffed, even as she arched against me when I grazed my thumb over one perfect, peaked nipple. I could never get enough of her. I wanted to tie her up and devour her all day, every day. The rest of the world didn't deserve her. Neither did I, but she was here, and she was mine, so fuck what I deserved. I took what I wanted.

"Nothing against music." I pinched her nipple, and she ground against my now rock-hard cock in response. "Just don't like singing."

I did it once at some stupid karaoke spot my uncle dragged me to, and I never sang again. Not because I thought I was bad—I was Alex Volkov; I could do anything—but because singing felt too raw, too personal, like I was baring my soul with each note leaving my throat. That held true even when it was a stupid pop song. All music, no matter how cheesy, was grounded in emotions, and I'd built my reputation on having none—unless I was with Ava.

Desire pumped through my veins.

I had her all to myself before Jules got home from work in an hour, and I was going to take advantage of every second.

"But if you really want an early birthday present…" I spun Ava around, and she laughed, the sound filling the room with its warmth. "I have something in mind."

"Oh? What's that?" she teased, looping her arms around my neck.

"I could tell you or…" I kissed my way down her chest and stomach until I reached the sweet perfection between her thighs. "I could show you."

I yanked myself out of the scene, my heart pounding. Like all my memories, it was so vivid it might as well be happening in real time. Except it wasn't, and all that surrounded me was emptiness and cold air.

My chest cracked. Now I remembered why I'd held off on reliving the good memories—every time I returned to reality, it was like losing Ava all over again. I was a fucked-up Prometheus, suffering for eternity, except instead of having my liver eaten by an asshole eagle every day, it was my heart breaking over and over.

I lay there until the shadows lengthened and my back ached from the hardwood floor. Only then did I force myself to stand and limp to my car.

The house next door was dark and silent, matching the weather. I'd been so caught up in my misery I hadn't realized it was storming. Rain fell in furious sheets, and angry bolts of lightning split the sky in half, illuminating the barren winter trees and cracked pavement.

Not a hint of sunshine or life to be found.

CHAPTER 39

Ava

Two Months Later

BRIDGET CONVINCED RHYS NOT TO TELL THE PALACE what happened in Philadelphia. I didn't know how, because Rhys was such a stickler for the rules—even if telling the truth meant getting himself in trouble, since Bridget had been kidnapped on his watch—but she did.

The press also never picked up on the real story. Other than a small item about an "accidental house fire that resulted in the death of former Archer Group CEO Ivan Volkov," it was like the worst six hours of my life hadn't happened.

I suspected Alex had a hand in both the fire and the lack of media coverage, but I tried not to think of him these days.

Once or twice, I succeeded.

"I brought cake." Jules slid a red velvet cupcake in my direction. "Your fave." Her face glowed with hope as she waited for my response.

My friends tried their best to put on happy faces around me, but I heard their whispers and saw their sidelong glances. They were worried. Really worried. So was Josh, who quit his volunteer program and moved back to Hazelburg for "moral support." He'd landed a few days after the Philly incident for his belated holiday break, and when he found out what happened, he went berserk. That'd been almost two months ago.

I was grateful for my friends' support, but I needed more time. Space. They meant well, but I couldn't breathe with them hovering all the time.

"I don't want it." I pushed the cupcake away from me. *Red velvet.* Like the cookies I'd baked for Alex as a welcome-to-the-neighborhood gift a lifetime ago.

I couldn't stand anything red velvet these days.

"You haven't eaten yet, and it's already late afternoon." For once, Stella wasn't glued to her phone. Instead, she stared at me with concern scrawled all over her face.

"I'm not hungry."

Jules, Bridget, and Stella exchanged glances. I'd moved in with Bridget because I couldn't stand living near Alex anymore. Even though he'd moved out soon after I did, I couldn't look at that house without thinking of him, and every time I thought of him, I felt like I was drowning.

Helpless. Unmoored. Unable to breathe.

"Your birthday's coming up. We should celebrate." Bridget switched topics. "How about a spa day? You love massages, and it'll be on me."

I shook my head.

"Or maybe something simple like a movie night?" Stella suggested. "PJs, junk food, junk movies."

"Movies so bad they're almost good," Jules added.

"Okay." I didn't feel like celebrating, but I also didn't feel like arguing, and they would bug me until I agreed to *something*. "I'm going to take a nap."

I didn't wait for them to answer before I pushed my chair back and went upstairs to my room. I locked the door and climbed into bed, but I couldn't sleep. I'd stopped having so many nightmares after I regained my memories, but it was now my waking hours that I dreaded.

I lay in the dark, listening to the rain outside and watching the shadows dance across my ceiling. The past two months had both flown by and dragged on, with each day bleeding into the next in an endless sludge of numbness. Yet I woke up every morning, surprised I'd survived another day. Between Michael's and Alex's betrayals, I had depleted my capacity to cry.

I hadn't shed a single tear since I returned from Philadelphia.

My phone pinged with a new email notification on the nightstand. I ignored it. It was probably a stupid ten percent off coupon for something I didn't need.

Then again, it wasn't like I could sleep, and the sound lingered in the silence.

I sighed and grabbed my cell, opening the new email with all the enthusiasm of a prisoner on their way to death row. It was the orientation package for the WYP fellowship, complete with a calendar of classes and activities for the year, a list of housing suggestions, and a mini travel guide to New York City.

I was graduating and moving to Manhattan in May. It'd been my dream since I was thirteen, but I couldn't summon a flicker of excitement at the prospect. New York was too close to DC for comfort, and to be honest, I hadn't picked up my camera in weeks. I even canceled my engagement shoot with Elliott and his fiancée because I didn't think I could do them justice. He'd been disappointed, but I'd steered them toward another photographer who could help. My clients deserved better than what I could give them, because at this point, I had zero inspiration or motivation to shoot.

I was entering the world's most prestigious fellowship in two and a half months, and my creative well was drier than the Kalahari Desert. One more beautiful thing in my life, ruined.

Out of nowhere, fury blasted through me, shocking me out of my stupor.

This should've been the best, most exciting time of my life. It was my senior year, and my dream program had accepted me. Instead of celebrating, I was moping like a...well, a heartbroken teenager. And even though that was half correct, I was sick of it. Sick of letting men who didn't give two shits about me have this hold over me. Sick of being the object of pitying looks and worried whispers.

Maybe I was that person in the past, but not anymore.

Anger and indignation rushed through my veins, compelling me to get out of bed and rifle through my drawers until I found what I was looking for. I put it on, covered it up with a hoodie and jeans, and shoved my feet into boots. I walked down the stairs and found my friends huddled in the living room. Rhys stood in the corner, stone-faced and watchful.

"Do you want a ride somewhere?" Bridget asked when she saw my outfit. "It's pouring outside."

"No, I have an umbrella."

"Where are you going?" Stella asked. "I'll go—"

"It's okay. I have something I need to do—alone."

A small frown took over her face. "I don't think—"

"I mean it." I took a deep breath. "I appreciate all you guys have done, I really do, but I need to do this for me. I won't hurt myself or do anything crazy. I just need you to trust me."

There was a long silence before Jules finally broke it. "Of course we trust you," she said softly. "You're our best friend."

"But if you need us, we're here." Bridget's warm, sympathetic gaze caused a messy knot of emotion to form in my throat. "You don't have to do anything alone if you don't want to."

"Just send a text, call, carrier pigeon, whatever," Stella added. "My Instagram inbox gets crazy sometimes, but that works too."

I swallowed the lump in my throat and huffed out a small laugh. "Thank you. I'll be back soon. Promise."

I grabbed the umbrella by the front door, feeling the heat of my friends' worried gazes on my back, and stepped out into the storm. My boots squeaked on the wet sidewalks as I walked toward a campus building I'd never visited in all my years at Thayer. One, because I was lazy, and two, because I was afraid...of a certain room, anyway.

I swiped my student ID at the front desk and consulted the map before winding my way to the back. It was a rainy Sunday in March, so there weren't many people here. The New Year's resolution people, the ones who'd vowed to exercise more in the new year, had given up by now, and the gym rats were apparently taking the day off.

I pushed open the door to the pool room, breathing a sigh of relief when I saw that it too was empty. It was a gorgeous space, with pale tile floors and a giant skylight over the pool.

I kicked off my boots and shrugged off my clothes until I had on only my swimsuit.

The smell of chlorine didn't nauseate me as much as it used to. I'd gotten used to it after all my swim lessons with Al—after all my swim lessons. Still, my skin prickled with unease at the undulations in the pale turquoise water, which seemed to stretch forever in its Olympic-sized concrete container.

I hadn't had a swim lesson in months. I *thought* I remembered the basics, but what if I didn't?

My chest tightened, and it took more effort than it should've to draw enough oxygen into my lungs.

It was worse when Al—when I was alone. If I drowned, no one would find me until later. There'd be no one to save me.

But that was the point of this exercise, wasn't it? To do this alone.

Breathe, Ava. You won't drown. You know how to swim.

I opened my eyes and took a few shaky steps toward the edge of the pool. It seemed bottomless, even though the markers indicated it was eight feet deep at its deepest.

Before I lost my nerve, I stepped in, trying not to flinch at the sensation of cold water lapping at my ankles. My knees. My thighs. My chest. My shoulders.

Okay. This wasn't so bad. I'd been in a pool dozens of times before. I could do this.

Not alone, a taunting voice in my head sang. *What makes you think you can do this alone?*

"Shut up," I gritted out, my voice echoing in the empty space.

I held my breath and, after saying a quick prayer, ducked my head beneath the water. I fought the immediate urge to panic. *You're fine. You're fine.* I was still in the shallow end of the pool, and I could lift my head at any time.

I closed my eyes, the events of the past eight months flashing through my mind.

Josh leaving for Central America. Me getting stranded in a rainstorm in the middle of nowhere. Alex—*there, I thought his full name*—picking me up. Alex moving in next door. Alex—

My head broke above the water, and I gasped for air. I allowed myself a minute break before I dove again.

Alex's birthday. Our first kiss. Our weekend at the hotel. Thanksgiving. My father. My kidnapping.

Sweet, trusting Ava, so eager to fix broken things.

Was any of it real?

Again and again. Head in, head out. It was the first time I'd allowed myself to dwell on Alex and our time together since Philadelphia. Razor blades pierced my chest at the memory of his voice, his eyes, his touch…but I was still here. I was alive. And for once, the water didn't seem like an enemy. It seemed like a friend, swallowing my tears and cleansing me of the past.

I couldn't change what happened to me or control what other people did, but I could control what *I* did. I could shape the future I wanted to have.

When the restless energy became too much, I stopped holding my breath underwater and started swimming. I wouldn't win an Olympic medal anytime soon, but I could move my body from one point to the other in the pool, which was more than I could say for myself this time last year.

All my life, people had coddled me. Josh. My friends. Alex. Or at least he'd pretended to care about me. I'd let them, because it was easier to lean on others than myself. I'd thought myself free because I didn't have a physical cage when in fact I'd been trapped by my own mind, by the fears that haunted my days and the night-mares that haunted my nights. I stuck with the safe choices because I thought I wasn't strong enough for anything else.

But I'd survived not one, not two, but *three* near-death experi-ences. I'd had my heart broken and smashed, but I was still breath-ing. I'd lived with my nightmares almost my whole life and still found the courage to dream.

I swam until my limbs ached.

After that, I stayed in the pool for a while longer, reveling in my accomplishment. Me, swimming alone, for—I snuck a peek at the clock—an hour without a panic attack. *More* than an hour.

I tilted my head up, my first real smile in months spreading across my face. It was small, but it was there.

Baby steps.

Above me, the storm had abated, the angry gray clouds giving way to blue skies. And through the domed glass, I saw, quite clearly, the pale glimmers of a rainbow.

CHAPTER 40

Alex

Two and a Half Months Later

"YOU LOOK LIKE SHIT." RALPH SANK INTO THE CHAIR opposite mine and appraised me with sharp eyes. "Haven't 'cha heard of a skin-care routine?"

I didn't look up from the screen. "Carolina!"

The door to my office opened, and my assistant poked her head in. "Yes, Mr. Volkov?"

"How the fuck did he get in here?" I gestured at Ralph.

"He's on your approved list of visitors who don't need appointments."

"Remove him from the list."

"Yes, sir." Carolina hesitated. "Do you—"

"You can leave."

She fled without a second thought. I didn't blame her. I'd been in a foul mood for months, and she'd learned it was best to stay out of sight.

Ralph arched his eyebrows. "Someone's in a bad mood."

"Don't you have a business to run?" I clicked out of the

spreadsheet I'd been examining and leaned back, irritation coiling in my stomach. I didn't have time for bullshit today. I barely had time for lunch.

Ever since I took over as CEO of Archer Group, the company's stocks had shot sky-high. Likely because I worked nonstop, more than I ever had. I barely left my office. Work kept me busy, and busy was good.

"Ah, about that." He rubbed the back of his neck. "I wanted to tell you in person."

"Whatever it is, make it quick. I have a phone call with the vice president in an hour." I picked up my glass of whiskey and drained the rest of the Macallan.

Yes, it was only noon. No, I didn't give a fuck.

"The vice president of the United—" Ralph shook his head. "Never mind, I don't wanna know. But since you asked, here it is. I'm retiring and moving to Vermont."

"Funny."

"I'm not joking. I'm retiring and moving to Vermont," he repeated.

I stared at him. Ralph stared back, his face calm. "You're shitting me."

Ralph was one of those guys I pictured working till the day he died, simply because he loved his job. He took immense pride in the fact that he'd built KMA into the city's best training center over the years, and he hadn't given a single indication he wanted to retire until now.

"Nah. I've been thinking about it for a while. I love KMA, but I ain't no spring chicken anymore, and Missy and I have saved up enough for retirement. Plus, the missus has been wanting to get out to the country for a while." Ralph drummed his fingers on the desk. "She grew up in Vermont. Always wanted to go back."

I needed another drink. "What the hell are you going to do in Vermont?"

"Fuck if I know. Guess I should find a hobby." Ralph flashed a crooked smile before it dimmed. "I know it's sudden, but I didn't decide until yesterday. I wanted to tell you first. Don't tell the other students, but...you've always been the biggest pain in my ass."

That was as close to a sentimental statement as Ralph would get.

I snorted. "Thanks. So." I assessed him with narrowed eyes. "What's happening with the academy?"

"My nephew will take it over. He'll do a good job." Ralph laughed at my grimace. "I know you're not his biggest fan, but he's been running things alongside me for years. He has what it takes."

"We'll see." His nephew may have what it takes, but Ralph was Ralph. "When are you moving?"

"End of August. Gives us time to put our affairs in order here, and fall in Vermont is nice as hell." My mentor's face softened. "You can call or visit anytime. My door is always open for you."

"Fine." I shuffled the papers on my desk. "We'll grab a meal before you leave."

"I mean it, Alex. Don't give me that I'm-an-asshole-who-doesn't-need-anyone shit either. I know it's been a tough couple o' months with Ava—"

"*Don't.*" My jaw clenched. "We're not discussing her. Period."

Ava had stopped taking Krav Maga lessons at KMA, which I'd expected, but Ralph hadn't stopped bugging me about her since he found out about our breakup. I didn't give him the nitty-gritty; I simply told him things didn't work out.

Which didn't stop him from prying. He was a persistent bastard.

"Never figured you one to run away from your troubles," he said.

"I'm not running from anything."

"Then why do you look like hell? Not to mention you've been in a foul mood since January. Whatever you did—"

"We're. Not. Discussing. It." A vein throbbed in my temple. *This* was why I abhorred human companionship. People couldn't shut the hell up. "Now, if you'll excuse me—"

"Sir?" Carolina poked her head in again, her face pale and not a little terrified. "Uh, you have another guest."

"If they don't have an appointment, I don't want to see them."

"About that, it's—"

"Don't bother. I'll announce myself." A statuesque blond swept in like she owned the place. The vein in my temple pulsed harder. "Princess Bridget of Eldorra, here to see Asshole—I mean, Alex Volkov." Her smile came off both polite and menacing.

I was impressed, if not annoyed.

How hard was it to find competent staff who could keep intruders out of my office these days?

"Princess." Ralph waved two fingers in the air.

"Ralphie." She nodded.

Ralphie? I wasn't going to ask.

Bridget's bruiser of a bodyguard stood behind her with his ever-present glower. He might be the one person in the world who had a better poker face and a shittier disposition than I did.

"I'm sorry." Carolina looked like she was on the verge of panic. "The princess—"

"Leave. I'll take care of it." My call with the VP was in forty minutes, and I'd already wasted enough time.

"That's my cue." Ralph rose. "I'll take you up on the meal, but it looks like you have some stuff to hash out first." He tilted his head toward Bridget but kept his eyes on me. "Think about what I said."

"Sure." I would rather eat rusted nails than visit Vermont. I didn't do country life.

When the door closed behind Ralph and Carolina, I leaned back in my chair and laced my fingers over my chest. "To what do I owe the pleasure, Your Highness?" I kept my expression impassive and tried not to think of the last time I'd seen Bridget—in her car, taking Ava from me.

Even if I was the one who'd pushed Ava away, I hated Bridget a little for that. For being able to comfort Ava when I couldn't.

The blond looked down her nose at me. "I know what you did."

"You'll have to be more specific. I've done a lot of things in my life, as you well know."

"Cut the bullshit." Bridget walked up to my desk and leaned forward, pressing her hands on the table. Her eyes glinted with steely knowledge. "You're having Ava followed."

My shoulders stiffened before I forced them to relax. "Princesses shouldn't say the word 'bullshit.' It's terribly undiplomatic."

"Don't deflect. Rhys"—she angled her head toward the bodyguard, whose gunmetal glare darkened the longer he looked at me—"caught him. It turns out it's a small world after all, because they served in the military together. In fact, Rhys saved his life, so it didn't take much before he spilled. Now, I want you to explain why, exactly, you're having Ava followed. Haven't you done enough?"

That fucker. No wonder the guy I'd hired had been avoiding my calls.

Navy SEAL of honor, my ass. Incompetency and disloyalty were a worldwide scourge.

"Perhaps you should check your facts, because I did no such thing," I said coolly. "Delusional much?"

"Don't lie, Alex. You're not as good at it as you think you are." Bridget pierced me with her stare. "He told us you ordered him to keep an eye on her. Not to harm her...but to protect her."

A familiar pressure built at the base of my neck and spread until it enveloped my skull in a crushing grip. "And you believed him?" I straightened my shirtsleeve. "Doesn't say much for your bodyguard that he would believe lies so easily. No wonder you got kidnapped."

A low growl emitted from said bodyguard's throat. He stepped forward, his eyes promising vengeance, but Bridget stayed him with a warning look.

"You're deflecting again." She relaxed, her hard expression melting into a thoughtful one that sent the hairs on the back of my neck rising. She slipped into Ralph's vacated chair and crossed one leg over the other.

"I didn't say you could sit." I didn't give a flying fuck that she was a princess. This was *my* office. *My* kingdom.

Bridget ignored me.

I'd already picked up my phone to call security when she said, "You secretly hired someone to look after Ava because you still care about her."

Why the *fuck* did everyone want to talk about her? Was it Torture Alex with Ava's Name day?

I slammed the phone down and stood. I was done with people today. The vice president could wait another day or week for our phone call. "I don't have time for this. I—"

"Still care about her," Bridget repeated.

"Take a pill for the delusion, Princess. I used her. I got what I wanted. Now I'm done. I've *been* done for months." I shrugged on my jacket. "Now fuck off."

"For someone who's usually so composed, you're awfully agitated," she said. "I wonder why."

"How about you mind your business, I mind mine." I flicked my eyes toward Rhys, who glared back at me with dangerous gray eyes.

Bridget tensed. "What's that supposed to mean?"

"You know what it means."

"Fine. Stay in denial." Bridget stood, her complexion a shade paler than before. "I guess you don't want to know about Ava."

"What about Ava?" The question slipped out before I could stop it.

Shit.

A small, triumphant smile spread across Bridget's face. Between her and Jules, "annoying as hell" must be a requirement for Ava's friends.

"Forget I said anything. You obviously don't care," she said.

"Just tell me," I gritted out.

"Not unless you admit it."

My blood pressure skyrocketed to alarming levels. I was *this* close to drop-kicking a princess, bodyguard be damned. "There's nothing to tell."

"For a supposed genius, you are *dense.*" Bridget somehow managed to look down her nose at me even though I was taller than her. "You didn't hire someone to follow Ava all these months to protect her for no reason. To be clear, I despise you for what you did, and I don't *want* her to forgive you. But I love her more than I hate you, and she hasn't been the same since Philly." A troubled expression crossed her face. "I didn't say anything at first because I thought you didn't care, but now that I know you do—don't insult me by denying it again," she said when I opened my mouth. "I may not have a Mensa-level IQ, but I'm not an idiot. I hate to admit it, but you're the only person with any hope of getting through to her. I've tried, Jules and Stella have tried, Josh has tried hard as he can…but it's not working."

I suppressed a flinch at the mention of Josh's name. "Ava's fine. She's healthy and thriving in school. She's even swimming on her own now."

There was no use pretending anymore. Bridget saw right through my bullshit.

"On the outside, Ava is fine," she said. "Not on the inside. She's...I don't know how to explain it. It's like she's missing the spark that makes her *her*."

I knew exactly what she meant, because I'd seen that spark die in front of my eyes.

I exhaled a ragged breath and tried to gather my swirling thoughts. They were usually crystal clear, each arranging themselves in the perfect pattern for me to analyze and strategize, but I'd barely slept over the past few months, and I hadn't eaten in almost twenty-four hours. I was a mess.

I'd been a mess since I let Ava go.

"I don't know if she'll forgive you for what you did," Bridget said. "Or if I *want* her to forgive you. But it's not about me. It's about her. Imagine how she must feel, finding out both her 'father' and her 'boyfriend' lied to her for so long—*and* finding these things out at practically the same time. She says she's over it, but you don't just 'get over' something like that." She glared at me. "At least tell her your true feelings. She doesn't trust herself right now, much less in love or other people. And an Ava who doesn't trust or believe in love...well, that's not really Ava, is it?"

My heart twisted into a knot that blocked the air from my lungs. "I can't."

"Why not? You care about her. Perhaps..." She paused, her face contemplative as she examined my tight jaw and rigid frame. "You even love her."

"Get out."

"You're being a coward. I thought you weren't afraid of anything, yet you're afraid to tell her how you really feel—"

"Because she's better off without me, okay?" I exploded, months of pent-up emotion bursting forth in one giant, scalding wave.

Rhys stepped forward, but Bridget waved him back, those blue eyes trained on me with fascination. I didn't blame her. I'd never blown up like that in front of another person. Ever.

It was strangely cathartic.

"I couldn't protect her. She was hurt because of *me*. My uncle kidnapped her because of *me*. And I couldn't stop him." I pressed my lips together, trying to calm my rampaging pulse.

Five months later, I still woke in the middle of the night, terrified something had happened to Ava. Envisioning all the things that *could've* happened to her had things gone sideways in my uncle's office. That was why I'd hired the private investigator-slash-bodyguard—I couldn't look after her myself without putting her in more danger, but I'd be damned if I left her defenseless and alone out there.

Of course, I needed to fire the guy for not keeping his mouth shut, but this was DC. There were ex-military and ex-Secret Service types everywhere.

Bridget's expression softened. "You saved her life."

"I was the one who put her in that situation in the first place," I said bitterly. "People around me always get hurt, and for all I have"—I swept my arm around my sprawling office—"I can't guarantee their safety." I raked a frustrated hand through my hair, glad my office was soundproof and surrounded by tinted glass. The last thing I needed was for my staff to see me lose my shit.

"Nothing in life is guaranteed, but you're Alex Volkov. Your uncle caught you off guard because he was your uncle, but now that he's out of the picture, do you really think anyone else can get the jump on you?" Bridget shook her head. "If you do, then maybe it is best you stay away from Ava. Like I said, I despise what you did to her, but I also believe you love her—even if you're too stubborn or stupid to see it—"

"I have an IQ of 160," I said, insulted.

"Intellectual intelligence doesn't equal emotional intelligence," she retorted. "And do not interrupt a princess. It's terrible etiquette. As I was saying, you're too stubborn or stupid to see it, and now it's too late."

I paused, letting her words sink in. Dread uncoiled at the pit of my stomach. "Explain."

Bridget and Rhys exchanged glances before she responded in a wary tone. "Ava's moving to London. She switched her fellowship location. Her plane leaves in"—she checked the clock—"an hour."

London. Another city, another country, another *continent.* She would be thousands of miles away from me.

Fuck. That.

The dread turned into full-blown panic. "Flight info," I snarled.

"I don't know."

I wanted to strangle her. I didn't care that Rhys was packing heat and looked ready to tackle me if I so much as twitched the wrong way.

"I swear to God, Bridget—"

"Why do you want to know?" she demanded. "It's not like you'll go after her. You said—"

"Because I love her!" I slammed my hands on the table. "There, happy? I love her so much I would rather give her up than hurt her. But if you think I'm letting her go to another country *alone*, with no protection, you've got another think coming. Now give me her fucking flight info."

Bridget did, a spark of triumph gleaming in her eyes.

I was well aware she'd baited me, but I didn't care. All I cared about was getting to the airport in the next hour—fuck, the next fifty-six minutes. I would figure everything else out later—Ava's protection, my enemies. For now, I just needed to see her. Hold her.

I brushed past Bridget and Rhys and stormed toward the elevator, ignoring Carolina's startled jump.

"Cancel my call with the VP—send my sincerest apologies and tell him I had a last-minute emergency—and book me a ticket to Europe that leaves in the next three hours," I commanded as I passed her. "Dulles Airport."

"You want me to cancel the—"

"*Do it.*"

"Certainly, sir." Carolina sprang into action, her fingers flying over her keyboard. "Which city would—"

"Doesn't matter. Just do it."

"Right away, sir."

I only needed the ticket to get past security.

On a regular day, it took half an hour to reach the airport, but of course, today was the day every construction crew in DC showed up in full force. Roadblocks and closures littered the streets alongside a shitload of drivers determined to win the World's Slowest Driver award.

"Get out of my way," I snapped at the Lexus in front of me. *Jesus, does no one in this city know how to drive?*

I broke what must have been a thousand traffic laws, but I made it to the airport in thirty-five minutes. Parking, security— fortunately, Carolina had the foresight to check me in online—and I was through, racing through the terminal searching for Ava's gate number.

I felt like the world's worst movie cliché. Running through

the airport trying to get the woman I loved to give me another chance...how original. But if it got me to Ava in time, I'd do it in front of prime-time TV.

Ava and I hadn't spoken in months, but there remained a thread tying us together despite what happened in Philly. Something told me that if she were to get on that plane, that would change. We—or whatever was left of us—would change. And I was terrified.

Beneath the fear, though, there lay a glimmer of pride. The girl who'd been afraid to go near water a year ago—who'd dreamed of traveling the world but never thought she'd be able to—was taking an international flight for the first time. Flying over an ocean. Facing her fears. I always knew she could do it, and she didn't need me or anyone else holding her hand.

I wondered if other people felt conflicting emotions like this every day. If so, I almost felt sorry for them. It was a pain in the fucking ass.

I dodged a mother with a stroller and a slow-moving group of students in obnoxious neon-green T-shirts. The gate numbers whizzed by in a blur until I found the one I was looking for.

My stomach sank when I saw the empty seating area and closed door leading to the Jetway.

"Flight 298. Did it leave?" I demanded of the attendant behind the counter.

"Yes, I'm afraid the plane took off a few minutes ago, sir," she said apologetically. "If you would like to book another flight—"

I tuned her out, my heart beating a desperate, lonely rhythm in my chest.

The plane had left.

Ava was gone.

CHAPTER 41

Ava

I LOVED LONDON.

I loved its energy, the posh accents, and the anticipation that I might sight one of the royals any day. I didn't, but I *could*, though I reassured Bridget she'd always be my favorite royal. Most of all, I loved that it was a fresh start. No one knew me here. I could be whoever I wanted, and the creative spark I'd lost in those dark weeks after Philadelphia came rushing back.

I'd been nervous, moving to a city where I had zero connections, but the rest of the WYP fellows and instructors were great. After two weeks of living in London and attending workshops, I'd already formed a small group of friends. We celebrated happy hour at pubs, went on photo shoots together on the weekends, and did touristy stuff like ride the London Eye and cruise on the Thames.

I missed my friends and Josh, but we video called often, and Bridget promised to visit me on her way back to Eldorra later this summer. Plus, all the WYP workshops and activities and the excitement of exploring a new city kept me busy. I didn't have time to be in my head, thank God.

I'd been in my head for months, and it wasn't a great place to be. I needed a change of scenery.

I also needed to send a big thank-you gift basket to the original London fellow who'd agreed to swap places with me—she went to New York while I came here. It was the only way the program would let me change my location so late in the process, but it worked out.

"You sure you can't join us?" Jack, an Australian wildlife photographer who was also in this year's fellowship cohort, asked. "Half-off drinks at the Black Boar today."

The Black Boar, located a few minutes' walk away from the WYP building, was one of the fellows' favorite pubs.

I shook my head with a regretful smile. "Next time. I'm behind on editing photos."

I wanted to make sure the final products were top-notch because they weren't for any ol' workshop—they were for Diane Lange's. *The* Diane Lange. I'd nearly had a heart attack when I first met her in person. She was everything I'd imagined her to be and more. She was smart, incisive, and talented beyond belief. Tough but fair. Her passion for her art radiated from every inch of her, and I could tell she cared about us. She *wanted* us to succeed and be the best we could be. In a cutthroat industry rife with backstabbing and undermining other creators, her dedication to helping us perfect our craft with no ego said a lot about her character.

"Fair enough." Jack chuckled. "See ya tomorrow then."

"See you." I waved goodbye and rummaged through my bag for my headphones while walking down the steps. That was the downside of carrying a large bag—it was impossible to find anything smaller than a full-sized laptop.

My fingers closed around the thin white wires right when I felt a prickle of heat on my neck. An electric awareness I hadn't felt in months.

No.

I was afraid to look up, but my curiosity got the better of me. My pulse quickened as I lifted my eyes slowly. Higher...higher... and there he was, standing less than three feet away in a black shirt and pants, looking like a god descended from the heavens to wreak havoc on my still-fragile heart.

I swore the poor thing stopped beating.

I hadn't seen him in person since Philadelphia, and the sight was too much. Too vivid, too overwhelming, too beautiful and horrifying. Those eyes, that face, the way I instinctively stepped toward him before I caught myself...

Oxygen grew scarce. My chest tightened the way it used to when I was near water. I could feel a panic attack coming on, and I needed to leave before I collapsed right there on the sidewalk, but my feet wouldn't move.

This is a hallucination. It has to be.

That was the only explanation that made sense. Why else would Alex show up in London in front of my fellowship headquarters after half a year of silence?

I squeezed my eyes shut, counted to ten, and opened them again.

He was still here. In London. *In front of me.*

The panic intensified.

"Hi," he said softly.

I flinched at the sound of his voice. If looking at him was a punch in the gut, hearing him was like getting steamrolled by a Mack truck.

"You can't be here." It was a stupid thing to say since we were on a public sidewalk and it wasn't like I could ban him from the city of London, but oh, how I wished I could. I was already drowning in him, and it'd been less than five minutes. "Why are you here?"

Alex stuffed his hands in his pockets, his throat flexing with a hard swallow. His eyes flickered with uncertainty as they searched my face for something I wasn't ready to give. In all the years I'd known him, I'd never seen him look so nervous. "I'm here for you."

"You don't need me anymore." I almost couldn't hear myself over the thunderous roar of my pulse. I regretted the falafel sandwich I ate for lunch, which threatened to make a messy reappearance. "You got your revenge, and I'm not interested in whatever new game you're playing. So leave. Me. Alone."

Pain slashed across his face. "This isn't a game, I promise. This is just me, asking you for...not forgiveness, not right now. But hope that one day, you won't hate me and we might get a second chance." He swallowed hard. "I'll always need you, Sunshine."

Sunshine. The word tore at me, ripped off the scabs on my wounds until I bled once again.

Stop calling me Sunshine.

Why?

Because it's not my name.

I'm aware. It's a nickname.

"Your promises mean nothing to me." I wrapped my arms around myself, chilled to the bone even though the sun shone high in the sky. "Even if they did, they're six months too late."

I'd lived less than a half hour's drive from Alex all those months, and he never once reached out. Now, he showed up in another country asking for a second chance? Unbelievable.

Almost as unbelievable as the small, shameful part of me that *wanted* to give him that second chance.

Stay strong. I'd survived multiple murder attempts. I conquered my aquaphobia. I could talk to the man who broke my heart without falling apart.

Hopefully.

"I know." Alex exhaled a shaky breath, his brows drawn tight over his eyes. He looked less polished than usual, with his rumpled hair and faint purple smudges beneath his eyes. I wondered if he'd been getting enough sleep, then mentally kicked myself for caring. His sleeping habits weren't my business anymore. "I thought I was protecting you. That you were better off without me. After what happened with my uncle, I couldn't risk you getting hurt again because of your association with me. But I never left you alone. I had someone keeping an eye on you—"

"Wait." I held up one hand. "You had me *followed*?"

"For your protection."

I couldn't believe it. "How is that okay? That's—that's crazy! How long…oh my God." My eyes widened. "Do you have someone following me in London too?"

He stared at me, his face stony.

"Unreal," I breathed. "You are truly psycho. Where is he?" I looked around frantically. I didn't see anyone suspect, but the most dangerous people were those who looked anything but. "Call him off. Right now."

"I already did."

I narrowed my eyes. That was too easy. "You did?"

"Yes, because I'm taking over his duties. That's why it took me so long. I had to make…arrangements for my absence in DC." Alex's mouth twitched at my stunned expression. "You'll be seeing a lot more of me from now on."

"The hell I will." The thought of seeing him every day sent me into a tailspin of panic. "I'll file a restraining order against you. Have you arrested for stalking."

"You can try, but I can't guarantee my friends in the British government will comply." His face darkened. "And if you think I'm leaving you alone and unprotected *anywhere*, you don't know me at all."

"I *don't* know you. I have no idea who are you are. I only know the person you showed me, and he was an illusion. A fantasy." Emotion clogged my throat. "I asked you that day if any of it had been real. You looked me in the eye and told me it was a lesson for the future. So consider the lesson learned."

Alex flinched. "It *was* real," he said hoarsely. "All of it."

I shook my head, my chest aching so hard it hurt to breathe. "I realize you're powerful enough that I can't stop you from doing what you want, but you're wasting your time if you think I'll fall for your lies again."

"They're not lies. Sunshine—"

"*Don't* call me that!" I couldn't stem the tide of tears gathering in my eyes. I'd been doing so well, but every second in Alex's presence eroded the defenses I'd built around my heart until it lay naked and vulnerable once more. "You've ruined everything I once thought was beautiful. Sunshine. Love. Even freakin' red velvet cake, because it reminds me of *you*. And when I think of you—" A sob ripped from my throat. "I think of every good memory we had and how they're now tainted by the fact that you were using me the whole time. I think of how *stupid* I was for falling for you and how you must've laughed at me when I told you I loved you. And I think of all those times you warned me about being too softhearted, but I ignored you because I believed the world was an inherently good place. Well, congratulations." I brushed the tears from my cheeks, but they fell too fast for me to make much of a dent. Thank God most of my classmates had already left and the surrounding street was empty. "That was the one truth you spoke. I *was* too softhearted, and the world is not the place I thought it was. It's cruel and it's vicious, and there's no place for soft hearts."

"Sun—Ava, no." Alex reached for me, but I instinctively recoiled. Hurt filled his face. His hand curled into a fist that he stuffed back in his pocket, and the tendons in his neck stretched taut. I detected a tiny tremble in his shoulders as he spoke. "That was what I believed because I'd never known anything else, but you showed me there *is* beauty in the world. I see it every time I look at you or see you smile or hear you laugh. You believe the best of people, and that's a strength, not a weakness. Don't let anyone, least of all me, take that away from you." His eyes burned into mine, bright with pain. "You told me once there was something beautiful waiting for me, something that would restore my faith in life. I've found it. It's you."

I wanted to sink into his words until they became my reality, but I'd been burned before. Who knew what he wanted from me this time around?

"You keep talking about protecting me," I said. "But you hurt me more than anyone else in my life, even Michael. Even when I thought you were an ass, I trusted you to tell the truth, and you turned out to be the biggest liar of all. Just…" I sucked in a deep breath, unable to look at him, it hurt so much. "Leave me alone."

Alex's chest heaved like he couldn't get enough air into his lungs. "I can't do that, sweetheart. I'll wait however long it takes, but I'll never be okay with a world in which you're alone."

"Who says I will be? Maybe I'll find someone else."

His eyes darkened to a furious shade of emerald, and his shoulders tensed even more. Somewhere, thunder boomed. I hadn't noticed the weather morph from sunny to its current gray, gloomy state, but I wouldn't be surprised if Alex had the power to control it with his emotions. "The hell you will," he snarled. "I'll kill any man that touches you."

"You have no right," I hissed back. "I don't belong to you."

The muscles in his jaw popped. "That's where you're wrong. I fucked up. Massively. But I will earn your forgiveness one day, and you *are* mine. Always. No matter how much time or distance separates us."

Do you know what it means to be taken by me? It means you're mine.

I shoved aside the unbidden memory. "I'm not arguing with you any longer." There was no way I could focus on editing tonight, but at least I could go home and cry myself to sleep like a pathetic moron. Yay me. "You can waste your time in London, but it won't matter. We're done."

I walked away before Alex could respond. Undeterred, he followed me, his every step matching two of mine. *Dammit.* Why couldn't I have been born tall like Bridget or Stella?

I ducked my head and picked up my pace, trying to ignore the man beside me as drops of rain splashed on my face and dampened my hair.

"Ava, please."

I clutched my bag to my chest, using it as armor while I bulldozed my way down the sidewalk.

"At least let me drive you home," Alex pleaded. "It's not safe, walking in the dark."

I'd been walking home for the past two weeks and had no issues. I didn't live in the best neighborhood, but it wasn't a war zone. I just had to keep my wits about me. Plus, I had pepper spray, and I'd restarted self-defense lessons at a local martial arts center.

I didn't say any of that to Alex though.

"It's cold and raining, and you're wearing a dress." No matter how fast I walked, I couldn't shake him. "Sweetheart, please, you'll get sick." His voice broke on the last word.

I clenched my teeth so hard my jaw hurt. I kept my head low, desperate to reach the warm safety of my flat. Eventually, Alex stopped talking and simply walked beside me, a glowering presence who ensured everyone else gave me a wide berth.

After what felt like an eternity, we reached my building. I

didn't look at him as I fished my key out of my bag and jammed it into the lock. Water streaked my face—from the rain or my tears, I couldn't tell.

Alex didn't follow me inside the building, but I could feel the heat of his gaze as I slipped inside.

Don't look. Don't look.

I made it halfway up the stairs before I caved. The glass pane above the door provided a clear view of the sidewalk, and although I was already in the building, Alex remained outside, soaked to the bone. His shirt clung to his sculpted torso, and his hair was plastered to his forehead, the light brown color almost black from the rain. He lifted his eyes until they met mine through the glass, his face stamped with equal parts anguish and determination.

And even though concrete, metal, and a good dozen feet separated us, he exerted a magnetic pull that almost convinced me to fling open the door and pull him in from the cold.

Almost.

I forced myself to turn away and run up the rest of the stairs to my flat before my stupid, soft heart got me in trouble again. Even after I changed and stepped into the shower, shivering, its seductive whispers caressed my ears and urged me to give in.

Ask him to come in. It's dark and cold outside... What if he gets sick? Robbed? Hurt?

"He won't," I said out loud, scrubbing my skin so hard it turned red. "Alex Volkov doesn't get hurt. He *does* the hurting."

The image of him standing miserably in the rain flashed through my mind, and I faltered before scrubbing harder. I didn't *make* him follow me or stand out there. If he caught a cold or...or hypothermia, that was on him.

I switched off the water with shaky hands.

I spent the next few hours eating instant ramen and attempting to edit photos, but I eventually gave up. I couldn't focus, and my eyes ached from crying. I just wanted to pretend this afternoon never happened.

I called it an early night and climbed into bed, resisting the urge to look out the window. It'd been hours. It wasn't like Alex would still be out there.

CHAPTER 42

Ava

ALEX LIVED UP TO HIS PROMISE-SLASH-THREAT OF showing up every single day. He was there in the morning when I left for my fellowship, usually with a vanilla latte and blueberry scone—my favorites. He was there to walk me home after my workshops. Other times, especially when I was with other people or exploring the city on the weekends, he was less conspicuous, but he was there. I felt his presence even though I couldn't see him.

I never thought Alex Volkov would become my stalker, but there we were.

On top of that, gifts arrived every day. By the boatload.

By the end of the first week, my apartment looked like I was opening an indoor garden. I donated everything to a local hospital—the roses of every color, the vivid purple orchids and sweet white lilies, the cheerful sunflowers and delicate peonies.

By the end of the second week, I owned enough jewelry to make the Duchess of Cambridge green with envy—at least until I pawned them. The sum I received for the pile of diamond earrings, sapphire bracelets, and ruby necklaces made my eyes water, but I donated most of it to various charities and saved the rest for living expenses. London wasn't cheap, and the fellowship stipend wasn't exactly princely.

By the end of the third week, I was knee-deep in gourmet chocolates, gift baskets, and custom-made desserts.

I didn't care about fancy jewels or flowers, so those gifts didn't matter to me. It was the little things that tore holes in my heart—the red velvet cupcakes that spelled out *I'm Sorry*; a rare, vintage Japanese camera I'd searched for for years but had never found for sale; the framed photo of Alex and me at the fall festival. I hadn't realized he'd kept a copy from the photo booth.

Why would I need photos?

For the memories. To remember people and events?

I don't need photos for that.

By the end of the fourth week, I was torn between tearing my hair out in frustration and crumbling like a sandcastle at high tide.

"We need to talk," I said Friday afternoon after I left my lighting techniques workshop. Alex lounged against a light pole outside the building, infuriatingly gorgeous in jeans and a white T-shirt. Aviators hid his eyes, but the intensity of his gaze seared through the glasses and burned into my flesh.

A group of passing schoolgirls looked him over, giggling and whispering among themselves.

"He is *so hot*," I heard one of them squeal when she thought she was out of earshot.

Spoiler: she wasn't.

I wished I could run after her and give her some unsolicited big-sister advice. *Don't fall for guys who look like they could break your heart, because chances are they will.*

"Sure," Alex said, unfazed by the girls' attention. He was probably used to it. While he followed me around London, women followed *him* around until we all looked like we were playing a giant game of follow-the-leader. "We can talk over dinner." His mouth twitched when I glared at him.

"That's not happening." I looked around and spotted a tiny alcove farther down the street. Not quite an alleyway, but private enough. I didn't want the other fellows seeing him and asking more questions. Most had already noticed Alex waiting for me every day and incorrectly assumed he was my boyfriend. "Over there."

I marched toward the alcove and waited until we were ensconced in the tiny space before I spoke again. "You have to stop."

Alex raised an eyebrow. "Stop...?"

"The gifts. The waiting. The games. They won't work." *Lies.* They were close to working, which was why I was freaking out. If he kept this up, I didn't know how long I could hold out.

His smile faded. "I told you, I'm not playing games. If you want me to stop with the gifts, I'll stop. But I'll never stop waiting."

"Why?" I threw my hands up in frustration. "You can have any woman you want. *Why* are you still here?"

"Because none of them are you. I..." Alex's throat flexed with a hard swallow. The nervous expression returned. "I didn't want to admit it, even to myself, but—"

"No." My heart broke into a gallop. I knew what he would say next, and I was nowhere near ready to hear it. "Don't."

"Ava, I love you." His eyes flickered with emotion, and my chest squeezed until I thought it would burst. "When you told me you loved me, I didn't say it back because I didn't feel like I deserved your love. You didn't know the truth about my plan yet, and I didn't think...fuck." He rubbed the back of his neck, looking uncharacteristically flustered. "This wasn't how I'd planned to say it," he muttered. "But it's true. And maybe I still don't deserve you, but I'm willing to work at it until I do."

"You don't love me." I shook my head, my eyes and nose burning with unshed tears. I'd cried so much lately I annoyed myself, but I couldn't stop. "You don't even know what love is. You lied and used me and Josh for eight years. *Eight years*. That's not love. That's manipulation. Insanity."

"It started out that way, but Josh really did become my best friend, and I really did fall for you." Alex let out a short laugh. "You think I *wanted* those things to happen? I didn't. They completely screwed my plans over. I held off on bringing down Michael for years because of you and Josh."

"How generous of you," I said sarcastically.

His jaw tightened. "I never claimed to be Prince Charming, and my love isn't a fairy-tale type of love. I'm a fucked-up person with fucked-up morals. I won't write you poems or serenade you beneath the moonlight. But you are the *only* woman I have eyes for. Your enemies are my enemies, your friends are my friends, and if you wanted, I would burn down the world for you."

My heart split in half. I wanted so badly to believe him, but... "Even if that's true, it's not about love. It's about trust, and I don't trust you anymore. You proved you're the master of the long game. What if this is just another one of those? What if one day, ten years from now, I wake up and you break my heart again? I won't survive it a second time."

If the source of the heartbreak were anyone else, maybe. But not Alex. He was embedded not only in my heart but in my soul, and if I lost him again for whatever reason, it was game over.

"Ava." Alex's voice cracked. Red rimmed his eyes, and I could've sworn he was on the verge of crying. But this was Alex. He didn't cry. He wasn't capable of it. "Sweetheart, please. Tell me what I have to do. I'll do anything."

"I don't know if there's anything you can do," I whispered. "I'm sorry."

"Then I'll just have to try everything until we find something," he said, his face granite, his tone resolute.

Alex wouldn't give up until he got what he wanted. It wasn't in his nature. But if I gave in to him the way my heart wanted but my mind screamed at me not to, how could I live with myself? A relationship without trust was built on a foundation of sand, and after a lifetime of drifting, I needed solid ground.

"Go home to DC, Alex," I said, exhausted—mentally, physically, and emotionally. "You have a business to run." Even as I said the words, my stomach lurched at the thought of an ocean separating us again.

I was a mess. I had no clue what I wanted, my thoughts raced too fast for me to latch on to any of them, and—

"I resigned as CEO, effective one month ago."

That shocked me out of my reverie. "*What?*" He was the most ambitious person I knew, and he'd been CEO for less than a year.

Why hadn't I heard about this? Then again, I didn't follow financial news, and I'd avoided any news about Alex himself.

Alex shrugged. "I couldn't stay on as CEO while spending all my time in London with you, so I resigned," he said matter-of-factly, like he hadn't given up his life's work on a whim. Except Alex did nothing on a whim. He thought through every move, and his latest one made no sense. Not unless...

I squashed the brief flare of hope before it could blossom into something greater.

"But what about money and expenses?" I realized how dumb that question was the second I asked it.

Alex's mouth tilted up. "I have enough in stocks, investments, and savings to last me the rest of my life. I worked because I wanted to. But now, I want to do something else."

I swallowed, my pulse thundering. "What's that?"

"Win you back. No matter how long it takes."

CHAPTER 43

Ava

One year later

THE FELLOWSHIP ENDED WITH A GRAND EXHIBITION attended by the movers and shakers of London's art world. The exhibition took place in Shoreditch, and every fellow had their own section in the pop-up gallery.

It was exhilarating, nerve-racking, and utterly surreal.

I stared at my little slice of heaven and the people passing through it, dressed to the nines and examining each piece with what I hoped were admiring eyes.

I'd grown by leaps and bounds as a photographer over the past year, and while I still had a lot to learn, I was damn proud of my work. I specialized in travel portraits like Diane Lange, but I put my personal spin on them. As much as I admired her, I didn't want to *be* her; I wanted to be my own person, with my own vision and creative ideas.

I took most of my shots in London, but the good thing about Europe was how easy it was to travel to other countries. On the weekends, I took the Eurostar to Paris or day-tripped to the

Cotswolds. I even booked short flights to neighboring countries like Ireland and the Netherlands and didn't freak out on the plane.

My favorite piece was a portrait of two old men playing chess at a park in Paris. One had his head tossed back in laughter with a cigarette in hand while the other examined the board with a furrowed brow. The emotions from both jumped out from the photo, and I'd never been prouder.

"How do you feel?" Diane came up beside me. Her pale blond hair brushed her shoulders, and her black-rimmed glasses matched her black jacket and pants combo. She'd been the best mentor I could ask for during the fellowship, and now I considered her both a friend and role model.

Me, friends with Diane Lange.

Surreal.

"I feel...everything," I admitted. "Warning, though, I might also throw up."

She threw her head back and laughed, not unlike the man in the photo. That was one of my favorite things about Diane. Whether it was joy, sadness, or anger, she expressed her emotions fully and without reserve. She poured herself into the world with the confidence of someone who refused to hold herself back to make others comfortable, and she shone all the brighter for it.

"That's normal," she said, her eyes twinkling. "I actually *did* throw up during my first exhibition. Puked all over a server and a guest who happened to be one of Paris's premier art collectors. I was mortified, but he was a good sport about it. Ended up buying two of my pieces that night."

I chewed on my bottom lip. That was another thing. All the fellows' photos were up for sale tonight. My cohort had turned it into a competition to see who could sell the most and therefore boast they were "the best," but I would be happy if I sold *one*.

Knowing that someone, anyone, liked my work enough to pay for it sent a swarm of happy jitters through my stomach.

"I hope I'll have as good a night," I said, because I hadn't sold anything *yet*.

The twinkle in Diane's eyes intensified. "You already have. Better, in fact."

I tilted my head in confusion.

"Someone bought all your pieces. Every single one."

I almost choked on my champagne. "Wh-what?" The exhibition started an hour ago. How was that *possible*?

"Seems like you have an admirer." She winked. "Don't look so surprised. Your work is good. Really good."

I didn't care how good my work was; I was an unknown name. A newbie. Newbies don't sell out their entire collection that fast unless...

My heart thumped—in warning or excitement, I wasn't sure.

I glanced frantically around the gallery, searching for thick brown hair and cool green eyes.

Nothing.

But he was here. He was my anonymous buyer. I felt it in my gut.

Alex and I had developed a new...well, I wasn't sure if I could call it a friendship, but it was a step up from whatever we had when he arrived in London a year ago. He still waited for me in front of my flat every morning and walked me home after my workshops every afternoon. Sometimes we talked, sometimes we didn't. He helped me practice my self-defense moves, assembled my new dining table after my old one broke, and served as a de facto assistant on some of my photo shoots. It had taken a *long* time before we reached that point, but we'd gotten there.

He was trying. More than trying. And while I'd regained a modicum of trust in him, something held me back from fully forgiving him. I could see how much it hurt him every time I pushed him away, but the wounds from his and Michael's betrayals—while they *were* healing—ran deep, and I was still learning to trust myself, much less other people.

Josh, who'd graduated med school last month, had visited a few times, and I made Alex stay out of sight while he was in town. Josh was still furious with Alex, and I didn't need them getting into a fistfight in the middle of London. Jules, Bridget, and Stella had visited too. I hadn't told them about Alex, but I had a hunch Bridget knew something was up—she'd kept looking at me with a knowing glint in her eyes.

Microphone feedback rippled through the air, and the crowd quieted. The fellowship director walked onstage and thanked everyone for attending, she hoped they were having a good time, blah blah blah. I tuned her out, too intent on my search to pay attention.

Where was he?

Alex wasn't one to hide in the shadows unless he didn't want to be seen, and I couldn't think of any reason he'd want to lie low tonight.

"…special performance. Please put your hands together for Alex Volkov!"

This was maddening. Had something—*wait, what?*

My head snapped up, and my stomach tumbled into free fall.

There he was. Black tuxedo, unreadable expression, his hair gleaming golden brown beneath the lights. There were almost two hundred people in the room, but his eyes found mine immediately.

My pulse thumped with anticipation.

What was he doing onstage?

I got my answer a minute later.

"I realize this is quite a surprise, as a live performance wasn't in the program tonight," Alex said. "And if you know me, you know

I'm not famous for my patronage of the arts—or my singing skills."
Soft laughter rippled through the crowd, along with a few knowing
looks. Alex waited for the chuckles to die down before he continued,
his gaze burning into mine. "Whether it's music, photography, film,
or painting, the arts reflect the world around us, and for too long,
I only saw the dark side. The seedy underbellies, the ugly truths.
Photographs reminded me of moments in time that never lasted.
Songs reminded me that words have the power to rip one's heart
out. Why, then, would I care about art when it was so terrible and
destructive?" It was a bold statement to make in front of London's
art world, but no one heckled. No one so much as breathed. Alex
had us all under the spell of his words. "Then someone came into
my life and upended everything I thought I knew. She was everything I wasn't—purehearted, trusting, optimistic. She showed me
the beauty that existed in this world, and through her, I learned the
power of faith. Joy. Love. But I'm afraid I've tainted her with my
untruths, and I'm hoping, with all my heart, that one day she'll find
her way out of the darkness and into the light again."

The room rang with breathless silence at the end of Alex's
speech. My heart was pounding, pounding so hard I felt it in my
throat. My stomach. My toes. I felt it in every inch of me.

Then he opened his mouth again, and my heart stopped
altogether. Because the voice that came out and filled the room? It
was the most beautiful thing I'd ever heard.

It wasn't just me either. Everyone stared at Alex with rapt
fascination, and I was pretty sure a few of the women straight-up
swooned.

I pressed my fist to my mouth as the lyrics flowed over me. It
was a song about love and heartbreak. Betrayal and redemption.
Regret and forgiveness. Each word tore me apart, as did the fact
that Alex sang at all. No matter how much I'd cajoled or begged
in the past, it was the one thing he'd refused to do.

Until now.

I understood why he'd refused. Alex didn't just sing, he *sang*. With emotion, with beauty, with so much rawness it took my breath away. He bared his soul with each note, and for a man who thought his soul was irrevocably damned, the thought of doing that in front of an audience must've been unbearable.

Alex finished to thunderous applause. His gaze lingered on mine for one long moment before he disappeared offstage, and the crowd broke up into excited chatter and gasps.

My feet moved before I could think, but I only made it two steps before Diane stopped me.

"Ava, before you leave, there's someone I want you to meet," she said. "The editor of *World Geographic* is here, and they're always looking for talented young photographers."

"I—okay." I looked around, but I didn't see Alex anywhere.

"Is everything all right? You seem distracted." Diane examined me with concern. "You've been talking about *World Geographic* all year. I thought you'd be more excited."

"Yes, I'm fine. Sorry, I'm just a little overwhelmed." Normally, I would've fangirled at the thought of meeting the editor of *World Geographic*, a travel and culture magazine famous for its stunning photographs and storytelling, but all I could think about was Alex.

"That was quite a performance, huh?" Diane grinned as she led me toward an older man with silver-streaked hair and a thick beard. Laurent Boucher. I recognized him immediately. "If I were twenty years younger..."

I forced a weak laugh.

"Not that it would do me much good. He seemed to only have eyes for you." She winked at me.

Heat rose on my face, and I mumbled an incoherent response before we reached Laurent.

"Diane, good to see you again." Laurent's deep voice rumbled with a charming French accent as he air-kissed her. "You look lovely as always."

"You're always such a charmer." Diane inclined her head toward me. "Laurent, I want you to meet Ava. She's the fellow I was telling you about."

"Ah, of course." Laurent turned his piercing dark eyes on me. "I was talking to Diane about your exhibit earlier this evening. You're quite talented—young still, and your work could use a little more refinement, but you have extraordinary potential."

"Thank you, sir." Between Alex's performance and praise from Laurent freakin' Boucher, this whole evening was surreal.

"Please, call me Laurent."

We chatted for another fifteen minutes, during which Diane excused herself to speak with the fellowship director. At the end of our conversation, Laurent handed me his card and told me to be in touch if I was interested in freelancing for a junior role at *World Geographic*. Um, *yes*. I was over the moon about the opportunity, but I couldn't help breathing a sigh of relief when Laurent was distracted by another acquaintance.

I thanked him and left to search for Alex, but I was interrupted *again* by a group of fellows who'd heard I'd already sold my entire collection and wanted to know who the buyer was. I told them I didn't know, which was technically true.

That kept happening the entire evening. I'd end one conversation only to get drawn into another. I was grateful for all the people who wanted to connect and congratulate me, but dammit, Alex was the only person I wanted to talk to.

By the end of the night, I hadn't caught a single glimpse of him since his performance. My feet hurt, my cheeks ached from constant smiling, and my stomach growled from the lack of food. I was always too nervous to eat at events.

Guests trickled out until I was one of only a handful of people left in the gallery, including the cleanup crew.

I couldn't believe Alex would leave without a word after what he did, but there was no denying it—he wasn't here.

"Hey, Ava."

I perked up, but disappointment slammed into me a second later when I saw who the speaker was.

"Hey, Jack." I fixed another smile on my face. "I thought you left."

"Nah. Seems I'm a straggler, just like you." His blue eyes twinkled. "You wanna grab a bite? I couldn't eat a thing all night. Nerves," he explained.

"I feel that."

"Nerves? C'mon, you sold your *entire collection*. That's incredible! Unheard of in WYP history." Jack hugged me. "We should celebrate. Maybe with a proper dinner and drinks? Doesn't have to be tonight if you're too tired," he added.

I blinked, sure I'd read his tone wrong. "Are you...asking me out?"

Jack had become a good friend over the past year, and I enjoyed hanging out with him. He wasn't unattractive either, with his longish blond hair, Australian accent, and sun-kissed surfer vibes. But when I looked at him, my stomach didn't flutter and my heart didn't skip a beat.

Only one person in the world could make me feel that way, and he wasn't here.

Jack blushed. "Yeah." He flashed a sheepish smile. "I've wanted to ask you out for a while, but I didn't want to make things awkward during the fellowship. Since the program is over now, I figured, why not? You're beautiful, funny, talented, and we get along well." He paused. "I think."

"We do." I placed a hand on his arm. "You're one of my

316 | ANA HUANG

closest friends here, and I'm so glad I met you. You're a great guy—"

"Ouch." Jack winced. "I feel like that's not a good thing when used in this context."

I laughed. "No, trust me, it's a good thing. You're cute and funny and talented too, and any girl would be lucky to date you."

"I sense a 'but' coming," he said wryly.

"But—"

"But she's busy," a smooth voice interrupted. "From tonight through the foreseeable future."

I turned, my pulse accelerating when I saw Alex standing less than five feet away. His gaze zeroed in on where I was still touching Jack's arm. I pulled away, but it was too late. I could practically taste the danger pulsing in the air.

Gone was the man who'd bared his soul onstage; in his place was the ruthless CEO who wouldn't hesitate to crush his enemies into dust.

"You're the guy who performed tonight and is always waiting for Ava outside WYP." Jack narrowed his eyes. "Who are you again?"

"Someone who will rip your entrails out and strangle you with them if you don't take your hands off her," Alex said in a deceptively calm voice.

It was only then that I realized Jack still had his hand on the small of my back from when he'd hugged me earlier.

"You're psycho." Jack tightened his hold on me, and I suddenly feared for his life. "I'm calling security—"

"No, it's fine. I know him," I blurted before Jack could get himself into more trouble. "He's, uh, prone to hyperbole." I took a step back, forcing Jack to release me. "I need to talk to him, but I'll see you later, okay?"

He shot me a disbelieving look. "Ava, he's—"

"I'll be fine," I said, my tone firm. "I promise. He's an old, um, acquaintance from DC."

Displeasure radiated from Alex in waves. His gaze bore into me with laser intensity, but I ignored it the best I could.

"Okay." Jack relented. "Text me when you're home safe." He kissed my cheek, and a low growl filled the room.

Jack flinched and cast another suspicious glance toward Alex before leaving.

I waited until he was out of earshot before I pinned Alex with my own warning stare. "Don't even think about it."

"Think about what?"

"Doing anything to Jack. Or hiring anyone to do anything to him," I added, because one always needed to cover one's bases with Alex. He was the king of loopholes.

"I didn't realize you cared so much about him," Alex said, his voice cold.

I clenched my teeth. "How is it possible you're the same guy who sang earlier tonight? One is an asshole, the other is…"

"Is what?" Alex walked toward me, and my mouth dried. "Is what, Ava?"

"You know what."

"I don't."

I exhaled a shaky sigh. "You sang. In public."

"Yes."

"Why?"

"Why do I do anything these days?" He brushed his fingers over my cheek, and shivers of pleasure skated down my spine. "I—" He paused, his jaw working before he said carefully, "I'm not the best at expressing my emotions. That's why I've never liked singing. It's all emotion, and it feels too vulnerable. I can't stand it. But I said I'm willing to do whatever it takes to win you back, and I meant it, just as I meant every word in that song. That song was for you. But I'm running out of ideas, sweetheart." Alex rubbed his thumb over the curve of my jaw and gave me a sad smile. "Do you know this is the first time you've let me touch you in over a year?"

I opened my mouth to argue because that couldn't possibly be true...except it was. A montage of images flashed through my mind of me shrinking back or turning away every time Alex reached for me over the past twelve months. Not because I didn't *want* him to touch me but because I didn't trust myself not to cave if he got that close again. He never said anything, but I'd caught the hurt and pain in his eyes.

"I looked for you after," I said, my chin wobbling. "I couldn't find you. You disappeared."

"It's your big night. I didn't want to take that away from you."

"I thought you left." I didn't know why, but I started crying. The tears dripped down my cheeks, and my sniffles echoed in the empty gallery. I was mortified, but at least we were the only people there. There had to be staff somewhere in the building or they would've kicked us out, but I couldn't see them.

"I would never leave you." Alex drew me into his chest, and I sank into his embrace for the first time in what felt like forever. It was like returning home after a long, lonely trip abroad. I'd forgotten how safe I felt in his arms, like nothing and no one could hurt me. That I felt this way even after what he did spoke volumes. "Do you *want* me to leave?" he asked gruffly.

I buried my face in his chest and shook my head. He smelled like warmth and spice, and it was so familiar it made my heart hurt.

I missed it. I missed *him*. Even though I'd seen Alex every day for the past year, it wasn't the same as touching him and actually *being* with him.

"Do you miss me, sweetheart?" His voice gentled.

I nodded, my face still buried in his chest.

All this time, I'd been afraid to let him back in, partly because I didn't trust him but mostly because I didn't trust myself. After being lied to for so long by two people I'd loved, I'd begun to think of my heart as my enemy and not my friend. How could I trust my instincts when they'd led me so astray in the past?

But the more I thought about it, the more I realized I *hadn't* been wrong. I'd thought Michael was my real father and that he'd saved my life, but I'd always felt uncomfortable around him. I never bonded with him the way a daughter should with her father. I figured it was because he'd been uncomfortable around *me*, and while that may have played a part, it had mostly been a sixth sense that warned me not to get too close.

As for Alex, he'd pulled the wool over both my and Josh's eyes. But in my heart of hearts, I believed him when he said our relationship and his feelings were real.

Was there a chance I was wrong, and this was yet another fucked-up long game? Yes, though I didn't see what else he could want from me. He'd targeted Michael based on false information, and even if he hadn't, Michael was already out of the picture— he'd been found guilty of multiple charges of attempted murder and corporate fraud, and he faced life in prison.

But I'd rather take a leap of faith than spend the rest of my life living in fear of something that *might* happen. I was sick and tired of letting my fears hold me back, whether it was over water, heartbreak, or something else.

The only way to live life was to *live* it. No fears, no regrets.

Alex pulled back but kept one arm around my waist. He tilted my chin up, his eyes boring into mine. "Do you want me to stay?"

He wasn't talking about the gallery, and we both knew it.

I swallowed hard and nodded again. "Yes," I whispered.

The word had barely left my mouth before Alex yanked

me toward him and crushed his lips to mine. It wasn't a sweet, leisurely kiss. It was fierce and desperate and everything I needed. A shudder of relief rippled through him beneath my palms, and I hadn't realized how tense he'd been until now.

"You know there's no getting rid of me now," he warned, his touch hot and possessive as he gripped my hands.

"That wouldn't have happened anyway."

He let out a soft chuckle. "Now you're getting it."

His mouth claimed mine once more, and I was so lost in his kiss, his scent, his touch that I didn't notice we'd moved until my back hit the wall.

"Alex?"

"Hmm?" He pulled my bottom lip between his teeth and bit lightly before chasing away the sting with his tongue. Full-on tingles spread from my scalp all the way down to my toes.

"Don't break my heart again."

Alex's face softened. "I won't. Trust me, sweetheart."

"I do." It was the truth. I'd seen the real Alex tonight, stripped of all his masks, and I trusted him with all my heart.

He gave me one of his real smiles then, the kind that could start a nuclear reaction and destroy the entire female population in one fell swoop.

"Also, I…" I blushed. "I miss when you call me Sunshine."

Alex's eyes flared with heat. "Yeah?" He slid my skirt up, inch by inch, until the cool air hit my ass and upper thighs. "What else do you miss?" He dipped his hand inside my already drenched panties and brushed the sensitive nub between my legs. "Do you miss this?"

A whimper escaped. "Yes."

"What about this?" He pressed his body against mine until I felt his rock-hard erection against my thigh. Heat sizzled through my veins. I hadn't had sex in a year and a half, and my sexual frustration was a volcano waiting to explode.

"Yes. Please," I moaned.

"I told the rest of the staff to leave before I came to see you. It's just you and me, Sunshine." His breath tickled my skin as he dragged his mouth down my neck until he reached the pulse fluttering wildly at the base of my throat. "I'm going to fuck you against this wall until you can't remember your own name, but before I do—" He grabbed my throat, his voice dropping to a soft snarl. My core spasmed in response. "Tell me about the blond fucker who asked you out. Did you let him touch you, Sunshine? Did you let him touch what was mine?"

I shook my head, practically panting from arousal.

Alex's grip tightened. "Are you lying to save him?"

"No," I moaned. "I swear. I don't think of him that way."

I gasped when he spun me around and pressed my cheek against the wall. The icy concrete dug into my heated skin, and my nipples hardened into painful points.

Alex yanked up my skirt and shoved aside my panties with his free hand. "You don't think about him *ever*," he growled. I heard his belt unbuckling and his pants unzipping. "I'm the only man in your mind. In your mouth. In your tight little pussy. Do you understand?"

"Yes!" I was so delirious with lust I would've said yes to anything at this point.

"Tell me who you belong to." He slid his cock against my drenched folds, and I almost had a mini orgasm from that simple action alone.

"I belong to you."

Alex hissed out a breath, and that was the only warning I received before he slammed into me. He clapped a hand over my mouth, muffling my screams, but I was so far gone I barely noticed. I could only focus on the sensation of his cock pounding into me and the pleasure crashing over me in waves.

The framed photos from the exhibition banged against the wall with each thrust, and I dimly heard something crashing to the ground. I was about to come when Alex spun me around again so we faced each other. His skin was flushed with exertion, his eyes dark with lust.

He was the most beautiful thing I'd ever seen.

He crushed his lips to mine, hard and demanding. I yielded with no resistance, letting him into every part of me—my heart, my soul, my life.

And you know what?

Alex and I, we fit perfectly.

EPILOGUE

Ava / Alex

Ava

"I KICKED YOUR ASS."

"You did *not* kick my ass," Ralph grumbled. "You got lucky with that last punch."

"It's all right." Alex adjusted his shirt sleeves, his eyes gleaming with a mixture of triumph and amusement. "Every student eventually becomes the teacher."

"Boy, I'll knock you upside the head if you don't stop talking nonsense." Despite his gruff words, Ralph was smiling.

"What did I say about arguing at the table?" Ralph's wife, Missy, raised her eyebrows. "Stop quibbling so we can all enjoy dinner."

I hid a smile when Alex and Ralph muttered under their breaths but complied.

"What was that?" Her brows rose higher.

"Nothing," they chorused.

"Teach me your ways," I whispered to Missy while the guys busied themselves with the roast chicken and garlic mashed potatoes. "How do you do it?"

She laughed. "When you've been married for thirty-plus

years, you learn a few things. Besides…" Her eyes twinkled with mischief. "Judging by the way Alex looks at you, I don't think you have to worry about keeping him in line."

Alex looked up at the same moment as I glanced at him. He winked, his mouth curving into a devilish smirk that had my toes curling in my boots.

I knew what that smirk foreshadowed.

Heat rose on my cheeks, and I pretended to be fascinated with my plate while Alex's low chuckle rumbled across the table.

Missy didn't miss a second of it. "Oh, to be young and in love." She sighed. "Ralph and I married when we were in our early twenties. I've enjoyed every minute—except when he leaves his dirty clothes everywhere and refuses to see the doctor—but there's nothing like the passion that comes with youth. Everything's so fresh and new. And the stamina. Whew!" She fanned herself. "We were like bunnies, let me tell you."

By now, my cheeks were the color of the cranberry sauce on the table.

I adored Missy. I met her a week ago, when Alex and I arrived at her and Ralph's Vermont farm for an extended Thanksgiving weekend, but I immediately took a shine to her. Warm, friendly, and down-to-earth, she baked a mean pumpkin pie and had a penchant for raunchy jokes—and raunchy personal stories.

This morning, out of the blue, she asked whether I'd ever had a threesome—I hadn't—and I'd nearly sprayed orange juice all over her cherrywood table.

"I didn't mean to embarrass you." Missy patted my arm, but the spark of mischief remained in her eyes. "I'm just so thrilled Alex is dating. I've known that boy for years, and I've never seen him look at someone the way he does you. I've always said he just needs the right woman to open him up. He was wound tighter than a Victorian corset."

I leaned toward her and said in a conspiratorial whisper, "Honestly, not much has changed."

"You know I can hear everything you're saying," Alex said dryly.

"Good. I was afraid l wasn't loud enough."

His eyes narrowed while Missy burst into laughter. Even Ralph chuckled as I flashed a cheeky smile.

"Sunshine, you being loud has never been an issue," Alex said in a silky voice.

My mashed potatoes went down the wrong pipe, and I erupted into a fit of coughs. Missy's laughter morphed into outright cackling. Poor Ralph turned bright red, muttered something about the restroom, and fled.

Once I got my coughs under control, I glared at Alex, who remained unfazed. "I'm talking about the volume of your voice during conversations, of course." He raised his wineglass to his lips. "What did you think I meant?"

"I have a feeling you won't be hearing my *voice* during conversations for a while," I huffed.

"We'll see." He sounded infuriatingly smug.

"I'll leave you two lovebirds alone while I fetch Ralph." Missy chuckled. "Poor thing is a lion in the bedroom but a blushing kitten when it comes to talking about sex in public—directly or indirectly."

That was something I could've lived the rest of my life without knowing.

After she left, I glared at Alex. "See what you did? You drove our hosts away during their own dinner."

"Did I?" He gave an elegant shrug. "Might as well take advantage of the situation. Come here, Sunshine."

"I don't think so."

"That wasn't a request."

"I'm not a dog." I took a defiant sip of my water.

"If you're not in my lap in the next five seconds," Alex said in the same calm voice, "I'll bend you over the table, rip off your skirt, and fuck you so hard Ralph will have a heart attack from your screams."

The bastard was crazy enough to do it too. And I must be equally crazy, because my panties dampened at his words, and all I could think about was doing the exact thing he'd just threatened.

Alex watched, eyes heated, as I pushed my chair back, walked over to him, and climbed into his lap.

"Good girl," he purred, wrapping an arm around my waist and pulling me toward him until my back pressed against his chest. His arousal nestled against my ass, and my mouth turned bone-dry. "That wasn't so hard, was it?"

"I hate you." I would've been more convincing had the words not come out so breathless.

"Hate is just another word for love." He slipped a hand beneath my sweater and cupped my breast while trailing a string of fiery kisses down my neck.

"I don't think that's right," I said, caught between laughing and moaning. God, his hands and mouth were magic.

I shot a furtive glance at the doorway to the dining room. Missy and Ralph were nowhere in sight...yet. But the possibility of getting caught made the whole thing hotter—I was so wet I was afraid I'd leave a noticeable spot on Alex's pants when I stood.

"No? Ah, well." Alex nipped my earlobe. "Close enough." He cupped my chin with his other hand and turned my face so I looked back at him. "Did you enjoy this week?"

"Yeah. It was the best Thanksgiving I've had in a while," I said softly.

I felt guilty because while all my Thanksgivings with Michael were tainted, I'd spent the holiday with Josh last year. He'd flown to London, and we had a blast stuffing ourselves with food—restaurant-bought because we didn't know how to cook a turkey—while binge-watching British dramas. But I'd been unsure about my feelings for Alex, and Josh had been pissed at his ex-best friend.

He still was.

When he found out Alex and I were back together, he lost his shit. He wouldn't talk to me for weeks, and even now, our conversations were strained. Josh stayed in DC for his residency, so we still lived in the same city, but he refused to see me if Alex was there. He'd ignored all Alex's outreach and seen through my schemes to help them patch things up. I'd invited him to celebrate Thanksgiving with us, but as I'd expected, he'd declined.

"I do wish Josh could've made it," I admitted. I missed my brother.

"Me too. But he'll come around." Despite his confident words, a small furrow creased Alex's brow. He didn't say it, but I knew he missed Josh too. They'd been as close as brothers.

Unfortunately, Josh was stubborn as a bull. The more you pushed him, the more he dug his heels in. The only thing we could do was give him time and wait.

"He will." I sighed and looped my arms around Alex's neck. "Other than that, though, this week was perfect."

We'd been in Vermont for six days, and the whole getaway had been a Pinterest-worthy autumn dream. Artisan fairs, a turkey trot, the best hot apple cider I've ever tasted... Even Alex enjoyed being here, though he refused to admit it. I'd overheard his conversation with Ralph when his old Krav Maga instructor called and invited him up here for Thanksgiving, and it took me forever to convince him to accept.

"Good." Alex dropped both his hands to my waist and kissed me on the lips. "Be glad I rented us our own cabin instead of staying here with Ralph and Missy," he whispered. "Because you're going to pay for your sass earlier."

My heart skipped with excitement. Before I could respond, Missy's and Ralph's voices drifted through the doorway, and I jumped up so fast I banged my knee on the underside of the table.

I lunged into my chair, my face beet red, right as our hosts reentered the room.

"Sorry we took so long," Missy chirped. "Hope we're not interrupting anything."

"Nope," I squeaked. "I was just enjoying your delicious chicken." I munched on the now-cold meat. "Yum."

Alex snorted out a laugh, which earned him another glare from me.

"Most of the food is cold, dear." Missy clucked in disappointment. "Do you want me to heat 'em up or skip straight to dessert? I made pecan pie, pumpkin pie, apple pie—"

"Dessert!" Ralph and I shouted at the same time.

"Alex?" Missy raised her eyebrows.

"One slice of pecan pie is fine, thank you."

"Nonsense. You're getting a slice of all three," she said firmly. "I made 'em for a reason, didn't I?"

What Missy wanted, Missy got.

By the time we left her and Ralph's house, I was full to the point of bursting.

I leaned into Alex for support as we made our way back to our rental cabin, which was a fifteen-minute walk away.

"We should come here for Thanksgiving every year," I said. "If we're invited, that is."

He cast an incredulous glance in my direction. "No."

"You had fun!"

"I did not. I hate small towns." Alex placed a hand on the small of my back and steered me around a small puddle I hadn't noticed.

I pouted. "Then why did you come this year?"

"Because you've never been to Vermont, and you wouldn't shut up about it. Now you've been, so we don't have to come back."

"Don't try to act all tough. I saw you buy that little porcelain puppy at the artisan fair when you thought I wasn't looking. And you drag me to that hot cider shop down the road every afternoon."

Crimson stained Alex's cheeks. "It's called making lemonade out of lemons," he growled. "You are asking for it tonight."

"Maybe I am." I squealed and broke out into a run when Alex reached for me. He caught me in, oh, five-point-two seconds, but I wasn't trying that hard to escape, and I wasn't exactly Usain Bolt after all the carbs I'd ingested.

"You'll be the death of me," he said, swinging me around until I faced him. The moonlight cast his features in sharp relief, making the pale lines of his cheekbones slash like blades through the darkness. Beautiful. Perfect. Cold—except for the warmth of his embrace and the teasing glint in his eyes.

I wrapped my arms around his neck and my legs around his waist. "So we're coming back for Thanksgiving next year, right?"

Alex sighed. "Maybe."

In other words, yes.

I beamed. "Maybe we could come up early and go apple pick—"

"Don't push your luck."

Fair enough. We'd go apple picking the year after next. Seven hundred-odd days should be enough time to convince him.

"Alex?"

"Yes, Sunshine?"

"I love you."

His face softened. "I love you too." His lips brushed over mine before he whispered, "But don't think that'll save you from the spanking you're getting once we're back in the cabin."

A shiver of anticipation rippled through me.

I couldn't wait.

Alex

Contrary to what Ava said, I hated Vermont. There were some not-terrible parts, like the food and the fresh air, but me *enjoying* the countryside? I didn't know what she was talking about.

At all.

I did, however, miss all the time I'd gotten to spend with Ava over Thanksgiving after I returned to work.

It was almost embarrassing how fast Archer Group took me back as CEO when I returned from London. I wasn't surprised—I was the best. The guy who replaced me was fine as a placeholder, but even he knew his tenure at Archer had reached the end of the road when I walked into my office four months ago.

That office had always been mine, no matter who occupied the chair.

The board had been all too happy to have me back, and Archer's stock jumped twenty-four percent when my reinstatement as CEO hit the papers.

I did have a better work-life balance now that Ava had moved into my Logan Circle penthouse, mainly because I'd much rather be eating her out on our bed than eating takeout at my desk. I left the office around six these days, much to the relief of my staff.

"Sunshine?" I called out, kicking the front door closed behind me. I hung my coat on the rack and waited for a response.

Nothing.

Ava, who worked as a junior freelance photographer for *World Geographic* and a few other magazines, was usually home by this time. Worry flickered in my stomach before I heard the squeak of the faucet turning and the faint but unmistakable sound of the shower running.

My shoulders relaxed. I was still paranoid about her safety and had hired a permanent bodyguard to look after her, much to her dismay. We'd had an all-out, knockdown fight over it, followed by equally all-out, knockdown makeup sex, but we'd eventually compromised—we'd keep the bodyguard, but she would stay out of sight and not interfere unless Ava was in physical danger.

I'd taken other precautions to ensure my enemies would think twice about going after her as well...including seeding detailed "rumors" about what happened to the last guy who'd dared touch her.

Rest in hell, Camo.

The rumors worked. Some people were scared so shitless they couldn't look me in the eye anymore.

Hauss Industries was also toast, thanks to Madeline's unwise decision to be in cahoots with my uncle. I'd had plenty of blackmail on Madeline's father. Embezzling, money laundering, deals with unsavory characters...he'd been a busy man. All I'd had to do was slip an anonymous tip and select pieces of information to Hauss's competitor, and they took care of the dirty work for me.

Last I heard, Madeline's father was facing years in prison, and Madeline was working at a skeezy diner in Maryland after the government froze all her family's assets.

The only person I was worried about was Michael, who Ava said kept sending Josh letters asking to see him. Josh had so far refused.

In an effort not to stain my hands with more blood, I'd dropped my plan to send Michael to an early grave in prison, but I had people on the inside monitoring him—and making his life more than a little uncomfortable. If he so much as uttered Ava's name, I'd know about it—and make sure he never did it again.

Out of habit, I turned on the flat-screen TV in our room and half listened to the evening news as I peeled off my work clothes. I should join Ava in the shower. What was the point of having a massive rainfall shower *with* a handy bench seat if we didn't fuck in it at least once a week?

My penthouse was huge but had had minimal furnishings until Ava spruced it up after she moved in. And by "spruced up," I mean she put art and flowers and framed pictures of us and her friends everywhere. Both Jules and Stella stayed in DC after graduation, while Bridget split her time between Eldorra, DC, and New York. Her friends were more accepting of our rekindled relationship than Josh, but that didn't mean I wanted their faces staring at me 24/7 in my own damn house. I'd only agreed to display the photos because Ava wouldn't stop giving me sad puppy-dog eyes until I relented.

"You should've said no," I muttered at a picture of myself and Ava at a Nats baseball game over the summer. It hung next to a more formal gallery of her work from London—the ones I bought in bulk at the WYP exhibition.

She had me doing all sorts of crazy things these days, like giving up coffee and sticking to a sleep schedule. She said it would help with my insomnia, and yeah, I slept more hours than I used to, but that had more to do with having Ava by my side than anything else. Besides, I still snuck the occasional cup of coffee at the office.

I was about to enter the bathroom when something the newscaster said caught my attention. I stopped short, sure I'd heard wrong, but the scrolling chyron across the bottom of the screen confirmed what I'd heard.

The sound of the running shower switched off, and the rumble of the stall door sliding open filtered into the bedroom.

"Ava?"

There was a brief pause and a faint rustle. "You're home

early!" Ava stepped out of the bathroom in a swirl of steam, hair and skin damp, with nothing but a towel wrapped around her slender frame. She beamed when she saw me, and my face softened.

"Slow day in the office." I dropped a kiss on her mouth. My cock stirred with interest, and I was tempted to rip off her towel and take her right there against the wall, but there was something she needed to know before we started one of our all-nighters. "Did you hear from Bridget today?"

"No." Ava's brow furrowed. "Why?"

"Check out the news." I angled my head toward the TV, where the newscaster spoke a mile a minute.

Ava paused, listening to the update before her jaw dropped.

I didn't blame her. Because what just happened? It hadn't happened in over two hundred years of Eldorran history.

The newscaster's high-pitched voice filled the room, so excited it trembled.

"...*Crown Prince Nikolai has abdicated the throne of Eldorra to marry Sabrina Philips, the American flight attendant he met last year during a diplomatic trip to New York. Eldorran law stipulates the country's monarchs must marry someone of noble birth. His sister, Princess Bridget, is now first in line to the throne. When she becomes queen, she will be Eldorra's first female monarch in more than a century...*"

Footage of an expressionless Bridget exiting the Plaza Hotel in New York, trailed by her grim-faced bodyguard and surrounded by shouting reporters, flashed onscreen.

"Holy shit," Ava said.

Holy shit was right. From what I remembered—which was everything—Bridget had chafed at the restrictions that came with being a regular princess. Now that she was first in line for the crown? She must be flipping out.

On TV, Rhys steered Bridget into a waiting car and leveled the reporters with a glare so menacing they backed up en masse. Most people would've missed it, but I caught the heat in Bridget's eyes when she looked at Rhys and the way his hand brushed hers for a second longer than it should've before he closed the door.

I filed that piece of information away for the future. Bridget was Ava's friend, so she was safe, but it never hurt to have blackmail material on a future queen.

Based on what I just witnessed, Bridget's feelings about her impending rule were the least of her problems.

BONUS SCENE

Ava

I'D DONE THE IMPOSSIBLE: I'D CONVINCED ALEX TO GO apple picking.

I *might* have cheated and tricked him into agreeing during sex—he was far more accommodating after an orgasm—but to be fair, I was sure he didn't hate the countryside and fall activities as much as he proclaimed.

Case in point: we'd been apple picking for hours, and he hadn't once complained. He hadn't gushed about it either, but it was Alex. He didn't gush about anything. The fact that he hadn't killed anyone was proof enough he was enjoying himself.

"A little to the left...a little more...perfect!" I plucked the apple I'd been eyeing off the tree and dropped it into my basket. Since it was too high for me to reach, Alex had hoisted me onto his shoulders and let me use him as my personal ladder. "I think that's the last one."

"Good." He lowered me onto the ground, his tone dry. "Any more and you would've picked all the trees bare."

I let out a small huff. "You're exaggerating."

We stared down at my overflowing basket. It was my fifth one that day.

Okay, I might have gone a *little* overboard, but Alex, being Alex, had booked the entire orchard just for us, and I wasn't about to let such a good opportunity go to waste.

"Think of all the delicious things we can make with these," I said a bit defensively. "Apple pie, apple cider, apple muffins, and...other stuff. You know what they say. An apple a day keeps the doctor away."

Alex raised an eyebrow. "Yes. It appears the doctor will be away for quite a while."

"Stop." I couldn't help but laugh. "You're enjoying yourself, and you know it."

"Verdict's still out on that," he said, still in that dry tone, but he was smiling. "Put the basket down, Sunshine."

I narrowed my eyes, my suspicion spiking. "Why?"

"Just do it."

I clutched the apples protectively to my chest. "What are you going to do with them?"

"Ava, put the basket down and come here. Nothing's going to happen to your apples."

My real name. *Uh-oh.* Maybe he hadn't liked being a human ladder after all.

I did as he asked with reluctance and edged toward him warily.

This time, Alex was the one who laughed. "You look like I'm going to bite you."

"You might."

A wicked gleam appeared in his eyes, and my cheeks flushed at the innuendo behind it. "Not yet." Once I got close enough, he pulled me toward him and brushed his lips over mine. "Are you having fun?"

"Yes." My tension eased as I melted into him. I loved a lot of places in the world—DC, London, our bed—but my favorite was in Alex's arms. "Today was perfect."

We'd arrived at the luxury Vermont farm resort we were staying at for the week yesterday, and while it had been too late for us to do anything more than eat and sleep, today had been packed with all my favorite activities. Breakfast in bed featuring the best pancakes I'd ever tasted, getting "lost" in the property's corn maze, a hayride where Alex and I made out the entire time, and, of course, glorious hours of private apple picking.

It was the quintessential fall day, and I couldn't have asked for anything better.

"Good." Alex gave me another soft kiss as his arms tightened around me. "Because it's time for you to pay."

My eyes flew open, and my heart thumped at the gleam in his eyes. "W-what?"

Alex smiled, and my heart gave another nervous thump, followed by a small thrill of excitement. That particular smile never boded well for my ability to walk the next day.

"Don't think I didn't notice *when* you asked me to go apple picking." He grazed his fingers over the small of my back, his touch deceptively light. "Very manipulative of you, Sunshine."

I gulped. I'd hoped he wouldn't realize I'd tricked him, but I should've known better. Alex was too smart not to know when he'd been bamboozled. I also should've known better than to get lulled into a false sense of complacency by the fact that he hadn't said anything about it in the weeks leading up to our trip. He was, after all, the master of the long game.

"But you had fun," I squeaked, my pulse hammering. "So you can't be mad."

Alex's smile darkened. "Not as much fun as I'm about to have." He lowered his head and whispered, "I'll give you a ten-second head start. *Run.*"

I didn't have to ask what he'd do when he caught me.

When, not if, because he always caught me.

I tore out of his arms without another word and bolted down the orchard path, unable to stifle my grin even as I tried my best to outrun him. I almost made it out of the orchard and into the field beyond when I heard Alex behind me.

I squealed, but it was too late.

The next thing I knew, I was on all fours with Alex's erection pressed tight against my ass. My pussy clenched with anticipation. It didn't matter we'd had sex just last night—several rounds of sex, in fact. I could never get enough of him.

"Caught you," he whispered. "Didn't run fast enough, Sunshine."

Sometimes, Alex liked to take his sweet time with foreplay, teasing and torturing me until I begged him to fuck me.

This was not one of those times.

He shoved my dress up and yanked down my panties, exposing me to the slight chill of the late afternoon air. I shivered, my heart racing with a mixture of nerves and arousal. The orchard had been empty all day, with not even a staffer in sight, but there still existed the possibility someone might see us.

Somehow, that only turned me on more.

"You know I don't like getting manipulated into things I don't want to do." Alex's hand closed around my throat, and as always, the pressure caused my core to pulse. "So you're going to make it up to me, Sunshine."

"W-what do I have to do?"

I had a good guess, but with Alex, I never knew.

"It's not what you have to do," he said silkily. "It's what you *can't* do. You're not allowed to come until I say you can. If you do"—his grip tightened—"I'll fuck you in the ass so hard you won't be able to walk for days. Understand?"

I gulped. We'd tried anal once, and it'd hurt like hell, even though Alex had done his best to prepare me. While I was open to trying it again—eventually—I wasn't ready *now*.

"Alex—"

"Understand?" he repeated. He tightened his hold further until tears sprang in my eyes.

"Yes," I managed to gasp out. I was so wet I could feel the juices dripping onto my thighs.

Alex released me. The sound of the condom foil ripping was the only other warning I got before he slammed into me, his hand returning to my throat, and I let out an involuntary scream at the viciousness of his thrust. Other men might've slowed down after the initial push, but Alex kept up a hard, brutal rhythm that drove every other thought out of my mind.

My breaths came out in shallow pants, my entire body a live wire waiting to explode. Shock waves of pleasure pulsed through me, and the chill in the air, coupled with the openness of our surroundings, only added to the thrill.

I was so loud Alex clamped a hand over my mouth, muffling my cries as he pounded into me so mercilessly it would've been painful had it not felt so good. The dirt dug into my hands and knees, and I was sure I would be sore as hell tomorrow, but that didn't stop the telltale ball of tingles from forming at the base of my spine.

Oh no. I squeezed my eyes shut, trying my best to fight the inevitable. *No no no no no. Not yet.*

My body tightened, and panic spiked with my arousal. I tried to plead with him to let me come, but his hand was so tight over my mouth only my unintelligible moans came through.

"You are so fucking wet," Alex growled. "Does this turn you on, hmm? Getting fucked on all fours in the middle of a field like a filthy slut?"

My skin flushed hot, and my clit throbbed with a heartbeat of its own.

He loosened his hold so I could respond, and my pleas fell out without thinking. "Yes. Please. I need to come," I gasped. "Please let me come."

Otherwise, I was going to go crazy. My heart beat an erratic rhythm in my chest, and even though the temperature was only in the midfifties, I was sweating from the effort of holding back.

"This is your punishment, Sunshine. It's not about what you need. It's about what I want." Alex reached into the V of my neckline and pinched my nipple, hard, and my core spasmed at the sensation. "And I want you to keep taking it until I say we're done."

Tears of frustration streaked my cheeks. At this point, I was beyond caring about anything except the tight ball of pressure growing inside me. "*Please.* I'm sorry," I sobbed. "Alex, I need to—I'm going to—"

I couldn't hold back for much longer. My orgasm was only a few thrusts away, and there was nothing I could do to stop it.

Alex yanked me up until my back pressed flush against his chest. "Tell me. Have you learned your lesson?"

"Y-yes."

"Are you going to try to trick me again?"

I shook my head frantically.

"For your sake, I hope you're not lying." He kept one hand on my throat while the other slid down toward my clit. If he touched me there, I would be done for. His lips grazed my ear as he whispered, "Come for me, my little whore."

Alex pressed his thumb against my most sensitive bundle of nerves, and I exploded. My orgasm ripped through me like wildfire, setting every nerve ending ablaze, and by the time it subsided, I was so worn out I would've collapsed facedown on the ground had he not flipped me around so I faced him while he hovered over me. He was barely out of breath, but his eyes glittered with lust, and a pale-pink flush colored his cheekbones.

And he was still hard.

"You were right, you know," he said conversationally, like he hadn't just made me come so hard I saw stars. "I did enjoy today, so I'm not mad. For the most part."

I was too wrapped up in postcoital bliss to do more than muster up a tinge of indignation. "That was mean."

Amusement flashed across his face. "Was it?" Alex pulled out until just the tip was inside me before lazily pushing himself in to the hilt again. "Judging by how hard you came all over my cock, you seemed to like it."

My fingers dug into the dirt as the tingle of arousal started to spread. Again. It hadn't even been five minutes.

This man was going to kill me one day, and I wouldn't even be mad about it.

"Alex," I gritted out. "I won't be able to walk tomorrow."

He didn't appear concerned. "Then I guess you'll have to spend the day in bed."

"You're impossible."

"Yes, but you love me anyway," he said, oozing smug male satisfaction.

I rolled my eyes but smiled. "Maybe."

"Maybe?" Alex lowered his head and nipped my bottom lip in admonishment. "*Maybe* you didn't learn your lesson yet."

My laugh was cut short by a gasp as he resumed his hard thrusts, and soon, all I could do was cling to him for dear life as another orgasm crashed over me. I cried out, my nails digging into his back, and there was no doubt we'd both walk away with more than a few hickeys and bruises after this was over. Not to mention my dress was probably ruined, I'd need to take a long, hot shower to get all the dirt out of my hair, and I would *definitely* have trouble walking tomorrow. But I didn't care.

Best. Vacation. Ever.

Thank you for reading *Twisted Love*! If you enjoyed this book, I would be grateful if you could leave a review on the platform(s) of your choice.

Reviews are like tips for author, and every one helps!

Much love,
Ana

If you can't get enough of Alex and Ava, type this link into your browser for a sexy bonus scene:
https://BookHip.com/HHKKMBF

HE CAN'T HAVE HER...
BUT HE'S TAKING HER ANYWAY. READ

NOW FOR A STEAMY FORBIDDEN
ROMANCE FEATURING BRIDGET AND RHYS.

Acknowledgments

Alex and Ava are two of my favorite characters I've written (shh, don't tell the others), and I want to thank everyone who helped bring my vision to life.

To my beta readers Aishah, Alison, Gunvor, Kate, and Kelly for their encouragement and feedback. It's always nerve-racking for me to send a book baby out to the world for the first time, but it was in good hands with these wonderful ladies!

To my editor, Amy Briggs, and proofreader, Krista Burdine, for whipping my manuscript into shape and putting up with my questionable love for special punctuation.

To Quirah at Temptation Creations for the beautiful cover.

To my editor, Christa Désir, and the amazing team at Bloom Books for helping this book reach its fullest potential. Nothing makes me happier than seeing Alex and Ava in such capable hands.

To my agent Kimberly Brower for all your support and guidance—I couldn't have done this without you!

And finally, to the bloggers and reviewers who've shown this book so much love. I adore you guys, and I am forever grateful.

xo,

Ana

Keep in Touch with Ana Huang

Reader Group: facebook.com/groups/anastwistedsquad
Website: anahuang.com
BookBub: bookbub.com/profile/ana-huang
Instagram: instagram.com/authoranahuang
TikTok: tiktok.com/@authoranahuang
Goodreads: goodreads.com/anahuang

Want to discuss my books and other fun shenanigans with like-minded readers? Join my members-only reader group: facebook.com/groups/anastwistedsquad.

About the Author

Ana Huang is an author of primarily steamy New Adult and contemporary romance. Her books contain diverse characters and angsty, sometimes twisty roads toward HEAs (with plenty of banter and spice sprinkled in). Besides reading and writing, Ana loves traveling, is obsessed with hot chocolate, and has multiple relationships with fictional boyfriends.

Also by Ana Huang

TWISTED SERIES
A series of interconnected standalones
Twisted Love
Twisted Games
Twisted Hate
Twisted Lies

IF LOVE SERIES
If We Ever Meet Again (Duet Book 1)
If the Sun Never Sets (Duet Book 2)
If Love Had a Price (Standalone)
If We Were Perfect (Standalone)